MW01132753

At the River

At the River

WRITTEN AND ILLUSTRATED BY
SADYE PETERSEN REDDICK

26 25 24 23 22 21 20   1 2 3

ISBN: 978-0-578-65910-7

∞ This paper meets the requirements of ANSI/NISO Z39.48-1992
(Permanence of Paper).

Book layout and design in collaboration with Ian Bright
Edited by Melanie Bright

Dedication

At the River is dedicated to those who love a good story
and desire to learn historical truths.

Table of Contents

Foreward

Sadye Reddick has managed to write a book that combines history, as the stage where *At the River* takes place, and fiction to tell about the characters that inhabit the world of early California life prior to the Gold Rush.

Historical fiction is not an easy genre, as both the historical and fictional components must weave together seamlessly. She did that superbly. Even more difficult, Mrs. Reddick managed to write the story from opposite points of view: that of the early inhabitants of California, which were part of the Spanish colonial empire, and the point of view of East Coast people who belonged to the United States of America. The people that, more or less, seventy years earlier, had been in British colonies ruled by the king of England.

I lived in Latin America until I was eighteen years old, where I learned the history of the Americas under the Spanish colonial era. Once I moved to the United States of America, I learned the history of my new country. In her narrative, Mrs. Reddick expertly switches between Spanish colonial life and early Anglo-Saxon culture points of view within each character, seamlessly and on the fly. Few persons can detect that her historical and cultural facts of the colonial life are spot on, and that she was burdened to provide parallel historical narratives that were culturally correct. She did it very well, since the average reader from this country will have no problems identifying the East Coast values brought here from United States citizens from that era, but might not realize the counterpart cultural values from the Spanish and then Mexican periods that are described very accurately as well. I must repeat, this parallel description of cultures was written superbly.

The human story captures the events of that era very honestly, describing both the good and the bad of the human condition. Virtues like honesty, love and the fear of God are contrasted against defects such as hatred, bigotry and domestic violence. The world of *At the River* is painted very realistically.

At the River tells a compelling story. It is a well-developed narrative where the characters, the locations and historical settings are properly described. Mrs. Reddick described in detail the physical features, clothing, and stance of the human characters very well. Likewise, the detailed description of the towns, houses, settings, and nature make the world of *At the River* come to life.

The historical basis for this story and the nitty-gritty details were woven well into the fictional element of the story. The nuances of the life of the Californios are properly described in this context. With respect to the historical details of California life prior to the Mexican American war and subsequent Gold Rush, I was not surprised about the descriptions of life, culture, institutions, and religion of the Californios under the Spanish empire. Their way of life was very similar to every other country controlled by Spain from California to the tip of South America.

What really surprised me was to witness the cruel and unfair erasing of the Californios story, culture and way of life from historical narratives. The academics and experts are the only modern people that truly know the life and history of the Californios.

The characters are well done, and the principal ones have traits that can benefit or hurt interactions with others based on their beliefs and culture. The dialogue accurately reflects the persona of each character and their cultural context. The interactions among characters also are in sync with the story and its environment.

I would recommend this book to anybody who likes a rich story that highlights the lifestyle of the early Californios under the control of the king of Spain.

-Eduardo Ortega Jr.
Engineer and Writer

Preface

While I wasn't aware of it, life had been preparing me, leading me, and, later, pushing me to write this book. This book came from a deep need to continue to learn, to teach and to communicate.

Looking back, I could see other hints or landmarks over time, not just my background living with, working with, and teaching Spanish-speaking immigrants, which was a large part of my life, but I loved the children, the families, the culture and the music.

When I was born, my father had a French Basque family living on the ranch with us. I lived with the Basque and the French language in the environment until we moved to Dixon, where I started high school. To make moving easier for my parents, they sent my sisters and I away. I was sent to Winters to stay with a friend, Phyllis Robbins. She was a senior in high school and Carmen Lopez, who came from an old Winter's pioneer Spanish family, was her friend. For the first time I was introduced to the Spanish language and family. Phyllis and I were invited to join her family for a barbecue. On the bank of Putah creek, they cooked a pig in the sand. That was a new experience for me, and the meat was delicious. I ate so much that the old grandmother came over to see if I was all right.

In high school, I studied Spanish and loved the language. Our teacher was marvelous and danced in the opera in San Francisco. I was fortunate to hear her stories and to see her dance in *Carmen*.

After my husband and I moved to the ranch in 1953, we had one baby and then I had two more within two years. I had little opportunity to use my high school Spanish with the Basque workers who lived with us. I learned how hard working, goal-oriented and respectful they were. They all spoke several languages, though they were not formally educated. They were good models for characters.

I became very ill, spent one year in bed and almost died. Since we lived far out in the country with three preschool children, I needed help. Sofia Torres y Ojeda arrived from Juarez, Mexico. She cared for me, our home and the children, and lived with us for four years. She was three years younger than I, but a woman of great wisdom. She was like my sister. She did not speak English, so I really began to learn Spanish with her. However, it was a crude Spanish. I had learned the way all immigrants learn- the hard way. I wanted to be fluent. I needed to study the language and master the subjunctive.

Later, I had the opportunity to return to the University at Davis. My family and I lived in Married Student Housing for four years while I studied

Spanish and received my lifetime teaching credential.

While there, I studied Analytical Poetry for one entire year in Spanish from a wonderful professor, Dr. Homero Castillo from Chile. One day, he stopped in the middle of his lecture and told us a story which stayed in my mind: the Spanish monarchy announced the Edict of Expulsion, which was composed by Torquemada, the church's Grand Inquisitor of the Inquisition. It stated that all Jews and Moors would speak Spanish, convert to the Catholic religion, or leave Spain or be sentenced to death. All lands and holdings would be confiscated. He explained that many Jewish people converted by changing their names and using the names of things like mountains, rivers, places, etc. I noticed my professor's name was Castillo, Castle, so I felt he probably was Jewish. I learned that many came to the New World. I was shocked. That story stayed with me always. This led to me wanting to know more, and it is why I put it into my story.

I watched a television novel, called a telenovela, titled "Ramona." It was based on a book written in 1880 about the Californios. Out of the hundreds I have seen, I never forgot it. That was when I first learned what happened when the Americans took over California. At that time there were no means of communication, so big posters were created and hung in back alleys and hidden high up under trees with thick foliage. The posters demanded that all Indians, who had no concept of land ownership, and landowners register/record their property. Anyone who couldn't comply lost their land. I was appalled. History did not teach that, and I never forgot it.

When genealogies for my mother's and my father's families were written, they triggered questions. I come from a long line of farmers and ranchers. How did they acquire so much property? They all immigrated here during the Gold Rush era, but they were not miners. They worked and bought land.

Another incident occurred that would become important to me. After I retired from the regular school system, I joined a writing group in Davis. It seemed an amazing coincidence that the hostess was the wife of my first Spanish professor when I returned to U.C. Davis, after the twins were born. I had been out of school for thirteen years and going back was difficult. Studying with Dr. Keller gave me the start I needed and the strength, back then, to stick it out for four years. What a small world.

I, then, remembered an incredible experience with Pir Viliyat Iniyat Khan, International Director of the Order of the Sufi's, who came from India, and spent a weekend in my home in 1972. As he was leaving and as his driver started to drive him away, he looked out the window at me and said, "Your destiny is Spanish." I stood there dumbfounded, watching them disappear down the street. That was forty-eight years ago. Pir Viliyat did not know that I spoke Spanish, and there was nothing in my home to suggest anything Spanish. I realized, then, the importance of the Spanish language for me in my life, and I knew it would continue.

During that time, I watched a Mexican movie with a famous actor, who was playing a strong, macho role. I wondered if I could write and capture his character. I didn't do anything with that piece of writing until I moved to Vacaville in 2007 and joined the Town Square Writers group. I read my character study to them. They really liked it and gave me good constructive criticism. The leader told us to expand and develop our character. The character and the time period captured me, 1848 – 1849, and so my story began and metamorphosed into a book - to my great surprise.

Acknowledgments

I was a bare beginner with writing fiction, but I kept trying due to the encouragement and constructive critiques from the Vacaville Town Square Writers. After moving from Vacaville to Grass Valley, CA, I missed the group dynamics, the intriguing stories other people wrote, and the help I received.

Author Rachel Howard, a wonderful professor of writing, came into my life, and kept pushing and encouraging me forward. There would be no book without her.

I also want to acknowledge the remarks, ideas, and suggestions from friends, family, and especially my daughter, Yvonne Read, for her insight and for lending an ear to my story.

A special thanks goes to Ernest for his constant support in taking care of me and for his clarity in picking up on areas of confusion and lack in my writing.

My uncle, Donaldo Francisco Gomez, Doctor of Veterinary Medicine, was a huge, positive and large influence in my life. He had such a love of life and sense of fun.

I would also like to especially thank the following people for their love and support: Nicolás Fagoaga, Vidal Echarte, and Javier Bereau from Spain, who lived with us many years on the ranch; Sofia Torres Ojeda, who came from Juarez, Mexico, to care for me and my family while I was very ill; Geraldina Sandoval from Mexicali, Mexico, who became a dear friend for years; Silvia Gil from Santiago, Chile, became a delightful friend during my time with the University of California at Davis and for years afterward; Fay Lavender Levoy, a longtime friend from my teaching days, who helped me research the hidden Jewish legacy part of the book; Amalia Medina, who helped me for many years; Silvia and Juan Gamiño are new friends and students of mine; and Eduardo and Margarita Ortega who are longtime friends, like family, from Nicaragua. These beautiful men and women have shared their wisdom and lives with me. They taught me the universality, the oneness, of all human beings regardless of birth, environment, education, etc. and that no one escapes the vagaries of life on this planet.

I found writing this book an amazing journey, and a fascinating challenge. I never dreamed how complex and startling California history was – it was quite an enlightening experience.

Prologue: The Land of the Californios

California received her name from a Queen Calafia of a mythical realm within a book of romance of chivalry written in the 1540s. These books were popular and spread about by Spanish navigators. The name California, from the mythical Queen Calafia, was predictive and appropriate with the later rise of Hollywood, the capital of illusions and dreams, drawing many into it as the feverish and delusional lure of the Gold Rush did earlier. Back then, California was a sparsely populated frontier and almost unknown. On the maps, California was considered an island and drawn as such into the 1700s.

Also, at that time, Spain was a strong influence in North America, controlling huge sections of land. She had also established a small occupation of Alta California, which guarded the route from the Philippines to Mexico.

In 1768, the Spanish monarchy demanded the colonization of upper Alta California. The colonization had occurred mainly along the coast with a small population made up of mostly military and convicts. In 1769, Fray Junipero Serra was sent to establish the missions in order to extend Spain's influence northward and stop the British and the Russians from coming down any further.

Many years later, gold was discovered in 1848 up in the Sierra Nevada mountains and the "Rush" was on. People flooded in from all over the world, but the Americans soon took over California. The Sierra was torn up by the gold diggers, who also stripped its timber, and the valley land was usurped from the Mexican Californios.

Jorge Luis Sandoval y Castillo, our hero, was born a Californio, into the pastoral life of early Spanish/Mexican California. Prudence Ann Mullen, our heroine, came from the faraway land of Maine in the United States. They were thrown together with their lives disrupted and shaped by forces beyond their control. California would be torn apart within an intense period of two years.

Our story begins in 1848.

Prólogo: La tierra de los californios

California recibió su nombre de una Reina llamada "Calafia" quien provenia de un reino místico, escrito en un libro de historias románticas de la época de la caballería medieval en los años 1540s y que fue esparcido por el mundo con los navegadores españoles. En aquel entonces, se creía que California era una isla y continuaba siendo dibujado de esta forma en mapas hasta los años 1700s.

El nombre California desde su principio estuvo destinado (y fue muy apropiado) para llegar a ascender más tarde en Hollywood, la capital mundial de las ilusiones y los sueños, atrayendo a mucha gente así de la misma manera como lo hizo el "Gold Rush" (la fiebre del oro) en el siglo anterior.

En esa época, España fue una influencia fuerte en Norteamérica controlando tierras extensas. España logró establecer una pequeña ocupación en California en la parte que protegía la ruta de las Filipinas hasta México.

En 1768, La Monarquía Española, con su autoridad, pidió la colonización de Alta California. La colonización ocurrió en las regiones junto a la costa del Océano Pacífico, que en su mayoría estaba compuestas por fuerzas militares, convictos (Los Precidios), y unos religiosos, Los Franciscos (Las Misiones).

El Francisco, Padre Junípero Serra, fue un gran ímpetu de esta época, estableciendo las misiones, dirigido para extender la influencia de España más al norte y ponerle un paro a los exploradores rusos y los ingleses quienes estaban llegando demasiado cerca con sus exploraciones intrusivas.

El Padre Serra llegó a San Francisco donde construyó la misión San Francisco de Asís, también llamada Misión Dolores.

Jorge Luis Sandoval de Castillo, nuestro héroe, nació siendo un Californio, entrando una vida pastoral, autosuficiente, sin cambios, con trabajo duro, una vida social activa, afable, y católica.

Prudence Ann Mullen, nuestra heroina, vino de tierra lejana de Maine en los Estados Unidos. Ella nació en un mundo agricultura, también de negocios bien desarrollados. Ella era inglesa, educada, y protestante.

La fuerza del destino los lanzaría juntos por fuerzas más allá de su control. California, también, sufrió esas fuerzas que la afectaron y la cambiaron con violencia dentro de un periodo de dos años.

Las misiones dejaron de recibir el subsidio de España y también la recompensa de la iglesia. Descendieron en decadencia causando un desarreglo entre los indios, lo cual hicieron trastornos dentro de Las Rancherías de los indios y muchos empezaron a formar grupos de bandidos. Los mercados de los Californios empezaron a descender y, entonces, se descubrió el oro en las montañas de la Sierra y, así, comenzó "la fiebre del oro." En sólo dos años, los americanos se habían apoderado de California. La Sierra casi fue destruído por los mineros de oro. Ellos deforestaron los árboles de los montes, mientras que las tierras del valle estaban usurpadas de los Californios.

Nuestra historia comienza en el año 1848.

Map of el rio Linda

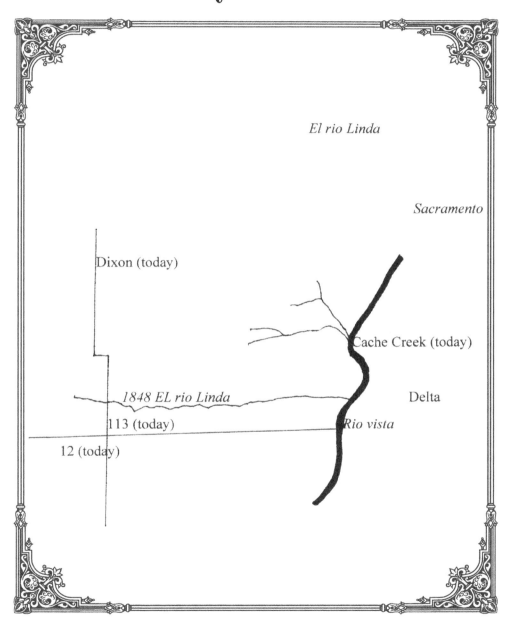

El rio Linda

Sacramento

Dixon (today)

Cache Creek (today)

1848 EL rio Linda

Delta

113 (today)

Rio vista

12 (today)

1
At the River

Prudence Mullens rested under the deep shade of a huge oak that rose up high on the bank of a slow-moving river. With the thick foliage it offered her, she felt protected and cooled from the hot June sun. "I miss home so much. I miss home so much," she whispered almost out loud to herself. She paused and allowed her shoulders to slump. *Maine is cooler and more civilized. I miss hearing English. I'm living in an incomprehensible world, and it's frightening.* A few tears came to her eyes while her thoughts went to her arduous, lengthy trip across the United States, and then to those who didn't make it and were left behind in unknown soil. *I made it.* She let her feeling of gratefulness out in a long sigh. *I will make it here, too. And when I can get enough money together, I will make it to San Francisco.* A sigh of sadness slipped slowly out and took her sinking thoughts with it.

She soaked up the view of the river, the hills, the lowering sun. She felt a wandering breeze wash over her face, hair and shoulders from time to time, which brought more relief from the heat. She felt a freedom here. No one knew her -- unlike Maine where she was under everyone's scrutiny. The memory of that pained her greatly.

She glanced at the accounting textbook next to her on the blanket that she had been re-reading for her new job. Her uncle gave it to her when he trained her to keep his books. She missed her uncle deeply. She wondered if he could ever make the trip out here. She had received no correspondence from him, and that worried her. *But what should I expect out here in this no man's land?* she thought with her feelings engulfed by bitterness.

I'm so lucky I landed here even if it is a hole-in-the-wall town, she said silently to herself, with a feeling of deep loneliness, allowing more tears. *At least I have a job, one I can do well, thanks to Uncle Lot.*

She rolled on her side, remembering the bandit who robbed her of everything except what was hidden under the wagon. *I have my gun. That's all I need, mister, if we meet again. I wouldn't be afraid to shoot anyone out here in this godforsaken country.* She hadn't realized the vastness of this new land, California. The emptiness within the country of human life, even Indians, shocked her. She had seen many animals like elk and antelope, but not many people, not even the Indians she had heard about. *Back home, there was always another ranch just a few miles away with friendly people. But, here? What's over that hill? And that one or that other higher one? Probably nothing*, she surmised.

Rolling back up, she rested on her elbows, now focusing across the river and enjoying the fragrances of the trees and grasses. She put her head back and let her hair swing in the wafting breeze. The cool, soothing air brought little whiffs of unknown smells as the memory of the many new smells of the cantina and her conversation with Facundo, the bartender, slipped silently in.

Facundo told me right. This is a lovely spot, and his directions were easy to follow. I'll thank him tonight when he's working in the cantina.

Prudence smiled, remembering what a handsome man he was. She had already noticed that he was married. He wore a wedding ring, and Pedro, his assistant, had to be his son. He looked just like him. *Facundo has such a big, generous heart; he's been so helpful to me, very giving, and strong, too.* She paused for a moment and thought a lot about last night: That unexpected brawl in the cantina had been frightening until Facundo had tossed the obnoxious drunk out by the scruff of his neck and the seat of his pants. *I am so grateful to be able to work with him even if it is in a cantina, and I have to live upstairs next to the brothel.* She shuddered.

She let go of her thoughts, took a deep breath, let it out slowly, and relaxed into her blanket on the ground. However, her thoughts seeped slowly in again. She swept back and forth in her thoughts and feelings between the gratefulness of having a job and the humiliation of where she had to work. No one in her societal class in Maine would be in such a situation. The willingness of her aunt and uncle to teach her everything they could had saved her from living the life of the brothel girls. During her reverie, her eyes perused the beauty of the countryside. She felt her muscles soften and her breathing slow down in the quiet peacefulness. She let out a long sigh of surrender to her new life.

Once again, absorbing the sights of the solid oaks and the meandering river, she realized the heat really didn't bother her. Serenity wrapped her and soothed her soul.

I will come here as often as I can. This spot is so peaceful and so inviting. I need this. She patted her gun, which she kept at hand. "I'm safe here. I'm so glad Uncle Lot made me take this big Colt Forty-Four for the long over-land trip. I definitely will come here again," she said out loud, feeling it, too.

The river, a rich, creamy coffee color, held her view as its slow, forward movement called to her, pulling at her desires. *I'm a good, strong swimmer. Next time, next time! Wish I could be in there now.*

She stretched and lay back on her blanket. Her eyes were attracted to a beautiful silver squirrel high in the big oak. She lay there observing it. *This is pure heaven. I could lie here all night.* But she knew that nighttime would not be safe. *I'll leave in time to find my way home, but that chicken leg, those olives, and that piece of freshly made bread in my basket are too inviting, and I'm hungry. I still have time to eat something,* she decided.

Lowering in the late afternoon, the brilliant sun left long shadows of darkening contrasts with the last hold-out of strong light. Glancing around, Jorge Luis knew it was time to quit. He needed a break, and he could hear his Peruvian Paso, Santón, whinnying for a good ride.

After he dismissed his workers for the day, he saddled up, mounted, and rode quietly for some time, relaxing into feeling one with his horse and its smooth, almost floating gait, the *paso llano*. He smiled as he saw the apple orchard in the distance, which almost hidden by the groves of oak trees. The oak trees thinned out as he left behind the hacienda.

Ahead of him was the open vastness of his family's land, granted to them by the king of Spain. His eyes swept across the land. Turning in his saddle, he looked back to the eastern horizon. He then moved slowly around to observe the hills that led up into the western coastal ranges. He took in a big breath of fresh air, filling his lungs. This was his favorite time of day as being out in nature always filled his soul, especially after a hard day's work.

"You, Santón. I want to give you a good workout. I didn't have a chance to do your training this morning, so we'll take an extra-long ride out to the river. I need to check out the land and evaluate the grazing situation for the cattle."

Santón twitched his ears, letting him know he had heard him.

Jorge Luis Sandoval y Castillo would someday inherit all this land. As he swept his eyes over the vastness of the property, in the depth of his soul, he felt that connection of belonging, feeling one with this land, his family, and his heritage - deep roots.

Riding silently in tune with the land and the lowering sun, Jorge Luis reflected upon his present life. *How good it is to be out here on land that has been in my family for generations.* He paused, feeling the pride in his chest.

Suddenly, his father's once ruddy and handsome face filled his mind. His light brown hair had now turned to white. His eyes, always bright and alert, had faded to withered grey. The image of his father's sunken cheeks filled Jorge Luis with an aching sadness – tinged with a feeling of a coming, unwanted loneliness. This image of his terminally ill father carried thoughts that rushed across his mind. *Papá was so alive, constantly active, hard-working. He was a great storyteller, full of fun, always laughing, and singing, and then hit with that slow, all-consuming illness? I can't believe God could want that.* He let his thoughts fly with the wind, while relaxing into his seat with the rhythm of his smooth-paced Santón. He kept checking out the condition of the grazing fields. The grass still looked good, thick and high enough, but *where are our sheep? I'll send Gregorio out here to check. I don't want them wandering away.*

Not much further on, the image of his father crept in again. *Why do I see him like this when my physical eyes see only the beauty surrounding me? He knows I am capable of managing our rancho, all of its almost one hundred and fifty thousand acres. Why hasn't he given me total authority? I can't make decisions without that, and it angers me. I know he feels I need to be married to the proper woman and be settled. But definitely not to that pretty, immature, and silly Elena. Besides, she has eyes for Edgardo, not me. Yes, Papá, someday, but not now. I will not be pressured.* Marina, with her exotic beauty and earthy voice, crept into his thoughts just as he heard an unexpected sound.

A neigh sounded on the air, interrupting his thoughts. He pulled the reins, stopping Santón instantly. Santon's ears rapidly moved back and forth in response. He calmed Santón and said to himself, in a low whispering voice, "My god, who could that be? The Indians don't come here anymore. A rustler? I'll hang that *ladrón* up myself! ¡Maldita sea!"

Full of anger, he hurried Santón forward. Adrenaline flooded his body and mind. He instinctively touched his holster. His mind and his pistol were at the ready.

A few minutes later, he quietly and slowly rode down the long path leading to the river, which was thick with oak trees, willows, and wild roses. He was almost holding his breath as he rode silently into the clearing. His breath stopped at a strange sudden sight. He pulled Santón up short. A woman! He had never seen a woman out alone in the country. No woman he knew would dare. And, she had ridden a horse!

¡Diós mío! ¡She's got a man's pants on! ¡What an abomination! Jorge Luis was speechless.

Meanwhile, a soft, caressing breeze had been ruffling the leaves of the old oak and the tulles along the bank of the river, masking the sound of advancing hoof beats as Prudence rested, until a man on horseback was almost upon her. Prudence, startled, reacted by kneeling, grabbing her gun, and pointing it directly at him.

Jorge Luis stared at her as if she had arrived from the moon. He couldn't believe what he was seeing. Not only was she a strange woman but, also, a gorgeous one. Her golden, long hair glinted in the sun. Her face was small, well-formed with big, green eyes that were focused right on him. Her gun was on *him.*

¡*Jesucristo*¡ *A Colt Forty-Four Dragoon. How dare she,* he thought. Then aloud, in Spanish, he confronted her, "Who are you? What are you doing on my property?"

Prudence stood up, looking him straight in the eyes, and held her gun steady, even though she felt shaky inside. It was as if everything stood still, nothing moved, no noises. Her heart felt like it had stopped. She was so intently focused that everything blurred her vision except that man in front of her. She couldn't answer. *Damn, I know French, but I can't understand Spanish. What did he say? What did he say? Oh, God, don't let me panic.*

"*Hola, Señor,*" was all she could say. Her heart was pounding, and her breathing was difficult. Her mouth felt dry.

Her stance told him to be cautious. His inner voice told him that she knew how to use that gun, and he did not doubt it. He couldn't put his thoughts together over this unexpected confrontation. He didn't move. Nothing seemed to move. The place was deathly quiet. Not even the crickets made a sound.

Holding his breath, because he had been taught to believe women were irrational, emotional, and impulsive, he thought carefully about what to do. He decided to be very cautious.

"*Me ba-jo,*" he said deliberately, pointing to the ground and carefully lifted his leg over the horse, lowering it slowly. He pointed to her gun, shook his head, and carefully pronounced, "*No me dis-par-e.*"

She stood solid as a rock. The gun never wavered. She watched him intensely.

On the ground now, he noticed her blanket and picnic basket. Pointing to a book on the blanket, he said, astonished, to himself, "¿*Está Leyendo?*" His eyes widened, and he glanced at her, puzzled.

Prudence did not understand what he meant but would not let up. Her gun was up and steady. She wasn't taking a chance on what he was up to.

Jorge Luis was thinking that a woman reading was extraordinary. He didn't know any who did. In fact, he didn't know many men who did.

Speaking in Spanish, he said, curiously, "I want to see your book."

Carefully pointing, he moved deliberately and slowly toward the book and, looking at her, picked it up, "You are reading a book about mathematics!" His eyes widened and he appeared totally confused.

Prudence understood the word mathematics, but all she could answer was, "*Sí.*" She kept her eyes and gun directly on him and made a mental note to find a Spanish teacher tomorrow.

Jorge Luis gazed at her in amazement. His mind was filled with mixed images. *She is a beautiful woman. She reads math. She rides like a man. She dares to put on a man's pants. She carries a gun. What do I do with her?*

Time was running out. He realized that soon the sun would be too low, and she would be in danger -- not only from men but the animals, also. Pointing to the sun, pointing back to her, and then to her blanket, he made hand movements to pick up everything. He pointed to her again and then to her horse.

He took notice of the horse and recognized it. *¡Ay caray! She rented that horse from our stable. That's one of our horses. That's Old Flojo.*

She looked at him, at the sun, and waved him back further from her, and motioned for him to put his hands up. She couldn't trust him so close. She decided to keep her gun in her right hand and pick up her things, even though it would be clumsy, with her left. She quickly did what he wanted, picked up her leftover food, water and bread, and placed them into the saddlebag to be put on Old Flojo, while her mind raced.

I don't dare shoot him. He acts as if he owns this place. Maybe he does. If he does, then, perhaps, I don't have to be so on guard. Those chaps he's wearing are well used, but they are obviously not a workingman's chaps. His belt is hand-tooled and covered with silver. He's got on expensive boots. He may work, but he's no cowhand. And look at that ring – but, I don't care who he is. I'll shoot him if he makes one wrong move.

She moved quickly and mounted her horse as he looked on in wonder. He was looking at her differently now, no longer taken aback by her unexpected appearance at the river but with a true curiosity. He noticed that, although she had on a man's pants, her blouse was the latest style and of a high-quality material, similar to his sister's and not a peasant cotton. Her boots looked expensive, he noticed, very different than what was worn here. *She's obviously a competent woman*, he thought. *She is no stranger to rid-*

ing. She is educated for a woman. Where did she come from? Is she one of those foreigners I'm hearing about? I've got to find out who she is.

He led the way, confident she would not shoot him in the back, but he guessed she was perfectly capable of doing it, if he were to make any inappropriate move. He would be cautious and considerate with his actions.

Prudence followed, plodding along on her old nag, admiring the horse in front of her. *He's not riding any old cattle mount. I know a well-bred horse when I see one. I've never seen a gait like that. What breed could it be?* Suddenly, she felt a turmoil of longing for her own horse. *My sweet Wilma, I loved her so, and how I miss Beauty, my uncle's Arab mare. I loved to show her, and she ate up the applause.* She could see Beauty in her mind doing her fancy prancing with her neck and head held high, so perfectly, in front of an audience.

She looked at Old Flojo and felt the sadness clinging. They hadn't ridden far when she decided she would not allow herself to become "Poor Me." She did not want to slip into comparing. She sat up straighter and looked at her mount. She whispered, "Flojo, I'm really grateful for you, so grateful." She sat up, stiffening her backbone, and let her sadness drift away on the evening breeze. *That horse in front of me, I'll bet he shows it. I wish I could ask him.*

Jorge Luis slowly pulled Santón back and soon they were riding side by side when Jorge Luis pointed out a magnificent oak and said, "*el roble*" in Spanish. She repeated the word. She then said the word "oak" in English. He responded by repeating her word. She suddenly felt more comfortable, safer, and found herself starting to relax and enjoy the ride.

On the other hand, Jorge Luis was still startled, challenged, and puzzled by this unknown woman with her dazzling green eyes and long, golden hair. He became very alert -- observing her from head to toe. *She sure rides like a man, pants and all, not sidesaddle like the women I know, if they ride at all. She rides well on Old Flojo. She has a good seat. I wonder how she would handle Santón?*

Dark came fast as they reached the edge of town.

Prudence was lost in her own mind. She was captivated by this man of impeccable manners; she observed that he carried himself with authority. *He cuts quite a presence*, she noted.

I've never met a man like him. He's not like those crude, ill-mannered cowboys or those repulsive foreigners from everywhere, showing up in the cantina, speaking so many different languages. Where on earth are they coming from? And why? I know I am a foreigner from Maine, and I know how and why I landed here, but all those men? I don't understand what is going on. She rode along quietly for a moment, contemplating the comparison of those rough and strange ruffians with the man riding beside her. She glanced quickly at Jorge Luis and thought, *I would like to know more about this gentleman, and - he obviously is a gentleman. He sure sits his horse with ease, and, I must admit, he's not only tall but very good looking. I will find out from Facundo. He seems to know everyone.*

They stopped and prepared to part. Jorge Luis, in his slow and careful Spanish, expressed his farewell in a tone that was smooth and very polite, "Don't go out there again. It is too dangerous for a woman out there alone. Anything could happen. Besides, you were trespassing." To himself he added, *Why haven't I heard about her? Where did she come from? Facundo will know.*

Looking him straight in the eyes and smiling, Prudence said, "*Grácias, Señor.*" Then, in her clipped-English, added, "I know what you are saying, mister. I will return there again anytime I want. I am not a servant to be ordered about."

She turned her back to him, spurred Old Flojo and trotted on. She did not look back. He sat on *Santón,* pensively, watching her until she disappeared into the village.

Turning his horse, he headed home feeling unsure if he would share this unexpected adventure with anyone. His concept of women had been shattered. His comfortable and controlled view of his pastoral life, that he had seen unrolling in his future, began to crack like the crackling of soil dried by the heat of summer. He rode uncomfortably with his feelings erupting and broiling from the shock of this unexpected encounter. His predictable world had, in one jolt, become unsettling and deeply unsafe.

2

Jorge Luis

orge Luis' dreams that night were full, heavy and bright in kaleidoscopic colors – a mix of two women, river scenes, flying among the stars, and many unidentifiable men. He tossed and turned, sleeping fitfully with black eyes and green eyes intruding, in and out, looking questioningly at him.

The morning came quickly, with its summer warmth, to this eldest son of Emiliano and Aldiana Sandoval. Jorge Luis Sandoval y Castillo could light up the eyes of any woman, young or old. Dark, wavy chestnut hair framed a high cheek-boned and strong-jawed face. Dark, intense eyes with a Roman nose gave him a clean and arrogant look. Tall for a Sandoval, he stood at six feet. Not only did he inherit from somewhere his height, but he also carried the broadest shoulders and the narrowest of hips from his mother's side, the Castillos. This eldest Sandoval at the age of 30 was at his prime.

This morning he woke to stiffness and some lethargy. He still didn't understand what had happened yesterday. "Unreal" was what he thought of it. He shrugged it off, dressed, and went down for breakfast. His workday would prove to be long, dirty, and sweaty, due to being a day at the end of June when the summer heat was beginning to augment.

The scourge of the angry, biting gnats that came out in full force in the middle of May had not been killed off yet. They should disappear by July fourth, as usual. It took a real hot spell to kill them. The men still had to cover their heads and necks to keep gnats out of their eyes, noses and ears, as well as tie their long sleeves to the gloves and tie boots over their pant legs to be able to work. The men looked forward to the stiff breeze arriving from the Yerba Buena Bay in the late afternoon, which would blow away the gnats. The big, old oak trees were lush with their foliage, and up in the hills the manzanitas still had a few remnants of their lovely pink flowers. During the late afternoon, the animals were all holed up somewhere, waiting for a cool evening.

Working in the heat was unpleasant and debilitating for the men, but that day, it was especially difficult for Jorge Luis when, across his mind, slid the memory of a gun pointed directly at him, held in the unwavering hand of a beautiful woman dressed in a man's pants. The situation was so far out of the realm of his experience that he found himself on the edge of denying its reality. On the other hand, there was a feeling of a buried, faint memory of a long ago, poking at him. It was too long ago, and it slipped away. He felt as if he had known her. *Maybe it was one of those deja vu memories my brother, Edgardo, mentions. Why would I feel that? No, no, can't be. I don't believe in that nonsense.* He felt an inner turmoil and didn't enjoy not understanding things.

Well, he thought, *that was quite an experience, but, in all likelihood, I will never see her again.* He closed his mind and turned his thoughts to his current lady, Marina. Suddenly, he looked forward to seeing her tonight at the cantina.

Jorge Luis wiped his sweaty forehead on his sleeve and called it quits, which was early for him, but his men would finish later. He headed for the house to clean up. He bathed and dressed impeccably in tan leather pants with silver conches down the sides. He wore a light jacket of cotton to match. A large silver belt tied his outfit together. His town-hat was carried on his back by his neck bolo tie so that he would be able to enjoy the evening breeze, as it flowed over his face and hair, while riding his horse to town. It would tell anyone who he was – the owner's son. He was quite dashing.

He left the hacienda riding his famous Peruvian Paso, Santón. His saddle, made to order of hand-tooled leather, was swaddled in the finest wool fleece for extra comfort. Jorge Luis rode with pride, his head held high. He rode as one with his horse. He had been riding since he was two years old and the rhythm of a horse was as natural to him as breathing.

The hour ride loosened the worries and problems of the workday. He let go of having to bark orders, maintain discipline, and think fast on his feet in order to solve the many problems that arose daily on a busy ranch.

Upon arrival in the small pueblo, which was a part of the Sandoval land grant, everyone on the streets recognized him. They stopped to watch as he halted in front of his family's stable. He dismounted in one fluid movement from his prize Paso. The reins were handed to a young, thin boy about eleven, who was generously tipped.

Jorge Luis pushed back his wind-swept hair, fingered his thick mustache, and brushed the dust from pants that fit only too well.

He glanced curiously at the boy, "Pepito, how's your father today,

¿mejor?"

Pepito lowered his eyes. His shoulders slumped, *"No, Señor."*

"Here then, *toma*. The stable needs your dad. Maybe this will help get him some medication. It's too much for you to do alone," he said as he pressed a few more coins in the small, dark hands. He paused for just an instant, as his eyes focused on the fading purples and golds of the receding sun. Then, moving with a quick, tight gait, he covered the distance to Cantina de Las Flores. He could hardly wait to get there. He loved his world, so predictable, routine, conventional – no surprises, no mystery – well, one.

Jorge Luis entered the cantina for his drink and his woman. He did this almost every night – the same *mujer* and the same tequila. He knew all the women, but his was the prize of the lot. Marina was a beauty and she was his. His head told him so, at least while he was there. His heart was wiser, and it said "no," but the message hadn't reached his head, not yet, and it wouldn't tonight. After all, he was a Sandoval, and the owner's son, wasn't he?

Sweeping the room with his dark, penetrating eyes, he visually placed each man, but not the women. He knew where his had better be. What would he do if some night she wasn't there? The thought chilled him.

He shifted his hip slightly, feeling the sensual security and power of his hand-tooled, silver-studded gun belt. He was as quick and accurate with his pistol as he was with his fists. He paused by the bar to acknowledge Facundo, the bartender.

Facundo, a childhood friend, held loyalty to his boss as sacred. The offers of bribes that came his way in the cantina had no effect on him. He was honest and trustworthy. The men who offered bribes learned that if they offered a second time, they were out the door and never allowed back into the cantina. Facundo was a man of his word.

Jorge Luis' quick glance confirmed that his woman was at his table with two waiting drinks. His Marina, her face glowing with expected happiness, was gorgeous in an alizarin crimson, satin gown. It set off her soft, very long, thick black hair. His eyes devoured her, but he had never let his feelings get out of hand toward her. She would never enter his life outside of the cantina. She would never be more than what she was tonight. This was a part of his world he had never questioned.

Jorge Luis nodded at Facundo, turned, and began to slip through the crowd to reach the table – his table. If anyone had sat there earlier, they quickly moved when Marina appeared. Marina looked up into his eyes with a warm and inviting smile.

"Sit down, *amor*. Your drink is waiting for you. So am I." Jorge Luis pulled the chair out, smiled at Marina, but stood a moment to check out the patrons.

"Facundo told me," he said to Marina, "more and more foreigners are slowly filtering in. I see there are more here tonight. They are not Mexicans or Indians, either. I don't like that."

"I agree with you. We are servicing more unknown men than usual. It seems they are headed up to the mountains for gold. At least, that is what we are hearing. Hard to believe."

They both picked up their drinks. They drank their tequilas in silence. When the drinks were drained, he quietly slipped his arm around her slim waist as they both rose from the table.

As they passed the bar, one of the men turned to get off the bar stool, caught the hem of her dress and stepped into her as if he were grabbing her. Without a pause, Jorge Luis pulled Marina tighter to his side with his left arm, punched the man down with his right and drew his gun -- all in one startling movement. Sparse words shot out like cold steel, "Turn around. No one touches my woman."

The man turned and looked at him, mouth open, eyes blurred in a stupor. Jorge Luis pulled the trigger and moved a tense, shocked Marina through the private door into the bordello. The crowd went silent, with all eyes locked on Jorge Luis as they disappeared. No one knew what to expect. He pushed Marina towards the stairs. In a breathless voice, she said, "Were you trying to kill him?"

"*Claro que no*. You know me better than that. I am a Catholic, a true Christian. I only kill out of necessity. We cannot allow more and more of those uncouth heathens to come in here and rough up the place. I won't allow it. Tonight, they needed to know that, and who I am. I think they do now." He pushed a shocked and trembling Marina up the stairs, a bit of passion squelched.

The men below whispered among themselves. Tempers simmered. A few threats were circulating, "Next time it will be him that gets the bullet in the foot. Just wait until the Americans take over. He'll get his come-uppance." Some left the cantina, but, eventually, the rest went back to their games as if nothing had happened. In that annoying incident, Jorge Luis did not recognize the warning of more changes to come.

3
Guests for Dinner

orge Luis' encounter with that golden-haired, green-eyed beauty, even in a man's pants, haunted him, stirring feelings that he tried to repress the entire ride home from the cantina to the hacienda. But her image stayed locked in his mind.

While riding back from town, he felt a little guilty about having taken off work early to leave, riding Santón while some of the men might continue working until sundown, even though they were told they could leave. They had to take advantage of the last rays of light. Working at night was too dangerous from fire with candles or lanterns in the barn. Now, his leaving for home was earlier than usual, but he did not feel like spending any more time in the cantina. He hurried Santón into his *sobreandando* gait. He didn't want to push him into a gallop in the dark for fear of stepping into a rut or hole, but he was looking forward to a hot bath, dinner, and early to bed. He would be up with the birds in the morning.

Arriving, finally, at the stables, Jorge Luis handed the reins to Juan, his manager for the horses, "Juan, tomorrow bring in three steers and keep them in corral number five for at least a week. I want you to begin *Blanca's* training. I know she'll make a good cow pony. Her instincts are quick."

"*Está bién,* Boss. Tomorrow I do it."

Jorge Luis removed his chaps in the equipment room, slapping them a couple of times against a saddle barrel – a little harder than usual to get the dust and his continued frustration of feeling out of his element with that woman. She kept slipping into his mind, and it really irritated him. He slung them over a hook on the wall, turned and hurried to the house.

Jorge Luis took the wide steps, leading to the front veranda, two at a time, his thoughts on the work for tomorrow and that – that – woman he met. The eight-foot, hand-carved double doors were too heavy to rush through. Jorge Luis stopped, pushed them open and made a dash for the stairs where his mother, Aldiana, stopped him.

"I'm sorry, *Mijo,* I know you don't know yet, and it is a little late, but we're having guests for dinner. The Ochoas will arrive about nine o'clock, and we will eat by ten o'clock. Please hurry and clean up. I want you down here when they arrive," she said. Aldiana already showed signs of being tired with wisps of hair flying around her face, catching in her mouth when she spoke. She couldn't brush them away, so she had to pull them out and poke them back into her unruly bun on the back of her head.

He kissed her on the forehead saying, "Mamá, another boring, boring, boring evening? I suppose Elena will be fawning all over me as usual! Ma, I can't stand that! I hope Edgardo's here. She likes him better anyway." Instantly, an image of that strange woman popped into his brain. *Díos, what a contrast to Elena she makes*, he thought. " Mamá, you look a little tired. Why don't you rest a while before they arrive?"

"No, no, I'm fine. But you, Mijo, what's the matter with you? You look distracted. *Mijo*, you are expected to be your mature, gentlemanly self. Elena has always been like a member of our family. I had hoped she'd become a daughter-in-law. You kids grew up together always having so much fun, and, by the way, where is Edgardo? That brother of yours had better be here also! Fiarela is not feeling well so she won't be down. Hurry, go, clean up. Come down and help choose the wines. Your father insists you have the best taste. Don't forget, bring a couple extra bottles. You know how Ignacio likes his wine."

Consuelo, *la mucama*, made sure his bath was ready as she did every evening. She put out soft towels, tested the water in the tub that stood on fancy lion legs one last time, and left his room quietly. After any day at work, Jorge Luis cleaned up and dressed for dinner, which was always formal in the evening.

He took as leisurely a soak as he thought he had time for, going over and over in his mind the events of the day. *My day went well, just as planned - except for ... that damned woman. I can't get her out of my mind. Who does she think she is*? He did not want to admit how much she got under his skin. The water was almost cold when he forced himself to get out. Later, dressed impeccably in black wool pants, embroidered in geometric designs down the sides, with a short jacket to match and a white shirt with a large white bow tie, he slipped on a heavy gold ring with a large, black agate. Looking quite elegant, he went downstairs in highly oiled, black dress boots and chose the wines for dinner. The wine cellar was small and on the side of the house close to the servants' area. At least choosing the wine gave him great

14

pleasure. He knew Señor Ochoa liked his wine. He would be tipping his elbow often.

A short time later, the Ochoas arrived in all their finery. Elena, he hated to admit, was especially charming, in a pink and gray satin one-piece dress with dainty, gray shoes. After a relaxing glass of wine and a general catchup conversation, they sat down for dinner. The chandelier had been lowered, the candles lit, and raised again. The candlelight created sparkling light around the room that moved as the candelabra swayed occasionally.

The evening was warm, so no fire burned in the fireplace. Elena made sure she sat next to Jorge Luis, but he kept turning away from her advances as much as he could.

His brother, the often-absent Edgardo, did not arrive until halfway through the meal, which set Aldiana and Emiliano on edge -- especially Emiliano who was ensconced on pillows to hold his weightless, almost bony body erect, and keep him as comfortable as possible. Edgardo sat down and almost missed his chair. He was already quite soused and looked as if he was ready to fire off a few belligerent words.

But, darling Elena, who had been all over Jorge Luis with her quick hands, pushy body, and sweet words, gave up and moved on Edgardo, who seemed to welcome it. Señora Ochoa remembered how well those two had always gotten along. She began to relax and tensions eased.

Señor Ochoa, well into his cups, broke into the light conversation, leaving the women to discuss the latest fashions by themselves while he addressed the men. Emiliano perked up and paid more attention.

"Say, I recently spent several days in Yerba Buena. You know they call it San Francisco now. They call Yerba Buena just that area in the south end where all the mint grows wild," said Ochoa, almost shouting because he was hard of hearing. "I must say the roads are better now for carriages, and, believe it or not, there is a ferry you can cross the bay with."

"Interesting," said Jorge Luis. "What took you there?"

"Well, I'm having a problem with the market changing." He picked up his napkin and held it against his mouth as he gave a loud belch, to his wife's embarrassment, "I went to talk to the market investors because I could not sell my usual amount of tallow or hides. The investors told me not to worry, that the market would turn around soon. I'm not convinced of that. I talked with too many people all over San Francisco to believe it."

"I'm sorry to hear that. How did you find San Francisco itself?" asked Edgardo.

"*Más o menos,*" said Señor Ochoa. "The city had a population of eight hundred people, but, now, unfortunately, a large number of the younger men are leaving for the gold fields."

"¡*Qué diablos*! That does not bode well. Did you hear anything about the missions? We've heard they are not doing as well. Something about not receiving their monies from Spain?" asked Jorge Luis.

"We-1-1," he said as he lifted his glass and took a long swig of wine, belching again with pleasure as the women looked on in exasperation. "I visited the Mission Dolores there. I didn't see as many Indians, but maybe they were just off somewhere. I should have asked. I did go over to the Presidio, which seemed to be in good shape."

Emiliano interrupted, "Well, it's about time. When I was in the military there, the Presidio was a disaster. One time, the ship from Spain didn't arrive for thirteen years - no pay, no supplies. That put us in a miserable position. We were not considered regular military, and you must realize that each Presidio was responsible for several missions. The conditions were so bad that we really couldn't do our jobs, which created problems, as you can imagine. The missions, especially, were upset with us."

Everyone stared in surprise, sat up, and listened. He paused to get a breath, "We lived in huts where the roofs fell in all the time, and in the winter the dirt floor ran with mud." Emiliano looked around the table and saw that everyone was focused on him, so he continued, "I heard they did, finally, reorganize the military to be like the regular army - so glad to hear it seems better." This time his cough stopped him from speaking, but the group sat politely to listen. "I must say, though, when my father retired, he was able to add to this land grant and then I added to it when I left the military."

"Interesting. I never knew that." Señor Ochoa looked at Emiliano, while wiping his mouth with a napkin, paused and then said, "They have a cannon up on the point now. I guess, in case some pirate" – another gulp of wine with another belch – "like Bouchard, that Argentinian pirate, might come again and lay waste to the few little coast towns. Say, I stopped in at my aunt's home, and she remembered that pirate. She lived in a small town near Monterey, and they got word that he and his two ships were nearing them very early in the morning. That was in 1810. They took the women and children and old men out immediately and hid them in the woods. They had to go in such a hurry that only two people had on shoes and none of the women had time to put on their dresses! She said they were half-naked, and when they returned home, every house was burnt to the ground, but the mission stepped in to help get clothing. After all these years, she says she still has nightmares occasionally."

"My lord, I can't imagine how frightening that must have been. I never heard about that," said Señora Ochoa.

"That's not going to happen. No pirate would dare come around here now. How about the harbor, many ships?" asked Edgardo, while the women sat silent now. This was man-talk. The women must not interrupt, or they would have to leave the table. With a bigger party, the women would withdraw to the *sala* and the men to the office or stay at the table.

"Oh yes, I saw many ships, but many of them unmanned. I was told the men simply jump ship and head for the mountains. In fact, the Chilenos have many ships there, and all came to mine gold."

"I understand they are the finest and most professional. They should be. Mining has been famous in Chile for hundreds of years," said Emiliano.

"Yes, yes," Ochoa started to say, but Señora Ochoa reached over and laid a hand on his arm, saying, "Enough business now, *Caro*. We have a long distance to go. We need to leave."

Aldiana offered her home for the night, but the Ochoas gave thanks for a lovely dinner, hugged everyone, gathered their things, and took their leave just as Jorge Luis ran out with a last gift of a bottle of excellent homemade wine and handed it to a grateful Señor Ochoa. "Ah, *mi compañera*, good company. *Gracias, hijo*."

"Oh, you will just snore like a lion and keep us all awake," said his wife.

"No, no, my nose might sing a little, but, between me and the noises of this coach, you two will sleep like the dead. I shall travel well with my little friend here, the best of the best, thanks to you*, joven*." He grabbed Jorge Luis and gave him a big hug, waved his bottle of wine, and climbed into the carriage, which began to roll soothingly along into the deep, dark of night.

As soon as the farewells had been said, and the carriage left, Jorge Luis and Edgardo rushed upstairs to their bedroom suites to retire. Jorge Luis turned to Edgardo to say, "Hey, *Hermano*, you didn't seem to mind Elena all over you tonight. What's with that?"

"I've never minded her. We've always been close since kids. Don't worry, there's nothing more than that there," said Edgardo.

The workday would come early, so they hurried to their own bedrooms.

Will Edgardo show up tomorrow morning? I should have said something. I can't let him get by with not being here to work any longer. I should have thought to ask him sooner, Jorge Luis thought as he slipped into bed.

Aldiana and Emiliano had stayed at the table when the Ochoas went outside to leave. Emiliano relaxed back into his pillows and seemed to breathe easier. Although his voice was weak, they chatted a moment at the table while they enjoyed a last slice of flan before expecting Donaldo, the butler and manservant, to come and carry Emiliano upstairs to his sickbed. That night had been a special treat for him to sit at dinner.

"*Cariño*, I realize once and for all that we cannot push Jorge Luis into marriage with Elena. He abhors her. Perhaps Edgardo, *¿Sí?* That would be good for both families, wouldn't it?"

Papá looked at Mamá with very tired eyes and retorted, "If so, she may suffer much. But then, who knows. ¿Quién sabe? It would have to be someone who would accept his sensitivity and talent. Aldiana, dear, I wish they would find happiness as much as we have. But you know the old saying: One cannot command the heart. He moved his hands and shrugged his shoulders as if to say that was just the way it was.

"Well, I only hope they do realize how important it is to marry well and maintain our name. Emi, *cariño*, I am beginning to worry about Fiarela. She is so depressed she would not come down to dinner. She is of marriageable age now. Somehow we must find a suitable young man."

Before they could carry on with their conversation, Donaldo suddenly appeared, nodded to both, and asked, "Are you ready to go upstairs or do you need more time?"

His chest tightened with a profound sadness, seeing his boss, his dearest friend of many years, so fragile and vulnerable. *Emiliano has been so good to me all our lives. We've been like twins, born here on the same day*. He held back tears as he gently lifted his old friend up from the chair. Emiliano was pale, as if drained of all his blood and just bones, light like a bird. It killed Donaldo to see Emiliano like this. He held him so gently. He would not do anything that might hurt him. They talked quietly on the way with Donaldo being extra cautious not to stumble or waver. He held his back as stiff as possible.

Aldiana went to her own room while Donaldo deposited Emiliano in his bed, helping his friend into his nightclothes. He settled him cautiously in the bed that had been warmed earlier with wrapped, hot rocks. He picked up a very light-weight, duck down-filled blanket and laid it softly, which was over his sick friend and tucked him in. He looked at the huge oak bed, hand-carved for Emiliano's father. *My god, his father died in this bed, and now he will. What will I do without him?* He wanted to pick him up and just sit and hold him. He loved this man who was like a brother. He crossed himself and sat down by the bedside. Emiliano had fallen asleep, but Donaldo waited until Aldiana entered to care for her husband. With eyes that drooped and a mouth that trembled, Donaldo bowed to her and silently disappeared. Tomorrow would be another day.

4
What About Edgardo?

The morning dawned warm. The day would be hot. The men would work in light shirts or none at all. Where the men worked, the shade was sparse unless they worked in the barns, but even there, the air was warm and stale. They prayed for the west wind from Yerba Buena to arrive early. Every day the winds arrived, sometimes weakly, but most often fiercely. A strong, cool wind would be welcomed by all.

Jorge Luis, pitching hay into the stall mangers, stopped to wipe off the sweat from his brow, all while thinking about his younger brother, Edgardo. *What's gotten into him? We always shared everything. Now, and for some time, he has told me nothing. Papá keeps asking me about him, but I don't know what to say. I don't like vacillating between worry and anger. Papá thinks maybe he is spending too much time with Shadowhawk up at the Ranchería. Maybe he is there, learning more about what he calls El más allá – that vision stuff he does, but I don't know.* He sighed deeply, rubbing the back of his neck. *Maybe I should talk to Juan.*

Juan was like a second father to Jorge Luis and Edgardo, and a life-long friend and confidant to Emiliano. Jorge Luis found him in the equipment room, checking the harnesses. By the time he entered the tack room, his anger had augmented with each step, though he was bombarded by confusing thoughts concerning Edgardo's absences and his lack of responsibility.

"Juan, where's Edgardo?" Jorge Luis received a puzzled look in return and a shake of Juan's head. "Juan, I don't know what is going on with my brother. I'm at my wit's end with him. I don't know whether to be worried or angry." Juan sat down on a saddle barrel and covered his mouth with his hand, looking pensive.

Jorge Luis stared directly into Juan's eyes and said softly but very clearly, "I want you to do a special job - a job *muy delicado*. I don't know why, but every so often, Edgardo just up and disappears. He's gone quite a while and won't tell me where he goes. Tells me it's none of my business, and he almost hit me one day. That's not the brother that I know. He's not showing up for work. What the hell is he doing? I want you to follow him. I need to know what he's up to."

Juan moved his hand, rubbing it over his chin and mouth, looking down in thought but did not say anything, and just listened to Jorge Luis, ranting on.

"I can't understand his surliness when I ask him. He was always carefree and happy, and now? Please, Juan," he begged, as he placed his hand on Juan's shoulder and lowered his voice, "Don't say anything to anyone -- *nadie*."

"*Está bién, hijo*. Not to worry. *Soy una tumba*. The dead don't talk. I'll follow carefully and watch." He stood up, turned, and started cleaning the saddle again with the saddle soap he had been holding.

Everyone at the hacienda considered Juan an unbeatable tracker, but three weeks passed before he had an opportunity to follow Edgardo unseen. When he returned, he found and approached Jorge Luis to give him the report about his brother. "Boss," he began, "yesterday was the first day I could get away. I followed your brother, but I don't understand what I saw at all."

"Why? What do you mean? Where did he go?" Jorge Luis felt at a loss. He couldn't second-guess Juan and the possibility of pain coming in the future was creating a build-up of anxiety.

"Well, I found him up by the Ranchería at the Indian gravesite. He spent the entire time at a grave. He appeared quite emotional, crying a lot, and he seemed to be praying a lot. He even lay on the ground as if trying to hold whoever is in there."

Jorge Luis stared at him, lost for words. Finally, he said, "Juan, did you see the name on the tombstone?"

"No, *Patrón*. There is no gravestone. It is a simple Indian grave. I cannot even guess why he was there. I'll follow him again if you wish."

"*Sí*, Juan. I would appreciate it. I don't know what to think, and remember, this seems to be something more than *delicado*." He felt his heart sink. He didn't know what to think. Nothing made sense.

"Sorry, Boss. I'll do the best I can, and I will follow like *un fantasma*."

Another ten days passed before Juan saw Edgardo slip out of the stables and leave. He quietly followed him on the horse he had kept ready. He had already tied sacking over his horse's hooves to keep him quiet.

However, this time, Juan was even more puzzled when he returned to report to Jorge Luis. Juan found Jorge Luis in the office with his nose in the financial books. Jorge Luis looked up, blinking his eyes to clear out the numbers, brushed his unruly hair back and said, "Sit, Juan, and tell me what happened this time." His breath was short from fear of what he might hear.

"*Jefe*, I followed Edgardo this morning, but it's even more confusing than before. He spent the time in the Indian *Ranchería* where I couldn't see him except for one time when he was carrying a tiny child on his shoulders, as if he were playing with it. He did not go back to the grave. Do you want me to continue?"

"I don't know, Juan. Let me think about it."

"*Está bién*." Juan sauntered off to the stables where he oversaw the management of the horses, the equipment, training, and breeding programs. He had been the stable manager for many years and knew horses thoroughly.

Jorge Luis sat there, feeling both dumb and numb. Nothing was making any sense. Somehow soon, he must confront Edgardo with his bizarre behavior. This situation had been going on longer than he realized. He began to let go of his anger and started to feel, instead, a deepening concern. *He used to follow me like a puppy. Could it be a woman? Surely, he would tell me. Is he upset that he can't inherit legally? His lack of authority? His absences are creating ill-will among the men.* Jorge Luis felt as if he had taken a punch to the gut, but he didn't want to deal with it now. "I've got too much to do. I'll wait a while and see if Edgardo explains everything," he muttered to himself.

Jorge Luis pushed the confusion and even the fear of discovering the truth out of his mind and his feelings. He pulled in his gut, pushed out his chest, now feeling more like the *Patrón's* son, and strode off to work outside in the hot, clinging air. He would spend the rest of the day training Santón. He wanted him ready for the next *charreada*, that is, if Papá was still living. He also spent time thinking about what he would wear as his costume when he rode *Santón,* leading the parade down the main street. Later, he would show off his horsemanship, his roping skills, and his skills with the whip. He looked forward to winning the chicken race. Santón would make sure of that. *I know there's no horse faster than mine. None of them, except mine and Edgardo's, will allow the rider to lean as far down to the ground as we can.*

He was focusing on the race. It was a strange one, and he wondered how it had begun. A rooster was buried up to its neck. Each rider had a turn to race by the buried chicken, lean way down and try to grab the chicken by the head and neck and pull it out of the ground where it was buried. The rider who managed to pull it out was the winner, and his prize was often to have the first dance with the prettiest girl at the fiesta that night. *How could I even think that Prudence would be there? She would be the prettiest - by far. However, my brother could win, and then what? Would he pick Prudence? Would she dance with him and not me? What does it matter anyway? It's stupid to think about it.* He couldn't help worrying about his brother because his horsemanship skills were unbeatable.

His brother, Edgardo, would demonstrate his famous riding abilities. He could ride like an Indian, no saddle, no bridle, and hang on the horse's side as if hiding from being shot by an arrow. He had felt so proud of his younger brother, but now, he was worrying about him. He and Edgardo, also, would be representing the family, so it all had to be perfect. *But, what if Edgardo did pick Prudence as his dance partner?*

His sister and mother would be wearing the traditional long, full-skirted, colorful dresses, and riding sidesaddle in the entrance procession to open the rodeo. *I wonder if Prudence would like to join them?* A sudden image of a golden-haired beauty riding like a man joined the images in his mind. He blinked it away, shaking his head, while he deliberately tried to force a vision of his dark-haired beauty, Marina. That didn't work, but he did manage to push his uncooperative brother into a tiny corner of his mind for the rest of a warm, and, now, an unsettling, routine day.

5
Facundo Knows

Prudence left her window open all night. In the morning, the sudden brightness of the rising sun woke her quite early. She went downstairs to the hotel restaurant for her usual steak, eggs, and coffee breakfast. After eating heartily, Prudence felt ready to tackle the cantina's financial books.

Entering the office, she looked around at a room that was bare bones. One wall had a small fireplace, closed now. A few shelves covered one wall, along with hooks to hang coats. There were three old wooden chairs. Clearly a *man's* room, she observed.

Prudence pulled out the desk chair and sat down. She started her morning ritual by checking her pencils, ink well, and quill pen. Opening one of the financial record books, Prudence was appalled by the state of the books. She noticed names so poorly written they were undecipherable. Some items were placed in incorrect categories. The book she was checking appeared to have been done in great haste with ink splashed and dripped on the pages. She realized money was being lost and wasted. Busy with her numbers, she did not hear Facundo's soft knock and quiet entrance.

"Good morning, Señorita Prudence. How you today?"

"Oh, good morning. I'm well, thank you. Facundo -- the river was delightful, a perfect spot. I loved the beautiful scenery and the peacefulness. I could have stayed there forever. But, Facundo, a very strange man came and made me leave. He was polite but a little arrogant. Who was he? Do you know? I wasn't frightened, but he was very insistent that I go."

Facundo, the bartender, did speak some broken English, "Oh, Señorita, I sorry. I no warn you. Sandoval family own all land. That was son, on *magnífico* horse ¿no?"

Prudence nodded, "Oh, yes, what a gorgeous horse." She opened her eyes wide with raised eyebrows and said, "What breed is it? Do you know?"

"Sí, Señorita, Peruvian Paso. The family receive land grant from king of Spain. They own town, cantina, *todo*! They good people. Good to us and want we obey, respect, remember position."

Prudence bristled when she heard the words "remember position." She felt insulted. After all, she knew she was more educated than any of these country bumpkins. *I am an independent woman. I was taught to think for myself, and I am a professional.* No one had ever looked down on her before, and she was not about to allow anyone to now.

She over-reacted with a growing resentment, remembering how handsome that man had been, and that he had such exceptional manners. He owned a Peruvian Paso, one of the finest horses. Her resentment turned into a hard anger, feeling as if she would be looked down on as a low-class woman and rejected out of hand without consideration.

"What? You mean I am expected to act like a servant? Well, he has another think coming. I may be a working woman, but I am not a common laborer! I won't kowtow to anyone," she said as she took in a deep breath and frowned. "I may be forced to work in this cantina next to the bordello - which is so humiliating. At least, as a woman alone, I can take care of myself. How dare he think about me in that manner." With furrowed brows and full of anger, she looked straight at Facundo, who was surprised at her boldness, and said, "What's his name, Facundo?"

Not quite sure how to handle this emotional intensity, he tried to be calm, and so he answered with a smile, "*Señorita*, he good man. He talk Spanish, no English. Name is Jorge Luis Sandoval y Castillo. You call him Señor Sandoval. So sorry, Señorita Prudence."

"Good lord!" She suddenly realized she had been too outspoken. "I hope I didn't cause you any trouble. I only wanted a quiet, peaceful day for a change and, except for him, I had it, thanks to you."

"No important. We children together. We have much ups and downs." Facundo produced a bigger smile, "He respect me. I his manager. Run business. Right-hand man."

"Good for you. I'm impressed," she said as she stood up, straightening her skirt. It was tight around the hips but flared out for walking. Facundo appreciated what he saw, his eyes lighting up. Her hair was rolled on the sides with a few tendrils flying about. She tucked them in under the rolls. "Facundo, I must find a Spanish teacher quickly. Do you know anyone?"

"*Sí, Señorita*. I ask Lola, sister of wife. She good teacher. No want much money."

"Thanks. I would appreciate that. I've studied French and Latin, so Spanish shouldn't be too hard." She looked at and pointed to the pile of registers on top of the desk, all in disarray, "These books are a disaster. It may take me weeks to clean these up. You are losing a lot of money here!"

She sounded angry which, again, shocked Facundo. He was unaccustomed to hearing a woman expressing anger toward him. *Hmm, Maria would never talk to me that way. This young lady is a foreigner all right. Do they all talk like that?*

"Do best, Señorita Prudence." With that said, Facundo gave a little bow and left to check the cantina supplies.

Meanwhile, at the hacienda, morning activities were in full swing. After Jorge Luis parceled out all the work orders to his men, and everyone knew what to do, he headed for the stables to saddle up Santón and leave for the pueblo. He had received a message that morning that Facundo needed him as soon as possible. He had Santón saddled in no time.

After he mounted, he struck a light spur to his horse, and Santón sped through the warming countryside at a fast gallop. He loved to run.

Jorge Luis arrived at the cantina not long after Prudence had talked to Facundo. He dismounted, tying Santón to the rail.

Facundo was taking inventory of his liquor in the cantina when Jorge Luis walked in, dragging his spurs across the floor, "¡Buenos! Faco, I received your message this morning. What's going on?"

"Hey, *amigo* – I need to talk to you. Do you have a moment?"

"*Claro*, Faco. Let's go into the back office."

"*Patrón*, the new bookkeeper is working in there right now," he said at the moment Jorge Luis opened the office door.

"What the hell? You? Facundo, what is she doing in here? Who is she?" Seeing her so soon shook him. He stepped back, banging a spur and scratching the floor. His eyes widened, seeing the image of her in a man's pants, holding that huge Colt forty-four directly on him. That took his breath away. He stared at Facundo with confusion and a little anger.

"*Patrón*, she is our new bookkeeper. And, a good one I might add."

Prudence sat in stunned silence. She never expected to see that man again so soon! If he owned everything, would he keep her on? A jolt of fear hit her in the middle of her stomach. She had to have this job to survive until her uncle arrived from Maine, possibly a good six months from now.

"Faco," he turned to look him in the eyes and said in a lower voice, "what's her name?"

"Sorry, Boss. I present to you *La Señorita* Prudence." In English, he spoke, "*Señorita* Prudence, to you, I present *Señor Jorge Luis Sandoval y Castillo*, your boss."

"Oh -" a small sound escaped from her mouth. She felt like sinking into her chair, but stood up for the proper introduction.

"Faco, tell her to leave. We need privacy."

Facundo was slightly taken aback by his boss' somewhat rude reaction and lack of politeness in not responding to the introduction. *What's going on here with him? I've never seen him act like this.* In his broken English, he explained to Prudence she needed to leave them alone to talk. She rose and gracefully left the room, but not without a fearful glance behind her.

"Let's sit down." Jorge Luis sat down in the office chair and motioned for Facundo to sit, but he remained standing. "Okay, now, what do you have to tell me?" asked Jorge Luis.

"*Patrón, amigo,* you know I stay here, working in the cantina, so I can be on top of what's going on. I hear everything. In here, the men drink. They talk. I listen. *And, I'm still wondering what went on between you and the girl.*"

Interrupting, Jorge Luis said, "I've always appreciated your information, Faco, and it has always been of great help. Now what's happening?"

"Jorge Luis, you have heard about the foreigners coming into town, but now they are arriving faster and more of them. They're coming for the gold in the Sierras, and I am thinking they will need pack animals, riding horses, mercantile goods and more. We could supply those."

Jorge Luis looked at him in astonishment and started to comment but Facundo continued, "Also, we need to think about a real hotel, not just a men's stop-over house. Since mainly men are coming, they will need women and some to marry, I think. I'm serious about this, Boss. We can't stop it. We need to act fast on this. What do you think?"

"Stop!" Jorge Luis reacted without thinking. "Those foreigners have no business coming here. All they do is disrupt everything. They need to stay out of here and off our property. We shouldn't need to deal with them at all. Just keep them off our land."

Facundo stood with his lips and brows pressed together, while looking off to the side, thinking, *come on, Boss, wake up. This is real. We could take advantage of this if you would get off that high horse of yours and open that brain. We need to face this head on.*

Jorge Luis paused for a moment to take in and consider the importance of what Facundo was saying about this new problem, "Facundo – my god, that is a lot to take in at once. I heard about the gold, and I hate the thought of more foreigners swarming into our country and the changes that may follow. We've never faced anything like this before." He stood up as if that would give him more authority but sat back down again quickly, "I don't like that. I would rather avoid them totally and keep them off our land!"

"*Jefe*, that is not going to happen. No matter how you feel about it, you cannot deny what is happening here, and we need to decide how to deal with it. Now, *Jefe*." Facundo had always had a strong inner-authority, and he used it now. He was not afraid of Jorge Luis. They were like brothers.

"You're right, Faco, *tienes razón.*" Jorge Luis stood up, his shoulders slumped, and he gave a big sigh. He caught himself, straightened up, and stood taller. He had to remember who he was. He took a deep breath and, looking Facundo directly in the eyes said, "I will discuss this with my father and Edgardo and get back to you. They are going to have a fit. If you hear anything more inform me immediately."

"*Sí*, of course, Boss."

"By the way, that girl, Señorita Prudence, does she also work as one of the women here?"

"Oh no, she is only the bookkeeper. Sometimes Madam Lisette makes her go out for a while to chat up the customers, but that is all. She doesn't like to do it, and she somewhat ruins it for a lot of the girls. She's such a looker; most of the men ask for her."

Yeah, who wouldn't, he thought. "Of course they would, but if she is out chatting up the men, that is too hard to believe. Are you sure she doesn't work with the girls, too? Where is she living? I really need to know more about her. Find out what you can and let me know as soon as possible," he said, giving his friend a pat on the shoulder and left.

"*A sus órdenes, amigo,*" answered Facundo, puzzled and a little annoyed by Jorge Luis' underhanded sarcasm, and, at the same time, his obvious interest. Prudence was not only a competent bookkeeper but very easy on the eyes. As he watched Jorge Luis walk out, a question formed in his mind. *What really happened out there by the river?*

6
A Plan for Fiarela

Back at the hacienda, Jorge Luis hunted up his mother because, on his way home, he had an idea based on his discussion with Facundo and wanted to run it past her. Since his father was very ill, he had to take over his responsibilities, and he felt overwhelmed. He needed help, and he had a plan where to find it. He knew the most likely and nearest place to look for his mother would be the kitchen and that's where he found her, discussing their meals with Teresa, the cook.

The kitchen was huge, feeding many people every day. Pots were on the ample stove, and the large table was full of produce. A huge pile of firewood was stacked next to the over-sized fireplace ready for use when needed.

"*Hola, Mijo*, you're back from town early."

"*Sí, Mamá, - hola, Teresa.* Do you have a little treat I could have? I'm really hungry after that long ride." He walked over to her and waited, rubbing his stomach while sniffing the food.

Teresa smiled, "Of course, *mijo*. I can see how hungry you are." She wrapped some meat and refried beans in a tortilla and handed it to him. He thanked her, took a bite, and turned back to his mother.

"*Mamá,* I have something I want to discuss with you, something important. Please, let's go to the office to talk."

"Teresa, can you handle things now without me?" asked Aldiana.

"Of course, *Señora*. Everything will be fine."

They left the kitchen through the large service room, where the servants and some of the men ate their meals, and entered the hallway. The sound of clicks from their heels and hard leather soles were heard along the parquet floor. They walked without talking until Jorge Luis stopped and opened the double doors into the office.

Aldiana peered up at her son's serious face, "*Mijo*, why do we have to talk here? I am becoming worried."

"No, no, not to worry. I just don't want the gossipy servants to talk.

That's all. Here, sit here so we can be comfortable." They both sat, with Aldiana adjusting her skirt, which was starting to twist around her, and Jorge Luis getting his courage up. He took a deep breath and started, "It's about Fiarela. *Mamá, y*ou know she is getting mopey, depressed, lethargic, and I worry about her. She really needs something to occupy her and get her self-esteem up."

"I know. I see it too. I really think she is jealous of you two boys, being free to go and do whatever you want, but she can't. She feels useless right now, and she won't even talk to me about marrying! That would be the proper answer for her. With your father being so ill, we have not been able to do anything for her."

"*Mamá*, forget that! Don't worry about her getting married at this point. Look, *Mamá*, I really need help in the office now that *Papá* is so ill, and Edgardo will not do it. He just refuses, and he is never around. I am stuck with it, and I do not have the time. Can't Fiarela help me? I realize she has no training, but she's a fast learner, and there is a woman bookkeeper in town who would be an excellent teacher for her. She's quite competent, according to Facundo." He stopped for a moment and just looked at his mother.

He realized that he didn't often see her as a human being. *Even though she looks matronly, she is a beautiful woman and always comports herself in such a dignified manner. She is working hard. Her hair looks clean and neat pulled back and shaped into a braided bun. I need a wife like Mamá.*

"*Mamá,* I suggest we hire the bookkeeper in town to show Fiarela how to do it. She was always quick with her numbers. Maybe she would feel that she would be a true-producing and important member of this family. *Mamá,* I am quite desperate. What do you say?"

His mother sat up straight with her eyes wide open, not believing what she just heard, "*Mijo*, are you serious? Fiarela working? A common bookkeeper? No, no! Someday she will be a head of a household. She needs to be able to run a home and care for her children. Besides, she represents this family. No, no, that would be unseemly. She is not to work. How could you even think that?"

"But, *Mamá*, I cannot have anyone outside the family take over the family financial bookkeeping. At least, I would rather not. Ma, I cannot force Edgardo to do it. Believe me I have tried! He absolutely refuses, and I understand that. He would not be good at it. Remember, this idea is also to help Fiarela, give her a boost. She is, after all, a Sandoval y Castillo and she needs to take her place in this family until she is married."

"*Sí, sí, claro,* I agree, but it is difficult for me to think of her doing such common, menial work! It would be beneath us, and we would be in the mouths of everyone. People would be shocked that we would allow our daughter to do such a thing!"

"*Madre mía*, it really is not common, menial work. You have to be educated and have specialized training in bookkeeping and be very good at mathematics. An ordinary person cannot do it. Please, for my sake and for Fiarela's, give it some serious thought, but act fast. I need the help now, and we would be quite remiss to allow her to sink into a deeper depression."

Aldiana turned and leaned away from Jorge Luis for a moment, mulling it over. Her eyes narrowed, and her lips tightened. She kept fingering her cameo brooch pinned to her everyday working dress which was, nevertheless, of good quality. She slowly turned back to face her son, looked him in the eyes, and said, "*Mijo*, I will seriously think on it, but I do not like it. However, I will talk with her. I don't want her to grow bitter and feel worthless. Find out if the bookkeeper would be willing to do it. You and I and possibly your father, if he is up to it, must interview her to be sure she will be an appropriate person to have in our home." Aldiana paused a moment, thinking about the different issues, and then continued, "Of course, they should have a chaperone while they are working. After all, Fiarela is quite an impressionable young girl. I don't want anything untoward going on." She tightened her lips and frowned thinking about that. "*Mijo*, we can afford to pay her a good wage. Although I am hesitant about it, you may be right. It might be worth a try. See what you can find out," she concluded. Jorge Luis' mother stood up, hugged him, gave him a kiss and said, "I am so proud that you care and think about your family."

Jorge Luis walked out with mixed feelings. He had an inner knowing that he was right, but he also didn't like to admit that maybe there was an ulterior motive on his part. Did he want to know more about Prudence outside of the cantina? What was she really like? She was just a woman, after all. Those thoughts made him nervous and no woman had ever made him nervous. It was all too complicated. Why was he wasting his thoughts on her?

He simply buried his feelings and went out to work. He made a list in his mind of what he needed to do: *Talk to Juan, check the cleaned stalls and the hay level in the hay barn, was that dead sheep in the south field removed? Did they fire the burn pile early? Ask Rómulo if the fig trees were harvested, talk to Gregorio about the condition of the cattle, and Paco about the sheep.*

I had better hurry, or I won't get it done before dark. If I don't get to town in time, Prudence will probably be chatting up another man in the can-

tina. A new feeling hit him – jealousy. *Okay, that's enough of that! It won't help me to think crazy.* Marina crossed his mind. *I don't want a mistress. I want a marriage as strong and loving as my parents.* He entered the stables feeling confused. *Work is what I need. Hard work solves a lot of problems.*

Early the next morning, Jorge Luis sat at his desk in the office looking at the pile of invoices, papers, and the many financial record books that needed taking care of. He knew he was right. *I've got to have help, and the only one who can do it is that woman, Prudence. Facundo doesn't have time, and there's no one else. Once she teaches Fiarela how to manage the finances and bookkeeping, I'll just let her go, and we will be fine. I know my sister can do it.*

After working out in his mind what he needed, he sat there with a clear vision of golden hair and green, mesmerizing eyes, while preening his mustache with his fingers. He figured out how to ask Facundo for her help without causing a sensation. He then got up and went out to the barns to check on his men. He made sure his workmen knew their orders before he left for town on Santón.

Once in town, he rose straight to the cantina. He found Facundo in the cantina's storage room where he was discussing the restaurant needs with Andrés, the chef. Facundo nodded at Jorge Luis, handed the chef a list of products and said, "Andrés, I will talk to you later." The chef turned and greeted Jorge Luis as he left the room. "A good man that," said Facundo. "Let's go into the other room where we can sit and talk."

Facundo lifted two chairs were lifted from the top of one table and set them facing each other. Both men sat and Jorge Luis began, "Faco, *amigo*, I have a big favor to ask of you – not as a boss, but a friend."

"Of course."

"Well, as you know, I am swamped with work with *Papá* so ill and worsening fast now. I have all the financial books to keep plus the books for the breeding programs for the sheep, cattle and horses. I really am desperate for help."

"I understand."

"Also, what you don't know is that Fiarela has become unhappy and depressed to the point where we are worried about her. *Mamá* agrees with me that she could learn to do the business bookkeeping, which would relieve me and give her something worthwhile to do. But I do not have time to teach her."

Facundo raised his eyebrows and looked knowingly at Jorge Luis, gave a little nod and said, "*Sí, sí, de acuerdo*, I get it. Do you want me to ask Prudence if she could teach her? Maybe you should ask her yourself?"

"No, no. I think that would pressure her too much, and she would refuse me." He shook his head sharply, "I don't think she approves of me anyway. Offer her a good wage and inform her that a carriage will come for her. She can evaluate Fiarela and accept to teach her or not. I know I cannot order her to do it."

"Fair enough, *Jefe*. I think she might do it. I will ask, carefully, that is. After all, she is methodical, efficient in her work, and her morals are above reproach."

Upon hearing that last remark Jorge Luis tensed his brow, giving Facundo a quizzical look, but did not comment.

"By the way," Jorge Luis continued, "we are discussing the problems and ideas you brought up. Of course, *Papá* is adamantly against anything changing, but Edgardo is enthusiastic, and he gives me the impression he would like to take over building the new businesses. He's already designing the new hotel."

"Ahhh, something finally caught his attention. That is good. Now, maybe, he will find himself and his direction in life."

"He will. Don't worry. I know it will be slow with *Papá*, but, in the meantime, start with the plans and prioritize everything. Find out what is most important to start with. When you're ready, Edgardo and I will meet with you and look it all over. How much time do you need?"

"Give me a week, and I will have the basics in order."

"By the way, is that woman working in the office right now?"

"*Sí*, she is."

"Well, I suppose I should at least greet her while I am here."

Facundo gave a knowing glance to Jorge Luis, got up and knocked quietly on the door, slowly opened it, and then returned to his work.

Jorge Luis, who had followed Facundo to the door, now stepped in and nodded to her as he said his polite morning greetings. He asked if there was anything she needed, even though he knew she probably wouldn't understand. He realized, seeing her work, that she truly was a competent woman. He was upset that they could not communicate.

Prudence, surprised at the friendliness, answered in kind, "Buenos días, Señor Sandoval." He gave a slight bow and left quickly, not allowing any conversation. The door was shut, leaving Prudence feeling puzzled and somewhat annoyed at how much he bothered her. *What goes on with him? One minute he is angry and distant, and now he is polite and friendly?* Her thoughts were in a muddle, disturbing, when she had so much work to do and needed to concentrate.

Jorge Luis took his leave of Facundo, having given him a rough hug, and with his spurs clacking across the floor on the way out, left on Santón for home and work. "One job out of the way," he whispered to himself.

On the hard-packed, dirt street, he put Santón through his gaits to the admiration of the few people on the roof-covered, wooden sidewalk. Passing the last building, he and his horse moved along a curving dirt road and up a slight hill. At the top of the hill, he halted Santón and looked back. *Facundo is working alongside her now. I wonder what that would be like?* He took a deep breath and shut down his feelings. *She cannot be for me. She's a foreigner. She doesn't speak Spanish, and*, he gave a big sigh, *she is a heathen.*

He slightly touched a perfectly trained Santón with the reins to turn him, when a kangaroo rat started hopping swiftly across the road. Jorge Luis' eyes swept over the vast, open land -- a rich, golden brown. Up behind him were the lower foothills spotted with oaks and manzanita. Ahead of him, a coyote loped across the road and into the field where it disappeared into a hole. *So that is where he lives. I'll have to come back and get him. I can't have him after our sheep. We lose enough already.* Far off ahead and to the left, his eyes followed the curving line of oaks, willows, and brush that flowed along the banks of the river. Although the river was large, he couldn't see it from such a distance, only the long line of trees, but he could see large blurs of green that were the tulles and the ponds used by the many water birds.

He was thinking about the ponds. *Man, I can hardly wait for the ducks and geese to arrive. I wonder if Prudence likes duck. Teresa cooks them to perfection.*

He almost reached the hacienda when he came to the creek that ran full of water in the winter to the ponds. It was dry. Instead of walking Santón over the bridge they had built, he walked him down and up the banks of the creek. He glanced over the open ground ahead, about one quarter of a mile, to the apple orchard. The fruit could not be seen through all the thick green leaves, but the sheep had kept the weeds eaten so everything looked neat and clean around the trees.

He enjoyed the ride home, and although he had, for a time, felt strange undercurrents of change, he simply dismissed them. After all, so far, his life was still ordered and consistent. *We do have the problem of the foreigners, but I still manage it all: the cattle for the hides and tallow market, the vineyards and the winemaking, the fruit orchards, and the sheep for meat and wool.* Then big green eyes and a pistol floated up into his mind. *Why can't I get her out of my head?*

Generally, he would be anxious to enter the hacienda, but not today. That vision reminded him that he had left something new behind, and the feeling pulled at him. He stopped Santón for a moment, staring but not seeing across the distant land. Suddenly, he pulled himself together, spurred Santón into a gallop and raced home.

7
Prudence Tells Her Story

orge Luis' order to get information on Prudence gnawed at Facundo's mind to the point he felt pressure to act. The next morning he waited in the office for her to come in to work. *How do I approach Prudence and find out her history? She may think I am impertinent and too nosey.* Facundo was truly worried. He knew Lizette never asked for references from her girls. She would know nothing. He felt stymied and concerned about losing Prudence's confidence, which was very important to him, since she took care of the bookkeeping for the hotel, the cantina, and the restaurant. Facundo rubbed his chin with nervousness, and then lifted and pulled his shoulders back to relieve his spine just as the office door slowly opened.

Prudence was on-time, as always. Facundo was not expected to be there and he surprised her. Seeing him waiting gave her a feeling of concern and a little jolt of anxiety. She worried that he might let her go. Even though her heart was beating faster than it should, she got her courage up and spoke, "Good morning. You're in here early. What are you up to, Facundo?"

"Well, Señorita Prudence, I want talk." He stood up from the desk chair and walked around the desk. He held up five fingers and said, "Five minutes. You have time? I no want bother."

"Of course. I always have time for you," she said as she pushed back her long hair to see him more fully and then shook it in place. Her hair sparkled from the light streaking through the window, impressing Facundo. "What is this about?" She felt her concern and worry drift away.

"Sit, please," he asked. He stood stiffly, as if in control, while she sat carefully and smoothed her skirt, then looked up at him with an anxious face. "You smart lady. You know numbers for business. That work important," he began. He looked directly in her eyes and nodded with a big smile, "The family Sandoval have daughter. Want that she learn numbers for books. The father very sick. He die soon. Cannot do numbers in books - too many books. I say you teach girl. They pay you much. They agree you teach.

They send coach for you. They return you. What you say*?"* And, to himself he said*, and I managed to avoid Jorge Luis' name!*

Prudence couldn't have been more astonished. She had been afraid of being fired, and here she was being offered another job. She sat, limply, sinking back in the chair, staring at Facundo. Words escaped her.

"Señorita, before teach, they want meet, talk. You must be good person, honest and talk never of money or family. What you say?"

Her hand flew to her throat, and her mouth flew open, taking in an unexpected gulp of air. "I am shocked that they would consider me." The memory of the river and Jorge Luis took over her mind for a moment. A blankness settled on her face before she could finally respond to Facundo. She answered slowly and hesitantly, "I should be flattered, thanks to you, I'm sure." She thought for a minute, "I'm assuming they can pay well?" Her hands went to the desk to steady herself as she stood up. She ignored her hair falling partly over her cheek and her skirt clinging to her thighs.

"Sí, they pay good salary. They bring horse and carriage."

"Facundo, I have time, and if the family and the girl are receptive, I would like to try it. I do need more work in order to earn enough money to move out of here and find a more respectable place of my own. What do you need to know about me?"

"*Señorita* Prudence, I think you know I not nosy person, but I need understand six things.*"* He touched a finger for each one, *"*Where born? Father, mother? Where get educate? Religion? Why you learn book numbers? Why you come here? This land big place, lonely. You young, pretty, happy girl."

"That's a big order." She nodded, "I'll keep my story as short as possible. First, I was born in Camden, Maine in the year 1826. I am twenty-two. My parents were killed in a horse and carriage accident when I was two. I was raised by my uncle and aunt." Prudence paused because Facundo had looked at her and taken in a sharp, loud respiration. With downcast eyes, she went on, "They had no children. I was raised very strictly and properly in the Congregational Church. My uncle had many business interests and needed office help, so he taught me. He believed I should be a useful citizen since I was not married yet. They also sent me to a girl's finishing school where I studied Latin, and I can speak, read, and write

French."

Facundo said in a low, quiet voice, "You good, good woman. You had husband?"

Prudence turned her head aside and almost in a whisper explained, "I am not married because my fiancé was killed in a hunting accident three years ago."

Facundo heard a long sigh, almost like a prolonged cry, but she turned and said, wiping tears away, "Sorry, unfortunately, my dear aunt, who was very active in our community affairs, died of consumption. Since I was a grown woman and unmarried, people in our community began to become suspicious of me living alone with my uncle. That was so painful. It was just vile."

"Oh, *Señorita* Prudence, so sorry, very sad. Why you come here?" said a very heart-stricken Facundo. He had children of his own and could not imagine his children hurt like that.

"We had to make a decision. My uncle has a business interest in San Francisco. He decided it would be best for me to come out to the west and study his business."

Facundo asked, "What happen? You no go to San Francisco."

Her fist tightened. She pounded the arm of the chair. She couldn't speak for a moment. Facundo didn't know how to react, so he remained silent. He had never seen her upset like this.

"I was robbed on the way and lost nearly everything. I could not pay for the rest of my journey and was dumped in this little pueblo. Lucky for me that Lizette took me in and put me to work with bookkeeping. Facundo, I am most grateful, but I truly want to get out of the cantina. If I could teach the young daughter, maybe, I could have a place of my own. Do you think so? By the way, what's her name and how old is she?"

"Name Fiarela. She has twenty years."

"What a lovely sounding name, and she is close to my age. That would be nice. If they will have me, I would like to give it a try. Tell me, what is Fiarela like? I would like to know what to do. Everything is so different. Will you help me?"

"*Claro, mi placer*. Fiarela es delight girl, energetic, humor. You like her." He paused and took her hands again holding them tight. *This little lady has suffered much more than anyone thought.* Even though he was the same age as Jorge Luis, he felt like he was a father for her. "I will inform Los Sandoval. I tell you. Es necesario you go first time talk, very formal. No worry. I help you. I help you."

Facundo turned to go, but quickly shifted back to face Prudence, "Oh, *Señorita*, I forgot ask how you come here from far? Boat? Horse?"

"Part way by horse. I rode my own horse, but it was stolen. Some Indians stole her one night, but a very gracious and generous family took me in, and I traveled out here in their Conestoga wagon. They had an adorable little four-year-old girl who was so cute on her little white horse. I loved playing with her. Once the Indians wanted to buy her, but the parents wouldn't sell her. That trip was long and, and," her voice caught in her throat and she suddenly looked stricken and helpless and began to pick at the lace on her long sleeve. "Facundo, it was so tough. People had to be strong and adaptable. One time an ox was dying. The owners were desperate because they needed it so badly. No one knew how to save it until, finally, someone told them to feed it bacon and lard and, amazingly, it lived. All we had to eat, when we got here, were blackbirds! I never want to make that trip again." She looked away, not wanting him to see the emotion playing across her face.

Facundo's heart went out to her and he made a vow to help her all he could.

"I think you very courage woman. You suffer much. Me no do it. I go now Señorita Prudence. Thank you."

Facundo took his leave, proud of himself that he did not mention that all this had been the idea of Jorge Luis. He realized that Prudence would have become instantly resistant, and she deserved to have this new position.

Prudence remained sitting, though now hunched over, letting the buried fears and held back tears loose. She wrapped her arms around herself and rocked with the letting go. She prayed Facundo would not hear her.

Facundo, back in the main room of the cantina, remembered that Jorge Luis said he would be in tonight. *I wish he could have heard her story in person. She's suffered a lot, and he needs to understand that. I'll try to explain it all. He's just too damn proud to admit he's smitten with her.*

Facundo had noticed a vase of wildflowers Prudence had picked and placed on the old desk. *Ah, she is competent, strong-willed, truly beautiful, and obviously needs beauty in her life, too.* His eyes lit up, and he broke out with a smile from the deep inner knowing of the heart. He knew what he felt with a certainty. *Jorge Luis has met his match! Finally!*

Meanwhile, Santón gave Jorge Luis a smooth, fast ride into town. Ordinarily, Jorge Luis enjoyed a more relaxed walk after a long day's work. He liked to regroup his day, evaluating how things went, and it gave him time to think over the next day. He loved to notice any changes in the countryside.

The seasonal differences in the trees and landscape always caught his attention. Sometimes, he would catch sight of an animal sneaking out after an afternoon of hiding.

But this evening his mind was on Prudence. He was anxious to learn what Facundo had found out about her. He had never seen her involved with the men in the cantina - supposedly, chatting them up. He presumed she would be doing that tonight, and he was very curious. Facundo's admiration for her was noteworthy, but he had to be careful who he hired to teach his sister. She must be above reproach.

Hadn't Facundo mentioned the words "good morals"? And, she's working in a cantina? I'll believe that when I see it, he thought. Then he kicked himself for thinking negatively, forming an assumption based on nothing. Lost in his thoughts, he suddenly realized that he was almost into the village and could see the stables up ahead.

Santón snickered, shaking his head and neck as he entered the stables. He knew all his fellow horses there. Jorge Luis laughed and gave him a pat on the neck and cheeks, turning him over to Pepe, who swelled with pride to have the honor of taking charge of a horse of that quality. He was the owner's horse, a big responsibility.

The Cantina de Las Flores was loud and lively when Jorge Luis walked in. He glanced over the crowd to a table where a woman, of noticeable style, sat by herself with two full drinks in front of her. That was his table and his regular woman. She caught his attention and nodded her head at his drink as if telling him to get over there, but he headed straight for the bar, while his eyes swept the rest of the room.

Then, he saw her -- Prudence. She was stunning, dressed in a gorgeous, lime-green gown, golden hair pulled up in some fancy style. A jolt of energy hit him in the solar plexus, but he couldn't define it or didn't want to. Besides, she was busy dancing and chatting up some cowboy.

She sure seems good at both, too, he noticed, more than a little.

In the back of the public room, at the bar, Facundo handed his towel to Pedro, his handsome, young son who was eager to please his father. He motioned Jorge Luis to come over to a back table where they could talk.

On his way over to Facundo, Jorge Luis noticed the pool tables had lively games going, the poker tables were full, and every stool at the bar was filled, keeping Facundo and Pedro extra busy. He could hear money clanging in the cash register, a very good sound to his ears. People were dancing and singing around the piano player and guitarist. *They are good. I wouldn't mind being out there with a beautiful woman in my arms. I'd waltz her all around this room. The piano player and that guitarist were a good hire,* he thought, watching them sing and play, as he wove through the boisterous crowd, to arrive at the private table.

"Big crowd tonight, Faco. Nice to see, and the noise is the kind I like to hear." He pulled up a stool and sat down, looked his friend in the eyes and said, "Okay, what's the news on Prudence? Just give it to me straight."

Facundo picked up on Jorge Luis' underlying tone of hostility and did not appreciate it. He needed to set him straight, "Listen, Boss, she is a woman of great courage – not just beautiful. You don't know it, Boss. She is exceptionally efficient and diligent in her work with the bookkeeping. And, did you know she is sewing baby clothes for our coming twins?"

Jorge Luis looked more than surprised at that information, "No, I didn't know that." Most of his unwanted suspicions slipped away. He watched her with a new awareness yet didn't like the guy she was talking to. He looked like a foreigner. *Probably one of those Americans,* he thought, because the man was fair in looks, and more and more of them seemed to be passing through on their way to the gold mines. He had been hearing more and more about the Sierra mountains and gold.

He decided to pay more attention to Facundo, who was saying, "She told me her history. Do you still want to know?"

"Yeah, sure." He wanted to know now more than ever. He swung around on the stool to listen, ignoring the woman at his table.

"Well, to begin with," said Facundo, "I have no complaints about her work. I am more than happy with what she does. She even cleans up the office when she leaves." He went on to relate as much of her history he found appropriate. "Amigo, this is a woman who has suffered and struggled much. She has seen difficult hardships at first hand, yet she is persistent and hardworking and truly is interested in the offer to teach Fiarela. We managed to work out the schedule. All the arrangements are now wrapped up. I personally believe it will work out well for everyone, and until she learns more Spanish, I will go with her and help translate. Numbers will not be hard. Lola teaches her Spanish already. Did you know that, *Patrón?*"

"No, I didn't. That will be an advantage. I know she speaks French with Lizette. My parents used to speak some French, but none of us children do." Jorge Luis felt somewhat humbled and a little deflated, a feeling that was unknown in his world.

At that moment, a movement caught their attention. The woman at his table glanced away from him toward the disturbance. Facundo jumped up saying, "*Jefe*, Prudence!"

Both men rushed to an ugly scene. Because they were intently talking, they had not heard the ruckus, but others had. The musicians both stopped and stared. The dancers came to a halt with the ending of the music and could not believe what was happening. Sudden silence filled the room. A drunken sot was pawing over Prudence who slapped and kicked, trying to get him off her. He was shouting obscenities and with a final grab ripped open her dress.

"Faco, get her back to Lizette!"

Jorge Luis grabbed the drunk by the scruff of his neck, swung him around and with each hard punch, shouted in his face, "Don't- you-ever-treat- a- woman- like- that- in- this- cantina- again- or- I- will- see- to- it-you- will- never- again - touch- any- woman- ever!" The drunk hit the floor like a sack of *masa*.

Trying to pick himself up, and out of a bloody mouth, he stuttered, "Hey, hey! I would have paid her! I got the money! That what's she's for ain't it? So, what's the problem?" Facundo appeared, picked up the drunken cowboy and tossed him unceremoniously out, forbidding him to ever enter the cantina again unless he was looking for more, and much worse.

"Faco, how is Prudence?" asked Jorge Luis as he shrugged his shoulders to adjust his jacket. He moved his belt back in place. "I don't want Lizette to allow her out here like that again. She doesn't belong out here."

"Boss, I think you should go check yourself. Your lady has given up waiting at your table, anyway."

"*Sí*, you're right," one glance, and he saw the empty table. Both glasses were empty. *How dare she*? A little anger surged. S*he'll be back,* he knew. With that, he strode off to Lizette's quarters. He found Prudence lying on a sofa wrapped in a blanket. She had obviously been crying. He saw the strands of hair that stuck to her face where the tears had run, but when he noticed her swollen and red eyes, his heart went out to her. His first instinct was to pick her up and carry her out. Instead, he turned to Lizette, "Tell her I apologize for what has happened. It will not happen again. She is not to go out there at night – ever. That is an order!"

"But *Señor*, she has to earn her keep."

"She is earning it! I saw what she is doing in the office and what she is capable of. Do not let her out there again! Now, tell her what I said."

Lizette, upset to have one girl, in her opinion, favored over any of the others, did what she was asked.

Prudence whispered, "*Gracias*."

Still looking traumatized and humiliated, she pulled the blanket up around herself tighter, even over her nose. She felt almost as though she needed protection from him, too.

He knew she would recover, but felt he wanted to reassure her. Instead, he turned again to Lizette, "Lizette, I will pay you for the dress. See that she is given another one of equal value at my expense."

No farewells were said as he left and strode out to the bar. He motioned to Facundo to tell him that an interview with Prudence at the hacienda would be arranged very quickly, "You were right about her, *amigo*. I think she will do exceptionally well."

His eyes sought his woman, waiting again at his table. He caught her attention, shook his head and left for home. She was out of his mind as soon as he walked out of the cantina door and later was surprised how quickly that had happened. *Marina is a flamboyant beauty. How could I forget her like that?*

Santón settled into a fast trot as Jorge Luis realized Facundo was right about those foreigners. He saw many of them tonight, and he must take action. His Cantina de Las Flores had always been above such brutish behavior. They had minor fights now and then, but Facundo was tough and brooked no nonsense.

He also realized, reluctantly, that Facundo was right about Prudence. *She is a lady, after all, who doesn't belong where she is at. Where does she belong?* He would have to give that some thought, but not now. He had enough for one night. He felt rather numb with all that chaos. There was always *mañana*, he believed.

However, he paused to reflect - he had received quite an inner jolt. His eyes had been opened. He had pre-judged Prudence several times: first at the river, then her morals, her residence above the cantina, and the dancing with all the cowboys. Somehow, she had become like a little magnet that stuck tight some place in his mind. Why? His ride home on Santón was one of introspection.

8
The Interview

Facundo poked his head in the office where Prudence was waiting for him. She had been sitting in the office chair, shifting back and forth, nervously curling a strand of her hair, and pinching her cheeks to pinken them. She had to face the interview with the Sandoval family today. Truly she wanted the opportunity to teach the daughter bookkeeping. The extra money would help her a lot. She didn't know what to expect or what they would expect of her. She jumped when the door to the office suddenly opened, and she heard Facundo say, as he entered the office, "*Señorita* Prudence, carriage here."

"I'm ready, Facundo, but I am, I admit, nervous." She stood up quickly, straightening her skirt and lace collar. She had dressed in a conservative sky-blue dress with a wide lace collar and lace on the sleeves. Fortunately, it had been packed in her small chest. Her hair was pulled back and held with her ivory hair combs, which allowed the back to hang loose, very appropriately. Nevertheless, she still worried.

"No, no, no be *nerviosa*."

She and Facundo crossed the neatly swept cantina floor, the heels of her only pair of good shoes clicking on the floor constructed of one-inch thick oak planks. The chairs were piled on the tables, ready for tonight's crowd. Facundo locked the cantina door behind them. He gently took her arm and lead Prudence outside. She was grateful and felt more protected.

They reached the carriage, which was only a wide one-seat cart that could seat three people, and it had no back. Facundo had expected the covered carriage driven by Benito. *What on earth? Who's driving?* Astonished, he looked twice at the driver.

"*¡Oye!*, Edgardo," said Facundo in Spanish. "Why are you driving? Where's Benito and why this small cart?"

Edgardo turned at Facundo's words, looked at Prudence with a sudden look of recognition and said, "It-is-you!" He stared at her, slack-jawed and wide-eyed, with puzzlement on his face. He paused a moment, then slowly replied, "Well, I just wanted to be a little more informal, get to know her somewhat ahead of time. I wanted a different experience than the formal one we will have in the office interview."

"Interesting," commented Facundo, raising his eyebrows. "And what was that 'it is you' about?"

"Ah, you know me, Facundo. I had a dream about her and didn't know why I was seeing this unusual woman. I learn a lot from my dreams. You know that. Now, seeing her in the flesh, I understand it. She is exactly as she was in my dream. By the way, has Jorge Luis met her yet?"

Facundo nodded.

Edgardo looked straight at Prudence with an intense study, *Oh, yes, and has he! She has made quite an impression, I think. She is a knock-out. Maybe this is his motive behind the new position. This interview may prove to be more interesting than I thought.*

Meanwhile, Prudence stood still catching a few Spanish words here and there. She heard the words know, learn, understand and Jorge Luis. Even though she was studying hard to learn the language as quickly as possible, the words meant nothing out of context.

Finally, she interrupted and asked Facundo, "Please introduce me and then help me up. Why are we sitting with the driver and in this small trap? There is no back on it. Where I come from this would be the sheep herder's cart."

"*Señorita,*" Facundo, ignoring her questions, said, "I present to you, Edgardo Sandoval y Castillo, the brother of Jorge Luis. Edgardo, *la Señorita* Prudence Mullens."

Edgardo gave her a big, welcoming smile, "Ah, yes, she is quite beautiful, ¿no?"

"For sure," answered Facundo.

As Facundo was helping Prudence up into the cart, Edgardo asked him, "How is Maria and your family? How many kids now?"

"We have five already. Maria is expecting again, but this time it is different, and we suspect twins. It is becoming difficult for her now."

After Facundo was seated and settled, Edgardo gave a little slap of the reins. He then leaned forward and looked past Prudence to Facundo. He could see the worry in Facundo's eyes and felt his sudden consternation. He responded with, "Don't worry, Faco, I will send someone to help as soon as possible."

"We would be most grateful, Edgardo."

Understanding parts of the conversation made Prudence realize she knew very little about Facundo's family, and she felt quite remiss. *I must do something more for them when we return. Besides the few baby things I'm sewing, maybe I could make some quilts or blankets. They will need a lot with twins.*

Facundo had placed Prudence between himself and Edgardo. Prudence felt a little trapped and unsure between the two men. She hoped it would be a pleasant ride. Edgardo surprised her with his relaxed, easy manner, not at all like Jorge Luis. She also noticed he was dressed casually but elegantly in a hand-knit, dark brown sweater over a white shirt. His pants were of a lighter brown wool. He did not wear boots but instead a light pair of shoes.

"Facundo, will you translate to English when I question Prudence?"

"Yes, but be careful with your questions!"

"Not to worry, Faco, she is meant for another."

Facundo gave him a questioning look, then understood, and smiled.

All the way to the hacienda they conversed lightly, with Facundo doing his best to convey what was said or asked. With each passing mile, Prudence was more impressed with Edgardo. His manners were as impeccable as Jorge Luis', but he did not have the underlying coldness. On the contrary, he was so open and warm. She hoped Fiarela would be the same. *I would really like to have a friend. So far only one of the brothel girls working at the cantina will acknowledge me at all. And Lizette is angry at me now because I'm not allowed to go out to chat up or dance with the men.*

She asked occasional questions of Edgardo, especially about the horses, sheep and cattle.

"I see sheep all over these fields but no cattle. Where are they? What kind are they? How many do you have? Back East we had about 200 Black Angus and Herefords."

"Most of our cattle are Corrientes. They are a small hardy, breed and they do well out here on this type of open range. It's dry and extensive for grazing. We have around 30,000 head," he explained. Edgardo heard Prudence gasp with surprise. "They are about a half day's ride from here," said Edgardo.

"I've never heard of that breed. I would like to see them. I also saw an apple orchard on the way. That surprised me out here."

Facundo translated clearly and Edgardo answered, "We also have apricots, peaches, some citrus, but you can't see those from here. We cultivate grapes closer to the hacienda."

Edgardo and Facundo both seemed surprised by her questions. They both believed that women only cared about clothes, parties, and children. Edgardo remembered, with sadness, one exception. He became more impressed than ever with Prudence. He thought, *Jorge Luis had better wake up fast. She's a real prize. She'll be good for Fiarela, too.*

They finally reached the hacienda and entered the main entrance to the home.

The horse halted, by habit, in front of the wide steps leading to the veranda. Edgardo waved at the hired hand, waiting to take the horse and cart while Facundo helped Prudence down. Together they walked up the wide, tile steps where on each side was a large pot full of colorful geraniums.

Prudence was wide-eyed with astonishment at the magnificence of the hacienda. She tugged at Facundo's sleeve and whispered, "I can't believe this is their home. It's huge. The veranda runs the whole length of the building. Why do so many doors and windows open directly out onto it?"

"Catch breeze in summer hot day," he answered.

Her eyes swept over parts of the tiled roof that were covered with deep red bougainvillea, which grew out of huge pots set on the ground in front of the walkway pillars. She noticed that the landscaping was kept immaculate, and the front double doors, which a manservant was guarding, were easily eight feet tall and beautiful. Obviously hand-carved out of oak, the doors were covered with images of local animals and fauna, such as deer, elk, and bear in among the oaks and sugar pines.

"Facundo, where did they find those incredible doors?" she asked.

He whispered to her that they were carved by the family's carpenter and wood carver, Nicolás.

She had not expected such magnificence. *What have I gotten myself into?* she wondered. As they approached the manservant, she began to feel nervous. She took a deep breath to prepare herself.

Edgardo approached Donaldo and informed him, "Donaldo, I present to you La Señorita Prudence Mullens because she will be coming here often. You need to know."

"Encantado, Señorita," Donaldo gave her a most welcoming smile, which she returned with a dainty curtsy, surprising all three men.

Facundo immediately pointed out, "Not necessary bow to servant, but well done."

Edgardo's face lit up with tremendous admiration. With such manners, she is obviously an educated lady, "Come with me, and I will escort you to the office."

Prudence felt completely overwhelmed by the luxurious size of each room, the combination of tile and inlaid parquet floors, the Middle Eastern carpets, antique furniture and all in exquisite taste. To her, this was what in Maine was called "Old Money." No flaunting of one's riches here. They were just a part of the lifestyle. Her happy thoughts slipped a little. *I can't imagine them hiring me. I don't think I could ever fit in here. Uncle Lot is quite wealthy but not like this. I'm not sure what they will want of me. What if I can't meet their expectations?*

Just then a double door opened, interrupting her worries, and standing in the middle of this wide opening was Jorge Luis. Prudence gasped. Edgardo eyed her wonderingly. Facundo simply said, "Here's the office. *Buenos días, amigo.*"

"Come in, come in. I will introduce you. Papá is not well enough to join us," said Jorge Luis, who then introduced his mother and sister, and raised his voice to introduce the chaperone, Catrina, who sat in a far corner of the room.

Prudence was astonished and wondered why on earth they would have a chaperone.

"I have some work I must do," said Jorge Luis, looking into her big, green eyes. He quickly blinked and looked out the window, feeling slightly embarrassed with a little veneer of guilt. "I'll be back later." Not looking at her, his eyes swept across the others, especially his mother, while he held his head high and left the room, closing the double doors with an extra flourish.

Both men looked at each other, shrugging their shoulders. Edgardo rolled his eyes at Facundo. Neither one said anything. Prudence looked around for a distraction, hoping she was not blushing. She suddenly realized how many record books were piled on the desk and on a separate table. She looked up to see Fiarela watching her.

Prudence took a minute to observe her. *What beautiful, big, dark eyes and creamy white skin. Fiarela is about my size, too,* she thought. She noticed her hair in a style that was pulled back off her full face with thick curls that swirled around her neck. Prudence was struck, not only by Fiarela intensely watching her, but also with her youthful attractiveness. Prudence put her attention back on the pile of books on the desk. *There are so many books here it will take forever to go through them all. Can I even do it? And, teach Fiarela at the same time?* Suddenly, she saw the mother come to the desk and stand beside it.

"Please sit down, everyone. I will explain why we are interviewing *Señorita* Prudence and what the criteria is for the job. Also, Fiarela has hopes that Señorita Prudence will be able to teach her the skill of bookkeeping." Aldiana, the mother, had taken charge, waiting for them all to find a seat before beginning the interrogation, "Facundo, will you please translate for us?"

"Naturally, I will be glad to."

Aldiana began to question Prudence about her educational background in bookkeeping and the possible difference with the books being in Spanish. To Prudence, she was detailed in her questioning, but, obviously, she had no knowledge about the bookkeeping itself. The business end was always left to the men. Aldiana expressed her worry about the teaching and could she do both jobs?

Prudence looked over at Facundo and asked, "Facundo, please ask Señora Sandoval if you can come for a while to translate for us. Tell her I speak French, and I am studying Spanish now."

Facundo spoke to Aldiana who, somewhat surprised, nodded in turn.

Fiarela, who heard, spoke up, "Oh, that is wonderful, and maybe I can learn some English, too."

Aldiana caught her daughter's attention with a strong look. "You have no need of any English. If you are to do this, you will be doing it in Spanish," she said, pointing to the pile of records, "And you will concentrate on learning these books with no nonsense."

Fiarela wrung her hands, her face flushed with embarrassment, but she assured her mother that she truly wanted to learn bookkeeping. She turned to Facundo, "Please, ask Prudence if she would mind spending the time to teach me. I am anxious to learn and, maybe, have a friend, too."

Again, Aldiana frowned at Fiarela, pressing her lips tight in disapproval and thought, *I will have to keep an eye on her, I think, if this is to work.* She noticed that Prudence was opening the books, examining them, and glancing at Fiarela. She also watched her daughter who focused on Prudence without turning away or interrupting.

Fiarela made an impression on Prudence. She noticed Fiarela's facial expressions, her quick movements to peek at the books when she opened them.

After Fiarela asked Facundo if he thought she could learn, Prudence realized she wanted this job and here was someone she would like to teach.

She said, with Facundo nodding, "Of course you can. It will hard at first, but, with perseverance, you can do it."

Fiarela looked at Facundo for a translation and broke into a wide smile, with brightening eyes. She grabbed a curl and rubbed it against her mouth while she looked apprehensively at her mother.

"Señora Sandoval," said Prudence with a soft smile and a slow and cautious Spanish, "I would very much like to teach Fiarela and do hope you will consider me for the position."

Facundo translated for everyone to make sure all were clear about what was going on. Although Prudence's Spanish was improving, it was still elementary. He made sure to prevent misunderstandings.

"I worried that the books, being in Spanish, would present a problem, but Facundo assured me they won't," said Aldiana. She turned to Fiarela and asked, "What do you say, *Mija?*"

"Oh, Mamá, sí, I want to learn. If she has patience, I know I can do it!"

Aldiana looked questioningly at Facundo who quickly nodded. Aldiana sighed. She looked at Facundo and said, "Please tell her she is hired." She smiled at Prudence, held out her hand and said to her, "Bienvenida." Then looking up at Facundo, she left instructions, "I must leave to care for Emiliano. Please explain our customs here. Fiarela, you will prepare to work diligently with her at all times."

"Oh, *sí*, Mamá. When can we start?"

"Work that out with Facundo and Jorge Luis. Jorge Luis is the only one who knows those books." With that, she left.

At that moment, Jorge Luis entered, looked around, asked, "¿Entonces?"

"Patrón, she is hired."

Jorge Luis noticed an extra big smile from Facundo, a know-it-all smile, which he ignored.

"Ask Prudence what time she will be able to give the lessons, since she already has a job keeping the books at the cantina and the hotel. Her workload is heavy."

The whole time he spoke, his eyes never left hers and, although Prudence felt like the air was being sucked out of her, she answered quickly, "I really need to come as often as I can in the beginning and then as Fiarela learns, I will taper off. Will that work?"

Facundo translated.

Jorge Luis answered, "Sí, está bién." He nodded, bowed and retreated.

Prudence, Facundo and Fiarela put together a workable schedule.

In the meantime, Edgardo had been silent, observing each person, thinking to himself, *She is going to be a breath of fresh air, a blessing for Fiarela and for our home. If only Jorge Luis knew what he was missing.*

With that thought, Edgardo wondered if his feeling of emptiness and longing would ever heal. He told them, "If Benito is busy, I will be glad to come for you, *Señorita* Prudence."

"Oh, no, I can drive myself if I have access to a carriage or trap," Prudence assured them.

"No, no, we don't want any woman out alone, especially when it is getting dark," remarked Edgardo quite assertively.

Prudence gave him a quick glance, but politely held her tongue. She knew he did not know she could shoot as well as any man, so she did not make a strong retort.

The arrangement details were soon completed, and everyone was happily in agreement. Edgardo drove them back to town, a very content and intrigued brother.

9
Another Rock in the Road

Peeking over an open and dusty windowsill, the low rays of the day's new sun brushed Jorge Luis' dreaming eyes. He opened them. He lay there thinking about the interview and how well Prudence seemed to be doing with the financial books and teaching Fiarela. *Having her come has certainly relieved me. My plan is working.* He made a point of checking on them every day, spending a little time in the office with them. He was embarrassed to admit how much he looked forward to that time. Suddenly, he realized he was daydreaming when he had another problem to solve. It was eating at him more each day.

Immediately alert, he leaped out of bed, and grabbed his clothes from the floor, cursing while stumbling into them. He dashed out the door, yet immediately slowed, tiptoeing fast. *"I don't dare wake anyone. That damn brother of mine is not getting out of work today!"* His mind raced as fast as his tiptoeing.

After knocking softly on Edgardo's door, he called in almost a whisper, "Edgardo." Neither an answer nor movement was heard.

He pushed open the door, allowing his anger to surge in a half-loud, crisply spoken demand, "Edgardo, wake up. Damn you, get up!"

No answer.

A subtle odor of staleness lingered in the darkness. His eyes required a moment to adjust to the dim light in the room. Then, to his shock, he could see a bed obviously not made by Edgardo but by a servant, neat and tight.

Clenching his teeth, unable to sort out furious thoughts, he took off for the stable at a fast clip, skipping breakfast.

He was breathing heavily from running, so he stopped at a stall gate to catch his breath. Jorge Luis found Juan in Blanca's stall slipping a halter over the horse's head.

Juan noticed his tense body, his heavy breathing, and felt his chaotic energy, which was unusual, he knew, for Jorge Luis.

"Morning, *Jefe*. What's going on?"

"Where's Edgardo? I can't find him!"

"Sorry, Boss, but his horse was gone from the stall when I got here. I don't know where he is. Do you want me to track him again?" he said, as he adjusted Blanca's halter.

"I don't know. He didn't sleep in his bed last night!"

"Not to worry, Boss. You didn't either at that age."

"Well, at least I was at work every day!"

Juan could feel the resentment in those words. Blanca, a pretty little Quarter Horse, stood quietly at Juan's side and now began to nudge him and with her lips nibble at his shirt.

"Go ahead, take Blanca out," Jorge Luis suggested. "She's getting restless." The anxiety over his brother calmed for a minute as he watched Juan with Blanca. Juan was a master with horses. They began to walk slowly toward the training corral. "She certainly has taken to your training, Juan. I was watching her yesterday and noticed that she is turning out to be an excellent, fast little cutting horse - thanks to your masterful work," he added.

"Yeah, she will be, Boss. Not much more work, either." Juan paused a moment and then added, "Look, don't worry about your brother. He is a different one - always has been since he was little. I need him here, too, right now. I have a mare ready to foal, and the foal does not feel right to me. I need his talent in checking her out."

Jorge Luis responded, "I'll check her out for you."

"No, thanks, but I need Edgardo. He has the gift to see what you can't."

With a sharp intake of air, Jorge Luis went silent. In his mind he could see the image of Edgardo as a child insisting Juan not leave a mare soon to give birth for even a second. He begged Juan to be with the colt while it was being born or it would die from the cord hanging him. That is exactly what happened when the foal was born. But Juan, being right there, had saved him. *And how did I react? How did I treat my little brother? I made continuous fun of him, ridiculing him arrogantly, telling him he was crazy and to not bother Juan! If he had listened to me, that colt would have died, and that is not the only time that something like this has happened.*

"Damn that kid!" he said under his breath, still mad at him. Remorse and guilt swept over him, but he cut the feelings off quickly. Being wrong was hard to admit, but he had been wrong and had to admit he had been cruel for ridiculing Edgardo for something he, himself, did not understand.

Jorge Luis was just beginning to realize that life was more complicated than he had believed. His was beginning to crumble around the edges.

"Damn that kid!" he whispered, feeling somewhat ashamed.

After Jorge Luis left the stable, Juan started thinking while walking Blanca to the corral. *I'm going to catch Edgardo and have a good talk with him before Jorge Luis gets to him. I don't understand why nobody acknowledges him and his abilities. We need Edgardo. I need him, and I owe him.*

His memory leaped back to a desperate time: He had been chasing a lone heifer in order to get her back to the herd when she ran straight for the river, slipped in and was carried away. He rode along the bank of the river for a minute when his horse tumbled down a muddy slope, throwing him out into the water. He finally managed to grab onto a rock above the rushing waters, but it was too slippery - he knew he wouldn't last very long. He wasn't a swimmer, and he would be gone. He started to pray.

Suddenly, he heard a shout. It was Edgardo with his horse as he jumped out into the water, yelling, "Hang on, hang on! I'll be right there." He swam his horse out to the rock, turned the horse around and shouted, *"Juan, grab his tail and don't let go!"* His horse pulled hard to get Juan out of the water and up the bank. Juan was a dead weight, but his arms were locked onto the tail.

After he recovered, Juan found out that Edgardo had had a sudden vision flash across his mind of Juan in the water, and he recognized the place at the river. Juan's heart raced thinking about it, and a strong chill ran down his body. Once again, he gave thanks.

Listening to Juan and not being able to find his brother left Jorge Luis feeling darkly depressed. Pondering his situation while walking and with his legs feeling like dead weights, he struggled slowly back to the house. *I'm going to the office to think about this.*

He sat in the office, passing time and feeling uncomfortable. His intellect continued analyzing and dissecting the problem to the point where he felt nothing but confusion. "I need a drink!" he said out loud to himself. But after more than one, he realized that drinking wasn't solving anything. *I need to get out of here. This whole situation is driving me crazy. I'm going to town.*

Jorge Luis took off on Santón and headed for the cantina and the arms of his black-haired beauty. He knew Marina would make him forget everything, including those intruding visions of golden hair and breathtaking eyes. It did not sit well with him to be unable to solve the problem with his brother. He was used to taking action and getting things done.

Jorge Luis, on Santón, talked to himself as he kept his horse to a gallop all the way to town. Burden after burden weighed on his thoughts.

Haven't I got enough to handle with running the whole place? On top of my overwhelming responsibilities, my father is dying, my brother disappears and won't do his share, Mother is unavailable taking care of Papá and my little sister, Fiarela, is depressed, and foreigners are arriving by the wagon loads. Facundo has already taken on more than his share. I have no one to turn to for help.

A flash of green eyes and golden hair crossed his mind. He put that aside fast, but not before he felt a pressure hit him in the chest. *No! No! No more tequila or whiskey for me! My drinking back there in the office didn't do it. I feel worse. I need Marina. That is all I need. Madam Lizette will be up by now, and she'd better get Marina up!* He reached the stables, threw the reins at the stable boy and dashed into the cantina.

Since the cantina's empty, he thought, *I'll go to the office and through the back hall to Lizette's apartment.* Briskly walking, he crossed the room and had the office door half-opened when he recognized the smell of cologne, subtle but compelling. Startled, he looked up, straight into green eyes widened in surprise.

Prudence stood up quickly, her face flushed. Using her new Spanish, she greeted him, "*Buenos días, Señor*. I did not expect you. *¿Qué necesita, Señor?*"

Hearing those last words, "What do you need?" said in Spanish, utterly embarrassed him. He only had one need on his mind, Marina, and he stumbled in answering, "Oh, uh, *nada*. I didn't expect to see you working."

Why wouldn't he? she thought, understanding his Spanish. "*Señor, yo tra-ba-jo* here every day." The surprise of seeing him directly in front of her so unexpectedly, left a vision of him in her mind that remained the rest of the day. *What is it with him? Why does he set me off guard so easily?*

Jorge Luis, staring at her, felt even more agitated and a little ashamed. He hadn't thought about her being at work in the office. The more he looked at her, the more his thoughts rang in his head. *I see her most days at the hacienda. That is a pleasant pastime and enough. What the hell is the matter with me? She is off limits to me and will always be. I won't allow myself to get mixed up with a foreigner.*

Her beauty still held him spellbound, but he said, pulling himself together, "Excuse me, Prudence. May you have *un buen día.*"

Prudence felt his eyes penetrating and holding hers. She stood, unable to move. She sensed a deep need in those brilliant, dark eyes. She responded, trembling slightly, "*Gracias.*"

Jorge Luis left feeling confused and disturbed on a level he didn't understand – a very new feeling for him. He couldn't seem to get control of himself. His desire had somewhat been taken down a notch, but old habits die hard. He walked down the hallway to Lizette's apartment, stopped at the door and called, "Lizette!"

Lizette opened the door a crack. "*Sí, Señor*, what may I help you with?"

"I need Marina. Wake her up!"

"*Señor*, she's been working all night. Now?"

"Yes, now!"

Jorge Luis waited impatiently for Lizette to call him upstairs. He paced the wooden floor while looking at all the stuffed animal heads hanging from the walls. He even checked the dust on the railing of the stairs, the chest, and a porcelain vase. *Damn, I've got to get on Lizette. There should be no dust anywhere. We run a high-class place here.* He pulled at his mustache and kept pacing.

Upstairs, Marina woke to Lizette's loud knocking, and with the hour being so early, was quite irritated. *What now? This is not acceptable.* But, when she learned it was Jorge Luis who was waiting downstairs, she rushed to the pitcher of water and bowl to wash quickly. *Why is he here? He has never done this before.* She hurriedly brushed her hair and threw on one of her best gowns. After she called out to Lizette to allow him to come up, she hopped into bed, postured herself, and made an effort to not look exhausted. *He'd better have a damned good excuse*, she thought as she rubbed the silky imported sheets from the Orient. This was her private room, a gift from Jorge Luis, and she was glad she had straightened it up last night before retiring. He had her bed carved by the hacienda's woodcarver, and he had bought her a colorful and plush rug imported from the Orient. She made an extra effort to be welcoming when he came in.

When he entered, his eyes locked on her as she held out her arms to him, scented with a lotion of lanolin and crushed rose blossoms. He stopped and apologized for coming in so early and unexpectedly, "Marina, I am overwhelmed by everything going on, and I need you. You look beautiful this morning. You don't mind, do you?"

"Of course not, amor, never would I mind. Hurry and join me."

Later, on his way down the stairs, he muttered to himself, "Something is wrong with me. Nothing felt right with Marina. I have never been unsatisfied before."

A fleeting image of Prudence, standing at her desk with her wide, startled eyes, slid across his apprehensive mind. *Never, never, don't even think it!*

He went straight home, and the ride was not a comfortable one.

10

Saving a Colt & the Lure of Gold

uan was on watch in the stall of Gema, a small Quarter horse. She was about to foal. *Something's wrong. I don't feel good about this one.* As he rubbed her gently, he talked to her in a soft, low tone, "Gema, girl, this time will not be easy for you. You've given us many strong, well-formed colts. What happened, huh girl? God, I wish Edgardo were here. I'm in trouble. I can't feel this one properly." Juan palpated her belly from all sides and underneath, talking out loud to himself, "The head is in a strange position, and I can't find that other leg. I can't do this alone. I will have to find Rómulo to help. Edgardo's not here, as usual. I don't know what has gotten into that kid, always gone. I really need him. Jorge Luis went off to town to meet with Facundo, so he won't be here to help. Rómulo's inexperienced and young, but he's the only one around right now." Juan was worried. He stood unmoving while rubbing his chin and mouth, pondering his situation.

Suddenly, familiar sounds echoed through the building. Juan wiped his hands on a towel, threw it over the side of the stall, and strode out toward the sound he prayed was coming from Edgardo and his horse. It was.

"Edgardo, *Mijo*, I don't care if you have ridden all night. I need your help with Gema. She's starting labor, and I can't get a proper feel for the foal. I'm worried, and I need you to tell me what's going on."

Edgardo turned, shut the stall gate and started walking along with Juan. "So far, what's happening with her?" He could see the concern and anxiety in Juan's face. It had to be bad. Juan was an old-hand at all this.

"Well, the colt is turned around, the head doesn't feel right, and I can't feel one leg. She's always thrown perfect colts, and I don't want to lose her or the colt."

Edgardo said, "Give me a moment. Let me see if something comes to me." He halted, took a deep breath, relaxed completely, and let it out slowly, closing his eyes. A few seconds later he said, "I see her, Juan. She's come into my inner-vision. I see the head pulled down with the cord around its nose but that's not all. Oh, god, it is in clear now. Not good, Juan. It seems as if it is around the neck also. I've never seen that before. That's bad. This may be difficult, but you can do it. I know you can."

"I'm going to need your help, please, Edgardo."

Edgardo gave him a silent nod.

Upon reaching the stall, Edgardo entered rapidly, talking softly to Gema in order to not startle her and placed his hands on her distended belly.

"This is a tough one, Juan. I see an extended leg and one pulled up tight. No wonder you couldn't feel it all." After checking her more closely, he questioned, "Has she been dripping like this, much?"

"For a couple of hours," responded Juan with despair in his voice. "I'm afraid we are also headed for a dry birth. I don't have much hope. Do we need Rómulo to help?"

Edgardo, realizing the seriousness of Gema's condition, turned and looked straight at Juan and said, with a sense of urgency, "Yes, get Rómulo as quickly as you can." Edgardo started talking softly to the heavy-bellied horse, patting her with strong, loving hands to quiet and calm her. She had started trembling from her own feeling of anxiety.

Juan rushed out to find the young man to help them.

Rómulo dropped his shovel, threw his shirt on, and joined Juan. He was born on the hacienda to one of the workers, grew up with the work and, it appeared, he would grow old there, too. A big, strong, young man, square-faced with wide-set, medium brown eyes, and short, cropped, wavy hair. Rómulo was a handsome young man, a sweet-talker, and quite popular with the girls.

As soon as they arrived, Edgardo gave orders to Rómulo, "Quick, run up to the kitchen and bring us a bucket of warm water, some towels or rags, and that long syringe that Teresa uses for cooking. Bring a bowl of that healing cream she uses for burns, too."

Rómulo returned quickly. Edgardo gave him more orders to bring in fresh straw.

He then turned to Juan, "Fill the syringe with warm water, cover it with the cream, and carefully insert it. Then, gently push the water out. I think we may have to do this constantly. Then, make your fist, go in and feel around those legs. See if you can feel that cord around the nose and neck."

"Yes, Boss."

The men worked hard. Juan repeatedly washed his arms and hands as he attempted to reposition the foal, and free it from the cord before trying to pull it out. The last thing he wanted was to pull it out in pieces.

Because this was Rómulo's first experience with a difficult birth, he learned more than he wanted to that day. He also realized what a help Edgardo was with his gift of "sight." Juan manipulated the baby very slowly and carefully with Edgardo's guidance. After he managed to position the foal better, he was able to deliver Gema's sweet baby with no more trouble. Gema turned to lick her newborn as Juan stood watching her. The fact that they were both alive was a miracle. He said a quick prayer of gratitude, relaxed, and a sudden tiredness hit him.

"Man, I'm done in," he said with a big yawn. "Guess I'm gettin' too old for this anymore." He leaned up against a wall. The men were a mass of sweat and felt exhausted. Their work was done. All three felt relieved and happy.

"Look at that little guy," said Rómulo, using his bandana to wipe the sweat from his brow and the back of his neck, "He'll make a great stud someday."

"He's got his mother's coloring - a beautiful buckskin with black leg markings," Juan quietly said. "His mane and tail are black, too. Couldn't be more perfect."

Edgardo dropped to one knee, said a silent prayer of gratitude and gave the sign of the cross. Gema was safe and the foal was alive.

To Juan and Rómulo, Edgardo said, "You guys did a great job. Thanks. All our work paid off."

Rómulo added, flopping down on the straw, looking up at the men, "Boy, I'm beat. I'll never forget this day." He beamed with pride. He now felt he would be considered a valuable ranch hand. He sat up, grinning, and watched as the colt wobbled around and exclaimed, "Look at him, he's almost up!"

"Yeah, he's a beauty. I can't wait to start working with him," Juan turned and looked at Gema, "Gema, girl, you sure threw a prize this time. It was all worth it."

Both Edgardo and Rómulo looked at each other and nodded in agreement. Rómulo actually stared at Edgardo and declared, "I've never worked with anyone who could work like you, man. Wish I could see things in my mind like that."

Edgardo smiled, "You were a huge help, too, thanks."

The men set to work preparing the stall with clean hay, feed and water for Gema and the new addition. While they were cleaning up, Rómulo began to talk and shared something neither Juan nor Edgardo wanted to hear.

"Hey, have you heard about all that gold up there in those hills?" Rómulo's voice quickened, and he became jumpy with excitement. "Me and some of the boys are thinkin' about gettin' some. We could be rich in no time. We just need to get a few things together, and we're takin' off!"

Edgardo and Juan looked at each other in dismay.

"Where are you headed for, *joven?* I hear those places are dangerous. Watch that temper of yours when they call you a 'greaser'," said Juan.

Rómulo gave him a disgusted look, "Nobody's callin' me nothin'!"

"Hey, I'm just warnin' ya! My cousin came back from the gold mines and told us they use the word 'Greaser' as a legal name for us Californios. He saw it written on one of their mining documents. Be careful, kid," said Juan, as he pointed his finger at him and looked very stern.

Rómulo shook his hands and his head back and forth, denying what he was just told, "There's no problem. We're headed for the Mexican camp up at Sonora. We'll be fine, it's safe, and I'll be back with a bag of gold." He held up his hand in the air and moved it up and down as if he already had that bag of gold.

"Rómulo, are you sure you want to try that? I see a lot of hard work. I don't see the gold. Who is going to replace you here?" asked Edgardo, his voice emphasizing the words with disapproval and growing impatience.

"You don't want me to go. That's why you don't see no gold," snorted Rómulo, beginning to look resentful. He pursed his lips and looked down. His eyes narrowed and he slanted them away from the men. He backed up, stiffened his body and crossed his arms. *These two men think they know it all. They're beginning to get on my nerves.*

Edgardo looked pointedly at Rómulo and said, "Well, you are leaving us shorthanded. Think what about what that means."

"From what I hear, anyone can find gold in a day or two. I won't be gone long."

"I can't ask you not to leave, but if you're taking four or five men with you, that puts the work at risk, and we won't finish up what has to be done before winter. If you go*, chamaco*, I expect to see a bag of that gold." Edgardo's voice had hardened.

"Gold, my eye," said Juan. "More like a bag of *mierda.*"

Rómulo ran out of the stall, leaving Juan and Edgardo staring at each other, shaking their heads.

"Juan, I don't understand men -- throwing everything to the wind and running after something as elusive as gold," he siad. Edgardo swept his hand across the sight of Gema and her foal, "Look what we just went through with Gema and look at what we have." He pointed to the colt, "He'll be a great cow pony and a major stud someday. That's our pot of gold right there."

"You're right, son. He'll be one fine show horse. In no time at all, you'll be riding him in the charreadas." Juan bent down to sit on the hay, feeling tired, "*Mijo*, thank god you got here when you did. I couldn't have done it alone." His lips trembled, and he breathed hard, overcome with emotion. He was hit with the realization that Emiliano was dying, his dearest lifetime friend, and he was just as old -- the same exact age. *We're given such a short time here, and I'm watching life go on right in front of me. I will soon leave this life, too.* He clenched his teeth to stop the trembling. He calmed down and said, "Everything's changing, Edgardo, and you'll just have to deal with it. Even with your gifts, you'll need the hope and faith you had here today."

"Yeah, I know I do. We got Gema and the colt turned around. Somehow, we have to do the same with what's happening to us now." He said as he stood silently. Juan, out of respect, also stood to watch the new life.

"Everything is unstable - falling apart. Now we have a frightening invasion of mad gold diggers, and I hear that our country may be taken over by the Americanos," Edgardo paused, looked down, rubbed his forehead several times, and then added, "Juan, it looks like we're in for some rough times."

Juan massaged his knees and legs, gave a shallow sigh, and said a prayer under his breath, "What do you see ahead? Any hope?"

"I haven't been able to see where help might come from," Edgardo shrugged his shoulders and shook his head, "but it looks like we might find some. I've seen Prudence in my mind with her uncle and her cousin. Her uncle is a businessman and her cousin a lawyer. *¡Ojalá!* Juan, maybe, just maybe, they can help us."

"Well, Son, as the old saying goes, 'There is no bad that comes that doesn't bring some good.' Look at the good we have down there on the straw."

Edgardo smiled and relaxed, saying, "Yeah, you're right, *viejo*." He walked slowly over to grab the pitchfork against the wall. He took a slow inhale as he carried it out of the stall to safety. He came back and gave Juan a quick hug. "Okay, let's clean up here. We both need a good rest," he said, rubbing his arms and shoulders.

"Sure, kid. I'll help. I've still got some juice in me."

They rubbed Gema down, covered her with a clean blanket, and left the new little guy standing on the fresh clean hay, wobbling and trying to nuzzle his mother.

Two days later, Rómulo and four young men were gone. They headed for the mountains - bitten by gold fever - and left the hacienda shorthanded.

Many ranches were left high and dry during that rough and chaotic time. Too strong was the lure of gold.

11

Changes in the Wind

Prudence had been teaching Fiarela about the complexities of keeping the financial books of the household, which were complicated. The work was beginning to wear on them when suddenly Fiarela asked, "Prudence, did you know Gema's colt came yesterday?"

"No, I didn't. Could we go see it?" asked Prudence, who had been thinking about Jorge Luis and was wondering if he would stop in, as usual, to check on them. She hoped so since he hadn't come by yesterday. *I know he is off limits for me, but he's the first man I've met that I really am attracted to since Jeffery died.* She sighed and felt a deep loneliness. *Why, why Jeffery did God have to take you so soon?*

Fiarela broke Prudence's reverie when she answered, "Sure. Let's take a break. Come on."

The girls walked out to the horse barn and searched for Gema's stall.

"Pru, here it is. Look, a little *macho.* Isn't he cute?"

"Oh, how precious," said Prudence, "He has beautiful coloring. What a gorgeous horse he will be."

Gema came over to the girls, who were leaning over the stall gate, and began to nibble on their fingers. They rubbed her nose and gave her a few pats on her cheeks.

"Fi, look at the little colt. Look, watch him. He's jumping around like a real bucker already. We should have brought a treat for Gema."

"Sorry, I didn't stop to think about it. We'll come out again. I want to watch him grow, and I wish he could be mine," said Fiarela.

They heard crunching sounds of someone walking on the loose straw on the floor behind them. Turning, they saw that it was Juan.

"Welcome, you two, to our new addition," said Juan, pointing over the stall gate at the new foal. He turned and lowered his head to Fiarela, giving her a big smile. "Wait until I train him. He's a beauty. Wouldn't you like to ride him in our charreadas?"

"Do you think I could?" She gave a look of askance at Prudence and hope and added, "Juan, I will need lots of riding lessons. I would really like to have him."

"Mija, I'm not sure about that but don't worry. You'll become one of our best show women in no time," said Juan, patting her on the shoulder. *To think it was just yesterday when I was lifting her up and putting her on the pony. Sometimes life moves too fast. Our pretty little princess is now all grown up.*

She reached up and gave Juan a big hug, "Thanks, Juan. We have to go now."

Fiarela skipped joyfully back to the office to finish up their work. They hadn't been back twenty minutes when Edgardo burst in, interrupting them unexpectedly. He was not in his work clothes but instead was dressed in casual buckskin slacks with a white full-sleeved shirt, covered by a vest that matched his pants. He wore a black bow tie. He carried his hat on the back of his neck with a black bolo cord under his chin.

Both looked up in amazement. Fiarela got up immediately, "*Hermano*, we're almost finished here. You look rushed and are all dressed up? What's going on?"

Prudence stood up, rearranged her skirt and sleeves that had been pushed up from work, and just watched.

"I have to be in town shortly. Instead of Benito taking you, Señorita Prudence, would you mind riding with me? No need to be taking two carts to town and back. I must pick up someone after I let you off and drive out to one of the *ranchos* for a meeting. Fi, can you clean up here? I need to leave as soon as possible."

"Yes, I can. I'll walk out with you." Once outside, she asked Prudence if she minded this last-minute change.

"Oh, no, I don't mind at all," Prudence said as she climbed in, set her cloth bag of belongings down on the floorboard, and settled her skirt to be comfortable. "I'm used to changes. If Jorge Luis shows up, please explain why I've left a little early, so he doesn't think I am skipping out on my responsibility."

Fiarela nodded and waved as Edgardo and Prudence set off. Leaving the hacienda with the horse at a fast trot, Edgardo turned to Prudence, saying, "Sorry to hurry like this, but I have an important meeting just out of town. In fact, I'm meeting a hide broker. Hides and tallow have been our biggest selling products, but our market has fallen. I'm hoping to work something out before it gets worse. I don't want to be late, so I hope you don't mind too much."

"No, no, Fiarela and I had a wonderful day today. We took a break to go see the new colt. He is just adorable, so cute and quite frisky already. He'll be one of your best show horses someday," said Prudence.

Edgardo laughed, "Oh, yeah, I agree. He's an example of perfect conformation and markings. He'll be a money-maker someday." Edgardo then went back to the original conversation, "How is the market for wool, tallow and hides back in Maine? We're having problems here because the missions, which have always been our biggest market, are no longer subsidized by the Spanish monarchy or by the church. They've been going downhill." He paused while he tapped the horse with the reins to speed him up after having slowed to a walk. "They can no longer cover their costs. And that is a big loss for us. The missions have always owned the best land, hundreds of thousands of acres, but they are selling off parcels now to private individuals. Some of the pieces are quite large, too."

"Edgardo, I'm astonished to hear that," said Prudence, turning her head to look at him. She was now listening intently. "I had no idea. I am not in a position to hear news anymore. I'm not allowed to go into the cantina alone, and Lizette does not receive a newspaper. I guess none come out here to California, and, if one did arrive, it would be hopelessly out of date. Does Jorge Luis know about all that? He has not mentioned anything when he comes in every day to check if I am teaching Fiarela correctly and - to make sure I am not wasting time," she said a little sarcastically.

Edgardo gave her a questioning look, but said, "I doubt that he knows yet. I just heard it myself. Also, I heard that many of the Mission Indians have been let go and sent off to the Rancherías. That will be a disaster. The returning Indians have not learned the skills to live an Indian life. They only know how to live in the mission environment, and they will find it very difficult to adjust. I don't know how the Rancherías will handle them. I am afraid it will only add more poverty to an already impoverished people. In fact, I have heard some of the young men are forming roving bands and creating havoc. Señorita Prudence, please, do me a favor and ask the women at the cantina if they have heard anything. I know the men talk. Also, ask Facundo and Pedro. If this continues, we could be badly hurt."

"Of course, I will. The problem is, I only know one of the ladies, Ana. If I see her, I'll ask."

Edgardo gave her a big smile, "Thanks, I'd appreciate that." He slapped the reins on the big rump in front of them. The horse gave a switch of its tail and began a fast trot. Prudence grabbed the seat for a tighter hold.

She gave a sideways look at Edgardo, who was intent on the horse, and said, "I hope the missions don't affect your family that much. I know all these foreigners coming in, like me, don't help. I hear complaints at the cantina. Thank you for sharing with me, Edgardo. I'll see what I can find out."

The news saddened her, and now that they were near the pueblo, she began to feel a prolonged loneliness seeping in. She saw the image of her empty room, where she could hear the music and noise from down below in the cantina.

"Yes, the foreigners are creating a lot of problems now. But, Señorita Prudence, I didn't mean to include you personally or to dump bad news on you. I've seen how hard working you are. You have been efficient, patient, and kind in teaching Fiarela. She loves you like a sister. And, I have a very strong presentiment that you will be an important part of our family."

What he said somewhat puzzled her. She wasn't totally sure about what he meant or how she should respond so she answered, "Thank you. Your family has been very kind to me, and I am more than appreciative."

They entered the pueblo, and Prudence stared at Edgardo, for a few seconds, until they arrived at the cantina. She was at a loss for words and couldn't quite grasp what he was getting at. She hoped it didn't mean he was interested in her. She did not want any trouble between the brothers.

The cart stopped. Edgardo stepped down and quickly went around to help Prudence descend the steep steps, which were difficult in a long skirt.

"Thank you, Señor Edgardo. I will keep my ears open and let you know if I hear anything. May all go well with your meeting," she spoke as she stepped carefully up onto the wooden walkway in front of the cantina.

"Gracias, Prudence, for permitting me to talk so openly. It has been some time since I have had that experience. My heart misses it so." He gave a big sigh, looking away for a moment, but then smiled and climbed up into the cart. He leaned back over the seat to say to her, "By the way, Señorita Prudence. I think we have long passed the time to be so formal. If you agree, I will call you Prudence and you may call me Edgardo. He smiled as she smiled and nodded. He waved his hand at her as he left. Little clouds of dust puffed up from the wheels of the cart, and ruts were pressed into the street as it made its way.

Prudence stood watching him disappear down the busy street, where people were trying to sidestep puddles and miss being hit by wagons or carts or a small herd of sheep. There were some mothers trying to keep small ones upright and their clothes clean.

Prudence tried to absorb the information Edgardo had shared but was mystified by his last words. She entered through the cantina doors, headed for the office and then upstairs to her room. It seemed to her that Edgardo must have something hidden in his background. She felt that was strange because he communicated so easily and openly with her. She felt a great need for that openness. *Would Jorge Luis ever be able to share like that?* she wondered.

12
The River Again

"It's beginning to warm up already, Octavio," said Jorge Luis, as he pitched another fork-load of fresh hay into the manger. He, together with his men, had been working all morning filling up the mangers.

"Yeah, Boss, it will be a hot one today, but we'll finish soon here. I'll tackle the horse troughs next. If I get too hot, I'll just jump in." Both men laughed.

Jorge Luis straightened up, rubbing his back and suddenly noticed young Pedro watching over the stall gate.

"Pedro, what are you doing here? Did Facundo send you? You should have yelled at me," said Jorge Luis, even though he knew how shy the kid was.

"My dad sent me, Señor. I have a message for you," said Pedro.

Jorge Luis leaned the pitchfork against the wall, brushed off the hay from his clothing, walked over to open the gate, and stepped outside of the stall.

"Okay, *muchacho*, what do you have to tell me?"

"Señor, I am to inform you that the lady, Señorita Prudence, is on her way to the river - alone," said Pedro.

That news did not sit well with Jorge Luis. "¡Maldición! Again?" he looked off to the side and shook his head. He took a moment to calm down and said, "Pedro, thank your dad. I will check on Señorita Prudence. Tell him to try to discourage her from going out there. She's headstrong, so it won't be easy, but try." He was walking outside to where Pedro had his horse tied. He wiped the sweat from his forehead. The heat had arrived.

"*Sí*, Señor, he did try, but she left anyway. As you say, she is a determined lady. Señor, please, thank Señor Edgardo for sending a person to help my mother. She needs more help now, expecting twins. She can't move around like she used to."

"Glad to, Pedro," he looked at his horse, standing in the sun waiting for his young rider, "Not too fast on that horse going home now."

Pedro laughed, "On Old Flojo? Don't I wish!"

After the kid left, Jorge Luis went back to the stall to let Octavio know he had to leave, "I have business to attend to in town, so don't fall into too many of those water troughs." He walked to where Juan was working, and got his attention, "Juan, find someone to take my place. I have to be gone for a while." *What's gotten into me? I can't even be honest with Juan about where I am going.*

He went to his bedroom, washed up, and changed his clothes. *She doesn't need to see the dirty chaps and clothes I had on the first time she saw me at the river.* He felt exhilarated, which he thought was silly, as he was only going to make sure she was safe.

His mother walked across the wide entrance foyer when he came down the high-winding stairway, "*Mijo*, where are you going all cleaned up? To town? Will you be back for dinner?"

"Oh, uh, Mother, I have some business to take care of. I'm not sure I can make it back in time for dinner." His heart started beating faster than usual. His mother would certainly not consider what he was about to do as anywhere near being "business". He was not used to telling his mother even a half-truth. Honesty had always been a strength of his. *Now I have told her an actual lie. God help me!* he said to himself, ashamed.

He gave her a quick kiss and strode swiftly out the front door. At the stable, Juan had Santón saddled and ready to ride. Jorge Luis imagined Prudence had been at the river for some time, so he spurred Santón into a steady lope.

When he arrived at the river area, he entered the path that led to the river, walking Santón silently and slowly. The path was overgrown with wild roses, willows and an occasional oak tree. He thought about bringing a machete to clear out the path the next time he rode out there. The shade did make it more pleasant, but the ground was rough with holes made from cattle hoofs during the wet weather. Santón was observant and stepped carefully. Jorge Luis still wasn't sure if he would let Prudence know he was there. He only wanted to see if she was safe and didn't know if he wanted her to see him. Suddenly, he was there, but she wasn't. Where was she? He slowly moved out into the open and dismounted from Santón to look around. He hadn't wanted to scare her, but now it was he who was scared.

Where is she? I see her horse tied to a tree, unsaddled too. Her picnic blanket is there on the ground. It's too close to the water - near the water. Oh no, she wouldn't. Would she? He then noticed a neat pile of clothes set on a tree trunk with her interior clothes hanging from a bush. *My god, she has. She is in the water with no clothes on!* He still couldn't see her. He turned his head and peered around a tree carefully. He walked closer to where her clothes were left. Then he could see her way out in the river, swimming and looking as content as could be. *Oh, I wish I could join her and be naked, too. How wonderful that would be, but I don't dare. What would she think of me then?* He called out to her, "Señorita Prudence!"

Prudence was obviously startled by his call. He could see water splattering all around her. Her head popped up, but that was all he could see. He knew she had seen him on the bank. Seeing her brought a sigh of relief to know she was safe.

He felt a real yearning to join her, but then he scowled, and his dark eyes darkened in remembrance of why he was there. He only came to see that she was safe.

His mouth set tightly in great irritation and disapproval, mainly brought on by the thought that she was in the water with nothing on, and he could not join in. He buried his feeling. *Someone will have to set her straight. She should never be out here alone. I sneaked up on her and so could someone else.* Those thoughts made him even more agitated, especially realizing he had no control over her.

He waved for her to come in. He realized that if she was naked, she wouldn't come out of the water while he was standing there, so he wandered around, searching to see what he could do and spied a big towel. He draped it over a bush closer to the water and walked several feet away, turning his back to her.

Hearing him yell, Prudence felt put upon and realized she should get out. But it irritated her that he had come out there and didn't want her to enjoy herself. *Blast him! What's he doing out here now? Well, he'll just have to wait. I'm not getting out quite yet.* She ducked under the water and swam so that he couldn't see her due to the thick, creamy coffee color of the water. *He may own all this land, but he doesn't own me, and I don't want to leave.*

She fooled around for a few more minutes before heading into shore. When she reached the muddy bank, she noticed he was standing with his back to her. *Oh my, he thinks I am naked. He sees my extra set of interior clothes I brought.* That amused her. *At least he is being a gentleman. I think, maybe, I will . . .* she yelled at him, "I'm coming out!" When she reached the bank, she made a big splash as if she had fallen. Then she did. She accidentally slipped down into the water and let out a small yelp.

He jumped, turned around and saw her thrashing in the water, "Señorita Prudence, do you need help?" He dashed toward her.

"Yes, I need help. I'm stuck in the mud. Grab my hand and pull me out, please."

My god, what will I do if she is naked? His fear for her safety over-ruled his thoughts, and he quickly grabbed her hand, with a look of concern crossing his face and eyes. Right at that moment, she actually slipped and fell, almost pulling him in. He grabbed her under her other arm and lifted her out, dripping muddy water. To his surprise, she had on interior clothes, sticking tightly to her. Every curve of her body was in open view. His thoughts slipped to Marina, but there was no comparison - none.

He was still holding her as he helped her up the bank. She shook her head in order to throw back her sopping-wet hair to remove it from her face. That action lifted her chest and raised her breasts, making the bodice stick more clearly. Her breasts were easily seen to be well-formed and tight under the cold, wet, and clinging material. His arm encircled her slim waist and when he pulled her upward, she bent over to get a better foothold in the mud. Suddenly, on his arm, rested the weight of both breasts. Desire hit him like a slap in the face. He quickly said, "Let me get your towel, and I will hang your picnic blanket up for you to dress behind."

"Thank you. That was awful! I'm all right now. I'm truly embarrassed." Her feeling of guilt made her cringe. *Why did I commit such a stupid and embarrassing act?* She never had done anything so silly before.

Not quite understanding her, he said, "Get dressed. I'll saddle up the horse for you. Oh, I must warn you about Old Flojo. He can be a tricky one. I know you can saddle him with no problem, but he will suck in air and blow up his stomach." He was making as many signs as he could to illustrate what he was talking about, "Then, after you have cinched him up tight and ridden him for a few minutes, he will let it out. The cinch will loosen, and the saddle and you will flip over his side. He can be quite nasty that way. You could hit the ground pretty hard and be hurt."

Prudence understood what he meant about the horse, not only by his hand signs but by many of his words, "Thanks, Señor Jorge Luis, but I always check that. Horses do that in Maine, too." *Who does he think I am? I'm not that stupid.*

He looked at her with a deep, penetrating look, "You really shouldn't be out here alone, Señorita Prudence."

She blushed, bending her head down, "I know, but I don't have anyone to come with me, and I need to be alone sometimes. There is so much noise and confusion at the cantina. I'm not used to that kind of life." She looked up at him briefly, then glanced down at the ground, wringing her hands in obvious distress, and talking in slow Spanish with hand signs the best she could, "We were only three in our home, and it was calm and relaxing. We lived on the edge of town, so it was very quiet. Señor, in my room, I hear everything off and on all night. I just needed to get away."

The implications of her having to live upstairs in the cantina had never occurred to him. *I never gave that a thought.* That was upsetting. He imagined her in contrast to the other girls. His heart went out to her. *She's a brave one, never complains.* He hurriedly hung up the blanket, then turned so she wouldn't see his concern or distress every time he glanced at her in her wet interior clothing. Her wet clothing defined her. Her hips were small, yet perfectly formed with legs that were long and straight. The clinging, wet material of the bodice shaped her breasts like the fresh, dew-covered melons from their garden in the early morning. Although smaller than Marina's, they had a perfect contour and an enticement about them that couldn't be denied. He shuddered and forced himself to focus on the moment.

"Señorita Prudence, you change while I saddle Flojo, so he won't dump you," he stated as he walked over to the horse, threw on the blanket and the saddle, and cinched it up tight. He led Flojo around and then tightened the cinch again. He did this several times until the saddle was safe. He turned and watched Prudence walk out from behind the hanging blanket. With all her clothes now on, she was still incredibly desirable. Her wet hair straggled against and around her neck. He wished he could use a towel to dry it. *She would probably kill me if she knew that. I want to know her better. She is the most intriguing woman I have ever met.* "Señorita, what are you wearing?" he pointed to her outfit, "You don't ride in a skirt."

"Oh, I had this outfit made by the seamstress that helps Maria, Facundo's wife. It fits me well. I designed it, and it's comfortable. It looks like a skirt because it has this long flap that comes down over the front and back." She flipped the flap aside to show her pant legs, "Clever, aren't they? Unless you'd rather me in those men's pants?"

"No, no, not in men's pants," he stopped for a moment, looking her over, "Yes, you did a good job." He felt himself blushing with embarrassment. He stared at her longer than he should have, "Quite practical, too. Come, let's pick up your things."

When all of Prudence's picnic and swimming articles had been picked up and packed into the saddlebags, Jorge Luis turned to her, "Señorita, did you know this open space where we are was the site of an old Indian summer fishing campground? They also have a sacred burial ground here. I'll show it to you if you like."

"Oh, I don't know." She looked somewhat embarrassed, "I'm not sure. At home I was always a little afraid of cemeteries, but I've never been to one in this country." She turned, glancing around at the campground, "I had no idea this was Indian land, but it is a perfect spot and so easy to get to the water. The banks are low for fishing, and it's well-protected with all the big oak trees, the willows, and the thick bushes."

She stopped, turned her head and look up and down the river, absorbing and appreciating the beauty and fullness of it. "You know, I never really noticed that island across the water from us, how interesting. Do you ever go over there?" she asked.

"No, not often, sometimes for duck hunting," he answered.

She stood still and remained silent for a few moments while soaking up the profound feeling of peace. An occasional splashing of a fish and the intermittent singing of the blackbirds were the only sounds. The river ran slow and silent.

Jorge Luis remained silent, too, appreciating how stimulating and enjoyable it was to be with her.

Prudence turned again to Jorge Luis and asked, "Señor, does the river have a name? Facundo only calls it 'the river'."

"Yes, but we only call it 'the river', also. However, it does have a name, *Linda*. The name fits. It is a pretty place. It should have a previous Indian name, but I've never seen any old Indian maps. On our maps the name is written as *Linda* and recorded as being situated just south of "Brazos del Rio" on the Sacramento river. We enjoy picnics and horseback riding out here. Maybe you would like to go riding sometime?" he asked, holding his breath in anticipation.

Her eyes were sparkling when she answered with a big smile, "I would love to." She turned back to the river and added, "Those poor Indians. They must have loved this place also. Are we even allowed around their burial ground? The Indians don't mind?"

"No, they don't. Come with me, and I'll show it to you," he said as he raised a callused finger, pointing in the direction down the river. "The Indians live pretty much in their Rancherías now, so they don't come out here anymore, except Shadowhawk, their shaman. Our family owns all this land now, but we gave him permission to come do his rituals for the dead."

"How moving. What does he do? Did you ever go with him?" she asked.

"I watched him once. I sneaked out to see what he did. Edgardo told me he always fasted for three days before he came. I followed him and saw him stand in front of the sacred ground, holding out his arms. He turned to the east, the south, the west, and to the north blessing each of the four directions. He had some herbs with him, and he waved them all over in the four directions as if he were cleansing the area. I heard him recite a prayer, but I don't remember the words."

Jorge Luis told her how Shadowhawk sat down in the Indian style and seemed to meditate for some time. "I didn't hear him say anything, but Edgardo told me he spoke mentally to the souls that were left there, trying to help them move on," he paused for a moment, waiting for a response from her. "Wouldn't you like to see the place? Come on, we can walk from here to see the burial mound. It's not like one of our cemeteries."

"Well, I do want to see it," she said, hesitating. She scrunched up her shoulders and looked unsure, "I'm just a little nervous." She took a couple of deeper breaths, looked directly at Jorge Luis, and then said, "Okay, show me the way." Prudence decided to get this over with and set off at a brisk walk, but the path was rough, beaten up by cattle hooves when the ground was wet. She stumbled and was grateful that Jorge Luis caught her before she fell.

"Hey, slow down. We've got a quarter mile to go, and it is rough walking here. Did you see the beaver dam over there in that pond? If you look carefully, you can see two brown things in the water. Those are beavers."

She stopped to look but didn't see the beavers. Continuing on, she did slow down and was grateful for her riding skirt, as she could never have walked in a regular skirt without constantly tripping and falling. Jorge Luis grabbed her by the arm when she started to stumble over the rough, difficult terrain.

"Señorita, do you see all this territory?" He pointed it out to her by waving his hand from the river and over the ponds and tulles. This river is all tide water and during the rains, or the high tides, the whole area floods."

"Really? No wonder the cattle make such a mess." Jorge Luis nodded when she asked, "Does it flood often?"

They talked a lot on the way, since there was so much to see. A lot of it made Prudence homesick. She noted the ponds with the tall tulles and another beaver dam in one small spot of water. She spotted water birds of many species, a few Teal and some Spoonies, just like at home.

"Do you hunt ducks out here?" she asked, looking at Jorge Luis questioningly.

"Yes, we do. Do you like duck?"

"Oooh, love it," she said, rubbing her stomach and closing her eyes with the memory. "I used to help my aunt pick and singe the ducks before cooking." She still accented her words with hand signals.

Jorge Luis looked at her in wonder. How well she fit into his kind of life was astounding to him and frightening, too. *Why does she have to be a foreigner and a heathen?* That question took a bite out of him.

Since Prudence had learned a substantial amount of academic Spanish from Facundo's sister, they enjoyed a mutually pleasant conversation. Both of them had relaxed and were enjoying the walk, even with the rough cow holes. They began to feel comfortable in each other's company. Jorge Luis often reached for Prudence's arm to help her over rough spots without considering the consequences. It felt natural and Prudence did not reject his help. Instead of getting huffy, she smiled, softened her eyes and said thank you.

He's been so kind and thoughtful of me. I've never felt so safe with any man before. I wish I knew how he really feels about me. I wish - but she wouldn't allow herself to say those words.

Yellows and oranges were splashing across the western skies from the setting sun, but they paid no attention. They were engrossed in each other and enjoying every step together on the way to the Indian mound.

Suddenly, Jorge Luis stopped by a huge oak tree that had a long, thick branch which curved down low and far enough over the ground to sit upon. "Come on, let's sit here for a minute," he suggested. Prudence had no idea why he wanted to do such an odd thing, but sat down beside him, causing the limb to bounce. Jorge Luis grabbed her as they flew up, and carefully setting her down, held her safely for a moment.

Prudence felt chills run down her whole body. She held her breath, not knowing what to expect.

He removed his arms and looked directly into her questioning eyes. His eyes were intense and dark, penetrating, while hers were like an astonished doe. He asked, "Señorita, I have had an exquisite time out here with you. I truly feel that we are friends now. I do not want to offend you, but I feel that it is time for us to speak less formally to each other. May I use 'Tu' and call you Prudence?"

"Of course, of course, I consider us friends now, and I am not accustomed to such formality. Please, just call me Prudence. May I simply call you Jorge Luis?" she asked, but felt that she was pleading. She did not know the custom well enough and did not want to be denied.

As he nodded a strong yes, he felt a surge of tenderness toward her -- a feeling that was new to him. A slight feeling of embarrassment swept over him. He rose up and said, "Let's go, amiga, the cemetery is close by."

Prudence was unsure how to react toward him. Even so, her face glowed with happiness and she felt her relationship had reached a new level. *I must be careful with my expectations, though. I don't want to be hurt*, she reminded herself as they moved on.

At the bend in the river, they both halted side by side. Jorge Luis pointed, "This is it, the gravesite."

Prudence, amazed, threw her arms out wide as if embracing the area, "Señor Jorge Luis, this is a huge area. There must be a lot of people buried here."

Jorge Luis explained, "Yes, there are, but these are the graves of men only because the wives and children stayed back in their villages. The men came for only short periods of time to fish and hunt. There used to be a lot of swamp deer here."

She walked back and forth, looking at all aspects of the large mound which was not high because the bodies were buried in the ground. She felt as if the bend of the river held the dead in its arms. She could feel a sensation of deep peace emanating from this sacred resting place. "What a lovely spot they picked, didn't they? Right in the bend of the river and protected by all those huge oaks." She paused a moment, "How sad to die way out here so far away from their families. May I say a silent prayer for them?" she asked, looking pleadingly into Jorge Luis's eyes.

He blinked in surprise at her request. Another surprising aspect of her.

"Of course, Prudence, I will join you."

They stood in silence, feeling a deep reverence for those at rest under the soil. Prudence realized that Jorge Luis was a mature man, generous, helpful, and to her surprise, very reverent. Standing together, they both felt each other's presence strongly, almost electrically. Today had given them a new, deeper understanding and acceptance of each other.

Jorge Luis was seeing her as a true lady, one of high integrity and one to be respected. She was beautiful and desirable, but that old, intolerant whisper came loud and clear through his mind: *She is a heathen. She is a foreigner.* Nevertheless, she certainly grew large in his admiration and esteem.

Again, on the way back there was much to see. "I didn't know you had pelicans and mud hens out here. Look! Look! What was that little animal running over the bank of the pond?" Prudence asked curiously.

"That was a mink. They have a fur that women like, but out here they're too scarce and too hard to catch to spend any time on them."

They stood for a while admiring the scenery, including the deep shadows on the water of the ponds. Some reflections of the clouds could still be seen at the surface. "Prudence, look. There is a huge flock of geese coming in for a landing for the night," Jorge Luis pointed to one of the larger ponds, which already had ducks.

"Listen to that noise! Hearing those geese calls make me so homesick. They used to wake me up at night sometimes while passing over our place," she reminisced.

She watched, nostalgically absorbing the symphonic sounds with the in sync rhythms of wings in the formation of their flight. Because the sun was setting rapidly now, a lot of wildlife movement was going on. Animals were scurrying to find shelter. They heard a lot of rustling through the tulles and an occasional fish splash in the ponds. Flocks of water birds could be heard landing in the water. Some of the larger birds were headed for the trees to roost.

Prudence suddenly noticed what is often a nightly routine. Without thinking, she grabbed Jorge Luis' hand and raised her own to point to a sky darkened with blackbirds, who were swirling and forming organic shapes in the air. They, too, were looking for their roost for the night. *His hand is so warm and strong. I wish he would hold mine all the way back.*

Her hand felt cold. He noticed she was beginning to shiver and watched as she lowered her arms, putting them tight around her body to conserve heat. Then, in what seemed like a dream, Jorge Luis snapped out of it and had a need to get home.

The temperature had suddenly fallen with the sun, which lost its color behind the hills. He quickly felt concerned. They had not paid attention to the passage of time. He spoke quickly, "Prudence, we have to hurry. We need to leave before it gets too dark to see."

On the way back to the horses, he guided her carefully in the dimming light, but he was lost in introspection. *Have we ever been together and simply enjoyed ourselves before? This has been one of the most pleasurable days I've ever had.* Jorge Luis did not feel his world crumbling. Instead, he felt it solidifying. How to explain that? He looked at her, mystified.

13
A Long Night

Prudence was frightened. She had never been alone out in a country so vast with a man she hardly knew -- and never after dark. Even though the sky was packed with stars above her from horizon to horizon, she had never experienced that type of deep darkness. Jorge Luis tried to comfort her by assuring her the horses knew the way, but she was not convinced. She did not know these horses, and she didn't know the way in the dark. She tried not to show her fear. The sky was clear. They could see the stars. They would not be lost, she told herself.

Jorge Luis paused the horses a moment to point out the billions of stars, "Look, Prudence, the stars are so thick and close, I feel like I could reach up and grab a handful. Isn't it beautiful? What would you do if I gave you a handful?"

She sighed, "Oh, I would keep them forever. Yes, the stars are re-markable out here like this. They are incredibly beautiful, so spiritual."

Jorge Luis looked at her in surprise. He had always felt that way out under the stars on a dark night.

"I wish I didn't feel so scared, but the darkness is overwhelming. Jorge Luis, please don't go so fast. Flojo can't keep up, and I don't know the way. I don't feel safe."

Jorge Luis halted Santón and dismounted, "Prudence, you're right. I'll tie Flojo to Santón and put you up here. We can ride double if you don't mind. You'll have to ride in front. I'm afraid you are so tired you might slip off the back." This was true, but he also was thinking about how he could hold her. He helped her down and tied her horse to his.

When he turned back to her, he noticed she was shivering and re-alized she had no coat. She was not prepared to be there after the sunset and the temperature dropped. The breeze from the bay was now colder and stronger.

He quickly removed his blanket and another coat from his bedroll, which was tied to the back of his saddle. He wrapped it with care around Prudence. "Okay, I'll mount and then pull you up. You'll notice that the pommel on my saddle is curved and wider than usual. There's no horn, so wait until I cover it with my coat. It'll be much more comfortable padded."

"*Gracías*, I'm ready."

Jorge Luis reached down and pulled her up in front of him, "Prudence, it may be uncomfortable for you, but at least I can hold you on safely."

"I'm so sorry. I hope it's not too bad for you." She took a deep breath and relaxed, leaning back into the warmth of his chest. His left arm cradled her trembling body while his right hand grabbed and held the reins. He gave a light spur to Santón, and they started off into the darkened night.

The half-full moon came up, floating, phantasma-like shadows across the landscape. Santón walked with a smooth, lightly rocking gait. With the strength of Jorge Luis's arms, and the rhythmic motion of the horse, Prudence fell asleep quickly. Jorge Luis held her close, occasionally bending his head to kiss her soft hair. He wished this would last forever.

When the lights of the village appeared, he did not wake her until they reached the kitchen at the back of the cantina. After sitting and holding her a little while longer, he had to wake her and set her down. He unlocked and opened the back entrance to the kitchen, escorted her in and said, "Sit here and wait for me. I'll take care of the horses and be right back."

She looked at him a bit puzzled yet too sleepy to complain or object for a change. *I don't care. I adore him.* She laid her head down on the table, instantly falling into a deep sleep.

In no time at all Jorge Luis took care of the horses. When he returned, he found her head resting on the table. Gently picking her up, without waking her, he carried her up the stairs from the kitchen directly into her room. He stood for a moment, taking in the view of the room, though not knowing what to do with her. At that moment, she slowly woke and stared at his face. A small smile slowly formed, and she drifted away again.

Oh, god, what can I do? Her clothes are a mess -- covered in mud, stickers, and burrs. I don't want her to sleep all night like that. I hate to wake her up, but I may have to.

Prudence suddenly opened her eyes. Jorge Luis was carrying her. Surprised and a little disoriented, she said, "Where am I? Where are we? Why are you carrying me?" She moved her head, "This is my room. How did I get here?"

"Prudence, you fell sound asleep. You woke up when we arrived, but then I found you asleep at the kitchen table. I didn't want to wake you, so I carried you up here. I was just going to lay you on your bed."

"You carried me all the way up here? Put me down. I'm fine, thank you. I couldn't help it. I was so tired." She regained her composure and felt guilty, "I'm sorry. I reacted badly. Thank you for helping me." Her face slackened. She started to tear up and appeared crestfallen.

Jorge Luis nodded and gently let her down saying, "Prudence, sit here and rest. I also am exhausted, but I'm going to the kitchen and bring some food up for both of us. I assume you are hungry, too?"

"I'm starved. Thanks. While you are doing that, I am going to clean up and change. I'm a total mess."

Downstairs in the kitchen, Jorge Luis found a pot of chili verde, which he heated by lighting a small fire. He hunted around and found some bread and cheese, a few boiled eggs and a thick slice of ham. The time it took for him to gather the food gave Prudence time to wash up and change into her nightgown and robe. She hoped he would not misunderstand, but she had been too uncomfortable, and it was too late to put on regular clothes again.

Jorge Luis, with a light knock, entered the room again. His surprise, upon seeing her dressed in nightclothes, showed on his face. All he could say was, "Prudence, you are beautiful."

Upon hearing his words, she felt her heart swell, beating faster. She almost walked into his arms without thinking. She caught herself and stopped, entranced by his face full of admiration. She did not doubt his words. Her eyes were bright, and her face flushed, which made her take a step back. A thin but happy grin stole across her face, "I'm sorry about these clothes, but mine were so dirty. I couldn't stand them a minute longer. I'll change them if you wish."

"No, no they are lovely on you." He took a second look at her clothes. They were quite elegant. Her gown was a thin, white cotton batiste with white thread embroidery. The shoulder straps were crocheted with thin white thread. Her robe was of heavier cotton material decorated also with white embroidery. He realized they looked imported - probably from faraway India, which spoke of family wealth.

He turned toward the table to hide his feelings of wanting her. "Come on, let's eat and enjoy ourselves. Here, take what I found in the kitchen. I'm sure we'll have enough," he said, sitting down swiftly. Watching her, he felt and thought, *she has everything a man could want, but I really don't know much at all about her and her family. Maybe I can find out while we eat.*

Prudence organized the table while he sat in one of the two chairs. His eyes followed her - full of admiration. He also realized how tired he was and did not look forward to another long ride to get home. Naturally, he would never complain.

"Let's eat. I know this is just a quick repast, but Jorge Luis, would you say grace?"

That surprised him. He had never done that. His mother was the one to say grace at the table. "Uh, uh, yes, I can do that," he said. They both bowed their heads, "Grácias, Señor, por tener que comer y poderlo comer, y te pido, Señor, que bendiga estos alimentos en el nombre del Padre, del Hijo y del Espíritu Santo, amén." He made the sign of the cross, looked at Prudence with respect, and a soft smile formed. They both began to eat. Only a small part of the grace had been said, and in a rather hushed and embarrassed manner, but she seemed pleased.

While they were eating, he heard unnatural, somewhat muffled noises outside of her room: boots walking, doors slamming, beds creaking, cries of pleasure, but, then, cursing with a dull bang was heard, which meant that a hole had possibly been punched in a wall. Suddenly, Jorge Luis sat up straight, looked at the far wall and realized where they were coming from. "My word, Prudence, do you hear that every night? How do you sleep? You should never have to hear that type of noise," he said, aghast. His face flushed from a surge of embarrassment, sinking quickly into dismay and then anger.

"I know, but I'm so grateful for this room that I will not complain, and, if you notice, I have a rug nailed to the wall covering the door to the bordello rooms. That helps keep the sound down, but I will be glad to get out of here."

He wished he could help her but did not know how to, so he changed the subject, "You know, I really know nothing about you and your family. Do you mind talking about them? Tell me about your uncle." He glanced around her room and took in her efforts at decorating. She had made it quite homey and comfortable. He admired that.

"Yes, you would like them," said Prudence, while she was snacking. "But, first, I need to say," she hesitated here, but began again, "Well, we are alone in my room." She looked at him directly in his face, as if to reinforce her words, "Jorge Luis, I trust you completely, but people may talk. I know your mother would have a fit if she knew you were alone with me."

"I know she would, but, Prudence, no one saw us arrive, and my horse is not outside. I know Facundo knows I went to the river. He doesn't know any more than that, and," his voice changed and became very soft with a protective feeling to it, "Prudence, I would never do anything to sully your reputation, never. If you think I should go, I will."

"No, no, I know you wouldn't," she swallowed her fear and found her courage, "Stay and we'll talk." Prudence opened up and began talking while they continued to eat. They talked, asked each other many questions and branched off into various areas of conversation. They talked animatedly with no attention to time.

Both were developing a deeper admiration for one another and neither wanted to quit. It became obvious to Prudence, who had a long sleep on the horse, that Jorge Luis was dead tired. She worried about him. She knew how far it was to the hacienda. He would ride back home, dangerous this late in the night, rather than take a chance on being seen in the hotel.

"Jorge Luis, I'm sorry. I have been selfish, keeping you up talking. I can tell how tired you are. I don't think you should be riding in that state all the way home alone, either. I don't want you to," she said, feeling truly concerned, even though she knew she was putting herself in an awkward spot and, maybe, a dangerous place. However, she did trust him. She waved her arms all around the room, "You own all this. Why not stay here? Here would be safer, and I would not worry all night."

Jorge Luis didn't know what to make of her. After their earlier talk, what was she offering? He looked her in the eyes and said, "I don't have a place I can stay, or I would. I don't want to be seen in the hotel."

"I know you will think I am either crazy or brazen, but please listen. I learned you are a man of integrity. You honored me by the way you treated me today and tonight. I can only reciprocate by letting you rest on my bed. That is all I am offering, so don't go and get any untoward ideas. I know what people would say no matter what we do, but I'm not sending you out in this condition. I would feel terribly responsible if anything happened. I'll get you a blanket. At least sleep a bit - enough to go home safely. I am going to clean the table and by the time I have finished, if you want to leave, I won't try to stop you. Take your boots off. Lay down on top of the bed. I'll get the blanket."

He looked at her with gratitude, silently pulled off his boots and laid down. She placed the blanket over him. He felt her tucking him in and thought, *Someday, she will be a wonderful mother*. Within seconds he slid into a dream – the dream was of her. He did not wake up.

She slipped into bed under her covers and she, too, fell instantly asleep.

Jorge Luis woke first. He felt dumbfounded and worried when he realized where he was. Then he looked at her, lying next to him under her blankets. His heart melted. *¡Madre de Diós*! That was a true first for him. *I need to get out of here now while she's asleep, or I may never get out of here.* The desire to stay with her hit him hard. He leaned over cautiously and lightly kissed her.

Slipping into the darkness of the very early morning, he went to the stable, bridled, and saddled Santón. He left town silently. He rode home absorbing that astounding experience. His mind was in a turmoil. *Will she be angry because I left before she woke? How should I act with her now? Where can this go? I want more of her. I've never wanted anything so much.*

Dawn was peeping over the mountains and beginning to break when he arrived at the stables.

Juan arrived just as he was unsaddling Santón. "*Oye, hijo*, it appears to me somebody must have had a very good time," Juan said, rolling his eyes. Juan tried to give him a bad time about arriving after a whole day at the river - and a night?

Jorge Luis returned Juan a squint-eyed scowl. He was too distracted to banter back, "Don't you have work to do?" He wasn't about to talk about yesterday or the night. He held that close to his heart.

Juan realized he had to tread carefully around that subject, as things appeared serious there. He wondered what the consequences would be. Jorge Luis was like a son to him, and he highly admired Prudence even if she was a foreigner. He could feel a future there and prayed that Jorge Luis would open his heart and mind. They both deserve to be happy, he felt.

Jorge Luis made it up to his room with no one seeing him, changed into work-clothes and went out to put in a hard day's work. Hard work takes care of a lot of things.

Morning had almost slipped into noon when Prudence began to move. She stretched, slowly opening her eyes. *Good lord, I forgot that Jorge Luis fell asleep on my bed last night.* She rose up, almost hoping to find him, but he wasn't there. *I wonder what time he left. I never felt a thing.*

She glanced at the window. The light was not an early morning light. *Oh, no, I'm horribly late to work. Facundo will wonder what happened. I've missed breakfast, too.* She rushed to wash and dress. Grabbing a bite of cheese and one boiled egg, left over from last night. She realized that last night had been a reality. It was not a wishful dream. *Now what? How should I act toward him? How will he treat me?*

Facundo was checking the liquor stock when he heard her enter the office. He then heard the shuffling of record books. He knocked softly, and opening the door, said, *"Buenos días*, Señorita Prudence. Well, well. You have good time, ¿no? You not come late before. Señorita happy, I think."

"I had a marvelous time. The best I've had since I've been here. Facundo, Jorge Luis showed me the Indian burial ground. I never thought about the Indian lives before your people arrived. I was touched by how hard their lives must have been, and so many had died there." She lost her smile for a moment in sadness, but quickly looked up into Facundo's admiring face, "There are so many ponds there, filled with ducks and geese. I even saw a few swans, a beaver dam, and some swamp deer. I almost felt like I was home."

She glanced out the window, fidgeting with her sleeves, and brushing her hair back. For a moment she felt lost in homesickness. She pulled herself out of that dark feeling to turn back and say, "Facundo, I went swimming! He didn't like that, but I did. I felt so refreshed and free."

Facundo took a deep breath, not wanting to hear that, but was relieved to hear how happy she was. He gave her a loving smile, "Señorita, how *mi amigo* comport self?"

"Oh, he was very much the gentleman."

¡Más le vale! Or answer to me! he said to himself. "I happy for you, Prudence, for all day and - night?" Facundo asked, glancing at her with a piercing look as he turned and walked out softly, closing the door. Prudence sat and blushed.

14
A Diversion

eather-bound books filled the ample shelves of the office. Tall cabinets with hand-carved doors held all the record-keeping books, pencils, pens, nibs, paper and ink -- all the needed equipment for an efficient office. Two fabric-covered chairs faced the desk and others were scattered about for guests.

In a far corner of the room was a settee and a comfortable chair. Catrina the chaperone sat there, or rather slept there, while the girls worked. The girls laughed at her. They felt it was a very old-fashioned tradition and ridiculous for their particular situation of working in the office. However, what people might think and gossip about, even the servants, was important to Fiarela's mother, Aldiana. Appearances were very important to her.

Prudence, sitting at the desk trying to focus on the figures in front of her, was caught off guard by sudden flashbacks of the travels she had been through since she left Maine. Her hand fell, thus dropping the quill pen which spilled a large drop of ink. Fortunately, it fell on the blotter and not on the record book. She sat numbed by the memory of the unforeseen and unexpected reality of her current situation. *Oh, God, please, I've seen too much, had to do too much and have learned so much to be worrying about appearances.*

Fiarela was oblivious, while concentrating on her assigned work, to notice anything going on with Prudence.

After the hardships she had lived through and the mixture of peoples she spent months traveling with, often under adverse conditions, she gained a greater understanding of them. She was much wiser. That came from her direct experience and she was quite different from when she left Maine.

I'll never forget that rich gentleman in his fancy Conestoga who made everyone believe he was so intelligent. He turned out to be a disgusting coward. The young boy who slept under his wagon was responsible for watering all the horses. He's the one who became our hero. I sure learned not to jump to judge people. No, Aldiana, you are not above me, nor is Ca-

trina below me and neither is anyone else.

She found herself deep in thought brought forth by those memories, *Why can't people understand that we're all in this together, whatever our station. I'll never forget how hard it was to learn to ask for help. I had to rely on people I didn't know and, probably, would never have wanted to know back home. I admit how innocent and unsophisticated I was. I can't believe how I allowed our lifestyle and other members of society to influence me. I had to learn the hard way, I guess.*

She scrunched down in her chair, remembering the malicious gossip - by friends, too- that had started back in Maine. She felt humiliated and helpless. There was murmuring about her being a young, unmarried woman living with her widowed uncle. People being mean-spirited was a cruel reality for someone so open, honest, and naïve.

When Uncle Lot found out, he was furious and took pity on her. He decided to send her to San Francisco to check on his business interests there. "Prudence," he said, "I have to settle up my affairs here, and then I will join you in California."

For six months she watched those who survived and those who did not, and those who readily gave of themselves. *I saw people who had to change. I did, too. I saw those men and women survive. I saw many women get out of their wagons and push and pull as hard as they could in difficult spots. I taught several women to shoot so they could fight alongside their men. I will survive here, too.*

For a couple of minutes she put her head down on the desk, feeling terribly alone. But then, she raised up and glanced over at Fiarela with her nose still in her book. *Fiarela, you are a lovely young girl. You've lived such a protected life. I hope you never have to experience what I have – leaders who gouged money out of people for any reason, men who forced themselves on any innocent girl, people who took and never gave. But - I met a lot of wonderful people, too. They added to my will to survive.*

She was pulled into the visual images of how close death was. Death rode with them. She clutched her hand to her heart, remembering the newborn that died after three days, and the two young ones who slipped into the river and were gone before anyone could get to them. She gulped air to keep from reacting out loud and disturbing Fiarela. The emotional pain was still sharp and hard to keep in, especially as she remembered the grieving parents who had to bury and leave their children where they died. Never would they be able to visit their gravesites to remember them.

Back home death was just as harsh and unjust, but I had family and friends around me. Our traditions always gave me closure, and my church was always there for comfort. I've got to stop feeling overwhelmed and sorry for myself for suffering all that. I'm here now, and those six months on the trail are over. I must make my life worth something.

She glanced at Fiarela, who was still so focused. Prudence took a breath in and let it out slowly when the memory of what happened at the end of the long trail suddenly slapped her – it was devastating and terrorizing. She gave a gasp, which caught Fiarela's attention.

Fiarela jumped up and ran to Prudence, "What's wrong? What happened?"

"I'm sorry, Fi, I didn't mean to disturb you," she answered. Her eyes teared up, causing Fiarela to give her a hug. Prudence wiped her eyes. "Fiarela, my – travel - memories," she choked, paused and then said, "I don't know why, but they suddenly appeared, and the last thing that happened to me took me over. I must try to forget all that."

"Oh, Pru, I had no idea you had such a bad time. Can you tell me about that last part? I hate to see you so upset," said Fiarela. "Prudence, I promise I won't tell anyone."

"Well – I – we - were way past Sacramento – close to here - when it happened. We were robbed, and they weren't Indians, either. They were dirty, filthy bandits. Their clothes stunk. I'll never forget the nauseating stench emanating from their leader. Oh, god, they were frightening and repugnant," she said, covering her mouth with her hand as if that might stop the memory.

Fiarela's eyes enlarged and her mouth dropped open, listening to what Prudence experienced. Unable to get any words out, she just stared at Prudence.

"Fiarela, I was lucky, because they missed taking my second trunk and my guns. They were tied underneath the wagon where they couldn't be seen, but they stole my purse, so I had no identification when I arrived here. I couldn't prove to anyone who I was. I was petrified."

"¡Diós mío!" Her hand flew to her throat as she remained speechless. She kept staring at Prudence.

"Thanks to those bandits, I had no money to pay the family that I had been traveling with for the rest of my trip. Since we were near to this pueblo, they brought me here and told me to get out in front of the hotel." She stopped a moment, barely breathing from feeling again the greatest fear and panic that she had ever felt. "Fiarela, you can't imagine the state I was in. I felt almost paralyzed. I had no idea where I was. I was in an almost somnambulant daze when I walked into the hotel. I prayed that no one would steal my things left outside by the door." Prudence stopped and turned her head away from Fiarela. She almost succumbed to the feeling of panic.

"I was scared and trembling," she continued, "and when the clerk saw me, he immediately left, scaring me even more, but he returned quickly with a woman he introduced as Lizette. Her attire shocked me, especially when I realized what she was. There must be a brothel here, and she must be the madam, I thought. That sure scared me. Why was she brought to talk to me? I found myself staring at her. I had never seen anyone dressed like she was. I'll never forget that first impression. She had on a very low-cut, bright maroon bodice that showed more than an ample bosom. They looked as if they would fall out at any moment, and the sleeves were off her shoulders! She sported a tiny waist that was tightly girded by a black sash. I don't know how she walked since her skirt was so tight. And, she wore a lot of jewelry that was obviously very expensive." Prudence's tears had dried. The trauma still showed through the emotion, tone, and speed of her voice.

"What happened next, I couldn't believe. To my amazement, she spoke French to me. French, Fiarela - I couldn't believe my good luck. When she asked me what I wanted, I answered her in perfect French that I needed a job and a room. That's when she sent me to Señor Facundo who gave me the bookkeeping job, and you know the rest. Really, I'm all right now. We should get back to work. But, Fi, I ended up so angry at that bandit that I could have pulled his flesh from him slowly, piece by piece."

Fiarela was horrified to hear such a thing but remained silent.

The two girls sat together quietly. Fiarela was feeling a great compassion and sympathy for Prudence, when Prudence added, "Good came out of it though. My pride and cultural beliefs were all put to the question. I felt as if they had been hammered on a heavy anvil."

Prudence felt that she shouldn't have told Fiarela about her meeting with Lizette. Fiarela was so naïve and unsophisticated. *She didn't need to know those details. They would never be important in her life,* thought Prudence. But she, certainly, would never forget their first meeting.

Prudence would not share all of that meeting, but remembered it well. She saw Lizette's eyes open wide in surprise as she looked Prudence up and down, appraising her. She could guess what was occurring in her mind, and she remembered every detail that occurred.

Lizette had her jeweled hand rubbing her mouth in thought. *She would clean up nicely, I can see, and she would make quite an addition to my girls.* "Are you looking to work here with the other women?" she asked with dollar signs in her eyes.

Prudence blushed, embarrassed, "Oh, no, Madam Lizette." She took a deep breath, regaining her composure. She stood straight and tall and announced, "I am Prudence Mullens from Maine, and I am a bookkeeper. I was on my way to San Francisco when we were robbed. Do you have any need for a bookkeeper? I am quite competent and have had lots of experience."

Lizette placed her fingers over her mouth again and squinted her eyes slightly, *I think she could be valuable. I'd hate to lose this one, but she'll probably end up with me anyway.* "Actually" she said, eyeing her again from head to toe with greedy appreciation, "we could use someone, at least part-time. I'll take you to our manager, Señor Facundo, and I am sure he can fix you up. If not, you can always work for me," she said, wishing she would. She could easily see what a draw Prudence would be.

"Thank you, Madam Lizette," Prudence said and followed her to the office.

Facing Lizette was embarrassing, but another blow to her upper-middle class upbringing was facing the fact that the only job available and the only place she could find a room was in the bordello connected to the La Cantina de Las Flores. She remembered how ashamed she felt, and how, if anyone in Maine knew, she would be talked about at home.

But she told herself, *I am so lucky. I'm alive. I saw too much of death to be concerned now about lowly gossip. I can do it, and I will.*

She was grateful to the manager for taking a chance by offering her the job. He was thoughtful enough to give her the room over the kitchen and not among the girls. However, living alongside those girls taught her how fortunate she truly was.

"Don't judge" became an important part of her convictions. At first, she had judged the girls out of old habits she had learned at home and in her religion. To her chagrin and shame, she learned that the majority of the women, or very young girls, working there really had no options in that small town. They were uneducated, did not read or write, had no other skills and most had no family. They tended to look at Prudence with some jealousy. They avoided her and she was unable to make friendships.

Having to depend on her own resources, her consciousness expanded and was deepened now by experience. Her formal education gave her skills to survive, but this experience gave her the understanding and insights to live her life fully in gratitude without bitterness. *Someday, maybe, I will be able to share this part with Fiarela. She would be too shocked by my story now. I don't dare tell her how I feel when I see the immensity of the hacienda and the grandeur of her home. I tend to lose my sense of self and feel that I'm not able to measure up.*

The memories stopped abruptly with the loud grunting, whistles, and snorts from the sleeping Catarina. The present moment broke the spell, and she was back in the office safe and sound, sitting quietly with Fiarela who was watching her. She hadn't realized that Fiarela had taken her hand and was holding it gently.

"I'm so sorry that this last year has been so traumatic for you. And I apologize for being so unaware. I feel so selfish now because I have been so happy working with you." Fiarela looked on the verge of tears.

Prudence reached over and gave her a hug, "No, no, no, you must never feel that way. I am grateful you were willing to listen. Let's forget all this and get back to work or, maybe, we need a break. In fact, I do need a break."

Outside, autumn was approaching and the afternoons were still quite warm. Prudence had been teaching Fiarela for several weeks. Speaking an excellent academic French and having studied Latin, Spanish had come easily for her; therefore, Facundo no longer accompanied her in order to help translate the lesson she had to teach.

In the beginning, Prudence had started teaching bookkeeping to Fiarela with the household books, which were extensive in themselves, containing many categories: the needs and the maintenance of the house, the grounds, the vegetable garden, water, the servants with their duties, needs, and quarters, seamstresses for clothing, bedding and linens, medicinal supplies, guest needs, entertaining, basic food needs, and the chickens. The larger animals came under husbandry.

Prudence took two or three deep breaths to calm herself. She pushed with her hands on the desk to stand up to say, "Fiarela, let's forget all about what happened here, okay?" She saw the agreement flash across Fiarela's face, so she continued, "You've been studying diligently. You're almost ready to take over the household books by yourself. I couldn't be prouder of you. We need to take some time off today. I still feel like a wreck. Could we take a tour of the hacienda? I would love to see more of it. It is so incredible. We have nothing like it back home in Maine."

Having heard Prudence's emotional tale of her journey and her having been dumped in an unknown place, with nothing, and all alone, Fiarela suddenly realized that she had never asked Prudence about her home life. Her lack of thoughtfulness struck her as if she were like Elena: a selfish, spoiled child. She looked lovingly at Prudence, stood up and pulled her skirt down, which was hitched up by so much sitting and scooting around in her chair. She fingered her neckline and felt as though her shame was being rubbed out. She stepped over and took Prudence by the hand, looked into her eyes while she caressed her cheek quickly and said, heartfelt, "Forgive me. I really want to know. Tell me, Pru. What do you mean? What's it like back there?"

"Well, give me a minute. There are so many things," she said as she hesitated, slowly squinting her eyes and looking off to the side for something. "For example, we have small towns near enough to each other that we can generally drive to one and obtain whatever we need. I've noticed that the hacienda must be self-sufficient for everything. You have to make and provide everything you need." Prudence looked around and pointed to some candles, saying, "Back home, we drove to a store that sells candles. A lot of people do make them, but we don't have to make them all the time like you do."

"I can't imagine your world, Prudence. You must miss it a lot. I never thought how different out here must be for you. I really hope you will share with me about your life." She paused, looking at Prudence with a compassionate smile, "I'm so lucky you are teaching me. I hope you consider me a friend. You know, even Mother is becoming accustomed to you being here."

In listening to all that, Prudence felt a true warmth with a small sense of belonging. She had felt so out of place. She would never belong at the cantina and had not belonged at the hacienda, but her situation was changing. She felt more comfortable now. Fiarela was such a dedicated student, and a lovely, thoughtful girl who was quite full of fun at times. A couple of times, when she heard Jorge Luis starting to open the double doors of the office, she would drop down behind the desk, shocking Prudence and leaving her with her mouth open when he walked in. A few times she snuck out to the kitchen when she knew no one was there in order to filch some leftover food. Prudence would hold her breath, hoping she wouldn't be fired if Fiarela got caught. But then, they both enjoyed the food while Catrina slept soundly.

Prudence remembered Fiarela's comments about wanting to become friends, "Yes, Fiarela, I definitely do consider you my friend." This friendship would be very welcomed as it would be her first. "You know what?" said Prudence, "I'm beginning to feel claustrophobic in here. Would you like to go out for some fresh air?"

"Good idea. I'll go ask permission from Mother, and we'll take a little tour. Should we wake up Catrina or just let her sleep and not tell her we're leaving?" said Fiarela somewhat impishly.

"Do we dare?" asked Prudence. "Okay, let's do it, hurry. I'll wait here and clean up the desk and you be very quiet."

Fiarela returned shortly with permission. Both girls sneaked out, leaving Catrina in the far corner, snoring.

Benito, removing the little coach from the carriage barn, was thinking about how Prudence had become like a sister to Fiarela, a real friend, which he knew they both needed. That thought brought him happiness. His big heart embraced them both. He brought the small carriage around and said, looking directly at the two girls with an endearing smile on his face, "Okay, girls, now, no getting into trouble and bring this back in one piece!"

"Yes, sir!" laughed Fiarela, while Prudence climbed up and took the reins.

"Where shall we go first? Which way?" asked Prudence with a grin.

"Let's go by the stables first," said Fiarela with a sly smile. "Maybe Jorge Luis is out there working." A quick brightness flashed in Prudence's eyes.

Prudence guided the horse carefully around the stables, turning at the back of the building to go by the working corrals and running track. She did not comment to Fiarela but couldn't help noticing the size and impressiveness of the working area.

Jorge Luis could be seen ahead of them working with Santón in one of the corrals. They stopped before they reached him, to watch, but not disturb him. Suddenly, they saw him halt his horse and jump off. He leaped the fence and was running over toward the blacksmith area where two men stood under the shade of a large tree.

Jorge Luis grabbed one of the men and gave him a hard, swift kick, yelling in his face, "I saw you kick that dog. How do you like being kicked? *¡Basura!*" He then grabbed him by the collar, pulled him up, and smacked him equally hard with his fist, shouting, "If you ever kick another animal or maltreat one on our property, you little wipe snot, I'll see to it you never see the light of day again!" He turned to Elías Yanci, another of his workers, whose eyes were open wide, staring, and obviously frightened. "Who is this, a friend of yours, Elías?"

"Oh no, he's my brother, Rafael. I'll see he never kicks another dog. He can be a mean one."

"Get your piss-ant of a brother off this property now! I don't ever want to see his face here again."

"Yes sir, sorry sir," Elías said as he grabbed his brother, dragging him away as fast as he could.

His brother stumbled and slinked along silently, turning purple from rage. He knew better than to make a sound, but he burned with fury. *You'll pay for this. A dog is a dog. I'll kick any I want to.* As he slumped over and moved faster, Rafael put his hand out of sight and made the sign of the horns. He knew that if he had been seen, he'd probably be dead. Under his breath he muttered to himself, "I'll get you yet. Next time, I'll bring my men and hit you where it hurts the most. It'll maybe be that looker back there in the cart."

Jorge Luis watched Rafael Yanci with a worrisome look on his face, feeling that this was not over with that mean cuss. He had heard too many rumors about those bandits in the gold mountains coming down and hitting the Ranchos now that everyone was hurting for lack of workers. They certainly were. He now lacked the men to ride the boundaries of the immense property to check the cattle. He wouldn't put it past Rafa to be one of the bandits, if not the leader. *He's a coward and a backstabber. Maybe I should warn what men we have left to be on the lookout.*

Jorge Luis turned back toward the corral and saw the two girls in the carriage. He was a gentleman and knowing they saw him using violence and cursing caused him a great embarrassment. He shouted at them, "Sorry, girls, that you had to see and hear all that. I apologize for the language."

Fiarela was sitting with her mouth open. Prudence yelled, "You were so quick to act. Never mind the language. My uncle would never condone cruelty, either. I'm glad to see you don't."

"What are you two doing out here anyway?" he called.

Fiarela yelled back, "We're taking a break from doing books. We'll see you later!" She nudged Prudence, who gave the horse a light slap of the reins and off they went.

Prudence quickly looked at her friend, "Which way, Fiarela?"

"Pru, it's getting late. Let's go back to the house. I need to ask Mother something before you leave."

Prudence turned the small carriage and headed back to the house while Jorge Luis turned and jumped back over the fence, fuming. To himself he said, "I'm sorry the girls saw that. Young ladies should never be exposed to something like that." Mounting Santón, taking control and putting him through his paces, shifted his thinking and allowed his anger to dissipate. Now, he began to think about how to reorganize the men, since they were shorthanded, and he hadn't been able to find new hands. *That damned gold rush is ruining us rancheros. It has put a huge damper on managing this much property. I may have to give up training Santón as much and do more of the actual work myself.*

On the way back, the girls were silent. Each was lost in her own thoughts regarding what they had seen and heard. Once they arrived at the steps to the veranda, Fiarela dismounted from the cart, turned to Prudence and informed her, "I'm going in, and I'll be right out again. I have to ask Mother something. Wait for me. Don't let Benito take you off." She ran up the steps and disappeared.

Oh dear, what is she up to now? wondered Prudence.

Benito showed up soon. "Ready to leave, Prudence?" he asked.

"No, not yet. I'm waiting for Fiarela. She told me to wait. She said she had to ask her mother something."

"Uh, oh," said Benito, "what is our little *Princesa* up to now?"

15
A Formal Dinner

Prudence stood with Benito by the carriage, waiting for Fiarela. She had run off so suddenly, yelling back to Prudence not to leave. Prudence informed Benito, surprising him as well. Fiarela left both wondering why. What on earth would she tell them when she returned? Benito stood there, remembering her and his past. He had taken care of the carriages, working with his father since quite young, and loved it. He had helped with Fiarela since she was born. She was his little *Princesa*, like another daughter for him. In fact, she was the little princess to all who lived and worked on the hacienda; a pretty and playful child who had grown up into a lovely young woman. *How time passes*, he mused.

As he waited, he looked at the beautiful young lady at his side, thinking, *Thank heavens for Prudence, so close in age to her. The time she has spent teaching her has brought Fiarela out of her depression. Prudence has so much exuberance. She has enlivened this family a lot.* He turned to her to say, "Prudence, what do you think Fiarela is up to?"

"I haven't the slightest idea," answered Prudence, fidgeting with impatience, standing on one foot and then the other. Then she started pacing.

Benito observed Prudence crossing and re-crossing her arms, smoothing her skirt, and walking back and forth to the carriage. He knew she was anxious to get going. *I don't understand why Jorge Luis hasn't seen her beauty and her competence. Or has he? I wonder.*

Just then, bounding down the wide veranda steps with great enthusiasm and a wide smile, came Fiarela, "Pru, Pru, you are invited to dine with us tonight. We're expecting three guests, so it might be boring, but much more fun for me if you are there."

Benito's mouth opened, first in surprise and then slowly into a smile. Astonishment showed on Prudence's face.

"Oh my, are you sure?" Prudence walked over to Fiarela. "I am quite honored to be invited, but would your family want me to come while you are having guests?" inquired Prudence with some anxiety in her voice. She would be eating dinner at the formal dining table with Jorge Luis. He would see her manners. Would they be correct? That thought made her very nervous.

"Oh yes, definitely. We are expecting three businessmen. We don't know them either, so it will help having you there, especially since you speak Spanish so well now. You know, Mother is a little distracted with Papá being sick. When I asked her about you, she didn't think about it. She just answered fine with her."

That information made her feel even more stressed. She looked down at her dress and ran her hand over her hair, saying, "But, I'm a mess. Do I have time to go home, change, and come back in time?"

"We won't eat until nine o'clock. Benito, can you wait for her and get back here in time for her to join us for dinner?" asked Fiarela.

"Of course, Señorita," nodded Benito.

"You can do it! Please, Pru. I want you to be here. Oh, I almost forgot. Bring something to sleep in, and clothes for the next morning because it will be too late to get you home. Bring your riding pants because they like to ride before breakfast."

"You already have three guests. I can't impose like that."

Fiarela was indignant. She said, quite authoritatively, "I am expecting you. Benito, take her home, wait for her, and don't forget her valise."

"Sí, sí, Señorita, *con placer." This may prove interesting. Wish I could be a fly on the wall in the dining room.*

Prudence grabbed the carriage door, pulled it open, and climbed up before Benito could reach her to help. *My, she is independent. I hope Fiarela doesn't tell her mother how bad my manners were, by letting her get up the steps alone.*

On the way home, Prudence had Benito stop as she wanted to sit on the driver's seat next to him. Her mind was a hurricane of thoughts. She finally relaxed and, for a few minutes, engaged Benito in light conversation.

"Benito, I have so much to organize and no time," complained a worried Prudence.

"Not to worry. You will have time and you are a very organized young lady. I will not leave without you."

I do have one elegant suit and the jewelry to match. It is quite conservative, so maybe it will be acceptable. What about my hair? Would Ana help me? She is amazingly clever with hair, and I could pay her a little. By the time they arrived at the cantina, she was mentally organized.

"Benito, you will wait for me? I'll hurry as fast as I can."

"Of course. Don't get yourself all agitated. We do have time."

Benito and Prudence entered the cantina. Prudence hurried to her room, while Benito went to Facundo's bar and helped himself to a drink. He took a chair off a table, put it on the floor and sat down to wait. *Man, this feels good, no raucous laughter, no stomping feet, and no shout outs.* He pulled down another chair and put his feet up on it. *Take your time, Prudence. Take your time.*

Benito removed his feet quickly and stood up when Prudence entered the cantina, who was ready to leave for dinner at the hacienda. He was startled as he watched her enter. He always had seen her as a very pretty young woman, but this evening she looked breathtaking. *Who will be more surprised, Jorge Luis or Aldiana?*

Her suit was a jacket fitted at the waist, flared at the hips, with a full wide skirt. A small, demure collar wrapped her neck and two rows of small ruffles ran down the front in the shape of a V. The color was perfect, a deep taffeta blue. The only jewelry she wore was a pair of beautiful gold, long, and thin teardrop earrings. Her hair was done in the latest style with three or four long curls, which hung from each side of her head. Ivory combs with exquisite rosettes carved along the top held the rest of her hair back, yet allowed it to flow loose. *Thank heavens I had put these in my smaller chest.*

She looked up to see admiration in Benito's eyes. Smiling, she gave a little twirl and a curtsy, saying, "Benito, do I look acceptable?" She stood up straight and straightened her skirt, "I'm very nervous, and I don't want to embarrass the family."

Benito remarked, "You couldn't look lovelier, Prudence. You will capture all the men's eyes tonight."

Prudence blushed, but with pleasure. She had not dressed up since she left Maine, and it felt exhilarating.

"If you are ready to leave, let me carry your valise, and let's go," suggested Benito. *Once Jorge Luis sees her, he'll fall like a ton of bricks. Wish I could see his reaction.* They walked straight outside to where the cart waited. "Prudence, please, let me help you up this time. I don't want anything to happen to your beautiful dress," he said, hoping she'd agree.

The ride to the hacienda was a quiet one. Prudence wasn't up for conversation while trying to hold so much nervousness at bay. The usual long ride this time felt short. Suddenly, it seemed to Prudence, they were there. She had to face her fears. Benito stopped the carriage in front of the hacienda.

While he helped her down from the carriage, he gave her some words of wisdom, telling her, "Be extra polite with Doña Aldiana. She's never seen you look like this, but hold your head high. Prudence, you are a true lady. Let them know who you are!"

Prudence took a deep breath, smiled and said, "Yes, tonight, Benito, I will." She walked up the steps to Donaldo, who was the doorkeeper for the evening, and curtsied.

"My, my, you are quite handsome tonight, young lady," he said as he let her in. Donaldo escorted her to the main parlor and deposited her with a flourish in front of Aldiana, happy to do so. *She is, obviously, a lady of alta categoria. She could fit in this family well*, he mused.

"My dear, how lovely you look," Aldiana spoke as she backed up a step and took in a breath. She was astonished by the Prudence she saw in front of her: a young woman of confidence, dressed in the best of taste, with her hair held with expensive ivory combs in the latest style and her earrings? *Where did she acquire those*? Aldiana easily recognized good taste and high quality. That suggested she came from previous wealth. She felt unnerved and taken off guard, but quickly regained her composure to say, "Permit me to present you to our guests."

Now, all eyes were on Prudence. She heard a glass drop on the rug and glanced over to the antique buffet to see where the sound came from. Jorge Luis was bending down to retrieve the goblet. It startled her for a second, but, fortunately, the glass was not broken. She turned back to Aldiana for the introductions.

Jorge Luis had been pouring wine from the crystal decanter on the buffet when he saw her enter. The glass slipped from his hand when he saw how beautiful she was, which embarrassed him in front of the guests. But their eyes were not looking at him. All of their attention was on Prudence, obviously finding her a fascinating surprise. It was more than apparent where their attention would stay tonight. Jorge Luis was unhappily aware that these were men of class, all good looking, and, he knew, unmarried. Like his mother, he too, was unnerved but for different reasons.

This may be a very long night. He sighed with almost a growl under his breath.

Prudence felt, for the first time, more like her old Maine-self – a woman of worth. She had been accustomed to an active social life and dressing formally and elegantly. She felt comfortable in the formal *sala*, as if she belonged there.

Aldiana introduced her to the three cattle brokers: Marco de La Torre from Mexico City, Antonio Echarte from Los Angeles, and Cecilio Fagoaga from Spain.

After the presentations, a maid announced that *la cena* was ready. Jorge Luis took his mother's arm and escorted her, leading the rest. Each person carried their own wine to the dining room.

The candles on the chandelier illuminated the room with a soft light, which reflected off the goblets and silver on the table and the long mirror over the buffet. The buffet was heavy Mediterranean style, an antique and hand-carved. Its light ochre colored rock was cut from a quarry up north. It was hauled by oxen to the hacienda, and used to cover the opposite wall and to form the fireplace. There was no mantel. The fireplace was flush with the rock wall and had handmade wrought-iron doors designed and made by the blacksmith. A tall, rectangular mirror of hand-worked tin and tile looked down on the guests.

Entering the dining room, Edgardo took Prudence on one arm and his sister on the other, while the cattle brokers followed, duly impressed by the taste and beauty of the room. Breathy oohs and aahs were heard.

Aldiana sat down at the head of the table, which was thick oak with barrel chairs made of hand-tooled leather. She placed her guests around the table. To her right sat Marco de La Torre from Mexico. To her left she placed Jorge Luis. Next to Marco sat Fiarela and on her other side sat the cattle broker from Los Angeles, Antonio Echarte. Across the table, between Jorge Luis and Prudence, sat Cecilio Fagoaga, from Spain, living now in Yerba Buena, San Francisco.

Edgardo sat on Prudence's other side, full of pride and admiration, and fully aware that Prudence had captivated their guests. To himself, he surmised, *Tonight should prove to be a most interesting evening.*

Aldiana noticed that everyone was looking at the empty chair at the end of the table in wonderment. "Unfortunately," she said, "my husband, Emiliano, will not be able to attend the dinner with us tonight, but we will honor him by leaving his seat at the table empty. He will be with us in spirit." She then announced, "Every Friday evening, we enjoy observing an old family tradition passed down for many generations. I hope all of you will not mind joining us? ¿Sí?"

Marco looked surprised, which Aldiana noticed, and he nodded in agreement with Antonio, Cecilio, and Prudence. Cecilio quickly noticed that Prudence was nodding, and realized she was not family. He smiled at her warmly, which was noted at once by Jorge Luis.

Aldiana turned to Fiarela and asked, "Fiarela, dear, as our female representative of the family, would you please light our main candle?" Fiarela rose and carefully lit the large candle while all sat in silence. Her face glowed and her smile was full of pride when she sat back down. Aldiana continued, "Fiarela has just lit the candle that symbolizes the light of life and the abundance that God brings us tonight. Let us praise God."

To everyone's surprise, especially Aldiana's, Marco immediately took part in the family response with the correct words, "Praised be the name of God, now and forever."

"Fiarela, please light the candles in front of the bread and the wine," Aldiana requested.

After Fiarela lit the two candles and sat down again, her face glowing, her mother stood up and put her hands together in prayer. She prayed softly, "May the Source grant peace to us and to all the world." She noticed that Marco took part again, but his eyes and brows were pinched in a puzzled look. Aldiana began to feel a little bit uneasy. *Why is he looking so puzzled?* she wondered.

Aldiana went on to explain, "Next we will give the blessing of the bread. Please wash your hands in the finger bowls and dry them with the little towels." Everyone did as they were asked. The servant came to the table and removed the bowls. Aldiana began to break the bread and to pass it around the table, "You may dip the bread into your salt-cellar and place it on your plate." While everyone took care of their bread, Aldiana spoke the bread prayer, "Praise to you, Eternal God, who brings forth bread from the earth." She glanced at Marco, but he was silent. To her, he looked deep in thought. *I'm not going to let what he might suspect upset me.*

Everyone looked at her with expectation. Aldiana picked up the goblet of wine, held it up and said, "Praise to You, our God of the Universe, creator of the fruit of the vine. In love and favor you have given Your holy abundance as our inheritance." Aldiana sat down and looked pleased. She turned to the servant, who was waiting a few steps behind her and requested that dinner be served.

Soup came first, which was a thick cream of dried salted Bacaloa Cod -- a favorite of the family. Cecilio's eyes lit up with recognition and pleasure. He said, "I haven't had this since I left home. What a treat."

Jorge Luis acknowledged Cecilio with a good-mannered smile, saying, "It's our favorite, too. Where do you come from in Spain?" He was attempting to be a gentleman.

"I come from up in the Basque country in the Pyrenes mountains,- from a little town called Lesaca. Do you know it? This is delicious."

Marco intervened with, "We always ate fish on Fridays as an ancient family custom, but it was usually freshwater. I'm from Mexico City, but I think, originally, the family came from the Toledo area in Spain. We have a prayer service on Friday nights, too, very similar to yours. I felt quite nostalgic."

Jorge Luis broke in with, "Where are you from, Antonio?"

"Me? Oh, I'm a Californio from Los Angeles. My family came from Mexico near Guadalajara, but, as I understand, my ancestors arrived from somewhere in the Basque country, too," he said as he looked at Cecilio.

Aldiana turned to Prudence and asked, "Prudence, you also are a visitor to our country. Tell us where you come from."

"Oh," Prudence felt surprised and perplexed at the word "visitor." *How did she mean that?* "I came from Maine," was all she said.

Cecilio quickly took up the conversation. "Prudence, you must speak English, ¿Verdad? I know English fairly well," and he began to speak it. "I was in Maine once. I sailed from England to Maine and had to stay there a month waiting for a ship to arrive that would take me out here to San Francisco. I learned English first in England and then more in Maine."

Prudence's eyes were wide with surprise, and her face glowed, "Yes, of course, I speak English. It is so good to hear it again, and you speak it very well." In Spanish she added, "You must tell us about your travels." She did not want others to be left out, even though she longed to hear him speak English.

"Yes, we would be quite interested. What about you other two? Do you speak English, too?" asked Aldiana.

Marco answered first, turning his head toward Aldiana, smiling, "No, Señora, but I also speak Ladino. You see my heritage is Jewish, and the language Ladino was a mixture of Hebrew and Spanish spoken by the Jews in Spain, especially the Sephardic Jews." Everyone looked up with curiosity, but Aldiana sank into her chair and became quiet and expressionless.

Antonio interrupted with, "Besides Spanish, I speak Italian, Portuguese, and a passable Basque. I'm interested in learning English. Are you available, Señorita Prudence, as a teacher while we are here?"

Jorge Luis looked daggers at him and almost choked on a piece of leg of lamb.

Prudence missed seeing Jorge Luis's dirty look at Cecilio, but worried about his choking. She kept peeking around Cecilio at Jorge Luis to make sure he was all right. She answered Antonio as soon as she heard Jorge Luis recover, "I would be glad to help you and anyone who is interested in learning English while you're here. Maybe Jorge Luis and Edgardo would like to join us?"

Aldiana, sitting quite regally at the head of the table, broke in with, "Why not boys. I hear the servants talk of many English-speaking people filtering into our country. You boys may need the English."

Prudence was surprised at Aldiana's approval, but, looking across the table, noticed Fiarela's crestfallen face and said carefully, "We'll decide on the time later, but I come out here regularly." She directed her attention to Fiarela and asked, "Fiarela, would you like to join in also?"

"Would I. I would love to!" She went from crestfallen to beaming with tiny bounces in her chair, charming Marco.

Aldiana looked shocked but didn't dare say anything in front of guests. She did not feel it proper for her daughter to be with a group of single, handsome young men, even though Prudence would be teaching them. Prudence being alone with them didn't register with her. After all, Prudence was a foreigner. What else could she expect?

"To change the subject," said Jorge Luis, "Cecilio, before I forget, I understand you rode a Paso mare here. Is that correct?"

Cecilio nodded, "Yes, she has papers, which show her linage. I'll show them to you," and added, "She is a pure Peruvian. She's a great little horse with a lot of stamina."

"Juan, our stable manager, mentioned she appears to be entering heat. Would you consider breeding her to my stallion, Santón?"

Everyone turned to hear the conversation, including Aldiana, as horse breeding was of the upmost importance. A good horse was worth its weight in gold.

Cecilio stared intently at Jorge Luis and answered with a strong, "¡Sí, claro! I had heard you had a good horse and was hoping you would agree to it. How would we arrange it?"

"Well, it depends," Jorge Luis responded, "on how much time you've got. We can turn them loose together in the small field and see if they get along, or we can place them side by side but separated and see how they react. Then, Juan, you and I could handle them. What do you say?"

"May I interrupt?" asked Edgardo. "I'm feeling the corrals may work the best. I believe she is further along in estrus than you think, and I see a beautiful little filly as a result."

Everyone looked at Edgardo with surprise and interest.

"Oh, that would be so exciting," said Fiarela. "I wish I could have my own horse. How about you, Prudence? You are an excellent rider."

"I would give anything to have my horse back. I really loved Wilma. She was special. Someday, I hope to have another," sighed Prudence.

"Sorry, Prudence. The loss of a good horse is hard. May your dream come true, soon. Jorge Luis, if it is okay with you, we'll try them in the corrals then. Feels good to me. I'll stay, if it is acceptable, until it occurs," said Cecilio.

"You are most welcome, Cecilio," Aldiana said, "and, so is everyone else. *Nuestra casa es su casa.*"

"We also need to talk about the cattle market, but let's do that tomorrow. Now, we need to decide on the morning ride," said Jorge Luis.

"You young people need to ride early and work up a good appetite for breakfast," suggested Aldiana, folding and refolding her used napkin and placing it on her lap, expecting the dessert to appear.

"Nothing like a brisk morning ride, and, of course, the ladies will be joining us, won't you?" asked Jorge Luis looking at Prudence. "In fact, Prudence, you can ride Blanca. I think you would enjoy her. Fiarela, should we bring Old Flojo from town for you?"

"Jorge Luis! Don't you embarrass me in front of our guests. You know I can do pretty well on horseback, although I can't ride like Prudence."

Prudence beamed with anticipation. She could hardly wait until morning.

Marco joined in with, "Fiarela, it won't bother me if you want to go a little slower. I would enjoy accompanying you."

Unaccustomed to receiving compliments from a young man, Fiarela blushed, looked the other way, and nodded.

The table was quickly cleared away for a lovely flan along with a final glass of the best house wine for dessert. Aldiana announced, when all appeared satisfied, they would retire to the parlor for entertainment and some piano music, followed by everyone singing and dancing, a common and pleasurable event for the Californios. The three guests looked at each other with anticipation.

Edgardo quickly said, "Mamá, we don't have enough ladies. Will you be dancing? Could you ask Margarita and little Eva to join us? They both enjoy dancing and are quite good, too."

Once in the parlor, Aldiana called for the girls who demurely and quietly entered. Their eyes widened and big smiles crossed their pretty faces when they saw the handsome, young men. They remained standing in the back of the room, properly, as the servants they were.

After everyone had settled, sitting on the settees and upholstered chairs with brocades, Aldiana asked Jorge Luis to start the festivities by playing the piano, which was a pleasant surprise to Prudence. He played a classical piece first called "Sabat Mater" by Juan Crisóstomo Arriaga and then a second piece titled "Los Esclavos Felices." He then switched to the guitar, playing a popular song, "Adiós, Adiós Amores", which was a Californio sing-along. Antonio joined in with the family to sing. Since he was a Californio, he knew the words. The feelings of anxiety brought into the room, caused by unknown expectations, dissipated quickly with everyone relaxing, singing, and, later, dancing.

Prudence got up her courage and offered to play the piano. Surprise showed on Aldiana's face. Here was something else she didn't know about Prudence. She was becoming more than an enigma, especially since she observed Jorge Luis's eyes constantly on her. Cecilio's attention to Prudence, she didn't mind, but she minded a lot about her eldest son's. She had not given much thought to Prudence as a woman. She was only a foreigner, but now, seeing her in a different light, was she to become a threat? Aldiana narrowed her eyes and pressed her lips tight in thought. She could not see beyond the bigotry and prejudice she had been taught.

Prudence played a small classical piece, *Minuet in G*, much to everyone's admiration. Then she explained that she would play a brand-new song just written before she left for Yerba Buena earlier that year.

"I know you don't know our national song written by a man named Stephen Foster, but the same man wrote this little, fun song. It is so easy to learn that we were singing it all the way across the country from back East. We sang it a lot at night when we sat around the bonfire after the caravan stopped to camp," Prudence explained.

The young people all clapped their approval, so Prudence played and sang "Oh, Susanna." She then played and sang it again while having them repeat the words. Soon, they all were gayly singing the little ditty. (Later, the song became the theme song for the Gold Rush 49er's and entered the favorite songs of the Californios as "Ay, Susana.")

After much dancing and singing, Aldiana called a halt to the evening. She thanked the two girls for joining the dancing, at which they nodded, and gave the boys happy glances as they retired for the evening. Aldiana then assigned bedrooms to all the guests. Fiarela begged to have Prudence stay in her room, so an extra bed was brought in. It was a standard rawhide one, tightly stretched, which Prudence had never experienced before. But, being so happily tired, both girls slept soundly, dead to the world.

16

A Morning Ride

Big smiles covered young faces when morning broke. No one wasted time dressing. Both girls threw on their fancy, new riding pants as fast as they could. Prudence had helped Fiarela sew an outfit for herself, although Aldiana did not approve. She believed women of child-bearing age should not ride like a man, but she did realize that the sidesaddle was too dangerous for the kind of riding these young people would be doing. The girls were dressed in a whirl and ran enthusiastically off to the barns. The young men all looked dapper and the two young ladies, lovely, when they arrived at the stables. All were anxious to be off.

Seven horses waited, snorting in the early air, stomping their feet, and switching their tails, anxious to get moving.

Prudence walked immediately to Blanca, saying, "You, white beauty, you're mine, aren't you?" She patted her neck and rubbed her nose. Turning around, she spotted Jorge Luis double checking each horse.

Marco helped Fiarela mount, much to her pleasure. She looked over at Jorge Luis and asked, "*Hermano*, where are we going?"

"Well, I think it is a perfect morning to take a ride out to the river. Everyone ready?"

All heads nodded but, suddenly, around the end of the building, came a horse and rider at full speed. He pulled his horse up short in front of Jorge Luis, spraying dirt and dust.

"*Patrón, Patrón*, may I speak to you quickly – ¿*A solas*?"

"*Sí, Gregorio,*" nodded Jorge Luis in quick agreement.

Jorge Luis dismounted rapidly and went to Gregorio's side, who leaned over his horse, and reported quietly, "Boss, we have rustlers! We found fifteen head of cattle butchered, hind quarters gone, over in the third field up the river. This rustling is getting worse, and we don't know who's doing it. Tracks show four horses, two shod and two not. The horseshoe tracks of one horse show a distinctive mark I've never seen. Sorry, Boss, to interrupt your morning ride. What do you want me to do?"

Jorge Luis turned his back to the group, hiding his furious anger,

"Ask Juan to study those tracks and take two men with you to clean up the mess. If there is any meat to save, save it. Look for any other clues. Thanks, Gregorio. We're headed for the river. I'll talk with you later."

Gregorio turned his horse, leaving with a fast bound and his arm raised in a farewell wave.

All eyes had been on Gregorio and Jorge Luis, but no one uttered a sound out of respect for their privacy and the obvious gravity of the situation.

"Okay, *amigos*, ready to go?"

Six voices answered "yes" in a relieved unison.

Jorge Luis, then, did say something not so happy to them, "Fellows, do you have weapons?"

Startled eyes opened wide, but the men all responded, "Yes, do we need them?"

"No, no," he paused and then added, "I hope not."

"Come on. Follow me. Prudence, you may ride up here if you wish," he said, giving Cecilio a quick glance.

The muscles in Cecilio's face hardened. His eyes narrowed and darkened, but he was gentlemanly enough to not give a retort.

Although dampened by the news, which Jorge Luis explained to the group, the ride was enjoyed. He and Edgardo pointed out many interesting landmarks along the way, with a little history thrown in. Much conversation took place as their horses slowly plodded along. They all admired the many different views across the vast property. Except for Antonio, el Californio from Los Angeles, neither Marco nor Cecilio had ever seen one family own such a large piece of land. Fiarela felt a joy she had never known and kept glancing at Marco often. Marco enjoyed observing how her pretty face glowed with happiness.

Cecilio observed, "I am amazed that you have successful orchards here and such a variety." He went on to add, "We'll have to work this out, but I can handle at least a hundred head of your Corriente cattle. I've been observing them, and they appear very fit."

Edgardo interjected, "They are. We have great grazing grounds here. How about you, Marco and Antonio, are you also interested in the Corrientes?"

"I certainly am," answered Marco with Antonio, adding, "I'm also interested in some of your sheep."

Meantime, the two girls were looking at each other with beaming smiles.

"It is beautiful out riding so early in the morning, isn't it?" said Prudence.

Fiarela's eyes lit up. She leaned over toward Prudence, "I am thrilled to my bones. Everything is so fresh and clear out this early. I have a perfect horse, and I'm not afraid at all."

With them appreciating the ride so much, and with so much to see, the river came up quicker than they expected. The small party was just entering the path, which led to the river campground, when Jorge Luis raised his arm suddenly, stopping everyone unexpectedly.

"Shhh! Listen! I thought I heard voices."

Silence reined while all listened intently. Jorge Luis was right. Men were at the river.

He dismounted quietly, walked to Prudence's side, and in a low voice told her, "Prudence, this may be dangerous. Please, take Fiarela home as fast as you can. Do you have your Colt Forty-Four?" She nodded. "Keep it at hand and be very quiet. Walk your horses back out of these oaks and willows, then go as fast and safely as you can. Don't talk."

Prudence nodded yes, shifted her gun, and leaned over to Jorge Luis with a soft, "Please, be careful." She turned her horse and motioned to Fiarela, who was wide-eyed and startled, to follow. They left slowly and quietly.

Meanwhile, the men dismounted and dropped their reins to the ground, which told the horses not to move. They were trained well, even Cecilio's mare obeyed. Jorge Luis informed Antonio and Cecilio to come with him. Edgardo was to walk with Marco in order to back up Jorge Luis, Cecilio, and Antonio.

Silently, the men approached the open campground and found a horrifying scene: Two men had a rope over a large tree limb, hauling a tightly bound Indian up over his horse, obviously a hanging.

To his men, Jorge Luis said, "Antonio, Cecilio, and I will rush them. You two cover us. We're going to stop this. Let's get their horses away so they can't escape."

"Okay," whispered Marco, "Let me move off the horses while you three take the men."

"I'll take the Indian," offered Edgardo. "I speak the Indian dialect. I'll find out what's going on."

That piece of information shocked Jorge Luis. He hadn't known that, and he didn't have time to react to it. Jorge Luis gave the signal. With guns drawn, the men bent down low so they wouldn't be seen over the bushes. The men moved fast and silently. The rustlers were so involved with their heinous crime that they did not hear the men approach and didn't have time to draw their own guns. When Jorge Luis yelled "¡Alto!," the two outlaws froze with their hands up. Edgardo ran and grabbed the horse to stop it from bolting and freed the Indian. Jorge Luis, and Cecilio kept their guns on the two men while Antonio went to help Marco round up the horses that he had let loose, and bring them back.

Edgardo became infuriated and shouted, "Jorge Luis! This Indian was being hanged to make our people believe the Indians are doing the rustling that's been happening. He says several other men are still at it."

Upon hearing that, the two rustlers began yelling, "Please, please, don't hang us. Don't hang us! We'll tell you where the others are."

"Okay, you'll take us to the rest of your men, and then we'll see what happens. Marco can you bring over the horses?" requested Jorge Luis.

They tied the men's hands behind their backs and made them lead the way in front of the horses. Not much time passed before they came into a clearing where the slaughter had taken place, though it had already been cleaned up by Gregorio and the other workers.

"There's no one here," Edgardo quietly said, glancing around in all directions. The open area was large, surrounded by groves of oaks, manzanita and scrub.

Jorge Luis approached the two rustlers, shouting into their faces, "All right you *miserables,* where are they? It's to your benefit to tell me the truth. Who is your leader and where do you come from?"

Sullenly, one of the men started to talk, "Jorge Luis - yes, I know who you are. You're too late. They've taken off for the mountains. We live in a huge cave up past El Campo de Los Angeles."

"What's the name of your leader?" demanded Edgardo.

"Oh, he's a mean one, that one – Rafael Yanci. I think his brother works for you."

"Ahhh, sí, Elías Yanci's brother. Rafa owes me big time. He'll be shot on sight or hanged!" hissed Jorge Luis.

"Amigo, what do we do with these two?" asked Antonio, "Shall we hang them up?"

"No, no," said Edgardo. "Leave them here to fend for themselves. We'll take the Indian back, so he can return to the Ranchería."

"Fine, let's go," ordered Jorge Luis.

Back at the river campground, they rounded up the bandits' horses and headed for the hacienda – exhausted and silent.

The Indian was given a horse. He went to Edgardo. Speaking in his

Indian dialect, he told Edgardo that he owed him his life. He offered to take care of the bad white man anytime Edgardo wished.

Edgardo thanked him and said, "You go now in peace, my friend."

He rode off quietly.

The three cattle brokers had heard of rustling but had never seen the results or taken part in anything like a hanging. They hoped they wouldn't be involved again. Antonio did say that in the Los Angeles area, where he came from, they did occasionally have some trouble, too. Horses and cattle were so prevalent and available that anyone, who needed one or the other, could just take what they needed with no questions asked. That was never considered a crime.

Cecilio and Marco both shared that they had been warned about going to the frontier. They were told that it was dangerous. Now, they had seen it for themselves. The men arrived at the hacienda to find an entire household anxious and frightened, yet deeply grateful to see them all safe.

After cleaning up, instead of a relaxing and fun breakfast, the men ate a hearty lunch while looking forward to a well-needed siesta. They informed everyone to watch out for the Indians being blamed for rustling and other crimes, when it was the bandits and the gold miners who were committing them. Everyone was aghast and found it hard to believe what was occurring. Their safe, pastoral way of life was unraveling.

After the men left to rest upstairs, Prudence approached Fiarela and informed her, "I wish I could remain, but it isn't right for me to stay longer when you have a house full of guests. I don't want to overstay my welcome. I'll thank your mother, and Benito said he would take me back to the cantina. Fiarela, I've had the most wonderful time, thank you so much."

"Oh, me too," responded Fiarela, "I really feel that we're sisters now!" Fiarela hugged Prudence and kissed her on the cheek.

"Oh, Fiarela, what a sweet thing to say," sighed Prudence and returned the hug.

Prudence left with a heavy heart, already missing the contact. She even felt closer to Jorge Luis and had enjoyed Cecilio's attention. *I need to start those English lessons right away*, she surmised.

"Come on, young lady," said Benito as he helped her up into the cart with her small valise. "The young men are all safe and sound. You'll be seeing them again soon, I assure you."

Relieved at his words, Prudence flashed him a full, wide smile, nodded, sat down, and waved goodbye to Fiarela with a lighter heart.

17
A Night to Remember

Candlelight reflected softly throughout the dining hall. The mirrors and highly polished silver cast shards of light back and forth wherever the guests gazed when they entered to dine.

"Oh, Mother," said Fiarela with a sigh, "The candles we added have created such an enchanting environment."

Aldiana smiled at her daughter as she headed for her place of honor at the head of the table. The others followed and sat where they had the night before. Emiliano's place was left empty in his honor, but his presence was felt as almost palpable. One other seat was empty, and all eyes were on it when Cecilio, the handsome young Basque, spoke up, "Where is Prudence? I assumed she would be here."

Irritation cut across Aldiana's face. Her tense eyes blinked rapidly for a moment. Her voice lowered. She answered rapidly and harshly, pronouncing all the words with emphasis, as all heads turned her way, "Cecilio, I am sure all of you are aware that Prudence is a foreigner. She is not Catholic, and she does not live here. Prudence is only Fiarela's teacher and lives in town."

Cecilio looked as if he had been slapped, and then appeared puzzled.

Antonio and Marco sat up straight, staring, and their intake of breath was audible. They could not believe what they had heard.

The three Sandoval siblings reacted with shock, blood draining from their faces, which returned with a reddish humiliation.

Fiarela, without realizing it, covered her mouth as she cried out, "Oh, Mother!" She averted her eyes for a moment, but then began to speak in a low voice, trying to be calm, "I don't understand how you can describe her like that, Mother. She has never been a common servant." And almost not daring to say it, she held her breath to get some courage, and said, "And in front of our guests. She has been very kind and a friend to me."

Jorge Luis added, with tight-lipped anger, but as respectfully as he could, "Mother, what you think and feel is very important to me. I have always respected that and always will. I have never heard you demean or put down anyone, let alone Prudence, who has helped us so much. It shocks me to hear that! You know she is a woman of the highest moral integrity."

"Dearest Mother, I beg you, please -- you know we love you and don't want to disappoint you or appear rude by what we are trying to say. I feel badly that I am addressing this here at the table but, Mother, that is not like you," said Edgardo.

The three cattle brokers, finding themselves in the middle of an emotional family squabble, felt very uncomfortable. They were embarrassed and sad. They listened to what was going on with eyes averted and were silent. Cecilio felt especially affected and felt bad for Prudence. *I would have grabbed her in a minute. Maybe now I might have a better chance with her, but I'm not sure, seeing how the family reacted. She is well-defended.*

"Please, Mamá," said Edgardo, "We love you, and Prudence highly admires you. I've never seen her do anything or heard her say anything that would be embarrassing to our family. She is highly intelligent, well-educated, and has brought a breath of fresh air to all of us." Edgardo's face was full of sadness, with his words spoken softly, yet in resolute, clipped emotional tones.

Aldiana, knowing her words had just tumbled out and she hadn't given any thought to them, realized she had stepped over an important line with her dearest children. Then it hit her they were grown children, and that line was one that should have held respect for them, their ideas, and opinions. But, she reacted in her old, habitual way. *I am their mother, and I know best what's good for them.* She almost stomped her foot, but that insight, and then that old feeling, caused her to see them from the depths of her being. She did not even see the guests, who had become a blur. She began trembling from feeling attacked by her children and from her feelings of inadequacy about a new family relationship developing. She appeared to be on the verge of tears. Turning, and without a further word, she left the dining room.

Looking around and seeing the consternation on everyone's face, feeling terribly humiliated himself from talking to his mother that way, Jorge Luis needed to clear the air and change the atmosphere. He suddenly stood up, suddenly, knocking over his empty wine glass. His eyes were dark and cold – his face frozen in anger. He took a deep breath, threw his linen napkin down on the table, tersely saying, "I have lost my appetite. Come on, let's go to town to the cantina. There will be singing and dancing. Fiarela, if you come along, I think, maybe, Prudence could be talked into joining us. How about it?" He looked around the table anxiously.

Heads nodded. Everyone stood up together, sorry about the incident, and wanted and hoped to change their mixture of embarrassment and sad-dened feelings. They were grateful to Jorge Luis for taking action. They felt that tomorrow the family would be all right and back to normal.

Benito brought the large carriage, and Fiarela was placed between her two brothers in order to be properly protected from the young, single men. Laughter and hearty conversation filled the vehicle, while Benito held the reins of the two horses that trotted toward a night of hopeful fun and joy.

Music and laughter filled the young people's ears when they arrived at the cantina's door. Their faces lit up as they entered the large social area where music was being played and dancing was going on. A hush covered the room as people realized this was the owner and his party, but it didn't take long to return to a normal level of vocal chaos.

"I am so excited," whispered Fiarela to Marco. "I have never been allowed to be here before." Marco moved closer and took her arm protec-tively.

"Jorge Luis, go get Prudence and insist that she join us," ordered Edgardo.

"I'm on my way. Get us a table near the musicians. We're going to dance all night!" He took off to the kitchen, crossed it, and went up the pri-vate stairs to knock softly on Prudence's door.

Prudence, while listening to the music coming from the cantina's main social room below, was sitting on her bed sketching a full, blooming Russian Thistle in a notebook. She had picked it on one of her many walks around the little pueblo. Startled by an unexpected knock, her hand with the pencil jerked across the page leaving a long graphite gash. Prudence threw down her drawing and quickly pulled her gun from under her pillow, holding it ready.

"Who is it?"

"Jorge Luis. May I come in?" The voice sounded a bit muffled behind the door.

Oh my god, now what? Why is he here now? Is it really him? "Yes, but open the door slowly."

Barely opening the door, he peeked in, saw the gun and said, "Prudence, put your gun away. I won't come in, I promise. We are all here, even Fiarela. We want you to join us, please. I'll wait in the kitchen."

"Oh, I would love to. I was sitting here, hearing all the music downstairs, and feeling sorry

for myself. I'm so glad you thought about me."

"Prudence, we all thought about you. How could we not? I need a dance partner, so hurry."

"Give me a minute, and I'll be right there." *He needs a dance partner?* In moments, Prudence, full of joyful expectation, had jumped out of bed. She washed her face and grabbed her celestial blue, satin gown. She brushed her hair, and with a quick glance, checked herself in the mirror. She dashed down the stairs with her golden hair flowing behind her.

One look blew Jorge Luis away, "Prudence, you look especially lovely. How did the robbers miss taking that gown?"

"This is new. A peddler came to the little store, and he just happened to have material. I couldn't resist this piece, and I do sew you know," said Prudence.

He stepped back, glancing up and down at her, feeling his desire for her in that gown, and said, "You are a woman of many talents. I admire that." He knew, for certain, that when he took her downstairs out into the open public area, that competition would be great. Pride filled his chest to be the one accompanying her. Taking Prudence by the arm, he guided her down the hallway, through the office and out into the cantina's public room. Jorge Luis was right to be worried. The crowd of masculine eyes locked on Prudence.

I knew it! I hope there are no ugly problems here tonight. I'll hang on to Prudence. I felt it was safe bringing the girls this evening, but those men have hunger in their eyes. I'll ask Facundo to put the waiters on watch and let me know if anything starts.

He led Prudence to the table where everyone greeted and welcomed her. Instead of sitting, he led her out to dance. Marco and Fiarela had already gone out to dance, joining other couples on the floor. Everywhere around the room feet were stomping to the music.

Antonio grabbed one of the working girls of the cantina and whirled her around.

Cecilio bided his time, while wondering if Prudence would dance with him. He also watched the other men at the tables, playing poker or just conversing, and suddenly realized they were speaking English. He sat up straight and thought, *I think I'll move among them. Practice my English.*

Edgardo sat pensively, observing the behaviors

of the people. He felt a deep aloneness, an unquenchable longing. His tequila was refilled a little too often. Finally, he began to sing with the crowd when the favorite Californio songs played. His voice rang out with a haunting clarity.

Marina appeared at a side door and stopped to listen. The electric green of Marina's elegant, tightly fitted dress, brought her porcelain skin and abundant blue-black hair into prominence. Men poked each other, directing their glances toward her. They watched as she went directly to Edgardo, lifted her arms, covered in gold bangles, around his neck and joined him with a strong alto voice. The applause was loud and accompanied by whistles and catcalls.

Prudence turned to Jorge Luis and got up her courage to ask, "Marina was putting the eye on you while singing. She's a beautiful woman. Do you still see her?"

Averting his eyes in embarrassment, Jorge Luis answered, "No, no, I have no interest there." Without a word, he pulled Prudence into him tighter and danced across the open space, "You look gorgeous tonight. You dance gracefully. You make me want to dance all night."

"I hope to dance all night, too," she told him with a smile that covered the stab of realization that he had not said - with you.

The singing stopped, and the applause faded away. Marina left Edgardo saying, "Wait, don't move." She threaded her way through the tables to the pianist and the guitarist. She leaned over and whispered in the ear of the piano player, made her way back to Edgardo, and announced to the crowd, "This next song is dedicated to *mi patrón*, Jorge Luis." Leaving off his last name and emphasizing the "mi" was a gross insult and insinuated more than Jorge Luis wanted. He felt his gun in its holster. It felt like it needed a new notch.

Marina and Edgardo sang a Californio favorite, "El ángel del amor."

That song title, "The Angel of Love," hit Jorge Luis like a bullet through his brain. His anger swelled at Marina. He felt like a fool. Any lingering feelings he might have had were cut off, dead.

As they started to sing, Marina stared directly into Edgardo's eyes but could see no emotion from him. Her eyes became slits, she raised her nose in arrogance, and her lips turned down in disdain.

Edgardo put all his emotion into the music and outdid himself. The crowd went wild, and he soaked up the applause. His eyes widened when he felt Marina grip his arm tightly and lead him away toward the girls' private door. *What the hell?* he thought. And then, with sudden resignation, said to himself, *Oh, what the hell*. He grabbed a bottle from a close table and sank his feelings into a submissive 'why not.'

Their action was not lost on Prudence, who was quite disturbed, and she hoped it would not hurt Jorge Luis.

Jorge Luis, looking surprised and disappointed, bordering on anger, hoped Edgardo would not be hurt. And, well – it was none of his business, not anymore. He could do nothing about it anyway.

Cecilio, wandering around while the singing was going on, found a table, after the duet had finished, where he felt he could try out his English. Most of the men seemed friendly, "Pardon me, may I join you? I would like to practice my English. Are you Americans or Englishmen?"

"Good lord. We are not British. We are Americans! The Brits are up north, and they are much too close. They had better stay up there. Here, sit down. And you? Are you Spanish? You don't look Mexican," said one of the men, who was much better dressed. He had the appearance of a gentleman.

"No, no, I am not a Spaniard. I'm not a Mexican, either. I am a Basque! I'm a cattle broker from Europe."

"Ah, a Basco, huh? And a cattle broker. Well, you should do well around these parts. There's not much but cattle. That's why you're with Sandoval and party then?"

"Yes," answered Cecilio, surprised at the man knowing the Sandovals. "On the long sea journey here, in one of the Chilean ports, I heard rumors of gold being found. Where? And is that where you gentlemen are going?" asked Cecilio.

"Yeah, there is some digging going on already. In fact, from what I hear, quite a lot," responded one of the other men.

"Well, good luck," said Cecilio as he nodded to the men, left, and headed for another table.

At the next table, the men appeared to be deep in intense conversation, as they were leaning close toward each other. *This might be interesting.* "Hi, there. I heard you speaking English. May I join you?" he asked.

"Not now. We're discussing business. Perhaps later," came the quick response.

With a glance around the room, he took note of another table where he was invited to sit. Here, at least two of the men seemed more knowledgeable, while two other men had women on their laps. Cecilio felt somewhat envious but ignored it.

"Say, I hear all of you are headed up to the mountains for gold. Is there really that much gold up there?"

One of the fellows opened the conversation with, "That's what we've heard. I'm going to try my luck. How about you?"

"Not going for the gold. Not yet, anyway. Although it does sound worth thinking about," said Cecilio. "I'm out here for cattle and maybe a few sheep. When I was in Maine, I didn't hear about the gold, but I did hear that the United States government was interested in acquiring California. Do you think it's true?"

"Yeah, it's true. They've already annexed it," spoke up one of the men, who pushed aside the woman he held on his lap. She pressed her lips in a pout and gave him a dirty look but walked away while he leaned into the table and began talking, "Before I caught the gold fever, I was working back east for the government in the Bureau of Indian Affairs, and, yes, way back in '35 President Jackson made an overt attempt at acquisition of California but that didn't work. The Mexican government wouldn't go for it. Then, in 1839, another attempt was made with a proposal to Mexico to write off their huge debt with the transfer of California. Forty million bucks was involved, but that didn't work either."

"I had no idea that was going on. I've heard no mention of it here with the locals," said Cecilio.

"No, no, they wouldn't know. There is no communication out here with such a small, spread-out population. But, also in 1839, a book was written --which I read-- called *History of California*. It was quite disturbing. The book was devoted to bringing about British colonization, of all things. We could not allow that," bristled the speaker.

"I never heard that," said one of the men at the table. The others nodded with surprise on their faces.

"Only people in the United States government knew what was going on," pointed out the man who, now, had another woman on his lap. "And, by the way," he continued, "The government was getting paranoid with warnings about the British designs on California. They are clear down to the Oregon border and the Hudson Bay company has been active all over that territory, especially up on the Columbia river. That's why the government, a couple years ago in 1846 ended up annexing California from Mexico, toward the end of the war with them - somehow they managed to."

Another man, in well-worn clothing, piped up with, "Well, Russia was a big problem, too, you know. They have a big fur trading business on the north coast up there at fort Ross. Those whalers and fur traders are one tough bunch. I wouldn't want to mess with them." The man sat up straight and looked at each person at the table intently. "Another thing - one of our big problems here that no one talks about, is that there are individuals who are buying up the mission lands, which are considered the best in the province. I don't know how that will work out, especially with Mexican secularization of the missions earlier and annexation now. They won't last long, is my guess."

"¡Carrumba! California is in for some big changes. I wonder how it will affect the Sandoval family and the other Californios?" said Cecilio.

The men at the table simply shrugged their shoulders and returned to their other interests. Cecilio excused himself and wove his way back to his table. To his amazement, Prudence was sitting alone. He asked her to dance and, with her in his arms, immediately forgot the unsettling news and impending changes. It never occurred to him to share them.

At 3:00 a.m. Benito came in and announced the carriage was ready for the trip home. Who was going?

Edgardo had long ago returned to the group. They all took their farewells of Prudence, who found it hard to say good night. She thanked everyone for the magical night and hoped they would have a careful trip home. Jorge Luis walked her to the kitchen to avoid any unforeseen problems with the last of the crowd. At the bottom of the stairs to her room, he took both her hands, kissing them gently as he looked deeply into her eyes and said, "Thank you for joining us and for a delightful evening. Sleep well, my lovely Prudence," he turned and was gone.

Prudence was left breathless. *What did he say? Did he really say that? Did I hear that correctly?*

She struggled up the stairs in her disbelief. Her bed was easy to slip into and sleep covered her with a blanket of dreams.

Meanwhile, the ride home was quiet, with Fiarela falling asleep on Jorge Luis's lap. Edgardo did not respond to anyone, as he held his feelings close. The three cattlemen were asleep instantly. Only Benito and the horses were alert.

The next morning arrived much too soon, with all the young people moving in slow motion. The young men spent the day with Jorge Luis and Edgardo checking the cattle and sheep, along with many discussions of prices and how to transport the animals. After returning to the hacienda exhausted, they cleaned up, and took a long siesta.

Aldiana did not socialize but took her wounded heart and lay down by the side of her beloved husband. He was failing fast now, and she knew it. His time was imminent.

Emiliano opened his eyes when he felt her presence. She saw his warm welcome in faded, unclear eyes. He seemed further away than ever before, but he surprised her. His voice was clear and stronger.

"Cara mía, the time is very near now. I've already seen my beloved grandfather and my mother waiting for me. I must speak to each of my children tonight before it is too late," he insisted.

Aldiana felt her heart wrench, and blood rushed up, flushing her face, "Of course, Amor. I will inform them later. They are all resting now." Feeling the huge loss that was coming, she said to herself, *I'm losing the love of my life and have lost my babies, all at once. It's too much.* Her brain roiled with anger, guilt, loss, and pain.

Later, Aldiana rose from the bed, having dozed for a while from exhaustion. The wind was blowing hard and banging against the windows and the large cacti that was planted around the house for protection. They were loudly scratching on the walls. Nevertheless, she could hear murmuring voices and laughter, and knew everyone was up. She changed her clothes, walked down the hallway, and tried to compose her mixed and fearful feelings. *How am I going to tell them about their father? How will they treat me now? I don't know if I can do it.* She stood at the top of the winding stairway, gulping air from her panic. *I must face my children - my grown children.* She clutched her chest, blinking her eyes to prevent tearing up. *My babies - they are such good, good people.* She took another deep breath. *But, why, oh why, does Jorge Luis have to be so attentive to Prudence? He should know better.*

She stifled her feelings, walked down the stairs with her head held high, and entered the patio. Immediately there was silence as everyone turned to look at her, unruffled as if nothing had happened last night. Aldiana announced that Emiliano had taken a turn for the worse and requested to talk to his family, one at a time that night.

She looked at the three brokers and said, in a trembling voice, "While you, our guests, are welcome to stay, would you mind, please, to dine in town and not come home until later?" The announcement came as an unexpected surprise. The three Sandoval siblings looked at each other in true distress, with Fiarela on the verge of tears.

The three young businessmen had no problem with the request. They felt quite badly for the family, but prepared for the trip to town, and looked forward to another night of gaiety at the cantina.

Fiarela went limp. Her two brothers held her up, their faces tight to not show their own emotions.

"Come on now, buck up. It will be all right," said Jorge Luis.

Edgardo whispered, "Fi, pull up your big-girl bloomers and be strong. Mother will need you. Don't worry. His time is not tonight. It is close – tomorrow night. You must remember he will be free of pain and suffering."

"Shut up! Don't talk like that," admonished Jorge Luis, almost in a whisper.

Edgardo lowered his voice and answered, "Sorry. I am only trying to help. It was shown to me very clearly, and I saw three angels standing behind him, waiting for him. Knowing what's going to happen will give Fi-arela the strength to face it when it does come." He stared as if he had gone inward. His eyes showing deep compassion. Jorge Luis knew he was telling the truth. They would have the strength together to face the inevitable.

The cattle brokers tried to have another night of gaiety at the cantina, but their joy and fun was dampened by the news of Emiliano's death hovering so near. Their friends would be highly affected and, maybe, need help. They sat saddened by the memory of their own father's death. They looked at each other, sighed, and all three agreed to head back to the hacienda early and turn in quietly.

The night watched the hacienda descend into a dark sadness, tinged with fear.

18
Final Words

innner was a somber affair. The family ate in silence, faces and eyes drooping in dejection. Fiarela was on the verge of tears, especially when Aldiana reminded them that their father wanted to see each one of them alone. "Donaldo will come to take you up when your father is ready for you. Children, when you go in, remember he is very weak. Try not to exhaust him further," their mother insisted. She was the palest her children had ever seen. However, she seemed, to them, resigned to her fate. This was far from what they felt.

"Mother," asked Fiarela, trembling, "what does he want to see us about?"

"I don't know, dear, but I feel he wants to take his leave of you. I think he feels his time is rapidly approaching now." Aldiana's eyes blurred with tears. She turned away and looked at the burning logs in the fireplace. *My life is burning out just like those logs. Soon they will be embers, no different than Emiliano's life force now. How can it have happened so fast?* The siblings looked at their mother, lost within herself, and then at each other, lowered their heads and were silent.

Shortly, Donaldo appeared and announced that their father was ready to receive Jorge Luis, and would he please follow him upstairs.

Jorge Luis stepped up behind him with a heavy heart. Fear took over his mind. *How can I fill my father's footsteps? Everything is changing too fast. I can't count on Edgardo. I'm afraid he will just up and leave. I will have all this alone. What will I do with it? I have Mother and Fiarela, too. We're already shorthanded. I can't count on anyone anymore.* He felt his world crumbling too rapidly. His stomach churned and tightened. *More and more foreigners arrive every day. I can't handle all these changes alone. Dad was my backbone. Now I have no one. Prudence? She's out of the question now.* His body suddenly felt sluggish, lifeless. His chest was tight and his breathing shallow as he followed Donaldo up the long, high stairs and down what seemed an endless hallway.

Before the door to Emiliano's bedroom was opened, Donaldo turned and reminded Jorge Luis, "Your father is very weak, his voice very soft. You must listen carefully. Let him know how you feel but don't spend much time. He wants to see Edgardo and Fiarela, too."

"Of course." Jorge Luis' eyes were already tearing, and he felt as if he were being smothered. He couldn't imagine how he could say goodbye to his father without falling to pieces.

The darkened room was lit only by a few candles which threw mysterious, dancing shadows with any little movement of air. Jorge Luis walked quietly to his father's bedside. His father looked up at him and with a weak smile reached out to take his hand. Jorge Luis leaned over and kissed his father. He then knelt at his bedside. *Diós mio, how frail he is. His eyes are the black of death and his cheeks are so sunken. Why does he have to be leaving now?* He put his head down on the bed beside his father.

Emiliano slowly raised his bony hand and placed it on Jorge Luis' head, patting him softly, "Son, I love all three of you, but you were special. You were my firstborn, the light of my life. You have proved to fulfill my hopes. You are a true Sandoval. I was always heartened at how responsible you were, even as a small child – you have become a man of great integrity and honor. I am incredibly proud of you. I want you to find the happiness that I found with your mother, and I want you to see that your mother, brother and sister are taken care of. *Hijo*, you are a mature man now and have always been an obedient son but – listen to me – you have a choice. You can always be daddy's boy, or you can be your own man. I am proud to be your father. Now go and call Edgardo. I love you, Son. Go, be true to yourself. Make a good choice."

Jorge Luis was too choked up to talk but whispered, "I love you so much Papá." He leaned over and kissed his father goodbye. He left the room, nodded to Donaldo, took a few minutes to collect himself, and walked alone downstairs. When he entered the dining room, he motioned to Edgardo to go. He then joined his mother and sister at the table and waited quietly.

Edgardo met Donaldo upstairs in front of the tall double bedroom doors. Knowing how emotional Edgardo was, he issued orders to be calm and collected. Donaldo hugged him and whispered, "Don't worry, it will be all right."

"Edgardo," said his father, trying to hold out his arms upon seeing him come. Edgardo leaned over to kiss him and then knelt at his bedside.

Holding in his emotions was not easy for Emiliano's second son. He wanted to hug his father, cry, and talk, but he didn't. He listened with a heavy, tremulous heart.

"Edgardo, my son, I have loved you so much. You brought so much humor, laughter, and joy to our lives, always sensitive and giving. Edgardo, please, open the drapes and the window. Let some air in. I don't know why they keep my room so closed and dark. I'm not dead yet." He paused to catch his breath. Emiliano watched his son intently as he pulled the heavy drapes open and cracked the window open a bit. He left the candles burning since the sun had set, and the light was now quite dim. He continued, "Son, I need to tell you while I can. I know about you. Shadowhawk came from the Ranchería with herbs to help me with the pain. I've known him many years, and we talked. You are well-esteemed by the Indians, Son. Please, I must see my grandson before I die, which is very near."

Edgardo sucked in his breath. His eyes widened in shock and fear, "But, Father, - is - is that wise? I don't want to upset the family. I'm not sure that is the best thing to do. I don't want to cause any problems." He felt found out, naked before his world, and felt he might sink down through the floor.

Emiliano's words came out clearly and emphatically, "I insist. By tomorrow I need to see him. I hear he is named after me. I'm also told he is already walking, only having nine months! I want him to be a true Sandoval." He sank lower into his bed, breathing heavily for a few minutes, resting. Then he began again, "I also understand that he shows signs of having your God-given gift of 'sight'. Now, Edgardo, you must take this to heart. You have been a wonderful, talented and caring son, but I will quickly be leaving. You have two choices to make. Your son will be precious. Teach him to respect his gift, thank God for it, and to use it for the benefit of all." He looked directly into his son's eyes.

Although his father's eyes had faded, they still held an intensity that Edgardo could feel. He moved closer and listened carefully.

Emiliano continued, "Son, you have another choice to make now. You can continue to be daddy's boy, my little boy forever, or you can choose to be your own man. Edgardo, I consider you a mature man now. Choose well." With that he sighed, slipped deeper into his pillow and requested to see Fiarela.

Edgardo, not quite sure of what being his "own man meant," walked slowly downstairs with a heavy heart and filled with anxiety. His father's words were echoing in his head. He felt shocked through and through that his father knew about Emilianito. He felt shocked that *Papá* did not want to castigate him, but, instead, wanted to see his namesake - his first grandchild. He was torn between his father, wanting to see the child and facing the reactions of everyone else - especially his mother.

To himself, he cried in grief, *I love my kid. I don't want him hurt. I don't want him to suffer because he is a Mestizo. His mother was the most graceful, beautiful, and kindest woman I've ever known. I can't live without her, I can't.*

He entered the dining room, and, without looking at his mother or brother, he motioned to Fiarela to go up to see her father. Aldiana sat praying the rosary. Jorge Luis sat with his elbows on the table and his hands holding his head. Edgardo poured himself a glass of wine and slowly sipped it. Silence reigned. Everyone dove deep into their own feelings and thoughts, in an effort to accept the loss that would soon come.

Fiarela's body shook as she walked up the high curved stairs. She had been her father's baby, his darling little princess. She stopped in front of Donaldo, who gave her the same directive he gave the boys. She entered the bedroom and tip-toed to his side. She looked intently at her father, a bare skeleton, and prayed he was only asleep.

"I'm not asleep, my little *Princesa*, come here."

Fiarela leaned over to kiss her father, knelt down on the floor, and began to weep.

"Here, here, none of that now. Listen, *Mijita*, I must express myself to you. You were the love of my life. Such a joy after those two rough boys. So much like your mother. I hear you are learning, very competently, how to take care of our bookkeeping records. Jorge Luis is very proud of you, and I only hear good things about your teacher. I wish I could have met her. I can tell by listening to everyone that she is well-esteemed by all. Evidently, she is quite beautiful. Is that true?"

"Yes, Papá, she is lovely in all ways. She has beautiful manners and very high morals, too."

Emiliano breathed heavily and watched his daughter for a moment, "Listen, Little One, if Jorge Luis chooses her, please tell him he has my blessing, but do not say anything before that, promise?"

"Papá, I will do whatever you ask, and I do hope he chooses her."

"Now, Fiarela, I want you to promise me you will be especially attentive to your mother. Help her with everything you can and support anything she may need. I must feel she will be safe and well-loved with you children."

With tears pouring down her face, she assured her father, "I will do it with all my heart. I will miss you so."

"Go with your heart," he said with a weak and raspy voice. "And Fiarela, stand by your family no matter what."

Donaldo entered, picked her up and carried her out. She wept all the way. He set her down in the hallway and suggested that she retire to her bedroom. Donaldo then went down to the dining room to inform the others that Emiliano had fallen asleep, and Fiarela had gone to her room.

Aldiana went up to stay by her husband's side. He heard her come in but felt too tired to talk. In the middle of the night, Emiliano awoke, strengthened somewhat by his sleep. He shifted under his blankets, waking Aldiana. He had something to tell her and prayed there would not be a blowup.

"Aldiana, dear, I have something to tell you, and I want you to remain calm. I don't want any hysterics," he said.

That scared her, thinking he was dying, right then.

"What, what? What's wrong? Should I call for Donaldo?" she asked. She sat straight up in bed, turned and stared to see if he was breathing.

"Aldiana, my dear, this is important. Now just *listen* to me. What I must tell you will come as a shock, but it should make you happy. Do not interrupt me," he said with an implied authority, but his breath came slower. She had to clench her teeth and wait.

In a couple of minutes, he began, "Do you remember Ramona, the daughter of Shadowhawk?"

"Of course I do," she said with emphatic impatience. "What's this about?"

"Edgardo, because of your prejudices, was afraid to tell you that they were married and have had a child - our first grandchild - our grandson. Shadowhawk will bring him to meet us tomorrow morning. I must see him before I die and – don't do that!" he said, as she jumped out of bed and started pulling at her hair and stomping her feet, shouting, "How could you!"

She yelled, angrily pointing a finger in anger at him, "How could you allow that? How could Edgardo do that to us? I won't have it! I will not be a grandmother to an Indian!" She broke out in gasping sobs. "You have let me down, Emiliano, and on your deathbed!" She could hardly get the words out.

"Oh, good lord. Stop that and get back in bed before," he started coughing and losing his breath, "before, before you catch cold."

The window was opened just a crack – just enough to let in the noise of the crickets and the wind moaning in the old tamaracks. Aldiana was too self-engrossed and upset to hear anything, but the sounds were nostalgic to Emiliano. He felt he would miss those comforting noises of this life.

Her husband's words and breathing shocked her more. Was he going to die right now? She gained some control and climbed back in bed, "Are you all right? Don't leave me now. How dare Edgardo bring a mestizo into our home! I can't face Shadowhawk and Edgardo alone. I just won't have it!" Aldiana stared straight ahead into nothingness. She heard nor saw anything. Only the thought of being a grandparent to a mixed-blood child consumed her.

Emiliano spoke to her very clearly even though in a weaker and raspier voice, "Aldiana, amor de mi vida, get a hold of yourself. I'm embarrassed and, quite frankly, disappointed in your behavior. Our neighbors are not going to run our lives. You've always been a loving mother and I want to see you set aside those ignorant prejudices and be a loving grandmother - one in every sense of the word," He stopped and said, "Aldiana, I-am-adamant-in-that," said Emiliano with as much strength as he had, slipping further down into his pillow, "he is our first grandchild, and I am going to live to meet him!"

Aldiana sat stone-faced, still in shock, and bit her lip. Sleep passed her by that night.

19
A Painful Regrouping and Emilianito

dgardo mulled over his father's words as he made his way down the stairs, which curved high over the large entrance. His shoulders were hunched as he walked quietly across the marble floor to the formal dining room where he joined his mother, Jorge Luis, and Fiarela, who had come back downstairs, at the huge oak table.

By the time he sat down, his emotions had taken over. He sat in silence with a face that showed nothing, but internally he felt terror raging through him. He felt cold. His breathing shallow. His heart was beating so fast he was trembling.

He had noticed his mother and brother looking at him when he entered the room. *What were they thinking? Did they already know about me?* Fiarela had such a scared, innocent look about her. *She is going to have a hard time when Papá goes. She was his little princess.* He nodded at her before Donaldo, who had come downstairs, motioned to her to come with him upstairs. He loved his little sister. Fear of being found out and judged washed over him again.

Oh, God, Ramona's death is killing me. Help me. No one will understand. I married an Indian. Why didn't I tell them? Will it mean anything to them? How could I love an Indian woman? What have I done to us all? What I have done will be in the mouth of all our neighbors and friends. Mother will be terribly hurt. She may never forgive me. Why did I have to be so secretive? Tomorrow they will find out everything. I know I have made everything worse. Will my parents accept their grandson? Will my siblings? Oh, god, Ramona, why did you leave me? He almost cried it out loud. He felt like his mind was betraying him. These fearful thoughts ran uncontrollably through his mind. The turmoil was eating him up. His stomach felt tight and painful.

He went to the sideboard for a glass of wine to calm his nerves. Jorge

Luis directed a strong frown at him, but he refused to acknowledge it. He held up the crystal decanter to watch the reflective candlelight on the glass, but it almost slipped from his hand, which augmented his nervousness.

Edgardo was on his third glass of wine when he rose from the table, still trembling. He could hardly contain himself. Fearful thoughts of impending doom streamed through his mind. The emotional pain ate at him as he left the room to enter the outdoor darkness. He felt enclosed by it, wrapped in its protection. Everything was dim, not clearly seen. He headed with an unsteady gate toward the chapel.

Why did Shadowhawk tell my father about Emilianito? My life might be torn apart tomorrow. Then what would I do? Would my family turn against me? Would Shadowhawk take the baby back and never permit me to see him again? What I have done would be exposed to the whole world.

Edgardo stumbled and almost fell. *I've got to get a hold of myself.* His thoughts then went back to his marriage with his beautiful wife, Ramona. *No one was more kind and giving than her. I can't live without her. When we were very young, Shadowhawk told me he knew we were meant for each other. Ramona told him long ago that I was the one she wanted.* That memory gave a jolt to his heart. He thought about the Indian custom requiring that he and his father-in-law have many discussions about what marriage meant and how to treat a spouse. *I enjoyed those talks.*

He stopped and took a deep breath. His memories carried him forward. *Thank God Shadowhawk was willing to overlook the ordinary requirements for an Indian ceremony. I didn't have to show that I could take proper care of a wife and family. He knew I could support her, so I was only required to take game to their door if I encountered one on the way to the Ranchería. Oh, God, I'm dying inside. Why did I hide things? I knew Shadowhawk disapproved of my deception, but I was terrified to tell my family. Mother would be horrified. Society would turn its back on me. My love for Ramona, present since childhood, was too powerful, and Shadowhawk was so good to me. He let me off the extra labor I should have done for him, and he didn't want any customary gifts.* Edgardo suddenly realized he was at the chapel. He let go of his remembrances, pausing long enough to make the sign of the cross as he entered. *I will pray for clarity and insight. I cannot go on this way. I have to face tomorrow.*

After entering the chapel, he lit the candles and knelt in front of the altar instead of sitting in a pew. He prayed long and hard. Things generally came to him from the great beyond easily, but not now. He was too shaken. First, he had to endure in silence the loss of his beloved Ramona, and now, the possible loss of his son and the security of his family. Time passed, and, finally, a deep calm seeped in and slowly settled over him. A feeling of profound peace was followed by a soft inner-voice saying, "Remember your father's words. Be your own man. Be true to yourself, and you will be true to your son. Show them you love him."

Edgardo sat absorbing the words in silence a while longer. Then, he made the sign of the cross, stood up, blew out the candles, and left the chapel. His mind felt clear and his heart full. He walked the pathway back to the house. This time there was no stumbling. He felt alive again.

On his way to the chapel earlier, he hadn't heard the sounds of the crickets or the deep calls of the bullfrogs in the fields, but now the noises were loud and clear. He stopped for a moment to listen. A big, silent barn owl swooped down over his head, which made him think of his father. *Papá used to take us out at night to teach us how to never be afraid of the dark. He taught us what all of the sounds meant. He was disciplined and firm, but he never allowed us to question his love for us.*

Tomorrow would be the beginning of a new chapter of growth in his family – his father leaving, his son entering. Edgardo let go of most of the worrisome thoughts and now accepted the consequences and responsibility of his actions. He would face the unknown resolutely. But his inner turmoil still had a hook in him. He felt calm with his inner authority intact, yet that tiny emotional hook said otherwise.

The night fell hard on all three of the siblings with emotions in a turmoil. Jorge Luis and Fiarela tore up their beds tossing and turning all night. Each felt totally alone and isolated in their bedrooms. Neither had a clue why their father demanded a family meeting after breakfast, especially after speaking his final words to each of them the night before.

Edgardo did not pull back his blankets and slip into bed. He paced the floor almost all night. His mind tossed thoughts around like oil on a hot pan. *Fiarela may be accepting. She would love anyone's child, but Mamá and Papa -- before he's gone? And Jorge Luis? Mamá tends to carry family prejudices, especially against the mixing of blood. She won't be able to face the gossip about her family. I understand that. My brother will probably be furious, but I don't care. Emilianito must be protected.*

Accepting the facts, and accepting that he could not control the consequences, he breathed a sigh of relief and slipped into bed. He slept deeply, not waking until the last minute before breakfast. He hurried, dressing while shivering in the cold. He excused himself for being a little late to eat breakfast, but no one responded. They sat, immobile, staring at their plates.

Breakfast was a disaster. No one had an appetite, and none of the guests were up yet. They returned in the early morning after spending another night at the cantina. Aldiana was not at the breakfast table, either. No one made eye contact, and no one spoke. The three siblings sat silently. No one ate, as each was lost in their own dark and worrisome thoughts.

Suddenly, Donaldo appeared at the doorway, breaking the silence by announcing, "Your father will see you now." Turning, he hurried back up the stairs, to wait outside the bedroom doors, in case he was needed.

The three siblings trudged solemnly up to their father's room, resignation on their faces. Even Edgardo felt resigned to accept his reception, though not willing to accept consequences that would negatively affect his son.

To their surprise, their father's room was bright with light. The window drapes were pulled back, letting in the sun, which was unusual during his illness. The candle wall sconces were flickering brightly. The room had the color of life. Aldiana sat in a chair by his side. Emiliano was propped up in bed with many pillows. He reached out slowly with his skeletal arms and smiled a welcome to his children. His arms were weak and wrinkled with loose skin. He dropped them hurriedly, but his children heard a strength in his voice that was not there last night.

"Good morning, children. Come in. Come in. Sit down." His sporadic arm gestures were now more energetic and expressive, showing a slight step up in the strength of his life force.

The three started to pull up chairs closer to the bed, but Emiliano said, "No, no, we need to have room. Push the chairs back and sit down." He then called, "Donaldo, bring in our guests."

All eyes widened as they turned toward the door with anticipation. Mouths dropped open with the appearance of Shadowhawk carrying a baby.

Jorge Luis gasped, "What's going on here?" just as the little boy, dressed in Indian clothing, opened his mouth with a big smile, eyes large and bright. His two little arms reached out to Edgardo. The sound of "Pá, Pá" was heard by all.

Stunned into silence, all of them could have heard a pin drop until Emiliano said, "Shadowhawk, thank you for bringing the child here. Now, give him to his father." All eyes followed as Edgardo stood up and took his son in his arms as Shadowhawk held him out.

Emilianito patted his father's face, repeating over and over, "Pá, Pá, Pá." He then turned and looked at everyone - all strangers. The smile stayed. No fear showed on his little face.

Jorge Luis was the first to react, "¡María Purísima! My god, my god, Edgardo. Why have you hidden him? Where is his mother? Who? Why isn't she here?" Incomprehension showed on his face. Suddenly, he understood all of Edgardo's disappearances and strange behavior. Looking at the little leather leggings and shirt with beaded designs that the child was wearing, he understood why the family had not seen him nor his mother before. He felt sick with sadness. With compassionate eyes, he looked at his brother. When he looked at little Emilianito, his chest filled with pride and wonder. He whispered in amazement, "I'm an uncle."

Aldiana, seated by the bed the whole time, looked stern, eyes cold, and her mouth pressed tightly, yet ready to snap and say something objectionable. Upon seeing the baby, however, she was shaken to see her youngest, precious son reflected back from the baby's face. Even though he was dressed in Indian clothing, he was his father all over again. She stood up quickly and in a tremulous voice said, "Edgardo, my darling, he looks just like you. He has received your heritage, not his mother's. He is a true Californio. He is a true Christian. I can't believe it. He is beautiful, my son." Her fears of her family's shameful truth being in the mouth of everyone, and passed around to the whole world, vanished.

Gasps were heard around the room. Her husband looked daggers at her, as he realized that she had only set aside her prejudice because of the baby's superficial, physical appearance. He gave a long and sad sigh. He had expected too much of her. He should have known that setting aside a lifetime of old beliefs would not happen at her age. She had buried them under her son's identity, seen in her grandchild and not the Indian mother's. No one else dared to say a word, holding themselves tensely, until Fiarela broke the silence.

Fiarela could hardly contain herself. Her face glowed; her eyes sparkled, "He's my nephew? Can I call him my nephew? What's his name, Edgardo? You're a father? Can we keep him?" She looked at him with an incredulous expression. Edgardo nodded but didn't speak.

At that moment, Emiliano interrupted, saying, "Bring him here, Edgardo. Let me see my grandson."

Edgardo placed him next to Emiliano, where the child gave his grandfather a sloppy kiss and patted him on the face. Suddenly, he turned and looked up above the headboard and smiled. He waved his little hand.

Aldiana and Jorge Luis spoke at once, "Edgardo, what's he waving at?"

Edgardo responded, "He sees three angels up behind our father. I see them, too, but he's waving at them."

Aldiana sucked in her breath, "Oh, good lord. He has been given your Gift." She looked directly at Edgardo and said, "You must teach him to use it with the utmost integrity and for the will of God."

Edgardo nodded, "Of course, Mother, I would teach him nothing else. That is of the upmost importance." Edgardo paused and looked at each person, saying, "I was horribly teased as a child. I was not believed, and it made me insecure and doubt myself. I don't want any one of you making fun of him or calling him a liar like you did to me, and - telling him not to make up stories!" He had everyone's attention, even his mother's, who wasn't sure she should respond. It was evident to all that he was going to be very protective of his son.

There was a consensus of nods and "of courses."

Shadowhawk interrupted to get them back on track, "Please, Ramona, my daughter, was his mother. I'm his grandfather, too. Edgardo, tell them."

The baby sat, held by Emiliano, as Edgardo glanced at Shadowhawk and then at his family. Everyone looked at him with wide-eyed astonishment.

"When I was young," Edgardo began, "I spent hours with Shadowhawk, who taught me many things. Ramona was my age, and we played and worked together all the time. As we grew up, we fell deeply in love. She was so beautiful with the kindest, most generous of hearts." Edgardo broke down and began to weep.

Shadowhawk moved over and put his arm around Edgardo. He looked at Emiliano and said, "My friend of many years, you have a good son here. He has become a solid, upright man. I was proud to give my daughter to him."

Jorge Luis burst in with, "Where is she? She should be here."

"It has been a hard tragedy and a painful loss, but our beloved daughter died after giving birth. During her lingering illness, she requested that little Emiliano be in his father's care, to know his family and to learn the ways of the Californios." He paused and added, "And the ways of the white men, who are coming soon." Shadowhawk bowed, turned and left the room.

Everyone was astonished to hear that, but no one addressed his prophetic remark. Edgardo was the first to speak, "Mother, I'll take care of him in my room. Will you have his things brought up and have the room prepared?"

"Of course, dear. I think we need to feed him. How about the rest of you?"

Jorge Luis spoke up, "Come on, everyone. Nobody ate anything earlier. We certainly weren't in the mood. Now, after such a surprising and wondrous event, I'm hungry. Let's eat."

He went to his father, leaned down, kissed him and said, "Papá, he is the most beautiful gift you could have brought to us. Now rest well." He then embraced Edgardo and said, "I am so sorry for your loss. You have a beautiful son." Long, golden hair and large, green eyes popped into his memory, surprising him and leaving him with a feeling of longing to touch and hold her. He looked at his brother and wondered, *How has he lived with such a loss?*

They all went down together to the dining room with Edgardo carrying little Emilianito, who occasionally looked up into the air, smiled and waved. No one seemed to pay any attention. When they reached the dining room door, Edgardo put him down. Emilianito grabbed his father's pant legs for security and walked into the dining room. He immediately caught sight of the men and gave them a big smile. The three cattle brokers had just begun to eat, as they had slept in from another night at the cantina. They looked up in complete surprise and disbelief to see a nine-month-old toddler, identical in looks to Edgardo, dressed in Indian leather leggings, a leather shirt and a tiny blanket around his shoulders, accompanied by a beaming family.

"What the hell? Who is that young one? Where'd he come from? He looks just like Edgardo. What's he doing in Indian clothes?" The family heard the outburst, spoken by all three of the men at once.

Edgardo picked up Emilianito and carried him to each man, saying his name. After he had introduced him to all three, Antonio said, "Okay, now sit down and tell us the story."

"This is going to be interesting," added Marco.

Cecilio had to put in his remark, "Obviously, he is yours, Edgardo. He is the spitting image of you. While we eat, tell us the story. I can't wait to hear it."

Everyone nodded in agreement except for Aldiana, who excused herself to go upstairs, saying, "Yes, Edgardo tell the story of my beautiful grandson." She gave the baby a quick little kiss and left the room with everyone waiting in anticipation.

"Well, as you can see, he is my son. He is truly a gift. His beautiful, loving mother left this Earth after he was born. Her name was Ramona, the love of my life. She left orders for his grandfather, Shadowhawk, the Chief and Shaman of the Ranchería, to bring him here to be raised as a Californio."

In the silence that followed, a pin could have been heard to drop. By the end of the tale, the guests were deeply moved. Each one in turn, left their seats at the table to embrace Edgardo, letting him know how much they felt his loss. Many eyes became misty. The three men were a long way from home and were beginning to feel the lack of their own families.

Just then, Prudence entered, escorted by Donaldo who bowed and left. All eyes turned to her as she started to say, "Here I am to – to - ." She was cut off by the unexpected scene, lack of understanding, and then, consternation.

Jorge Luis stood up and immediately told her, "Come here and I will tell you all about it."

She went to Jorge Luis and sat down in the chair he pulled up for her. As she stared at the baby, now in a highchair brought in for him, she heard him say, "Prudence, just listen, and I will repeat the story. You are sensitive and compassionate. I know you will understand."

She listened in silence, tears coming to her eyes. When the story ended, she got up and kissed Edgardo and the baby.

Everyone ate quietly, lost in their own thoughts, feeling the hurt and the loss, but not knowing what to say. The energy finally began to shift into feelings of joy as they watched the newest little family member happily playing with his food.

20

A Prediction Comes True

rudence arrived extra early that morning for work, just in time to join the group for breakfast. Except for Aldiana, Prudence, all the family, and guests enjoyed a hearty breakfast of crispy refried beans, chorizo, and huevos rancheros and a pitcher of orange juice. The previous night and day were forgotten for a while as good conversation held forth. Once breakfast was over, Prudence and Fiarela were ready to leave for the office.

"Before you two leave, Señorita Prudence, what time is our English lesson?" asked Marco. "I'm anxious to learn."

"I'm sorry, Marco, but we'll do that the next time I'm here. It's late, and we have much to do today." All three cattlemen showed obvious looks of disappointment on their faces.

Edgardo picked up and held Nito in his arms, who waved his little hands at the girls as they left, giving them big smiles. They waved back, while the servant gathered up the baby's things, and headed upstairs, following behind Edgardo. The little boy had to be settled into his new family home. Jorge Luis and the other men left for the stable and the barns.

Back in the office, the girls shuffled figures and books for the rest of the afternoon. Prudence noticed Fiarela rubbing her forehead, looking spacey. She finally closed the books and said, "Fiarela, we've had a long day. I'm tired. Let's call it quits." She started to pick up the books to place them in the cabinet.

"Whew, I agree. Thanks, Pru. I'm done in. I'm feeling looney," she shook her head and then pushed her hair back, smoothing it out. "I'll go out with you to meet Benito, and then I need a nap."

They called for a servant to inform Benito that Prudence was ready to leave. The carriage was immediately brought to the front steps. Prudence left with Benito, looking forward to her room above the cantina - her little home. In fact, Prudence fell asleep immediately on the way to town. Benito just gave a small, warm smile and was quiet. The carriage went on with its usual rocking motion and the soft plodding of the horses' hooves. The usual sounds and motion were soothing and comforting, keeping her asleep the entire time. Her dreams were free of any negativity or fear.

Fiarela felt exhausted from so much concentration, checking and re-checking figures. She could still see figures jumping around in her head.

Fiarela went straight to her bedroom, which was large with a sitting room in front of the bedroom area. She also had a bathroom with a large standing tub and an area for her chamber pot. All three rooms had fireplaces. She was so exhausted that she headed straight for her bed. She threw herself over her cow-hide mattress, which was covered with a thick wool pad, and fell directly to sleep.

Still asleep in the carriage, Prudence did not awaken until she felt the jolt of the carriage coming to a halt in front of the back door of the kitchen. As soon as she descended the steps, she sleepily thanked Benito, went upstairs to her room, divested herself of her dusty clothes and slipped under the soft, clean sheets.

She awoke later with the feelings of a recurrent nightmare. *Not again. That horrible smell of that robber. I'll kill him in a second if I ever meet up with him.*

She went downstairs to dinner and afterwards walked over to see how María was doing with her pregnancy. Later, she spent time sewing baby clothes in her room, knowing that María would need many more than she had planned on. Listening to the music from downstairs helped pass the time. Sewing baby clothes was fun and gave her a chance to be more creative by embroidering many of them. Piecing different materials together would make some of them unique and that would be fun for twins.

At the hacienda, while the dinner meal of thick lentil soup and home-made adobe bread with bread pudding for dessert was an enjoyable dinner, everyone retired early. The day had been long, emotional, and one with a lot of hard work added.

Two hours later, deep in the silence of sleep, loud cries started waking everyone. The noise was startling and puzzling to all, especially coming out of a sound sleep. No one knew what was happening.

"¡*Madre de Diós*!" cried Jorge Luis, almost forgetting to grab his robe. He ran out to find what was going on. Everyone was up, confused and frightened by the screaming -- even the servants.

The three siblings immediately ran to their mother and the body of their father. Fiarela latched onto his empty body sobbing, "Don't go, Papá!

Don't leave me."

Jorge Luis gently lifted her up and placed her carefully in a comfortable chair, wrapping her in a blanket.

The inhabitants of the hacienda had discovered that Emiliano had died. Wailing could be heard as they approached the house. People began to enter the room and were standing around, many weeping.

Aldiana had collapsed by her husband's side.

Teresa took over and gave orders to the other servants in the room to bring hot, calming tea for Aldiana and Fiarela, and to prepare a room to wash, dress and prepare Emiliano's body for viewing and burial. She then sent everyone else out. The loss of his lifelong friend and boss left Juan dispirited. Nevertheless, he arrived and quickly stepped in to handle the men. Sadness and grief prevailed, but there was order.

Edgardo, even knowing his father was leaving that night, still felt a deep and lonely grief. He quietly moved to Jorge Luis's side, *"Hermano,* when will the priest be back?"

"Not for over six months. We'll have a viewing immediately here and then a small burial in the old family cemetery. When Padre Serrano returns, we will have a formal mass." Jorge Luis felt like a guillotine, hanging over him, had come down. It was finally over, and he was left standing with the weight of the world on his shoulders.

"That sounds good. Remember that mother and us have to privately say our family prayer for the soul of anyone who has died on the hacienda. The one she said her mother and grandmother always practiced, and they called it the Kaddish, I think. I don't know what that word means, and she told me that no one else could perform it but us, just the family, and we were not to talk about it to anyone," said Edgardo. He stood silently reverent for a moment and then said, "Someone needs to go to town and inform Facundo, and, I think, Prudence. Who could we send?"

"Either you go or send Benito. I can't afford to send Juan right now in the middle of all this, and, really, I shouldn't leave Mother, but I will arrange with her to have the prayer service sometime tomorrow. I don't know if I am up to it. It will be too emotional," said Jorge Luis. His shoulders slumped, and his eyes and his lips drooped.

"For me, too. Being right there with Dad will be very difficult for me." He took a deep breath and added, "I'll send for Benito." Edgardo gave the orders to one of the wailing servants. He informed her to have all the mirrors covered with sheets and to put pillows beneath so that anyone who is grieving can sit on them. He also reminded her how important the old traditions were to his mother.

She answered, weeping, "Yes, sir, I understand, sir." Within a few minutes, she was back with Edgardo and told him, "Benito's very sick, and he's in shock because of your dad's death. Sorry, he can't help."

"We could ask one of the cattle brokers to go, but they don't know where either one lives and it's late. They would get lost without Benito driving them," said Edgardo.

"You're right, and I don't trust Cecilio around Prudence," said Jorge Luis.

Nodding, Edgardo said, "It's best if you go, Jorge Luis. I'll tell Mother you are taking care of details. I can't leave with Emilianito here. You may have to give Facundo orders, and, I imagine, Prudence may want to come back with you to help, especially to comfort Fiarela."

"You may be right. That will give me time on the way to think through what I need from Facundo. I'm not sure about Prudence, though."

Edgardo thought a moment, "Jorge Luis, I think she deserves to know right away and not from some stranger in town. She has become a part of this family, and Fiarela will need her and don't deny it – you will, too!" Edgardo was quite emphatic.

"Okay, okay. Give those cattlemen something to do. If they're going to stay longer, they need to help out also."

"I agree. Now, get going," said Edgardo, "Things will be smoother here when you return."

Jorge Luis left on Santón, trying not to push him too hard, but he had a head and heart full of anxiety and anguish, and needed to hurry. *How can I live up to Papá's expectations? How will Edgardo feel not inheriting anything? That old primogeniture law is so cruel. I must tell Prudence. How will she take it? So much is unknown. I don't know if I can handle it all. I feel so alone. I wish I had Prudence by my side, but that is impossible.* His old, comfortable life was gone. What was ahead? *I will face whatever comes. I know I can do it. No, I can't do it alone.* A vision of Prudence flashed before him. *Please, Pru,* he begged, *be with me.* His journey seemed lonely and long as he hurried Santón on, but, in reality, the ride was a fast one to town, and Jorge Luis had it all worked out in his mind on what to do when he arrived.

When he rode up to Facundo's, he noticed the lights were on, which did not bode well. Was his wife in labor with the twins so early? Jorge Luis didn't know what to expect. He strode up the steps and knocked quietly.

Facundo, fully dressed, opened the door and stepped back quickly with his eyes wide open and mouth partially open, "My God, Jorge Luis. What the hell are you doing here at this hour? What's wrong?"

"Someone had to come. I wanted to tell you personally, as soon as possible, that Papá died tonight," choking back his grief. "May I come in?"

Facundo grabbed Jorge Luis, hugging him tightly, saying, "Oh, sorry, sorry. When? What happened?"

"He died in his sleep, Faco. At least he had a peaceful death, but everything is in an uproar, and we need your steady, strong hand to help us get things done. I noticed your light on." His face showed a puzzled concern as he glanced around, not seeing any of the children, but heard noises from their bedroom. "Is everything all right here?"

"Oh, God no. This is a bad time. My wife has gone into labor a month early. The midwife is here. I don't dare leave. The twins' birth is immanent. We may lose them." He looked stricken, shaking his head. "Are you going to inform Prudence? Could she come and help out here for a while?"

"Look, *amigo*, don't worry. We have a lot of help and what you and I need to do can wait. I'll see if Prudence can come over."

"Thanks, Boss."

Jorge Luis was at the back door of the cantina and up the stairs in a flash. He woke Prudence with a soft knocking.

Prudence sat up, startled, grabbed her gun from under the pillow. "Who is it?" she asked, trembling slightly.

"It's I, Jorge Luis. Please, let me in." He sounded frantic to her. Prudence shoved the gun under her pillow, jumped out of bed, and ran to the door, forgetting her night robe. "What is it? What's wrong?" she said as she opened the door. She was truly frightened of what it might be.

"Oh, Prudence, I had to tell you that Papá died tonight. I knew you would want to know and I - -." It was then he noticed her, all of her, in her barely opaque cotton batiste gown with thin shoulder straps. She took his breath away.

She saw his drawn, tense face and felt his pain, and thus rushed into his arms, "Oh, I'm so sorry, so sorry. How did it happen? Can I help?"

"Yes, yes, please can you come and help Fiarela? She is so lost and torn up. Oh, I almost forgot. Facundo needs you tonight. His wife is birthing their twins, and it is too early."

"Oh my god, of course. I'll go there first and see how I can help. Then, I'll ride out to the hacienda, probably right after daybreak. Would that be acceptable?"

"*Sí, sí, por supuesto*," he said, clinging to her tightly. It was hard to let her go.

Prudence suddenly realized, and was shocked, that she had raced into his arms so quickly and easily. It felt so natural and right under the circumstances. She stepped back as he let go and heard his intake of breath as he looked at her. She was horrified that she did not have a night robe on. *Too late now*, she thought. *I hope he does not think badly of me and criticize me.*

"I apologize for the lack of my night robe, but I was taken by surprise and just reacted."

"No, no, Prudence, not to worry. I will look for you at the hacienda later. You know Edgardo told us it would be tonight, but, still, it was a shock, and the loss is great."

"Jorge Luis, I understand. I know exactly the feeling of deep loss. You go now, and I will be out as soon as I can."

He left silently, carrying the warmth of her body in his arms with him. That feeling sustained him during the ride home.

21
Both Cycles of Life

rudence hurriedly dressed, still feeling embarrassed for forgetting her night robe. Even so, she could still feel his strong arms around her, and his welcoming acceptance of her. She threw her coat and hat on and started downstairs. *María, María, I'm coming. I'm coming. I want to get there in time. I hope they aren't born before I get there.* She walked the short distance unaware of how dark it was. She was trying to remember how she helped her aunt take care of twin babies at home in Maine. They were incredibly tiny and delicate. She remembered how fearful she was, but they had saved them. *Please, Lord, help me.*

Facundo heard her soft knock and ushered her in, "Prudence, I am so grateful you are here. They need you, and I'm a wreck."

"Oh, don't worry. They're going to be fine," she said, patting his cheek as she rushed through the living room and into the bedroom with María and the midwife just as the first baby was pushed out – a tiny one, a boy. The midwife hurriedly wrapped it and handed it to Prudence, who was thrilled. Taking the baby out to show Facundo, who was waiting anxiously in the living room, she spoke rapidly but clearly, saying, "I know what to do. I helped my aunt birth twins in Maine who were just as tiny and fragile. Quick, Facundo, help me. You know where everything is. I need olive oil, a small box, and soft cotton or wool, and I need your oven on."

"*Sí, Señorita*, first, I check oven. Then I bring oil and wool."

She returned to the midwife and María, still holding the first baby to keep it warm. The second baby arrived, a tiny girl. Prudence held her, too, protecting them against her warm chest. Facundo moved swiftly and was back within minutes.

"Facundo, heat the oil until it is warm on your skin. Get me a box and some wool quickly. They are precious, but too tiny," said Prudence with anxiety. Facundo obeyed immediately. She knew that he felt these twins were a special gift from God to him and María, chosen as the twins' parents to take loving and firm care.

Within minutes, Prudence had the babies rubbed with the warm oil and wrapped in the warm wool. She lay them both carefully, side by side, in the box and placed the box on the open oven door to keep them warm. She and the midwife both gave orders to Facundo and María about the babies: The oil must be kept warm and the oven must not ever be turned off; they were not to put the twins anywhere but on the open oven door; and they must be fed often. The midwife suggested they find a lactating neighbor to give María some relief.

Prudence felt proud. The twins were so very tiny and sweet little things. She felt she had done all she could and prayed the twins would both live. While handling the newborns, she had felt their tiny little bodies next to her and wanted one of her own. Her thoughts went to Jorge Luis. *What kind of father would he be?* In her mind she could almost see him holding one, loving it, causing her heart to beat faster. *How - how I wish* . . . but she was stirred out of her reverie by Facundo, slipping up quietly by her side. In almost a whisper, he took her by her arm and turned her around to face him, "My dearest Prudence, I owe you so much. I just couldn't face the loss of those two little new ones. They're going to be fine, thanks to you."

"I know they will be. You and María are beautiful parents. You two have the most alive and happy children. I hope, someday, to be so lucky." She paused and seemed far away in her thoughts for a second. "María's asleep, so I will say goodbye. Thanks, Facundo, for letting me help," said Prudence, as she was putting on her coat and hat.

Facundo gave her a tight hug of gratitude, while thinking, *I wish I could wake Jorge Luis up. He needs her. She's one in a million.*

Prudence walked briskly back to her room, feeling exhilarated from the excitement, being the first to hold two new little souls in her arms. Walking in the dark was no problem. She felt so buoyed up with the love for those two new babies. *Someday – someday.* A vision of Jorge Luis, sitting and holding a child on his lap, bouncing it up and down, and laughing shot into her mind, surprising her. A smile broke forth on her face. When she entered her room, she quickly set to packing her valise in case she stayed at the hacienda. It only took a few minutes.

She noticed that it was about two o'clock in the morning when she walked to the stables for a horse. The streets were empty, where not even a dog barked. She woke up Pepito, whom she found sleeping in the hay. He jumped up and had her Arab ready in no time. Mounting Cámila was such a pleasure, and she was trotting along at a good gait.

She left with her buoyed-up excitement slowly slipping into a feeling of profound sadness. With the death of their father, big changes were in store for the Sandovals. She pulled her coat tight around her and put a wool cap on, as it was cold but there was no rain. As she rode, she glanced up into the dark heavens with its billions of stars. The sky above was clear. It was close to freezing. The predicted storm had not arrived yet. She had no idea what was in store for her now that Emiliano had passed, but the feeling of Jorge Luis's warm body, his strong arms, and his sincerity when he came to her, sustained her for a ride that was going to be long and cold.

The trip to the hacienda on Cámila did seem longer than usual and was quite cold and dark. When she arrived and knocked softly on the entry doors, Donaldo was immediately there. She thought, *Poor Donaldo, he must have still been awake.*

"Ah, Miss Prudence, you are most welcome. Fiarela is in her bedroom. She will be grateful you are here," said Donaldo, as he opened the great front doors for her.

"Thank you, Donaldo. I am so sorry for you and the family. I will go up to Fiarela's room. I know the way. Oh, by the way, would you please have someone take the horse to the stables?" She noticed his worn, stricken face and realized how much he would feel the loss of his old friend.

"*Sí*, I will call someone immediately."

Prudence found her way easily and entered Fiarela's room quietly. No noise could be heard inside except her light breathing. *Poor thing. She must have been overcome with exhaustion*, Prudence thought, as the sudden darkness overwhelmed her. She stopped and opened her valise for a candle. *Oh, damn. I forgot to put one in.* An old saying of her uncle's came to mind, surprising her*: Haste makes waste. Boy, it sure does*, she thought. She felt her way carefully through the dark and began to softly call Fiarela's name, "Fiarela*, amiga*. Wake up, wake up."

Fiarela opened her eyes, leaped from her bed and rushed out to embrace Prudence.

"Fiarela, I'm so sorry about your father. It is a huge loss for you. I came to help, if I can."

"Prudence, Prudence, I am so glad you're here." She pulled her long sleeves of her nightgown down as far as she could. She felt cold having jumped out from under a warm, duck down, home-made blanket and a mattress pad full of wool. Even though she had on a long, cotton muslin winter nightdress, the cold was a jolt. She crossed her arms across her chest to warm herself and shifted her feet, which were getting cold. "I feel broken apart. I can't stop crying," said Fiarela, agitated. "I don't understand how I fell asleep."

"Don't worry about it," Prudence looked at her winter nightgown with all those tiny pleats and thought, *I'm glad I'm not the servant who has to iron it*. "Come on. Go back to bed. I'll stay with you, and when the sun comes up, I'll help with everything. I'll be okay. I have a warm coat on. Slip into bed, and I'll lay on the bed by you. Here, you can put your head on my shoulder, if you want."

Fiarela did as she was told. She felt safe and warm on Prudence's shoulder. Soon both were asleep, but Fiarela tossed and turned, sleeping fitfully for what was left of the night.

Aldiana, on the other side of the house, was experiencing the same, even though Teresa had given her a strong sleeping draught.

Both Jorge Luis and Edgardo talked until late. Many responsibilities were discussed that would fall on Jorge Luis' shoulders now. They talked about how much he needed Edgardo's help, even though he could not inherit. Jorge Luis hoped his brother would help as much as possible, and later, they would work out the legalities of the primogeniture law that affects everyone's inheritance. Jorge Luis made it clear that he felt, by right, that Edgardo should have his share. Finally, exhaustion took over and both brothers slipped into their beds.

Jorge Luis had worried, as he slipped into his bed, *I hope Prudence didn't ride way out here alone. I wish I'd told her to wait for morning. She's so independent and unafraid. I'll bet she's here. I hope nothing happened in the dark – oh, god; I forgot Facundo's twins. I'll say a prayer for them.* He lay down, falling asleep before the last words of his prayer were uttered.

Tomorrow would bring a new era and the start of many changes.

At breakfast the next morning, most of the family arrived with swollen, reddened, and bleary eyes. The cattlemen were seated when they arrived and, seeing the strained faces, they nodded good morning and remained quiet.

Exhausted, the family sat silently while being served a substantial breakfast. Teresa, the head cook, hoped to give everyone the strength to hold themselves together and face what must be done.

Aldiana lay prostrate in her bed, having been given a calming tea and a sleeping draught. She would awaken later to step up and take charge of her husband's *velorio* and funeral.

Jorge Luis, feeling dead from the lack of sleep and the emotional blow, stepped up to the challenge and took charge at breakfast. He had everything organized and began giving out the orders, "Cecilio, Antonio, and Marco, I'm putting you under Juan's charge. As you know, due to the lure of gold up in the Sierras, we are shorthanded, and, especially now, we need your help. If you don't mind, Juan will give you your instructions." The three men nodded in agreement.

"Please, can Prudence stay to help me?" asked Fiarela. "I will need help with Mother, my changes of clothing and – and," she began weeping.

"Of course, *hermanita querida*, she may stay as long as she can."

Prudence nodded as Jorge Luis looked directly and inquiringly at her. She turned and patted Fiarela's hand, giving her a reassuring smile.

Jorge Luis then spoke directly to Prudence, "Prudence, Facundo sent a message this morning. He is sorry he can't be here, but the babies are doing well, thanks to you. He said you were magnificent. You literally saved their twins. He and María are eternally grateful."

"That was such an honor for me. I know they'll do well." She paused, looked up, and smiling said, "I love hearing you call me Prudence."

Jorge Luis' face flushed. Before she could say anything more, he changed the subject and continued, "The *velorio* for Papá will start today for whomever wishes to come and express their *pésame*. Teresa and Mother are taking care of that. Fiarela, can you and Prudence help with the food and drinks to be served? As well as those for after the funeral?"

He watched for their response, then turned to Edgardo, "Edgardo, will you take charge of the old family cemetery? It needs cleaning. The grave must be dug and readied. The funeral will take place three days from now at noon. Maybe our guests can help. Check with Juan."

"Don't worry, we will have it all cleaned and ready by then. What about the *novenas*?"

"Probably, we will start those in the chapel the day after the funeral. I will check with Mother. We'll need someone to prepare the chapel, too," said Jorge Luis.

Fiarela spoke up and offered to help with the chapel, "I'll ask Teresa if she can spare a couple of women to help me."

"Fiarela, don't forget me. I'll be glad to help," said Prudence.

Breakfast ended with all the guests and the servants feeling relieved, knowing they would all help the family in specific ways. By helping, they would show how much they cared about this family having been so generous to them.

Upon leaving the room, Prudence turned to Fiarela, "Tell me, what is a *novena*? I didn't understand that part."

"Oh, sorry, we have a tradition that for nine days after the funeral we gather in the chapel for prayers and readings, and we allow people to share the experiences they had with Papá. If Padre Serrano were here, masses would be held. The *novenas* help provide comfort for us in our grieving and for protection of Papá in the afterlife."

"Oh, how nice. That does sound comforting and a welcome solace for those left behind. I would like to help and take part. Let's go to your room now, and I will help you sort out your clothing," said Prudence. "What do you have in black? You will need several dresses. Should we call your seamstress? I can sew, too." She paused and added, "Fiarela, I have nothing in black. What about your mother and your brothers? Do they wear black, also?"

"Oh, yes, everyone will. I'll go talk with Mother, if she is awake. Would you look through my things and see what I need?"

"Of course, send the seamstress, and we will get right to work."

Everyone had their orders, which lessened much of their anxiety by being physically active and feeling useful. The workers of the hacienda were organized. Calm came with the security of knowing what was expected of them and who was in charge. The day marched forward with sadness, but with a clear, directed energy.

22

The Funeral

Edgardo was asked to take charge of the cemetery. The three guests offered to help. The men felt grateful that they could help in some small way. Marco, Cecilio, and Antonio had felt rather at a loss as to what to say to the family or what to do for them. Their business at the hacienda was not completed. None of them were ready to leave. Cecilio was concerned because Juan had not let him know for sure if his mare was even impregnated yet.

The men walked to the small cemetery, which was situated on a hillside overlooking a small creek that ran by the hacienda. Running full, the sound of the water was music to their ears. A few oak trees were there for shade and over the years rose bushes had been planted. Even though Aldiana had not been able, with her husband so ill, to keep the grounds and the plants taken care of, a few of the roses were blooming. The deer loved roses and kept them eaten back so that they did not grow too wild.

Edgardo and the three cattle brokers arrived early, knowing they would be in for a long day of hard cleaning. Luckily, it didn't look like rain, though it was overcast. The dark clouds swirled in from the southern horizon, which meant there would be several days of rain soon.

The men walked around and looked at the gravestones, which were hard to read due to so much debris.

As they moved around, Antonio remarked, "Edgardo. This is a well-chosen spot for a cemetery. It's a neat place with a nice view."

"Look here," said Cecilio, "Here's a child's grave, a girl. Could it be a sister?"

"Yes, it is," said Edgardo. "Every year on her birthday, Mother has a prayer session for her in the chapel, but I was too little when she was born. I don't remember anything."

Edgardo handed out the tools and orders for each of them. They cut the weeds and loaded them into a cart pulled by a mule. The small number of headstones were scrubbed and the dirt brushed out of the lettering. The family names were once more visible. The stone mason had cut a new one for

Emiliano, which stood out in sharp relief from the old ones. The new hole for the casket was dug. Chairs had been brought for the family and close friends. The rest of the mourners would stand. A lot of conversation and joking was carried on. Meanwhile, the clouds blew over, and the sky cleared.

Marco remarked to Edgardo that the oldest headstones had a six-pointed star on them. He turned, pointing with his finger, and said, "Edgardo, my family is Jewish, and we use this star on our family gravestones. Since you are all Catholic, why is the star used?"

Edgardo stopped cutting grass with a sickle. He looked puzzled, "Honestly, I'm not sure. I always thought it meant that the deceased had gone to a heaven full of stars." Suddenly, he looked pointedly at Marco. The other two men had stopped to listen, their interest being piqued.

But Cecilio interrupted with, "You know, when I was in England, I saw headstones with that star, and you're right, Marco. They were Jewish." They both turned and stared at Edgardo.

"I have heard," said Edgardo, leaning on the sickle, "That in the old days, when the Jews were persecuted, that many pretended to convert to Catholicism, but still practiced their Jewish traditions. They had to hide it. They said many left Spain and came to Mexico, but I don't know how that would relate to our family." As he said it, a strong wave of chills swept over his body and startled him. He had learned long ago that this was the way his angels touched him. He had not felt that since Ramona died.

¡Jesús y María! he said to himself. *Jewish? Could it be?* A swift visual image of an old trunk flashed before his mind. One that, as a child, he had never been allowed to touch. *I tried a couple of times. I caught hell for that. Why? Could it really be?* He thought again. *I think I know where that trunk is stored.* He knew what he would do later.

Just then he was shaken by another memory. As a small child, maybe four or five, he had found a ring and played many times with it. He had gotten into trouble, but he loved that ring. He could see the top of it again with its beautiful silver cross. What he found the most fun was to open it up. Inside was a six-pointed star. It was shiny gold. He had not seen it since the day he was caught with it. That image hit him again - that of the six-pointed star. Now, it took on quite a different meaning. *Oh, my God, that star had six-points just like our ancestors' gravestones. What does that mean?*

"Edgardo," said Antonio, "You look like you have seen a ghost. What's wrong?"

"No, no, I'm just tired."

"We're done here, aren't we? Let's load up and leave. I need to clean up. I'm going back to the cantina tonight," said Antonio.

"Not me," said Cecilio, "I'm turning in early." He looked at Antonio, "It's that little cutie pie, Desiré, isn't it?"

Both he and Marco looked at each other, rolled their eyes and made exaggerated lip-smacking sounds that looked and sounded like kissing.

Antonio, his face beet red, turned and started picking up tools, muttering loudly, "At least I have a pretty girl."

The tools were set on top of the cut grass piled in the cart. Edgardo led the mule. The three men followed on foot quietly, tired from a day of physical labor, and each lost in his own thoughts of the loss of his own father, and how hard it was to grow up, be independent, and become responsible.

On the way, Edgardo's thoughts raced. *I'm going to find that trunk. Should I mention it to Jorge Luis? No, he's too upset and busy. I'll go it alone. Besides, tomorrow is the funeral. I'll just have to go it alone.*

At noon the next day the family was dressed in black, and sat together in the carriage, which was also draped in black. Benito, his face sagging from his feeling of deep loss and sadness, drove slowly to the cemetery. The cattle brokers walked with the other people.

Prudence had been asked to attend, but she did not travel in the carriage. The young people felt she should have, but she was not family; therefore, they did not complain, and kept silent in honor of their mother, the widow, and, now, the matriarch.

Prudence walked with the few workers who had been closest to Emiliano. She felt as if she was a stray cow, sticking to the herd but didn't belong. She believed that Jorge Luis, at this time, would need her more than ever. He had no one to console him, she felt. She glanced often at the carriage but couldn't see within it.

Many of the laborers and their families had spent their entire lives on the hacienda, as many had been born there. Juan, Emiliano's closest friend, kept by Prudence's side. He, too, felt she should have been in the carriage as she was such a part of this family now. He felt Jorge Luis would have wanted her near. He, also, knew that Aldiana's attitude toward Prudence was not one of approval. He understood it was because of Jorge Luis' growing attention to Prudence, and he was well aware of Aldiana's need for family appearances and prestige. He walked protectively beside Prudence. *With the scarcity of good women here,* he thought, *Jorge Luis couldn't do any better. His mother's prejudices are hurting their family. Look what happened to Edgardo. Well, I'm not the matchmaker. Wish I was. I just pray he will be strong enough to stand up for himself.* He glanced back inside the carriage and could see Jorge Luis watching Prudence from the side window. He looked rather forlorn and not just from his father's death. It was cold out. There was no rain in sight, though, just a scattering of puffy white clouds against a bright cobalt sky.

The funeral service would not be presented by a priest. Father Serrano was getting old, and, with the decline of the missions, he was finding it harder and harder to travel such long distances to service the haciendas. However, the burial could wait no longer. Once everyone had arrived at the cemetery and all were seated or standing close, Jorge Luis and Juan took charge of leading the prayers. Jorge Luis found it very strange, realizing that from now on, this would be a duty of his - to reign at funerals. Looking down at his father's casket, he thought, *Oh, Dad, how I have always taken you for granted. You taught me everything, but there are so many extra duties I forgot about. How did you do it all?* He began to feel a huge weight settle uneasily on his shoulders. He glanced over at Prudence. She was looking at him sadly, but he lowered his eyes with a feeling of deep longing. *I've got to be strong like my father was.*

Many of the hacienda workers and servants, along with people from the pueblo and friends who came from distances away, had meaningful stories to tell at the funeral about their lives with Emiliano.

Juan told about the many unexpected things that happened when they were breaking horses, like those close calls and a few broken bones. He talked about how Emiliano had trusted him to begin teaching the boys to ride, and at the age of two they were galloping a horse safely in the corral.

A fast rider with a spare horse had been sent immediately after Emiliano's death to Monterey to inform the government officials. A couple of government men were able to make it in time for the funeral. Each man spoke at the funeral and praised Emiliano for coming haste forth, when word was sent that they needed his advice. He was said to be highly respected by all for his generosity, strong ethics, and honesty.

When the ceremony ended, both Aldiana and Fiarela felt relief. They found it physically and emotionally difficult to sit out in the open for so long with their loss right in front of them - ready to be dropped into the ground.

Each person placed a few red roses on the casket. As each family member left, they threw a handful of dirt upon the hand-hewn box. Emiliano's two sons bowed down in respect and made the sign of the cross before they stood and tossed in their handful of dirt.

The funeral was over.

Edgardo had maintained a calmness during the ceremony. He was only too aware of the stars on the older gravestones and their implication. He kept seeing them in his mind, and he wondered if, possibly, one should be on his grandfather's. He felt a queasy feeling hit the pit of his stomach. He churned and debated within himself about whether it would make a difference to know that his family was once of the Jewish culture and religion. *I remember that Shadowhawk told me once that I did not have the soul of a Catholic, and then he said that I didn't have the soul of an Indian, either. I didn't understand what he meant. I wonder if he meant Jewish. He didn't say anything more though, and I was afraid to ask.*

The carriage left with Edgardo feeling a profound sorrow as he was deep in thought. This change was, for Edgardo, like a snake that shed its skin, its old life peeling off. He felt raw and exposed to the threats of unknown storms that could sweep in, blow over, but hit hard unexpectedly. He lowered his chin against his chest for a moment and shivered. When he looked up and glanced through the window, he was distracted by a flock of geese up in the sky flying in a V formation, while they made a big circle around the funeral walkers, as if saying goodbye and, like Emiliano, heading for the prospect of a new home and new adventures. They would come back, but Emiliano's work here was over.

Emiliano's death marked the end of an era. He would never see the forces of change looming on the horizon - like a lowering, black cloud that would touch everyone.

23
A Fateful End for Alberto

The hacienda was silent. Nothing moved. Fiarela cried herself to sleep. Aldiana prayed and wept. She succumbed to exhaustion. The two brothers, spent from all their hard work, tried to allow slumber to take them early. Edgardo laid his head on his pillow and was gone. The baby was sleeping undisturbed but not Jorge Luis.

Papá is gone and I am it. Now, I have no one to turn to. I know the business part but there is so much more to it. How can I be responsible for all the people here in the hacienda and in town, too, and the pueblo itself? I shouldn't have to be head of all that and don't want to be. Jorge Luis sat up on the side of his bed, tired of tossing and turning. His thoughts raced in a whirl. *I can't manage all that like Papá did. I didn't count on all that. It's too heavy a load, especially with so many changes hitting us.* He rolled back into bed and under the covers. *Edgardo has been a big help. He's got to do more. But why should he when he didn't inherit anything. How do I fix that? I can't have a family now with all this mess, and I want one. I need one. No one is going to pick out a wife for me. I won't stand for it.* Too exhausted, he let go and fell into a deep, dreamless sleep.

About two o'clock in the morning, all hell broke loose. Loud knocking woke most of the household. Donaldo, groggy from sleep, staggered to the front door to find two men from the pueblo. Shocked, he stuttered, "Ay, ay, ay, what's - what's happened? Shall I call Jorge Luis?"

Both men started speaking at once, rapidly and excitedly together, "Sí, sí, get him quick - quick!"

Jorge Luis and Edgardo reached the door at the same time, still struggling to get into their winter bathrobes, "What's going on? Paco, Diego. What the hell are you doing here at this hour?" asked Jorge Luis, tightening his belt.

"Boss, Edgardo," said Paco. "Sorry, sorry, bad time with father so soon dead, but something has to be done and done now! Because father dead, we came to you. You are the law now. It's Alberto, that *bastardo*. If Diego hadn't stopped me, I would have shot him through the window. We can't take no more."

Jorge Luis leaned forward to make sure he was hearing correctly.

"He's killing her. This is worse than ever. He's crazier, meaner, and we can't let him beat her to death with those little kids," said Diego.

Paco said, "I'll kill him. She's near to death. Then what? He'll start on his children!"

"Stop, stop," said Jorge Luis, thinking, *Why now. Oh God, why have you brought this mess to me now? I've got to have some sleep. We have to be up early to work. My having to deal with that miserable drunk is a waste of time, when I have so much weighing on me.* "Stop. I thought you talked to him a few months ago, after talking to my dad about him and his drinking behavior. We heard he was better."

"I heard he was," said Edgardo.

"Yeah, we did, but it lasted only two months. Then he slipped into a brutal downslide. We've had it. It's affecting my family to hear this night after night. My wife is beside herself and tries to help his wife, but when he finds that out, he beats her twice as much."

"Same on my side," said Diego, his hands punctuating every word. "Our houses are too close. We hear everything. I can't let my family endure this any longer. We are serious about this. We need to act now. Tonight."

Is this what I have to put up with? How did Papá deal with something like this? He never talked about this crap at all, except for Alberto, that miserable cobarde. I am the law. I guess I had better resign myself to it. "What the hell can we do?" asked Jorge Luis, "If we take him to the court in Monterey, they will just reprimand him and tell him to be good and stop drinking. A lot of good that will do. That's a waste of our time and money."

Edgardo was quick to respond, "You'll have to get rid of him. Make that *puta madre* disappear."

"That's strong language coming from you, Edgardo." He gave his brother a surprised stare and paused momentarily. "I'm afraid you're right. Obviously, his brutal behavior has accelerated with no letup," said Jorge Luis, still thinking, *What can I really do though?*

"I should have shot him tonight," said Paco. *"¡Qué barbaridad!* He threw her to the floor, put a hammerlock around her neck, and, if she moved at all, he pulled her hair. I mean hard. I saw some chunks in his hand."

"¡*Madre Purísima*!" blurted Edgardo.

"That's not all, one night I saw, through the window, him grab her by the jaw and swing her around the room and throw her on the bed! Another time, that *desgraciado* knocked her down, stood over her, grabbed his penis, and yanked it right out of his pants. That *loco borracho* stood there and wagged it at her, laughing. I can't handle that kind of crazed behavior. It's brutal. What if my wife or one of my kids saw that? I would have shot him on the spot if Diego hadn't stopped me."

"Last time," said Diego, "*La violaba* for four hours on the floor. I decided then that he was sinking deeper into depravity, and we had to come to you. You are our only hope. I'm serious. He's killing her, and he will kill her. She's a good woman. Everyone knows that. Jorge Luis, it is lamentable that we have to drop this on you so soon after your father's death."

"You, being the law now, no choice. Sorry, *Joven*," said Paco.

By that time, Aldiana and Fiarela had come down. "Boys, what's happening here? It sounds bad. The noise frightened both of us," said their mother. Both had grabbed warm robes and slippers. Aldiana's hair was braided for the night, hanging to her hips while Fiarela's hair was loose, which she had cut to shoulder length – against her mother's wishes. She shook it back, looking directly at her brothers, eyes wide and mouth partially open, as if she were going to say something.

Jorge Luis said, "Mother, Fiarela, go back to bed. This is men's business. We are going to take care of it. You are not to worry. Now, please, go before you get cold."

The women retired knowing it was useless to ask questions. Whatever happened, it would be up to the men to solve it, but Fiarela was very curious. "Mamá, what do you think could have happened?" said Fiarela.

"I don't know, *Mija,* but whatever it was, it must be bad for those men from town to ride all the way out here in the middle of the night. Maybe something happened at the cantina," said her mother, pulling her robe tighter against the cold.

"Will they tell us about it tomorrow? I really want to know."

"Women are not allowed to hear about things that are very bad, but, of course, I would like to know. Maybe we can get them to talk at breakfast," said Aldiana.

"I know, let's ask Teresa. I'll bet she will know. She usually hears all the gossip from town," said Fiarela.

"Well, I'm not sure we should. The men may not want us to know, but it doesn't seem right that they don't tell us. We have a right to know what goes on. You go ahead and ask. I shouldn't," said her mother, pulling her robe up around her neck.

Fiarela shrugged and went on to her bedroom. She didn't like being left out of things. When she got married, it would be different, she thought.

The men were still mulling over what to do when Jorge Luis suggested that he, Edgardo, Paco, and Diego go to the office to work out a plan.

Just then, the cattle brokers, having heard the commotion, ran down the stairs to join the men. They had rushed so fast that they were only in their pajamas, but all had their guns. "Anything wrong? All the loud voices woke us up, and it sounded scary, serious. Can we help?" asked Antonio with Cecilio and Marco, nodding, now looking suspiciously at Diego and Paco.

Jorge Luis said, "It is serious, but put your guns down. We've got a problem in the pueblo with a guy badly beating and violating his wife. You don't need to be involved, but we have to act quickly."

Edgardo added, "If, by chance, we need help from one of you, would you be willing to help out?"

"Absolutely," all three answered.

"I had to deal with that once," said Marco, "That guy disappeared! I made sure of that. I'll help you any way I can."

"So will I," said Cecilio, breaking a shocked silence, "Just let me know."

"Thanks," said Jorge Luis, "Would you sit down with us in the office and help us make up a plan? We can't shoot him."

After they all sat down and were offered something to drink, Paco started by saying, "Look, let's tie him up and throw him in a shed of yours until we can get rid of him."

Edgardo said, "Sure, we can do that. We've got one empty right now, but then what?"

Diego suggested throwing him in the river, but no one wanted his body to be found and fingers pointed at anyone.

Marco said, "I'd like to hang him high. Leave him there as a lesson to others!"

"That won't work," said Jorge Luis, "Everyone will know who did it. The authorities in Monterey would come out here and tear the place apart. Since they don't care about wife beating, they won't come unless there's a body that has been murdered, and then, they probably would hang *her*!" said Jorge Luis. *Ay, mi Papá, why aren't you here to help us? This is nasty business.*

"You're right. What about the swamp?" asked Antonio, "Would that be a possibility?"

"It could be, but, yet again, the body could be easily found by the dogs," said Edgardo.

Cecilio spoke up, "Look, I'm leaving soon and taking my mare with me home to Yerba Buena, San Francisco. I could haul an extra cargo." He paused momentarily. Then he said, "Say, I have an idea. If I take him, I could dump him at one of the wharf bars on the bay. He would be immediately shanghaied and thrown on board one of the ships in the harbor. And, believe me, he would deserve it. He can't escape. The work is grueling and debilitating. If he gets drunk and goes crazy on board, those sailors will have no problem taking care of him."

All the men looked at him and then at each other in great surprise.

Jorge Luis said, "That's it! Cecilio, I am taking you at your word. No one will ever guess what happened to him." *And you will finally be out of my life.*

"That is a lot of risk you are taking," said Edgardo, "but, we would be grateful."

"No problem," said Cecilio. "Glad I can help."

"Okay, that's settled. Paco, you and Diego go get him and we'll keep him in the shed until Cecilio is set to leave," said Jorge Luis.

"A little bread and water might help him to sober up," said Edgardo.

Antonio added, "I would like to tear him apart with my bare hands. My sister was violated, and, believe me, that guy paid big time. He'll never do that to another woman ever again."

With that said, horrible as it was and understood by all, eyes turned quickly to Antonio. Antonio had just stepped up in esteem and admiration in their eyes. They all sighed with relief. The plan was set. Paco and Diego left for Alberto.

Deep, dark clouds, pushed by freezing winds, suggested a coming storm. The two men tightened their scarves, pulling their wool hats down further on their ears. They bent over their saddles and made a swift trip back to town. They walked their horses as silently as possible through town and approached Alberto's home cautiously.

"Diego, he'll be passed out by now, so hog tying him shouldn't be a problem," said Paco.

"If he's not, we're going in anyway. We'll get him no matter how Yolanda objects – if she is conscious."

"Oh, God, this is disgusting. I'd like to gut him and feed him to the vultures," said Paco, dismounting and clutching his coat tighter.

"We should have done this a year ago," added Diego, glancing around to see if anyone nearby was up. He didn't want any extra trouble.

"Here we are. Diego, get your gun ready in case he's awake and still violent."

They tied the horses to the hitching post and walked silently to the front steps. Diego said, "You stay down here. Have your gun ready. I'll go up first."

Diego stomped loudly up the stairs, across the porch, and pounded heavily on the door. No one came. Paco joined him, and they both pounded. Yolanda opened the door and promptly slid to the floor unconscious.

Diego caught her and carried her to the couch. Her eyes were swollen, turning black and blue. Her lip was cut. Her arm was bloody and so was her leg, which the two men could see as her skirt was torn off. She had nothing left on except a scarf around her neck, which looked as if it had been used to choke her. He wrapped her in a blanket and felt her pulse, "She's barely alive Paco, poor thing. She needs help. Do you think Prudence could help? At least for tonight and tomorrow?"

Paco answered, "I'll go down the street and send Facundo to get her because she doesn't know me. He is going to have a fit. He already beat Alberto up for treating his wife like that. I'll have my wife take the children. They should not be here." He shook his head in disgust. He felt like smashing the drunk, passed out on the floor, to a pulp.

"I'm going to put a gag on him right away in case he starts coming to," Diego said.

"Yeah, okay, and as soon as I tell Facundo, I'll get an extra horse to carry him," said Paco.

Everything was carried out like clockwork. Prudence, who was quite shaken by what she was told, dressed and ran to the house. Even though she felt sick to her stomach upon seeing Yolanda, Prudence stepped in and got right to work. Her thoughts took over, running wild. *My god, I didn't know a man could do anything like this. No beating is like this. Why, why? What could have caused this? Can any man do this?* Fear and doubts crept into her mind. *No, no, Jorge Luis would never do something like this. Would he?* Doubts again assailed her. These things had never happened in her life before. She knew women were raped but this? She planned to kill any man who ever did that to her. *I have got to be careful. Thank god he has been taken away, and I hope he never returns. I would have shot him long ago*, she thought, not realizing that there would be harsh consequences for her as a woman. Also, there were children to be considered. *Those poor little souls. How they've suffered.*

Earlier, before Prudence had arrived, the men had thrown Alberto, still passed out, over the horse, tied him on, covered him with old blankets, and rushed him to the hacienda where they secured him in the empty shed, tied and gagged. Edgardo had obtained a large canvas to cover him and prevent him from freezing. Outside the shed, no one heard anything. So far, the plan worked.

After it was all over, Jorge Luis placed a few logs on the coals in his fireplace and sat on his bed. He gave thanks that he had so much help, including Prudence, who should never see anything like that, and prayed that something like this would never occur again. *I have so much more respect for what you had to do, Dad. I hope I can measure up.* He did feel a real sense of accomplishment and felt his leadership strengthening. His pillow was soft and the chill was now off the room and his bed warmed quickly. Once under the blankets, sleep overcame him swiftly.

Prudence listened, very alert, to Yolanda's cries of pain and torment, off and on, while in and out of consciousness on the couch. Her thoughts rolled around her mind, searching for what to do -- a solution, some way to calm Yolanda. She realized that she would have to clean up the bedroom before she could manage to get Yolanda into the bed. Yolanda, herself, would need a good cleaning, also. She was a mess after being in the middle of that depraved and frightening situation. Prudence prayed that sordid and violent life would never touch her own self. She looked at Yolanda, who was covered under many blankets to keep her warm. She could see only her face. She wanted to pat her to comfort her, but didn't dare, "Yolanda, even though you are black and blue, you are a beautiful woman. You didn't deserve any of this. Don't worry, we will get you well."

24
The Healing Begins

olanda remained unconscious on the sofa while Prudence held her breath to keep from breathing the putrid air. She gagged repeatedly while throwing open the windows to let the cold fresh air in. Prudence removed all the terribly soiled bedding and put it into a pile for the women to wash at the creek. She remade the bed and wiped clean the headboard and side table. She warmed several large stones in the oven. Then, she wrapped them in towels and placed them in the bed to warm it.

By the time she had the bed ready and had straightened up the room, Prudence was fully furious. What had been a warm and attractive bedroom was in complete shambles from Alberto's drunken rages. Yolanda's beautifully embroidered curtains were pulled off the rods. One rod was broken. *Had he used that on her? My uncle would never have treated my aunt that way. Why would a man do that? Is that what happens when a marriage goes bad? What if I was having a bad time, would Jorge Luis do that to me?* She shuddered. *No, I don't believe it.* But the seeds of doubt entered.

She picked up the rod and set it and the curtains aside. She had done all she could. She would take care of them tomorrow. A home sewn quilt lay dumped on the floor. Seeing muddy footprints and yellow urine soaked into it was sickening. Prudence picked it up carefully and put it on the pile to be washed. She gagged and felt like crying.

A soft knock drifted in from the front door. Prudence perked up her ears and went quietly to answer. Facundo had returned to ask if she needed help.

"Yes, I do. I do. I'm so grateful you came back. Please, carry her to bed. It's all clean and warmed." She whispered in a low but emphatic voice, "Facundo, I've never seen anything like this. It is beyond belief. I feel filthy, and Yolanda is in seriously bad shape. Facundo, there is no food anywhere in the house."

Facundo looked at Prudence, shocked. He had not thought about that. He glanced down at Yolanda, sighed, shook his head, and began to lift her up gently.

"If you can bring me a chicken, I will make soup," she said as she watched Facundo carry Yolanda into the bedroom. "Could you also obtain a leg of lamb or some beef? She will have a hard time healing. It's going to take time."

"Prudence," he said, as he slowly maneuvered Yolanda, heavy and still unconscious, down into her bed. "You have done a tremendous job here already." He looked around and said, "I will bring plenty of food for you." He noticed that Prudence had found clean bedding and left the soiled ones in a pile. He picked up the pile, saying, "I will take all these in the morning to have them washed. Prudence, you need a good rest. Tomorrow, I'll bring Lola's oldest girl, Estela, to help you out. Do not worry about the bookkeeping or her children. Paco's wife is caring for them."

Facundo stood holding the dirty clothes, waiting for Prudence while she took a deep breath with a long sigh. He could see the emotions steal across her face and respected that. He gave her a minute or two.

Prudence, overtaken with the exhaustion setting in and the sight still in her mind of what she had encountered upon coming into the house, felt lost for a minute. She had wiped Yolanda's face, arms and hands, and, with difficulty, put a clean nightgown on her. Very carefully, she had brushed her hair, which was difficult with her still being unconscious. While being kind and gentle with her, doubts crept in. *I really don't know men. I never had a brother and only one boyfriend. Why did he have to die so soon? I've never seen Edgardo do anything harsh or mean, but Jorge Luis can get a little strong at times. I saw him take down that guy who kicked the dog. Would he ever turn on me?*

Suddenly, she came back to herself, looked up at Facundo, and in a low but emphatic voice said, "I don't understand this at all." She stood still and stiff. "I have never seen anything like it. I pray Alberto does not return. I would like to kill him myself for what he has done to her and his family." She began to brush back the hair strands that had fallen over her face, which stuck together from the sweat of cleaning.

"Prudence, when drink takes over a man, it seems to open the door for evil to enter, and most don't seem strong enough to stop it. Alberto was not like that when he was a younger man. Anyway, he won't be back. I can guarantee that," said Facundo. "Please, let Yolanda know that she and her children will be taken care of and not to worry. Get some rest, Prudence. You will need it. Jorge Luis would be proud of you tonight." He left as quietly as he came.

Yolanda began moving nervously in bed, whimpering, making Prudence quite upset. This continued for an hour until she suddenly became conscious with a painful cry.

"No, no, stop!" she screamed, pulling the quilt over her head.

"Yolanda, it's Prudence – Prudence. You're safe now. He's not here. He can't hurt you. I'm going to bring you some tea. Don't be afraid. I will not leave you alone."

Yolanda reached out and grabbed her hand, crying, "My children, where are my children? Did he hurt them? He said he'd kill them." Her voice was weak, and the words were drawn out.

"Your kids are safe. They are sleeping at Paco's house," assured Prudence, horrified at what she heard. "Yolanda, you are too weak and sick to take care of them right now. We will take care of you and get you well and strong again. Don't worry. Now rest. I'll bring your tea."

With help from a soothing and calming tea, Yolanda slept through the night, moaning in pain now and then.

Estela arrived early the next morning and what a relief for Prudence, who had hardly slept at all. With Estela's help and two weeks of hard work, Yolanda finally gained enough strength to have her children brought regularly to visit her, but they remained with Paco's family. Her recovery was slow and hampered by a lack of understanding and a feeling of guilt about Alberto's abusiveness. She had the tendency to take on the blame. One day, Prudence brought up the subject.

"Yolanda, I didn't know Alberto, and I don't mean to be nosy, but was he always mean?" asked Prudence.

"Oh, no, not in the beginning, but he did occasionally drink quite a bit, and, after a while, it increasingly became a problem because he began to spend all our money on drink."

"What do you think happened that he became so abusive?" said Prudence.

"I don't know, but he changed. It must have been something I did because my mother told me that if I ever had a problem in my marriage, it would be my fault. He just kept getting worse, and the children cowered behind their beds. I tried everything, but nothing worked, and he threatened to kill the children if I left him." Yolanda looked stricken by the memory and turned her head away as if humiliated.

Prudence was horrified but did not pursue the topic further. Later she would carefully talk to her with the help of others. Eventually, Yolanda did comprehend that Alberto would not change. She understood that she was the victim and did not cause the abuse. She also came to terms with the fact that she had many people willing to help and support her, and that she deserved it. That was a huge step in her healing. Her fear took longer to ease. Her nerves were shot, and she startled at the slightest sound and movement.

One evening, they heard the quiet noise of the doorknob turning. Yolanda panicked and immediately started to shake. She scooted down in her bed and hid under her blanket. Prudence went to the door and found out that it was Facundo - wanting to know if they needed anything. These events happened off and on until she learned to tell herself, after several flashback experiences, that that was then and this is now. She no longer needed to be afraid. Prudence stayed with her for two weeks until she could organize others to take over, but then it was many weeks before Yolanda could be left alone, even with her children, for very long.

During this same time, Jorge Luis and Edgardo were kept hopping as they took over the family business. There was so much to it – 150,000 acres of land, some 20,000 or more cattle, 4,000-5,000 sheep, orchards, hired men and their families, seeing that Aldiana was cared for and that the household ran well. They were having more trouble with rustling, and the markets were failing. They found it hard being shorthanded. Both men were worried. The times were slowly getting worse.

Fortunately, Fiarela had stepped up, putting in full days of hard work, helping her mother with the household. The annual fall charreada had been postponed earlier due to the failure of Emiliano's health. Christmas festivities had to be postponed also, much to everyone's disappointment. There was no time or much desire to organize the events.

Even with the heavy responsibilities, Jorge Luis stopped to see Prudence every time he arrived in town, which wasn't as often as either wished - the wishing still unsaid. He simply couldn't visit the girls working in the office as he used to. One day, Jorge Luis arrived with a letter sent by Cecilio.

In the letter, Cecilio sent profound thanks to the Sandoval family for their generous hospitality. He apologized to Prudence for not being able to take proper leave of her when he left. He wanted everyone to know that his mare was doing well, and that he would write again when the colt was born. He informed them that the cargo that was sent with him was delivered, and that it all went as planned. He signed it: Many regards, Cecilio Fagoaga. The letter was passed around, and those who read it gave a grateful sigh of relief.

Jorge Luis was content with the news and accepted Cecilio being thoughtful in having written them a letter, but he felt he had an ulterior motive to contact Prudence. *I know she'll be happy to hear from him but how happy?* He felt a crunch in his stomach. He tried to wave it aside to no avail.

I felt like not delivering it, but I couldn't do that. No one would have been the wiser, and I wouldn't have had to stand here and grit my teeth while she read it. No, I don't want to hide anything from her. It wouldn't be right, and Cecilio was a good man. Why do I fret? He's not here.

Jorge Luis recognized his feelings of jealousy, and his responsibility to his family weighed heavily on him. He really didn't know what to do about Prudence. He considered himself a good Californio, a loyal son, and a stalwart member of society and his church. *How could I have fallen in love with her?* These confused thoughts dumped a load of guilt on already heavily weighted shoulders.

Fiarela also came as frequently to Yolanda's as she could, when her mother did not need her, and happily helped. Of course, Edgardo stopped often, bringing teas, salves and poultices from Shadowhawk. Emilianito occasionally accompanied him to the joy of Yolanda and all who were present. Her children loved to play with him.

As soon as he would arrive, Emilianito would rush to Yolanda, placing his tiny hands on her heart or face. His bright, dark eyes looked deeply into hers. His endearing smile was a joy to see. Yolanda looked forward to this little tradition. A warm flow of energy emanated from his small hands and passed through her body. She welcomed the feeling with a prayer of gratitude. She could feel a step up in her physical, mental and emotional well-being. Although much damage had been done to the little family, and the healing was slow, the family's love was strong, and it would hold them together.

Needing to get back to her own work, Prudence organized others to help, which was a blessing. Three of the cantina girls offered to help and were accepted. Yolanda had reached the point of having her children home and was now strong enough to do most of her own work. She was becoming, again, a young and joyful mother. Prudence, due to her role in the whole affair, became a woman highly esteemed and respected throughout the pueblo.

Prudence had always been the outsider, the foreigner. A lot of the women were jealous of her beauty and her relationship with Jorge Luis, their *patrón*. This horrifying episode with Alberto and Yolanda was eye opening and had awakened people. Facundo, hearing everything in the bar, revealed to Prudence the change in the town's perception of her.

"Prudence, everyone is amazed at how much you have done for Yolanda," said Facundo. "They knew you had helped with our twins, but this is different, and they now accept and admire you."

Prudence was quite surprised, "Thank you, Facundo, but how was it different? I only did what was needed."

"I know, but other people were involved this time, and they saw the difficulty of the situation. In fact, they found it truly frightening and disgusting. Prudence, they watched how hard you worked and how organized you were. They truly admire you. And, not only that, but Jorge Luis constantly tells me how proud he is of you. His eyes light up when he talks about you. He's madly in love with you, Prudence."

She stepped in front of him, looking straight into his eyes. She really wanted to know, and she trusted Facundo, "But, how can that be? He's always so crotchety and sometimes standoffish with me. Are you sure?"

"Be patient. He has a lot to deal with right now, and his mother is worrying him. She is so despondent and difficult."

"I'm sorry. Thank you for telling me. It has been hard since Señor Sandoval died." She stood up on tiptoes and gave Facundo a kiss on the cheek. She turned back to her work as he walked out with a smile.

Everyone in the pueblo now knew her, trusted her, and admired her. Aldiana did not know much about what was happening except for the twins. She had not made an attempt to get to know Prudence. She did grudgingly respect her, but she still considered her the foreigner and, worse, a heathen. However, to the pueblo, she was no longer the stranger in town.

Although Aldiana did hear some of the gossip from Teresa, the cook, she did not know much and did not ask.

One day Jorge Luis sat down beside her and began to talk about how Prudence had stepped in and took care of poor Yolanda. Aldiana, hearing that, began to get a queasy feeling in the middle of her stomach. He continued, "Mamá, the townspeople have been so impressed with what she has done that she is respected and considered one of them now."

Fiarela walked in on the end of the conversation before her mother could respond, "Yes, I heard the people thought the whole thing was dreadful. I know she saved Yolanda's life. When I visited, Yolanda looked half dead, pale as a ghost, bruised all over, and skinny as a rail. I would kill my husband if he treated me like that."

Jorge Luis looked at her and smiled but thought, *Oh, God, Fiarela, if you only knew. I hope you don't ever.*

Aldiana had always looked at Prudence as a servant, a foreigner. She did not belong to the hacienda, so why would she make an attempt to know her. She grudgingly admitted that she had heard good things about her.

"I've heard from Teresa about how admired she is with the people in the pueblo, but isn't that what we expect of our servants?" Aldiana said.

"Good heavens, Mother, with all due respect, you can't be serious. You know she isn't a servant. Surely, you have recognized how educated and professional she is. She has taught Fiarela long enough for you to know how competent she is - really, Mother, it disappoints me to hear you talk like that," said Jorge Luis.

"Me too, Mamá." Upset over what she had heard, Fiarela said, "I know it has been very hard for you since Papá died. I miss him so much, too, but it embarrasses me to hear what you just said. Prudence has been so patient and kind to me. She's not just a teacher, but a real friend."

Aldiana came back with, "Really now children, don't get carried away with your generosity toward Prudence. I do admire her work, but she is definitely not of our class or our society, and, Jorge Luis, it's time for you to seriously consider marriage."

Jorge Luis gave his mother a dark look but refrained from responding. He was thankful that Edgardo was not there to hear this. *I don't want this to blow up into a family war, and I doubt if Edgardo would have held back his feelings or words. What is wrong with Mother that she is so prejudiced?*

He said to his mother, "Mamá, I am losing patience. I will always love you, but, when I choose, and I mean when *I choose a wife*, I will expect you to love her as I will love her and treat her as beautifully as you treat others."

"I'm sorry, Son, but I insist you marry a well-behaved Californio, a good Christian Catholic - not a heathen, and no Indian." She rose from her chair and walked out, leaving two very frustrated young people. Fiarela rolled her eyes at her brother.

"Stop listening to your head and hear your heart for once. No matter who you choose, you've got to get your courage up. Mother won't like her anyway."

Jorge Luis nodded, recognizing she was right. He leaned over and kissed her on the top of her head. "Thanks, little sister. I love you," he said as he left, feeling buoyed up, supported, and hopeful.

Aldiana knew, from hearing Teresa relate the goings on, how much the pueblo admired and respected Prudence. She considered that hearsay. She thought of her still as the foreigner and a heathen.

25
The Chest and Another Try

Edgardo was exhausted emotionally and physically from the funeral, two months of intense hard work with the ranch, all the legalities associated with his father's death, and, on top of all that, that horrible problem of the violent drunk Alberto.

He thought about the last couple of months, as he dragged himself up the stairs and into his bedroom. He excused the servant, who had been sitting with Emilianito while he slept. Edgardo slipped silently into his bed, which was warm and inviting. The *mucama*, Consuelo, had wrapped hot rocks and heated his bed with them. He lay relaxed, warmed from the wrapped rocks at his feet. He listened to his son's soft breathing in and out and fell into a deep sweet sleep.

He awoke from a dream in the middle of the night – a dream of a chest. He saw it clearly, just as he had seen it as a child. Now he was awake. He had almost forgotten it with all the turmoil and extra work demanded of him and Jorge Luis. He remembered the accumulation of events that implied something about being Jewish - the six-pointed stars on the old graves and Marco knowing most of their Friday night tradition. *Marco was Jewish, wasn't he? Why was it all so secretive? It didn't seem to bother Marco to tell me. How did it involve his family?* He wondered if the chest had a connection. He could still see it from his dream. *Where is it? I thought I knew, but I'm not sure. I know I would recognize it. It's smaller than our old, big trunks. Could it be in one of the storage rooms? Maybe the stables. I'll check around tomorrow.*

With that decision made, he slept soundly until, suddenly; he awoke with a start. *Oh, lord. What time is it?* He lit a candle and picked up his grandfather's watch off the nightstand to check the time.

It's midnight. Everyone should be asleep. Maybe I can find that small antique chest now.

He walked over to check little Nito in his crib, straightened his blanket, and then added a soft woolen one since it was quite cold. The small fire had gone out in the fireplace. His long nightshirt was cotton, not as warm as wool would have been, so he grabbed a warm robe, tied it securely, pulled on warm boots, a woolen hat, and silently slipped out of his room. He felt a little guilty about sneaking around, yet ready to tackle the task.

As he made his way down the dark hallways with just the flickering candle and creeping shadows, he thought about his experience that morning in the stable with Juan. He had explained to Juan about looking for the old chest of his dad's and had he possibly seen it?

Juan had answered, "No, I don't remember ever seeing a chest like that. There is an old trunk out here in the storage room, but it is full of horse blankets. You can check the storage, but it seems to me that it most likely would be up at the house and, maybe, in your dad's own rooms."

Edgardo had thanked Juan, and did rummage through the storage, but found nothing. Therefore, he had decided to check the storage room right now while everyone was asleep. Juan was surely right after all.

Edgardo walked as quietly as possible, listening for any noises of the large household. All was silent as he stealthily moved through the dark hallways. He went down the stairs, through the kitchen area, grabbed an apple out of the fruit bowl on his way, and stuffed it into the pocket of his bathrobe. *If Emilianito wakes up, I'll give him one. He loves apples.* He moved on and into the wing that housed the servants and the storage room.

No sounds were heard in the hallway when he found and entered the room. He lit another candle and placed it safely off to the side in order to allow enough light to survey the jumble of stuff piled in there. Within minutes he noticed what looked to be a trunk. *It looks too big, like the one in the stables. I'll move it out from under all that stuff and see what's inside.* He moved aside, an old hand-carved headboard, a delicate, antique tea table with a broken leg, and a small broken-down settee. The trunk was covered in dust but, to his surprise, it was unlocked. He wiped it off, lifted the lid and sighed in disappointment when he saw only old quilts occupying it. Nevertheless, he rummaged through the trunk and picked out two quilts, one for Nito and one for himself. He closed the trunk, blew out the candle, left the stuff the way it was, and slipped out of the room.

Suddenly, Edgardo stopped, holding his breath upon hearing the soft closing of a door, and then footsteps moving toward him. He stood frozen with nowhere to hide. He covered the candle with one hand. At the last minute, he removed it to shine directly into the young face of Danilo.

"Danilo, what the hell are you doing coming out of Loretta's room at this hour?"

In the candlelight, Edgardo watched a deep red flush flood over

Danilo's face.

"Sorry, Boss. I – I –," said Danilo in a low voice, lowering his eyes, expressing shame.

"Hmm – are you two serious about each other or is this just a pastime?" Edgardo was not sure whether he should be angry or sympathetic.

"No pastime, Boss, very serious," whispered Danilo, trying to shrink back into the shadows, "But her parents think little of me."

"Look kid, I understand. I will see what I can do to help. Sneaking around is not the way to do anything. Now, get going. No more of this. You have to be up early for work."

"*Sí, sí*, thank you, Señor Edgardo," Danilo said, still embarrassed. Not looking at Edgardo, he slinked away.

A deep feeling of loss settled tight in Edgardo's chest. A memory washed over him and took hold. Before they were allowed to consummate their marriage, he and Ramona were required to sleep on the same floor but far apart. *I didn't dare get up and go near her. I knew he wouldn't, but I was scared to death Shadowhawk might slit my throat. Each night we slept closer and closer until that final night. Her parents left us to be alone, and I thought I would die of desire - watching the rays of the moonlight caressing her body as she slowly came to me. She was all I ever dreamed of. We lay on a bed of soft bear fur, and I could have loved her forever. Lucky Danilo -- he has his love to hold. My arms are empty.* He let out a deep, lonely sob, treaded lightly back to his room, and into an empty bed that was no longer warm.

When he awoke the next morning, the sun was up - full in its brightness coming through the open window. A slight cool breeze swept over Edgardo's cheeks and forehead. He moved and slowly opened his eyes. Once open, he realized how late he had overslept. He glanced over at the crib to see Emilianito happily playing. Edgardo sat up to watch him intently – his concentration, his physical movements. His heart leaped when he saw clearly his nose, hair, and ears matching his wife's, in this child of theirs.

He's such a good little kid. I'm so grateful to have him. I would have nothing if it weren't for him. Edgardo stood up, rubbed his neck to get the night twists out, and stepped over to the crib. Emilianito pulled himself up, and stood, hanging onto the top rail, looking up at his dad. He began to try to climb out of his crib.

"No, no, little guy. You're too small yet." Edgardo lifted him out and put him down on his bed to dress him. All the while, he was concerned about being late, as he feared Jorge Luis would come down on him hard as he'd been doing lately. *Being the new hacendado, I know he's under pressure with all the requirements and demands. He's really being run ragged, and I have not always helped much. He's having a hard time accepting that he is the law. His is the final word on anything. That is a huge responsibility, and he's missing Prudence, and I don't want to add any more hardship.* Nito was demanding attention, and he needed to get him dressed and delivered to the kitchen. His mother and *ama de cria*, Amalia, would be waiting and wondering why they were so late.

"Come on, kid," he said, dressing him. He washed his little face and his own with water from the basin quickly and began to brush Nito's hair with a very soft brush. Nito grabbed the brush and hit himself in the head trying to be independent. "Hey, good job, Nito. Here, let Papá finish." Edgardo ran his fingers through his own to tame his unruly hair. Picking Emilianito up, he carried him to the door, feeling a delight in his tiny warm body against his. He set him down in the hallway and talked constantly to him while finding their way down to the kitchen, "Okay, Nito, we're going to the kitchen. Which way do we go?" Nito pointed correctly. "You're right. Come on now, you show me the way." They made a game of finding his grandmother and, in the game, teaching him the labyrinth of the hallways.

In the larger part of the kitchen, where there was a box of playthings, Edgardo gave Emilianito over to Aldiana and Amalia. His grandmother took him immediately and turned to Amalia, asking her if she would look after him until she returned from the chapel. Upon hearing that, Edgardo wondered, *Oh man, maybe that will give me the time I need.*

"Amalia, do you have everything you need for Emilianito?" asked Edgardo.

"Yes, thank you. We'll have fun, won't we Nito?" She reached out to Aldiana, who pressed him into her arms, "Señora, you really should eat something before you go out to the chapel."

"I'm fine. Teresa will call me for lunch."

Edgardo, trying not to look impatient, quickly wrapped an apple and a tortilla in a napkin, saying, "Mother, I want you to take this. We worry about you." He hugged her and brushed her with a quick kiss, hoping she would get going. He did not have much time left. *I've got to hurry now, but I don't want them to suspect anything.* He wanted to look perfectly natural, so he walked over to Nito, already in his toy box. He leaned down and gave him a kiss. Edgardo raised up his hand and poked his cheek, saying, "Kiss, Nito, kiss here."

Nito looked up, smiled, and gave him a big, sloppy kiss. Edgardo walked out, wiping his cheek, laughing. *That's my kid. Now I'd better hurry.*

I don't think they caught on to anything. Knowing that his mother would be in the chapel for some time, he did not go to work, even though he knew he'd be in trouble for not showing up. He glanced around to make sure no one was around to see him and hurried to find that chest. He took the stairs two and three at a time and sped his way to his parent's bedroom suite.

Standing in his parents' living area, he slowly surveyed the room. *Everything feels so empty without Papá. I sure miss him. He used to sit reading on that antique settee that Mother was so proud of. It came all the way from Spain. The import taxes were so high; I wonder how they managed it. Once in a while, I used to come in and sit down, and we would talk. He would pull the rope on the wall and Teresa would bring us tea and fruit. How I enjoyed those times with him. I know he didn't approve of my spending so much time with Shadowhawk, but he never forbade me.* His eyes caught sight of the old brass spittoon. *I wanted to see him spit into it so bad, but I could never catch him. He wouldn't swear in front of us either. He was a true gentleman. Papá, I miss you so.* There was a huge oak roll-top desk on the far wall. *Oh, that desk reminds me, Jorge Luis and I have to go through all the stuff in it. Nothing's the same anymore. No, the chest is in the bedroom, not in here. I know exactly where it is. It flashed through my mind – his wardrobe, that's where.*

He quickly made his way across what, in the old days, had been a plush Persian rug, well-worn now. It lay under an antique mahogany table, which held a fresh floral arrangement.

I'm glad to see Mamá is still keeping the vase full. No flowers now, but she cut sprays of tamarack - how unusual. But that's Mamá, creative. He passed around the table and peeked through the bedroom door just to be safe, although he had heard nothing.

Once in the bedroom, he stopped again before he headed to the antique wardrobe. He stood admiring the hand-carved bed of his father's, which had belonged to his grandfather. The previous carpenter had carved the animals and trees of the countryside, the oaks with herds of elk, the manzanita, and the river willows. There were deer, grizzlies, antelope, a wolf and coyote. Edgardo had always wanted that old headboard. Above it was a large, wooden cross, also handmade. Edgardo had always loved that big bed. Memories flooded his inner vision of childhood mornings - of him crawling into bed with his parents and sometimes his siblings. He remembered breakfasts eaten there as a special treat. *How lucky Papá was. Mamá slept with him all of her life until he was too sick.* A swift depression hit with a heavy desire for his beloved. He stood up from sitting on the edge of the bed and let it go as he looked at the tall windows, with heavy brocade drapes, which were pulled aside to let the light softly flow through the sheer curtains. Edgardo could see the myriad of dust particles dancing in the light rays hitting the floor. *I remember trying to grab them when I was little*, he thought, feeling a fond sense of nostalgia.

The wardrobe was against the opposite wall. With a deep sigh, he took hold of its golden doorknobs. Deftly opening the aged, ill-fitting doors, he knelt to pull out the chest, which was back underneath the clothing against the wall. He stealthily looked around behind him, just in case, and then pushed aside his father's clothes and peered in. There was the chest. The clothing had hidden it all these years.

That's it! The one I remember. Boy, it's dusty and sure smells musty and stale. It's been in that wardrobe a long time. I'd better rush it back to my room before someone discovers me. Funny, how much smaller it looks now. I remember it being bigger.

In his room, he shoved it under his bed, but, suddenly realized that he had no key to open it. *Damn! I have to go back again. Where would she hide it? Of course, her jewelry box.*

Once again, he quietly crept through the hallways to his parent's suite. He cracked the door to peek in, expecting, possibly, *la mucama* to be working, but Consuelo was not there. He made straight for the jewelry box, which sat on a long antique dresser. The box was a focal point in the room, constructed of a highly-polished, dark, rich wood and painted with exquisite miniature roses. It was full of jewelry.

Diós mío, she has so much. Papá was more than generous with her. I wish I could have given Ramona fine things. She deserved so much and got so little. He paused for a minute as a flow of pain and guilt washed through his heart.

The key was in plain sight. He lifted it out, turning to go back to his room – Jorge Luis stood in the doorway, hands on hips, stiff, with jaws clenched, watching him. Edgardo was speechless, but not Jorge Luis.

"What the hell are you doing stealing from Mother? I ought to beat the tar out of you. Okay, Edgardo, out with it. Let's see what you took."

"I haven't stolen anything. It's just a key. Come with me to my room, and I'll show you what it goes to. And – I'll explain what I suspect."

"You're crazy. You 'suspect' – what are you talking about? You've crossed the line this time, little brother," said Jorge Luis, but as he followed him, his anger subsided into anguish. *I don't know how much more I can take. Papá why did you have to go? You were my backbone, and now this?*

"Here we are," said Edgardo. "Come in and sit down on my bed and shut up. This is not going to be easy to get through that thick skull of yours."

"I'm sitting, I'm sitting. Now start talking, and this better be good."

Edgardo pulled the chest out from under his bed. Jorge Luis' eyes widened, then narrowed in puzzlement, "That's just an old chest of *Papá's*. What are you doing with it?"

"Did Father ever let you see what was in it?" asked Edgardo.

"No, I only saw it once. He never mentioned what was in it, and I never saw it again – okay, I'll listen. This will be some story, I imagine."

Edgardo started his explanation with what first piqued his curiosity and stimulated his growing suspicion – the Friday night dinner with Marco, who was Jewish. Edgardo stopped and stared intently at his brother, saying, "He seemed to know much of our ritual and joined right in, remember?"

Jorge Luis interrupted, "Jewish -- this has something to do with being Jewish, in knowing a lot of our ritual? Give me a break. That's nonsense!"

"You, brother, were too occupied with keeping an eye on Cecilio going after Prudence to notice anything. Now don't interrupt, but listen." Edgardo told him the entire suspicious story, especially about the stars on the oldest graves in the family cemetery.

"I've heard enough," said Jorge Luis, "Open the damned chest."

"Hold on, hold on. You're making me nervous. This is an old key. It's rusty." He took a deep breath and inserted the key, wiggling it several times before it caught.

"*Jesús y María*," said Jorge Luis, "You're slow. You're making me nervous. What if we get caught? There will be hell to pay and you and your cock-eyed story – what if it's all stupid and not true at all?"

"I got it." Edgardo removed the key while Jorge Luis sat tapping his foot, looking annoyed. Edgardo set the key carefully on the nightstand.

Jorge Luis sat up straighter, tensed, took a deep breath and said, "*Por favor de Santa Atocha*, open that chest."

Edgardo pressed his hands down on the top of the lid, and turned to look at an obviously impatient brother. "Maybe Mother should do this? Now, I'm feeling like a thief. We shouldn't be doing this," he said.

Jorge Luis stood up with a fist tightly closed, ready to use it, and looked at Edgardo. In a low, intense voice he said, "Open that chest before I lose it."

"Okay, okay." Edgardo slowly lifted the lid. Peering in, he suddenly exclaimed, "It's there, the ring. I used to play with it until I got into trouble for it. Look, I'll show you."

Jorge Luis saw a beautiful silver cross on the top of a large man's ring, "It looks old, probably our ancestor's, maybe Grandpa's."

Edgardo opened up the ring and deep inside, well-hidden, was a solid gold Star of David.

"Oh, my god," whispered Jorge Luis. He looked up at Edgardo with knitted brows and eyes clouded with concern, "What have our parents done? Lord, Edgardo, aren't we facing enough without this?" He felt as if his energy was draining out of his body, deep into the earth. What would this do to his family on top of everything else? *This is just too much.* "Okay, Edgardo, what else is in that chest?"

"A lot. Here's a parchment paper with a list, but it is all in Hebrew. I can tell the first item." He pulled out a candlestick, "It's called a Menorah, but I don't know what it is used for."

"Edgardo, we're not going to know any of that stuff. We ought to confront Mother. You wear that ring, and I'll carry the chest. She's in the chapel."

"How do you think she might react? I don't want to hurt her, and this might be a big shock," said Edgardo, looking concerned and worried now, after what he had done.

"We have to do it. Well – maybe we don't have to do it right now, but how will we bring up the subject to her? No matter when we do it, it's going to be a blow for Mother. This chest, obviously, has been hidden a very long time. It's all your fault, Brother. But since you've found it, we need to know what it all means. We'll be as careful as possible with Mother – come on, put on that old ring and let's go find her. I'll carry the chest. Hurry up, before we chicken out."

Aldiana was kneeling and praying in front of the altar. The mid-morning sunlight, shining through the windows, bathed the statue of the Virgin Mary and Aldiana in spectacular rays of sunlight and shadows, creating a look of divine love from above. Aldiana, deep into her prayers, was startled to hear someone entering the chapel. Looking over her shoulder, she was astonished to see her two boys. *They never have interrupted me before. What are they doing here?* She started to get up, pulling up her skirt so as not to step on it, when she saw what they had. "Where did you get that? Oh, God, help me," she murmured as she doubled over and fell unconscious onto the tiled floor.

"Mother! Help me, Edgardo," said Jorge Luis as he put down the chest and ran to her.

"What have we done?" said Edgardo, choking up.

"The shock was too great. Help lift Mother into my arms. While I carry her, you take the chest." Jorge Luis, as usual, cut off his feelings and his thoughts. He needed to get her into the house. That was all. His concern showed on this face and in how carefully he carried her. Edgardo felt terribly guilty and was on the point of breaking into tears as he trudged along behind his brother, thinking, *What have I done? How could I not have realized how she would react?*

They carefully made their way to the kitchen and found Teresa, who was horrified upon seeing them, "Oh, my god. I was so worried this would happen if she didn't start to eat better. She's been spending all her time in the chapel. Take her upstairs, and I will make some tea and sustenance. In fact, I will bring enough for all of you. You'll need it too."

Once in the bedroom, Jorge Luis carefully laid her on the bed while Edgardo brought a thick, warm wool blanket to cover her.

Jorge Luis, feeling numb, turned to his brother, saying, "Listen, I think you'd better go get Fiarela. She should be here before we try to talk to Mother."

"You're right. What about Prudence? They are both at Maria's helping with the twins."

"No, no, this is a private family matter. Just tell Fiarela that Mother has taken sick, and we need her here at home. Explain everything on the way home, but don't say anything to Prudence. I'll see that Mother is taken care of," said Jorge Luis.

Edgardo nodded, left the room and headed for the carriage barn. He harnessed up Buñalito to a small carriage and left as soon as possible. He felt torn up. *What have I done? I almost killed my mother. Everything I do turns out wrong. I seem to make everything worse. Why didn't I leave things alone? It's all my fault. Why can't I do things like my brother? He looks at me like I was still his little nuisance brother - no good to anyone.*

"Come on, Buñalito, you're slowing down. We need to hurry," he said as he gave his horse a little slap of the reins and moved him into a smooth gallop. Sitting outside on the driver's seat, with the fresh air pouring over his face and hair, he felt his mind clearing, and he worked out how to tell his sister without scaring her too much. It felt like he reached Facundo's much quicker than ever before. *I hope I can carry this off,* he thought, as he rushed up the front stairs and knocked on the door.

When Edgardo pushed the door open slowly, he could see Fiarela holding one of the babies, a boy named Tomás, while María nursed the other, Luisa. Maria's and Facundo's twin babies were thriving. Fiarela and Prudence enjoyed their time caring for them and helping with the other five children. Prudence was teaching the eldest girls to sew, while the three boys were pretending to be big men by carrying in wood and stacking it by the fireplace and stove. When they heard the knock at the door and saw Edgardo, one of the boys ran to welcome him. The other two boys stopped their work in anticipation of fun, but, seeing his somber face and sad eyes, their little faces changed to disappointment and consternation.

Fiarela had glanced to see that it was Edgardo and then looked back at the baby she was holding. "Come on in, Brother," she said. Upon hearing the sudden silence of the children, she turned and stared at him, "Are you all right?"

"Hello, everyone." He tried to give something of a smile and said, "How industrious you all are. I'm impressed to see that, and you boys are quickly learning to be big, helpful men."

The three boys and two girls responded with big smiles and bright eyes, but the adults looked at Edgardo with frowns instead.

Edgardo turned to them and said, "Actually, I'm not all right. Fiarela, Mother has taken ill, and you are needed at home."

"Is there anything I can do? I would be glad to come and help," said Prudence.

"No, no, but thank you. You continue helping María. She needs you. Oh, by the way, have you heard anything from your uncle or cousin?" He waited, glancing around somewhat impatiently. *God, I wish I could have given Ramona a little cottage like this. We could have been so happy.*

Prudence shook her head, saying, "No, I haven't heard a word. I'll let you know if I do. I do hope it's nothing serious with your mother. If you need me, I'll come as fast as I can."

Since Benito had driven Fiarela to Facundo's and then returned to the hacienda, she had no horse to ride home. She climbed up on the driver's seat with her brother. On the way home, Edgardo slowly, and in detail, explained the whole story to Fiarela, who could not grasp what he was really talking about.

"You frighten me, Edgardo. I don't understand any of this. It's too confusing. I never heard the word 'Jewish' before. I don't know what that is," she snuggled closer and felt safer with her big brother holding her. "How sick is Mother, and what are we supposed to do?"

Edgardo pulled her close to him, saying, "Don't worry, *Hermanita*, Mother has had an emotional shock. She is not ill, but we need her to explain about the things hidden in the chest, what it all means to us, and why she was so agitated."

They both rode in silence as Edgardo kept the horse at a fast pace and with Fiarela attempting to keep her fears abated. Her mind raced with all kinds of terrible scenes. Being next to Edgardo, and not alone on her own horse or in the carriage, gave her a solid feeling of support and caring.

The hacienda was quiet when they arrived. The morning chores were completed, so the servants were taking their break, drinking tea, and smoking out on the kitchen patio.

Fiarela and Edgardo rushed to enter the front door where they met Teresa, in front of the stairs, carrying a tray of tea and a snack for their mother. "Oh, I'm so glad to see you are here. Jorge Luis is upstairs with your mother. She is conscious, but very upset still, and he is trying to keep her calm. Please do not agitate her more. I will wait and come in after you" she said. When they reached Aldiana's room, she whispered, "Now, go quietly, and I will follow." She stood back to lean against the hallway wall, as the tray was heavy.

Two anxious, worried faces nodded and turned to go in. The door shut softly.

Teresa closed her eyes, taking a deep breath and waited respectfully and quietly, praying that all would be well. She would go in when called for, no matter how long it took. There was a wall niche above a table by her side, which held a statue of Our Lady of Guadalupe. She set the tray on the table, knelt and prayed for Aldiana, her lifelong friend and *dueña*.

26
The Outing

iarela and Edgardo paused before opening the door to their mother's bedroom suite. Looking at each other, Edgardo gave his sister a loving pat on the back. Both took a deep breath, and then they tiptoed into the room.

Teresa waited in the hallway to be called in with the tray of tea and a small repast. She wanted to be very respectful of whatever was going on. She felt badly. She had warned Aldiana several times about staying so long in the chapel without having eaten anything. *I've been so worried about her.* She wrung her hands, hoping they would call her quickly.

Inside her mother's suite, glancing across the room at her mother, Fiarela couldn't help it, but ran to her, and dropped on her knees at her bedside, crying out, "Mamá, are you all right? What happened?"

Fiarela glanced questioningly at Jorge Luis, who was still sitting holding his mother's hand and lost in thought, while his other hand held his head, covering his eyes. She had never seen her older brother look so despondent, and he appeared to be unaware of them. He didn't look up or acknowledge either of them. Fiarela turned and stared back at Edgardo, standing behind her.

The room was dark, reflecting the heavy feelings of desperation that filled the room. Fiarela shuddered, looked around the room, and noticed the two windows covered with dark blue velvet drapes. She quickly pulled them open. The windows seemed to her to sigh in relief, and light reigned in Aldiana's sanctuary.

Edgardo ignored both Fiarela and Jorge Luis. He was too concerned about his mother. "Mamá, we are terribly worried about you," said Edgardo, trying to maintain his composure and not break down with guilt. "Teresa brought you some tea. Can we help you to sit up to drink some?" He went out into the hallway and asked Teresa to please come in.

Teresa came in very quietly, and placed the tea and food with care on the table, "*Señora,* if you need anything, I will be in the kitchen, waiting."

She backed out silently.

Jorge Luis suddenly lifted his head, pulled his shoulders up straight, now coming out of his dark confusion and fear, turned, and gave a glance at Edgardo and Fiarela. He turned back to his mother and said, "Please, Mamá, let me help you sit up to drink your tea, and then we can talk."

Aldiana lifted her head and looked at each of her three children. Tears streamed down her face and little strands of gray hair loosened from her bun, now sticking to her wet cheeks. The light filled the room, showing off her hand-carved headboard. Emiliano had it specially made for her as a wedding gift, but she was oblivious of the simple beauty surrounding her. Her three children held their breath with anticipation and fear. Suddenly, Aldiana threw off her blanket, sat up, and covered her face with both hands, bursting out with, "Oh, my God, oh, my God, I am so sorry. I prayed and prayed for guidance, but it fell on deaf ears. I couldn't go to Father Serrano. I would never put any of you in jeopardy."

The children saw such anguish in her face and heard her weak voice shake with fear. No one said a word. They sat, watching in shock and silence. They glanced around the room to avoid looking at their mother in such a state.

They noticed the oriental rug, worked in blues, was showing its wear. The European wallpaper covered with the Fleur de Lis design, still regal looking, was losing its color and had seen better days. They realized they had not paid attention to this aging before. No matter how worn the room was, it still retained its beauty.

Fiarela sat stiffly with her hands in her lap clasped so tight that the circulation was almost cut off. Finally, Edgardo made an attempt to speak, but Aldiana went on, "My whole life has been a lie. I've been so afraid. I'm going to die and go to hell forever."

The three siblings jerked and sat upright in their chairs. They sat stiffly and frowned. They looked at each other with astonished consternation. Their chests tightened with growing fear.

Not believing what he heard, Edgardo interrupted, "*Adorada* Mamá, please, don't talk like that. You are frightening us. Everyone respects you highly. You've always been wonderful and loving with us."

"Mamá," said Jorge Luis, "You aren't making any sense. Papá loved you dearly, and your religious devotion has been exemplary. I have always known you loved me."

"Mamá, here, sit up a little and take your tea. You worry me," said Fiarela, getting up to help her, and giving her brothers a puzzled look.

Jorge Luis stood up and took charge, "*Hermano*, go downstairs and inform Teresa we will have lunch here, and bring Nito up to eat with us. He will help calm his grandmother." Jorge Luis took over from Fiarela and helped his mother to a chair next to her family's old oak table, which stood in front of the window. A rocking chair sat on one side that, at one time or another, for three generations, had held all the Sandoval children. The other chair was upholstered and comfortable for reading or writing on the table. The color was dark oak. However, there were a few water-stained areas and a few chips on the edges made by small boys with little hammers or play knives.

Aldiana remembered her grandmother working on her embroidery there. Occasionally, she would go out into the garden to sketch a favorite flower for her work, and the table sometimes smelled like lanolin from being cleaned. In fact, as a child, she had to learn to clean it by getting down on her knees and rubbing lanolin on the trunk and legs with their scary bird-claw feet.

Aldiana loved her table and frequently sat at it. That table was the only place Aldiana could become quiet and would occasionally feel the presence of her dear departed mother. If and when her mother appeared, the atmosphere in her room smoothed out and was enlivened. Aldiana didn't ordinarily see her mother but always felt her presence, her energy. Generally, she'd feel her first, very softly, on her arm and shoulder like a soft, comforting breeze. A few times she saw before her a form of pallid, vibrating light. The energy always felt loving and supportive, and her mother would impress upon her insights and understanding. Feeling buoyed up was always the result. She felt her now, immediately, because she felt a soft infusion of a calm strength settle over her. Her mother had been a strong woman with great inner-authority. Aldiana knew then that she could face what was coming.

Fiarela quickly retrieved a round tablecloth to place on the table, which was made of fine cotton and embroidered with her mother's favorite flowers from the garden.

Aldiana reacted with more tears saying, "Thank you, Fi, dear. That was Mother's and her embroidery was always perfect. I could never do it that well. If only she were physically here; she would know what to do."

At that point, a light knock was heard and in walked Adela carrying a tray with silverware, napkins, a bowl of chopped eggs with olive oil and seasonings, slices of lamb, olives, bread and a plate of fruit. She also set on the table a pitcher of chocolate and small cups. She was almost through setting the table when Edgardo walked back in with Nito, who ran to his grandmother and climbed up on her lap. He paused for a moment, looked over toward the window, and smiled and waved, as usual. Since his vocabulary was meager, everyone had to wait to find out whom he waved at until he learned to speak more clearly. He then laid his head upon her warm, soft chest. Everyone waited quietly, knowing he had seen someone in spirit. Could it have been Papá, they wondered? Later, Nito looked up. Upon seeing his highchair, he sat up, and looking at his grandmother said, "*Abue, Abue*, me eat, too," while reaching out toward the table with his hands. Seeing her nod, he climbed down, ran to his chair, and climbed up onto it so fast that everyone, including Aldiana, laughed.

Jorge Luis, when he noticed everyone waiting, began to say grace since his mother was obviously indisposed. Suddenly, his mother dropped her head on the table.

"*Diós mío,* Mamá, what's wrong?" he asked his mother, while Fiarela and Edgardo sat wide-eyed with incomprehension.

"Everything, everything, the grace is wrong for us."

"Mamá, saying grace is never wrong. We've been saying grace our whole lives," said Jorge Luis.

"Almost every group of people in this world say some form of grace, even our Indians here," said Edgardo. "In Shadowhawk's family, they always said grace with a 'thank you' for what was put before them."

"I know, I know, but . . ." she whimpered.

The siblings looked at each other, sighing deeply with lack of understanding and deep concern.

Jorge Luis thought and felt deep within himself that, *Thank God, your father is gone and he didn't have to experience this on top of his illness, but I needed him.* He felt lost. *Papá, where are you? I need you. I don't understand this with Mother. Never in my life have I seen her like this, and I can't do a thing about it. I'm supposed to take your place now. How can I? I don't have your experience. I don't have your knowledge, and I certainly don't have your wisdom. I need help to calm Mother down. Please, Papá. Please, God, help me.* Then it came to him. He felt a surge of confidence. He stood up and took charge, saying, "Nito is hungry. Let's eat." He turned to his mother, "We love you no matter what. Let's all relax and enjoy the meal."

There was no small talk. Peace and calm reigned, with everyone eating quietly, though deep in thought. Little Nito was the only one who occasionally engaged in conversation, which brought the overall tension into a quieter place.

The small, delicious meal combined with Teresa's calming tea settled Aldiana's anxiety. In her inner-mind and heart, she began to let go of so much fear. She truly realized she had a loving and supportive family. Emiliano, her true love, was gone, but she still had her children. *They will not turn against me for what I am about to tell them.* She felt more at ease, and with little, innocent Nito in his highchair happily eating, Aldiana began to relax somewhat.

A short time later, the table was cleared, and all put to order. Nito was taken out for his nap. Aldiana looked at each grown child with a little more composure, but it was hard to hold back new tears. She sucked in her breath to get up her courage to say, "What do you need to know? Where shall I begin?"

Fiarela, brushing her hair back, took a deep breath and tried to slow down her hammering heart, "*Mamá,* are we Catholic or what are we? What is happening?"

Aldiana felt a blow to her solar plexus, as if the air had been knocked out of her. She hadn't expected something so straight and to the point so quickly. Her true identity had been hidden her whole life. Now she would be exposed. She closed her eyes with a staggering thought, *I can't hide any longer. Oh, God, help me do this.*

"No, Fiarela, you are not truly Catholic. All three of you, by birth, are Jewish." She stopped to gauge the reaction of each of her children, "In the Jewish culture and religion, if the mother is Jewish, then all the children automatically are."

Gasps were heard from all three and then silence. Fiarela began to fidget in her chair, and Jorge Luis stared without blinking, appearing almost absent.

"Then our grandmother was Jewish?" asked Edgardo.

"Yes, Son, but your other grandmother, your father's mother, was not Jewish. So your father was not born Jewish even though his father, your grandfather, was. That is why your father was able to join the military and ended up here in Northern California."

"¡Madre Purísima! Why has this been so secretive, so hidden away? Why did the family have to denounce their heritage and religion?" Jorge Luis paused, trying to think. "The Inquisition? - - Out here, so far from the mother country, Spain?" He was grasping to understand the implications of what his mother was saying.

"I don't expect you to understand, *hijos,* but back in the preconquest days, our ancestors suffered horribly. Grandmother was the one who used to tell me the history, as I spent so much time with her when my mother was busy working. I would sit and listen and get so scared." Aldiana pushed her hair off her cheeks and tucked it back into her bun. She was feeling a little calmer now that she was finally telling her family's history. She continued, "Grandma told me they'd been Jewish forever and owned large properties and prosperous businesses for hundreds of years in Spain."

Aldiana paused. The tears that sparkled in her eyes were wiped away quickly by her hand. "Grandma had a hard time telling this part of the story." She looked down and closed her eyes for a moment. She then said, "I will, too - In Spain, the Grand Inquisitor Tomás Torquemada, was infamous for his cruelty and his extreme torture. Grandma said that he petitioned the monarchs for years to expel the Jews because the church considered them heretics. Evidently, on March 20, 1492 – grandmother never forgot a detail – Torquemada presented a draft decree to the monarchs. They signed his decree - the Edict of Expulsion on March 31, 1492. That edict required all Jews to convert to Catholicism, speak Spanish, depart, or die. If anyone did not comply within four months, all their properties and businesses would be confiscated, and they would face the death penalty."

At once, all three children began to ask questions, but Aldiana raised her hand to silence them. After a long sigh, she began to speak again, "Many converted, but more hid their Jewishness and pretended to be Catholic. That is what our family did, but the church with its Holy Inquisition considered the Jews as heretics. So many Jews were sent to the torture chambers and so many killed that my family had to escape to the New World. It was a horrifying and terrible time. Even here, in the New World, our ancestors had to hide their Jewish roots and pretend to be Catholic publicly because the Inquisition followed from Spain - its arm was long. A cousin of my mother was arrested in Los Angeles and burned at the stake."

Attention did not drift from her story.

"No, no, Mamá, that is horrible," said Fiarela, almost breathless. She clasped her hands to her mouth. Her eyes widened in horror. The air felt smothering in the room.

Jorge Luis clenched his fist and felt an anger he had never known, "My god, Mother. That was an atrocity and certainly cannot be called Christian in any sense of the word. I had no idea," he said, rubbing his hands through his hair as if he might tear it out. He looked frantic.

"I had no idea, either," said Edgardo, who slumped down into his chair feeling an oppressiveness washing over him. His lips trembled with a sense of deep betrayal, but then felt a great tenderness for his mother fill him. *How could anyone be treated so brutally?* The thought that it could still happen sent chills up his spine. Since this atrocity had been done in the name of God and the Great Spirit, it was doubly appalling and frightening.

The three siblings sat up attentively. This was a part of her they had never seen or known before. It was a shaky place to be and more was coming. They sat stiffly, afraid to miss anything.

"Mamá, are you still afraid of the Inquisition, even though you have been a perfect Catholic since you were born?" asked Jorge Luis. "And way out here in the frontier of Northern California?" *I've got to be as careful and kind to her as I can. I need to watch my words and be more patient. She doesn't deserve any of this.*

All three immediately noticed their mother's body start shaking as her eyes darted toward the door.

"We are so isolated out here," said Edgardo. "I don't think most people have ever heard of the Inquisition."

Fiarela said, "Mamá, why would you still be in danger?"

"When I listened to her stories, my grandmother would warn me and warn me to keep quiet and never say a word about anything Jewish, because being a heretic was an automatic death sentence. All Jews were looked upon as heretics. Sometimes, at night, I would shake in my bed, cover my head, and pray I wouldn't be found. Remember, Father Junípero Serra, before he built all the missions here in Alta California, was head of the Inquisition in Baja, and all the priests of the missions were trained in methods of hunting out heretics and Jews. I know Father Serrano would not want to, but he could arrest me if he knew." She wiped away the tears off her cheeks and brushed back her loose-flying hair again. She felt much more at ease now that everything was out in the open.

"Oh, no, no, he wouldn't, he couldn't," cried Fiarela.

"But, he might," said Jorge Luis, "If he considered it his Godly duty after he found out." He paused, "I completely understand your fears, Mamá. I don't blame you for not telling us anything. Do you feel able to tell us about the contents of this old chest? I have seen them and am quite anxious to know what they are."

"Sí, Mamá, I've seen them, too. They are most curious," said Edgardo.

"I've never seen them," said Fiarela, her face and voice full of excitement and anticipation.

Aldiana took a deep breath and braced herself, "Hijos, I don't know how much I remember, but I will do my best. We were never allowed to touch the chest at all. It's as old as anyone can remember. Edgardo, dear, put the chest on the table and open it for us, please."

Edgardo cleared off the table, placing the chest on the far side so that he could put the items in front where everyone could see. "Mamá" asked Jorge Luis, "would you like to rest for a while and do this later?"

"No, no, no, let's get it over with. Go ahead, Edgardo."

Edgardo removed the parchment list first. Before he took out the first item, he looked at his mother sadly and compassionately and then at his siblings and said, "Remember, what is in here represents a past that happened, but it isn't written in our history. Our family, as Jewish exiles, originally came to the New World with the title of 'La gente prohibida,' and I found out that the Holy Inquisition has a High Tribunal in Mexico City. Mother's fears are correctly founded because the Franciscan Missionaries are invested with the Spanish Inquisition powers."

His family looked at him with eyes wide with astonishment. Jorge Luis asked, "How on earth did you come to put that together for yourself?"

"After Marco left, I became curious -- thinking about our Friday night dinners, and Papá's funeral. I thought on it and wrote Marco with many questions because he is Jewish. I was lucky to receive his response two days ago." He stopped and looked around at everyone, "Ready? Okay, here is the first item." He took out the small, golden Menorah.

"What a beautiful candle holder," remarked Fiarela.

"Yes, my mother took it out every year sometime before Christmas, and I remember how I loved to watch the candlelight at night in her room. It would flicker shapes against the wall, and I would make up stories about them. But she never told me anything about it that I remember," said Aldiana.

Edgardo reached in and held up a small, silver container that was engraved. It had tiny legs and a lid. Edgardo checked the list and said, "I think this is called an Etrog box. Do you know, Mother?"

"No, but my mother kept it on her dresser. I think it should have a ring inside. I remember my grandmother allowing me to play with it. Open it, please."

When she saw the ring, she exclaimed, "Oh, let me have it. I want to open it. It was my mother's wedding ring. Look, the two clasped hands over the top open, and the word engraved underneath says 'Mazeltov,' which means 'congratulations.' Here, this part opens, too. It is where she kept her wedding document. Everything was hidden behind those clasped hands." She held the ring to her heart and then set it back inside the Etrog. "You know, the engraving on it said 'Carvajal,' which was an ancient family name."

Her three children were silent, immobile with fascination. Edgardo broke the silence by pulling out a few things she did recognize but did not know much about, such as the mezuzah, which is placed on the door and holds a prayer of protection; and the yamulka, a man's small, hat-like cover, which was sewn of wool and so well worn that it was coming unraveled. There was a lace head covering for a woman, which was beautifully wrought with fine, thin thread, as well as a prayer shawl. He pulled out a prayer book, which was written in Hebrew and fashioned with an ivory, hand-carved book cover. Well-known biblical scenes decorated the ivory cover. They noticed the yellowish tinge of the ivory showing its age. There was a Passover plate with Hebrew letters around the edges, and a golden goblet with the Star of David as the nob on its lid.

"Look at that star," said Jorge Luis, "Mamá, it is true then. This is all Jewish."

"*Sí, sí, sí,* Jorge Luis, it truly is. Edgardo, please put everything back, and put the chest into my wardrobe."

"Mamá, why?" said Fiarela. "Why can't we use some of the things in it like the gold candlestick? It would look very pretty on the table. No one would know. Would they?"

"Fiarela, I would never take that chance because I know Father Serrano would recognize it, and, besides, that chest holds my heritage of who I truly am, even if I didn't know it or understand it. I cannot deny it." She turned to Jorge Luis. "You can bury it with me," said Aldiana, finally accepting who she was now once and for all. She felt safer than she had ever felt.

Edgardo picked up and returned everything, then closed and locked the chest, and gave his mother the key. The chest was put to rest in the back of her wardrobe and would never be opened again.

Aldiana, Jorge Luis, and Fiarela sat in silence, lost in their own personal thoughts until Edgardo returned.

Jorge Luis stood up, looked at them all, and reminded them they had to find a solution to this unfortunate situation, "All of us must give thought to how we want to handle this. This is very personal to the family. Mamá, do you know what you want to do?"

"I don't know. Now I understand that, when I was born, I was automatically born Jewish. My mother was Jewish, but I was never raised Jewish, and I don't know how to be Jewish. There is no one else out here who is Jewish," said Aldiana.

"Mamá, you don't have to make a decision right now. Take your time," Jorge Luis said. Looking at his brother and sister, he paused for a moment. "We will love you no matter what you choose," he added as he leaned over and held her. The other two nodded in agreement.

Fiarela, who had been fidgeting with her hands, rubbing them back and forth and then pushing her sleeve up and down, spoke up softly and slowly, "Our Catholic religion is all I know. I'm not going to change, at least not now. Besides, maybe my husband, someday, will be something different, and then what? I don't know what I will end up being." She sighed a barely audible sound and sat with her head bowed.

"For the first time," said Edgardo, looking off into the distance, "I am beginning to understand what Shadowhawk told me a long time ago." Everyone looked at him questioningly, intrigued. "He told me one day, while we were in the sweat lodge, that I did not have the soul of a Catholic, but I didn't have the soul of an Indian, either. Then he stared at me as if he were looking at me from some far place but didn't say anything. I got nervous, frightened a little, and why, I don't know, but I felt guilty. He never mentioned it again, and I was afraid to ask."

Fiarela ran to her brother and hugged him, saying, "I love you. We all love you. You will always be my brother, and I don't care what else you might be."

"Edgardo, go back to Shadowhawk and see what he says now," said Jorge Luis. "Take Nito with you and make his Grandpa happy. You're my brother. You'll always be my brother and that's all there is to it."

"*No lo sé.* I don't know. Here we are, born to be Jewish, but we're Catholic. What are we to learn from all this?" asked Edgardo. "You're right. I will take Emilianito and visit Shadowhawk."

"*Bueno, hijos*, I just cannot make a change at this age. It's too hard. I wouldn't be accepted. I would be ostracized. No one would understand, and how would I learn and from whom? There is no temple anywhere. Here I have my own chapel, which I love. I feel the presence of spirit there, and that's where I find my peace," said Aldiana.

"I'm not sure about you two," said Jorge Luis, who stood up and looked at his siblings, "but I'm satisfied with Mother's decision." He gave his mother a smile and added, "For me, I have no reason to change now. I've got too many responsibilities, and I need to think about forming a family of my own soon. I'm not getting any younger." He said all that deliberately to set a seed into his mother's mind.

Aldiana nodded in agreement, but Fiarela and Edgardo looked at each other in surprise, and then exchanged a knowing look -- with big smiles.

"Oh, *Mijo*, if you are serious, then you must plan a trip and stop in Los Angeles, Mexico City, and, maybe, you will have to go to Spain. You must be quite cautious in choosing a proper wife, one that will fit well into our family and our traditions."

"Forget it, Mother," he said with a furrowed brow and a tone of annoyance. "I'm sure you realize that I could never be away that long. Even with Edgardo's help, the work is overwhelming now that Papá is gone. I don't have time to be running all over the world looking for some woman whom might meet certain specifications for this family. And I won't just accept anyone, just so that I can produce an heir. I will have to live with her, not any one of you. I either marry the woman I want, or I will never marry." He had meant to plant a seed, but it was obvious that all it did was make his mother upset.

Aldiana looked away with a bit of anger at his rejection and then let out a disappointed exhalation of breath.

"Jorge Luis, I've been thinking about going to the Ranchería with Nito as you suggested, but I'm going to have Shadowhawk come here," said Edgardo, a little surprised to hear his brother speak so forthrightly and with such authority. "I know it's been a while, but I just can't face going over there yet." He turned his back and stood looking out the window. The three others sat still, allowing him to steep in his feelings of having half of himself yanked away. He never again would hold her in his arms and feel her warmth. His heart felt empty. He turned and said with words barely heard, "I'll be back soon." He left and went to his room where he threw himself on his bed.

He fell into a sudden deep dream. She was there. Ramona came into his arms, "Edgardo, my love, I am fine. I want you to be happy. I will wait for you. Earth is not your home you know, and your time there may seem long, but, in reality, it will be very short. I must go now." She was gone as quickly as she had come, and he awoke with a start. *Oh, God, what have I done*? He checked his grandfather's watch on his bedside table and found he had been gone for only five minutes. However, he felt a greater inner-strength. He quickly joined his family.

"Edgardo," said Jorge Luis, "we talked a bit, and have decided to just continue on as before. We're not sure what you want to do, but we will support you, and all this must never be spoken of again -- not one word."

Edgardo nodded in agreement.

"All right, from this moment on, we go on as if none of this happened. Our secret is dead."

The adult children left their mother, adrift with her thoughts and feelings. The siblings went out to face what was left of the day. No questions were ever asked again. But each one wondered what the future might hold. Their lives, turned upside down, seemed surreal. Could they hide this for the rest of their lives? Was nothing as it seemed?

27
The Letter

Benito rushed the horse on his way to pick up Prudence. In town, although winter was more than half over, the weather was biting cold and cloudy, with a wind coming up, but Prudence still had a job to do at the hacienda. She had a lot remaining to teach Fiarela about bookkeeping. The record books of the big *rancho* were complicated and extensive.

Upon helping Prudence into the carriage, Benito suggested, "Prudence, you should bring a valise with you in case you might have to stay. The weather is unreliable, and it looks somewhat menacing."

Prudence glanced at the sky and said, "Oh, no, I'll be fine. There's no wind, and it doesn't look like rain. Besides, I don't have time to go get my carrying case. Let's just go."

After arriving at the hacienda, Prudence went straight to the office and started preparing each financial record they would work on that day. When Fiarela came in, to Prudence's surprise, she was her usual chipper self. The grief that had gripped her was lifted, but Prudence was puzzled to see her wearing an apron. "Fi, what's that apron for?" she asked.

Fiarela pulled her apron out wide and twirled around, showing it off. She started laughing, "I was feeding Nito. Then I thought, some of these old books are so dusty I would just keep it on."

"You're right, they sure are, and that is quite an apron. Okay, let's get to work. It looks a little stormy outside, so I don't want to be too late getting back to town."

The girls worked most of the day without a break. "Fiarela," said Prudence, standing behind the office table, which was covered with accounting records. "You have mastered all the books except the last ones. There are only three left." She paused, looked at Fiarela directly in her eyes, and said, emphatically, "I'm so proud of you."

Fiarela was busy making notes at the desk with invoices, papers, her quill pen, and the ink beside her. She glanced up at Prudence's words, and her eyes brightened. Her smile was contagious. She stood up and responded,

"Thanks to you, Pru. You're always so patient with me. I couldn't have a better teacher." She moved over and gave Prudence a soft kiss on the cheek. "You are just like having a sister, you know."

It was Prudence's turn to smile, "It's been a pleasure, Fi. And you are just like being my little sis."

Fiarela walked over to a small round table, which held a silver tea set on a tray that Adela had recently brought in, and said, "I want you to be my real sister. Jorge Luis is crazy about you. It's obvious to all of us. You're in love with him too, aren't you?"

Prudence looked away, saying, "No, he can't be in love with me. I'm a foreigner, Fi, and I'm not a Catholic, either." Her voice dropped, and she whispered, "I'm a nobody in this country, and I don't have anything to offer. I know he will be expected to marry well – into a highly esteemed family."

"Pru, you have everything he needs. I've never told anyone this, but Papá held you in high esteem, and he told me that Jorge Luis has his blessing if you two were to marry, but I was not to tell him unless - that idiot brother of mine. He needs to wake up before it's too late."

"Your mother looks at me as a common servant. She would never accept me as a daughter." Prudence looked downcast and avoided Fiarela's eyes.

"Listen, she won't accept anyone he chooses. Edgardo and I think you are a perfect fit him and for us."

"Don't you tell anyone, Fi, but I fell in love with him the first time I met him at the river. We seem to have a lot in common, but I want equality and partnership in a marriage. I won't kowtow to any man. I want to be chosen from the heart, not from a man's head."

Meanwhile, it was getting late when Jorge Luis quit work and took time out to pop in and check on the girls. He felt he should make sure they were properly attending to business. He wouldn't admit to himself that he needed the contact with Prudence. He needed the rush of just seeing her. To him, she was far and above any woman he had ever met - so competent, efficient, and incredibly beautiful. Her energy fed his desire. This time, he told himself, he had a legitimate excuse to interrupt their bookkeeping. Facundo had sent a letter from her uncle out to the hacienda. *When her uncle arrives, will he take her from me? She's all alone here. She'll want to be with her family. I'm sure. Without her in my life, I'll be nothing.*

Jorge Luis swung the office door open without knocking, interrupting Fiarela and Prudence. He rushed in, seeing them standing by the tea table and not working, saying, "Hey, what's going on here? Why aren't you girls at work?"

Prudence quickly responded, "I knew you'd come checking up on us. It never fails."

Oh, god, why did I have to say that. I'm such an idiot, he told himself.

"We're taking a tea break," said Fiarela, who had long ago taken off the apron and looked quite business-like. "Prudence has had me working hard all day, and I'm tired."

"Your sister is a hard, persistent worker, and she deserves a break." Prudence felt so attracted to him, yet so annoyed. "Why don't you join us?" she asked, trying to control her irritation and be polite to her boss. *What is the matter with him? He doesn't need to be so irritating. He can be such a stick in the mud.*

"Well, I guess I could take a few minutes," said Jorge Luis, looking around the room. He noticed Conchita's absence. "Where's your chaperone? Why isn't she here seeing that you two do what you are supposed to do?"

"All she did was sleep and annoy us with her snoring," said Fiarela. "I finally convinced Mother to remove her. It was ridiculous. We were just paying her to waste her time."

"It sure was. It was boring for her, too. She couldn't talk to us, and our conversation made no sense to her," said Prudence.

Just then a soft knock was heard. Prudence excused herself to go answer the door, "Edgardo! What a pleasant surprise. You are just in time to join us for tea. Come in."

"Hey, *Hermano*," said Edgardo. "You're here, too. I should've known. Yeah, I'd like to have a cup of tea. I need it. This had been one hell of a day. How about you, Jorge Luis?"

"Yeah, one of many. Edgardo, I need to meet with you and Shadowhawk about the Indian marauders and those other problem makers -- the white robbers coming down from the mountains. I think Rafa is the leader. He's got a big grudge against me, and the horseshoe tracks show he's been rustling a lot of our cattle."

"You two can talk business later," said Prudence. "Grab a chair and join us for tea."

They all settled down while Fiarela poured. Suddenly, Jorge Luis said, "Oh, Prudence, I almost forgot. I have a letter for you. I believe it is from your uncle." He pulled it from his jacket pocket and handed it to her.

"I can't believe it, a letter," Prudence said. Clutching it to her heart, she sat down and set it on the desk.

"Read it. Go ahead, read it. It must be important. Maybe they are going to be here soon," said Jorge Luis.

"Yes, yes, yes, read it," added the other two.

Prudence excitedly retrieved the letter. She held it for a moment in her hand, and then she opened it with a silver-jeweled letter opener. Taking a deep breath, she began to read, "Oh, it seems strange to read English again. I'll try to translate it."

My dearest niece, Prudence,

I am praying that you will receive this letter and that you are well and happy as you always used to be. Bryant is with me and can hardly wait to see you again.

We have been stuck here in the port of Valparaiso, Chile, for over two months due to ship repairs. We think the real reason is that the captain has a lady here, and we know he likes the bottle. We were able to send this letter ahead on a different ship, but we were not allowed on the ship as passengers. Bryant is already speaking a good Spanish, and I am stumbling along.

We have missed you greatly, and we will be looking for your small pueblo as soon as we arrive in Yerba Buena. I'm hoping that is San Francisco. They say we can sail in two weeks, but I'll believe it when my feet are on board. I hope this letter reaches you before then.

We have much to tell you as we are sailing with Washington D.C. government officials who will be taking over the government there completely, now that California is no longer a part of Mexico. It belongs to the United States. One of them, a Texan, is looking forward to getting married there in California. It is an arranged marriage by his family and the lady's relatives back in Texas. As I understand it, the other officials don't know anything about it, which seems rather odd to us, and we were asked to not mention it, strange. I'm not sure what to think of him. He seemed quite ambitious and somewhat arrogant. The name of the family they mentioned as being there in California was Ochoa. Maybe you might know of them. I understand they have a land grant somewhere in your area. He seemed quite assured of raising his society stature with this marriage. We were not impressed with him.

I can't wait to give my little niece a big hug and kiss, Uncle Lot

Tears streamed down Prudence's cheeks as she finished the letter. "I'm sorry," she said, embarrassed.

"No, no," said Edgardo, "You have every right to cry."

He looked at Jorge Luis, who said, "Ochoa? Do you suppose? There are no other families by that name, and they're our neighbors. Elena certainly is of marriageable age. I'll bet it must be them, and an arranged marriage makes sense for silly, flighty Elena. My god, what kind of wife would she make?"

"Oh, come on. She could make a good wife - if she could get away from those parents who spoil her so much. She's always had a good heart, and, as kids, there was never a time that we didn't get along well," said Edgardo, with disapproval on his face.

"Ay, Edgardo, be realistic. *Pobrecito, ese hombre*, if what they say is true. It will certainly be a marriage of convenience for him. Elena is so immature and unaware. You know - I think it might just work, especially if he is a little on the shady side. She would never know. Maybe Mamá will know more about him and the wedding," he said as he moved closer to Prudence and sat down by her. "Please, Prudence, don't be embarrassed," said Jorge Luis. "It is a very emotional thing for you to receive news of your family after so long apart."

Fiarela arose from her chair to give her a hug saying, "Pru, I am so excited that they will be here soon. I can't wait to meet your uncle and cousin."

Jorge Luis stood up as he had been nervously shifting in the chair. He had been watching Prudence's every move as she cleaned up the desk and all the books, in preparation to leave. There was nothing awkward about her. He noticed how smoothly and efficiently she moved physically. *Madre mía, her beauty overwhelms me. I seem to turn into a blithering idiot every time I am around her. I can't help but want to run my fingers through that incredible hair. When her uncle arrives, would I have the nerve to ask permission to court her?* He had been overcome by her emotional reaction. He felt anxious and uncomfortable. His heart began to race with increasing anxiety. He wanted desperately to hold Prudence in his arms and support her, seeing her so vulnerable, but he didn't dare. *Oh, God, why can't I? Why am I so afraid to approach her?* He stood silent for a moment when a few nagging thoughts entered his mind, putting a block on his desires. *I know better than to love her. I don't think she'd have me anyway. I need to stay away from her. I've got to control my feelings. She's a foreigner, and mother will never accept her.*

But – yet - his desire to be near her overrode those negative thoughts, and he told her, "Prudence, I am happy for you. I need to go into town. I want to check on some rumors I've been hearing regarding the Americanos confiscating land. Why not let me drive you and give Benito time off? In fact, I will check the hotel to make sure they have the best rooms reserved for your uncle and cousin while they're here."

"That's very kind of you. I'll accept the offer, thank you." She looked down, shyly, not wanting him to see how much she wanted to be with him, if only for a short ride.

Fiarela and Edgardo exchanged looks, rolling their eyes and raising their eyebrows, but they kept their mouths shut.

"I have work to do in town, Prudence. I must meet with Facundo. We have a lot to discuss with all these changes happening, and I am looking forward to meeting your family."

"I must say, it is disconcerting to think of our being taken over by the Americanos. I had heard rumors, but I didn't pay any attention to them," said Edgardo.

"Yes, neither did I. Now, I am hearing more rumors about us Californios losing our lands," said Jorge Luis. "They can't take our land. We own it legally. I knew no good would come from all those foreigners. They've already started moving in and taking over the Sierra. I won't stand for losing our land." His body stiffened, his words tensed, and his eyes darkened.

Edgardo spoke up, "Calm down, I think the Treaty of Guadalupe de Hidalgo guarantees that we keep our land." He set his teacup on the table and stood up.

"They have another think coming if those Americanos believe they can grab *our* land. Prudence, your uncle should know about this. Maybe he can shed some light on it." Before Prudence could answer, he pounded the table with his fist, "Never will anyone touch our land – over my dead body!"

"Take it easy. I'm sure Prudence's uncle and cousin will be able to explain the situation," said Edgardo. *"¡Madre mía!* I hope they can because things don't feel good or right from what I'm sensing." He stepped back, his lips and jaw were tight, and he kept his hands in his pockets.

Prudence and Fiarela stood in stunned silence, not accustomed to hear an outburst by Jorge Luis. Watching him in such distress pained Prudence, and she addressed him with heartfelt hope, "I'm so sorry. I've never heard any of those rumors. It can't possibly be. I know my uncle will do what he can, and my cousin is a lawyer. I'm sure he would be willing to help, too." She saw a look of gratitude pass over Jorge Luis' eyes, and Edgardo heaved a sigh of relief. "Fiarela, would you mind putting the record books back where they belong? I have my heavy coat and basket, and I'm ready to leave," she said, looking up at Jorge Luis.

"Of course, I will," said Fiarela, giving Prudence a sly wink, which turned Prudence's cheeks red.

Jorge Luis kept telling himself not to, but he got up his nerve and took her arm to escort her out. His touch was almost an electrical shock to Prudence, and she hoped he did not hear her intake of breath.

Jorge Luis did not loosen his arm from her until they reached the cart, "I hope you don't mind that we are riding in the small cart. It is faster, and it was ready."

"No, no, not at all. I am just grateful for the ride," said Prudence. She started to pull herself up into the cart when Jorge Luis quickly grabbed her arm and helped her.

"Thank you, but I am quite capable of getting up," said Prudence, somewhat testily.

"Prudence, I would feel quite remiss if I did not help a lady," said Jorge Luis. *Weren't proper manners taught in Maine? Why is she always so prickly?* he wondered.

Jorge Luis had the horse in a good strong trot as soon as they left the hacienda grounds. Prudence complained about the rough jostling, which resulted from the wheels hitting all the ruts in the dirt road.

"I'm afraid if this gets any rougher, with all these ruts, I might fall off backward. There's no back on this seat," she said, just as they hit a deep one, throwing her sideways and backwards. She let out a loud cry of alarm. Jorge Luis leaned over, grabbed her, and pulled her up to him.

"Don't worry, don't worry, I won't let you fall," said Jorge Luis. "Hold on to me if it gets rougher or, better yet, here, let me hold you so you can't fall."

Prudence couldn't believe her ears. *That is why he took the cart instead of the carriage. He really wants to hold me.*

She moved closer to him, and, although trembling at his touch, she allowed him to put his arm around her.

He felt her trembling and, misunderstanding, said, "Prudence, if you are cold, you may have my extra-heavy coat. It is folded on the floor, and I have a warm jacket on."

"Oh, no. I'm fine," she told him. She did not want a heavier coat between them. *I want to feel his warmth and strong arm. He makes me feel safe. I wish the ride would last forever, but it won't and then what? Will he just dump me off?*

Jorge Luis was lost in his own thoughts as he held her. *She fits so well next to me. As a woman, she always seems to fit well in whatever we do. I don't want to see this ride end. Why does she have to be a foreigner and a heathen? If only she could have been Catholic. And, now, worse yet, she's one of the conquerors. She will never be acceptable to my mother or our society*. He paused a moment. He breathed in her scent. He wanted to kiss her. *She'd probably push me off the cart if I tried. She's already made herself a part of our world. What am I really afraid of?* His mind held a mishmash of thoughts and feelings. *I need to say something to her but what? Damn, I feel so stupid.*

"Prudence, this time of year, it's still wintry and can get very cold. I'll put the coat across our knees."

"Please, it's getting chilly, and that would be nice," she responded.

Jorge Luis slowed the horse to a walk, and she wondered why. She really knew why but was afraid to accept it. She did not believe a man of his standing and class could want a foreign nobody like her. Even so, she snuggled in closer to him and he held her tighter.

I'm not Marina, Jorge Luis. Don't forget that. I know how much I want you, but what do you really think of me? Look where you bring me home to - the back door of a cantina.

Jorge Luis drove the cart to the kitchen door at the back of the cantina to let her off. He rushed to hold her and help her down the high steps of the small cart.

"That was a most enjoyable ride for me. I hope it wasn't too rough for you," he said to her. His face very close to hers. She could feel his breath, and it took hers away.

"Not at all. I found the ride comfortable and too short," she answered, looking up into his dark eyes, which were full of something she didn't want to recognize. Her hopes would be too easily dashed.

"Prudence, there is a storm coming in," said Jorge Luis. "I know it's late in the year, but this storm looks like it might be a bigger one. I want you to be prepared for it. I'll bring you some firewood for your small stove." Thoughts of a different sort ran through his mind as he looked into her green eyes, darkened by the night. *If I kiss her, will she slap me or push me away? At least she can't push me off the cart. I want more time with her. I need her.*

"Thank you, I do need some," she said, with a longing in her eyes. "Good night," she said softly. She started to turn with a sinking disappointment, feeling he did not want to talk more.

He moved closer, stopping her and said, "Prudence, I, I would, se puede - ?"

Now he scared her. She looked at him with lowered eyes and whispered, emphasizing each word, "Jorge Luis, I-Am-Not-Marina."

Her words cut like a broadsword, slicing deep. They stung. *How could she? How could she think that?* As she turned again to go, he hissed,

"Never think that!" He suddenly reacted, grabbed her, pulled her to him in one swift embrace. He kissed her with a passion that left her breathless and speechless. Swiftly he pulled his coat tight, left, and in another moment, he was gone. The dark swallowed him up too fast.

Prudence stood, stunned, in the dark doorway, watching him until he disappeared. *Damn it. I can't help it. I love that man.* The emptiness she felt with the unexpected suddenness of his kiss and his departure was deep, but the emotion of wanting him and wanting to be in his arms was even deeper. *What is to become of us? What am I to him? I am a nobody out here, and I live right on the other side of the wall of a house of prostitution, of all the horrible places. How can he even consider me? I will not be a pastime. I don't care how acceptable that would be. I am not Marina. My husband will know me when we marry -- not before.*

Prudence trudged slowly up the stairs carrying conflicting emotions and unrequited desires. She entered a dark, empty room. She didn't even light a candle. She laid in bed for what would be a long, restless, empty night.

28
A Surprise Visit

Prudence pushed herself up from the desk, leaning heavily on her hands and letting out a long sigh. "Fiarela, I'm done in. How about you?" asked Prudence, twisting her head and rubbing her neck. She stretched her arms out, shaking them. "Now that it's beginning to be warmer in the afternoons, this room stays cool with those extra-thick walls, but now, it feels stuffy and warm. Must be really heating up outside." She had taken off her shoes, but the floor tiles no longer felt cool as she walked to the window and peered out, "Nothing's moving out there. Usually, we're getting a breeze by now."

"I'm blurry-eyed. We should've taken a break earlier," said Fiarela, shaking her head, trying to fan herself with one of the thinner ledgers. "If this keeps up, we're headed for an early, hot summer." She walked over and plopped on one of the chairs with an extra-soft seat, stretching her legs out. "Give me a minute, Prudence, and I will go to the kitchen and bring back some lemon and mint water," she added.

"Boy, that sounds good. I am so thirsty. I'll push the shutters closed to keep the heat out, and then I'm going to lie down on the rug for a while. We need a sofa in here, but we'll never get that. I've had it. I think we should quit."

Fiarela raised herself up as if she weighed a ton, taking forever, but, once up, she shook her body and stomped her feet, gaining some energy. "Be right back," she said, leaving with a flourish out through the double doors. She didn't stop to close them, but Prudence didn't care.

Once comfortable on the carpet, Prudence promptly dozed off for a moment. She caught herself and laid there thinking. She realized how far Fiarela had come with her studies. Prudence felt that soon she might need to come only once a month instead of weekly. She really preferred to come out to the hacienda two or three times a week, depending on which financial book they were working in. Fiarela was a fast learner, had worked hard, and was, fortunately, methodical. And above all, she was as dedicated as Prudence.

It seemed like only minutes before Fiarela returned with the tray of lemon and mint water, which they drank down with a relish. They both felt refreshed, though not ready to tackle any more financial figures.

Prudence, with Fiarela, had struggled all day, working between the piles of the hacienda records. That day felt quite long because Jorge Luis had not popped in to check on them. *I miss his visits and his teasing us every time I'm here. I shouldn't count on seeing him, but I do*, thought Prudence to herself, feeling a strange loneliness.

Fiarela, whose thirst was quenched and was feeling human again, pushed her hair back, tucking the loose hairs behind her ears. She gave a quick glance at Prudence, stacked the record books in order, and placed them in the cabinet. They were ready for the next lesson.

Meanwhile, Prudence was putting the desk in order with cleaning the quills, covering the ink well, and putting down a fresh blotter. Both Fiarela and Prudence were thinking the same thoughts, *Oh, how I will miss working together. We have become true friends.*

Fiarela, my only friend and my excuse to see Jorge Luis. The Sandovals are my family. What will I do alone in this god-forsaken country? Will Jorge Luis stop seeing me? Why doesn't Uncle Lot arrive? Prudence wondered. She felt like melting down into one of the chairs and putting her head in her hands. She caught a glimpse of Fiarela's face, holding a pensive look. *She's watching me. No, I won't feel sorry for myself. I won't lose the gratitude I have for what they have done for me.* She took a couple of steps toward her student.

"Okay, Fi, I am ready to leave. Thanks for putting the books away and can you close up here in the office? Jorge Luis didn't come in today, and he usually locks the doors. Should we do it?"

"Of course, Pru, don't worry. I will lock them. Will you be here to-morrow?"

"I'm not sure. I've got a lot of bookwork to do in the office at the cantina, so not unless I finish early." Prudence continued thinking, *Jorge Luis always popped in every day and Edgardo occasionally. I will miss that.* She saw herself becoming lonely and possibly isolated. A sadness descended, settling on her like a wet, cold towel after a warm bath. She shivered and turned to look out the window to prevent Fiarela from noticing.

For a second, she focused on the silhouette of a horse, standing with its head down, resting in the distance with the undulating hills behind, which was still bathed with some green patches here and there. Her eyes followed two swirling vultures high about the hills as they floated on the updrafts.

What might be dead out there? she wondered, as a red-tail hawk sped across her view. The beauty of nature lifted her spirits. She turned and smiled at Fiarela, a true companion. She did feel as if she were her little sister at times. Prudence wished she was and thought of Jorge Luis. *Could it be possible for us? Can I really trust him? What about his mother? What about Marina?* She lifted her shoulders to regain her composure and straightened her skirt, which was wrinkled from so much sitting, "Come on Fiarela, walk out with me to the carriage."

Fiarela went out with Prudence to meet Benito at the carriage and say their goodbyes, giving her a heart-felt hug.

Benito and Prudence made light conversation on the way home, which relaxed her as they rode into the pueblo. He dropped her off at the kitchen door. When she entered, she was hit with the smells of breads and desserts baking for tonight's dinner. *I'm so hungry. I wonder if Andrés would give me a treat.* Before she could ask, Prudence was greeted by an excited cook.

"Hey, hey, Prudence, family here. Go hotel desk. See."

Prudence ran as fast as she could down the back hall to the hotel desk. "Prudence, Prudence," yelled the young boy behind the counter.

"Your family here, nice people. Upstairs in two-bedroom suite. They brought you something. You be happy. Go see," shouted Carlos, the clerk, beaming and waving his arm, pointing up the stairs. He stood and watched her dash toward the stairs, wanting to shout, *My God, you won't believe what they brought you. I should be so lucky. Well, she deserves it.* He felt a joy he hadn't felt for a long time. Trying to do all the tasks that the hotel required him to do, and keeping an eye on those unpredictable ladies who worked here, was hard. He felt Prudence was always a breath of fresh air.

Prudence, joyous, took the stairs two at a time, pulling up and holding her long skirt. The thought that they had brought her something didn't enter her mind. Her family was here, and she couldn't wait to see them. She stopped in front of the double doors, caught her breath, brushed her hair with her hands, and knocked. The doors opened, and she burst into happy tears, hugging her family, and speaking Spanish until she realized they were speaking English, "Sorry, sorry, I haven't spoken English for so long. I can't believe you are here. Uncle Lot, Bryant, I am so happy to see you."

"Prudence, Prudence, my little darling, you look wonderful. For a while, we weren't sure we'd ever see you again," said her uncle, holding her tight. Bryant, her cousin, pulled her to him and gave her a strong hug. All three were talking and laughing at once.

Bryant, at last, in a pause within the hurried conversation of catching up, said, "We're starved, at least I am. Let's go down to the restaurant. We can catch up while we eat, and then we have something to show you. Uncle Lot has a gift. One you'll love. I can't wait for you to see it."

"I can't wait to give it to you, but I'm starved. Let's eat first," said her uncle.

"Yes, yes, let's. Just let me clean up a bit. I've been working all day." She noticed how good they looked. It had been a while since she had seen such smart American business suits on men. "I'll meet you in the dining hall. Only be a minute," she added.

In the dining room, sitting at a table by the window, the two Americans sat drinking whiskey, while taking in all the scenes: the dining room, the people, the help, and the view out the windows.

Soon, Prudence appeared in a lovely suit, her best conservative one, the color of wine, which drew attention to the color of her eyes. The light jacket had a raised lace collar, which came down in a V where a large lace bow fell over her chest. The sleeves were full and pleated to her elbows, caught by a ribbon, and flared out in more pleats. She did not look like her usual working-girl self. Her ankle-length skirt flared out softly. She wore her best shoes with moderate heels. She had pulled her hair back with her ivory combs, which she knew her uncle would recognize because her aunt had given them to her.

Everyone who worked at the hotel and in the cantina popped in to look at Prudence's transformation and her American family. "Oohs" and "aahs" were heard over Bryant, the handsome young lawyer.

Whispers circulated fast, "He is a famous lawyer from Maine, you know."

Andrés had whipped up a special cake for their dessert. The other diners watched with envy while they ate. Facundo, in his best suit, and María, in a black jacket and skirt, looking very elegant with her hair done up high and held with ornately carved horn-combs, walked in to present themselves to Prudence's long-awaited uncle and cousin. He introduced himself and María, speaking to Lot in broken English, while Bryant, from their stay in Chile, conversed well with them in Spanish.

The two Americans impressed everyone, as both were tall, handsome, impeccably dressed in worsted wool business suits, and demonstrated the best of manners.

Facundo noticed that they were just finishing eating, and, after some small conversation, said, "Señor Mullens, you ready show Prudence the gift?"

Bryant said, "Yes, come on, Uncle, let's do it."

"Of course, but let me take care of the bill first, and then we'll go," said Lot.

"Oh, no, meal on house. We wait long time meet you."

"That is very kind, thank you. Let's go then," said Lot. "Prudence, come. I hope you will like what we picked up for you."

Bryant added, as they were walking, "We found it in Chile and brought it all the way here."

"Where are we going? That's the stables in front of us. Do we have to ride somewhere to see it? I'm not dressed to ride."

"No, no," assured her uncle, "but we had to park it somewhere."

Now Prudence was so curious she could hardly stand it, and she knew she would never be able to guess what it was, "María, María, tell me what is it? I bet you know."

"No, no, Facundo wouldn't tell me, and I wouldn't tell even if he did," said Maria. "Have patience."

When they entered the stable, Facundo said, "Wait here. Bryant, you come help take out."

Prudence held her breath in anticipation. She began dancing in place, almost like an impatient child. María put her arm around her with a loving smile, "Wait, wait, they're coming. I hear them."

Out walked Bryant and Facundo leading an elegant, whitish-grey Arabian mare with dark gray, almost black markings, head held high, jerking up and down, with her larger-than-life black eyes, eyeing everybody.

Prudence nearly fainted, looked at her uncle, burst out with, "She's amazing, she's amazing. Oh, Uncle Lot, she's beautiful. For me? You couldn't have brought me a more precious gift." She went to the horse to rub her black nose and pat her neck, all while tears of joy streamed down her face, "Oh, how I've wanted a horse. I missed mine so."

"She's called a steel gray," said Bryant. "Look, Prudence, see her dark gray, almost blackish legs from the knees down?"

"Yes, yes, I see them. They're beautifully matched." She reached up and brushed the hair falling over the head between the ears. She pushed her new horse's mane back and forth, checking her neckline for a continuation of the same colors. She stood back a few feet, viewing her in astonishment - her horse. She continued, "Her conformation is perfect. Uncle Lot, how could you have picked out a more beautiful Arab?" Her Arab purity was obvious. "Look, everyone, she has the scooped head," she pointed to her nostrils, "See how big they are? And her eyes?" She walked up and slid her hands over her back, which was shorter than the average horse. Prudence was afraid to breathe in case that, maybe, her new horse would evaporate like an unfulfilled dream. She stood staring, entranced, until Bryant broke the spell.

"Prudence, yes, she has bigger-than-life eyes. She is a show piece. Did you know that Uncle Lot obtained all the accoutrements for her? Wait until you see the saddle and bridle."

"I saw," said Facundo, "You be one fancy lady." He couldn't help but think of the Sandovals reactions when they see that horse. *If that doesn't change things, I don't know what will.*

"I can hardly wait to ride her. Maybe tomorrow we can ride?"

Facundo said, "Yes, *mañana,* you ride to hacienda. When I see family arrive, I send Pedro pronto. Give them news. Family excited meet you. They want you come for dinner. They want you appear early, have big tour. See hacienda. You be guests, pass night in hacienda and have morning ride."

"Oh, Uncle Lot, you will love it, and you too, Bryant. The family are wonderful, and the hacienda is amazing. You can see where I work." She hugged her horse and turned to Lot to ask, "What's her name?"

"My dear, she has papers with a legally recorded name, but you will have to give her an ordinary name for yourself."

"Really?" Prudence leaned her head softly on the horse's neck, rubbing her back. "Cámila, I'm going to call you Cámila. You are so beautiful." She petted her one more time, and ran to her uncle and hugged him, "I love you so much, Uncle Lot. I can't thank you enough. I missed Wilma terribly after she was stolen."

"We thought as much, so Bryant and I talked it over when we saw this young lady for sale. I'm just glad we didn't have to pay in dollars. I got a good deal, and we'll be happy as long as you are happy," smiled Uncle Lot.

Facundo had his arm around Maria's waist. He looked down at her, smiled and nodded. Everyone stood with joyful smiles and admiration for a horse of obvious high quality. She had a sheen to her hair that cow ponies didn't, and no horse holds it head as high and bowed as a full-blooded Arab.

Uncle Lot said, "I wish we had one of those new-fangled cameras here to take a picture of you, Prudence, standing by her. What a photo that would be."

When they returned to the hotel, María and Facundo stayed to join them for a few drinks in the cantina, where, again, the Americanos were the object of everyone's interest and talk.

Lot was impressed with Facundo and his wife and the fact that Facundo was the hacienda's manager. "Facundo, will you be there tomorrow at the hacienda?" asked Lot.

"No tomorrow. Have much work here. Why?"

Lot paused and rubbed his knees, hesitating to talk, but finally said, "Look, Facundo, we spent months on that ship, damned thing always needing repairs. We were never sure if it really did or if the captain was putting us on. He seemed to like spending time in the wharf bars. We should have waited for the ship from Maine."

"Very sorry, Señor Mullens, but here now and all happy, ¿no?"

"Yes, yes, of course." Lot paused long enough to bring heads forward toward him, wondering what was next. His long, unusual pause caused them to watch his face closely. Lot rubbed his chin, pondering. He folded his napkin neatly and placed it by the plate on the table saying, "We'll talk more about this later, but you should know we had three United States government officials, land management men, with us the whole time, and we often talked, and, I must say, listening to them was disturbing." Bryant had been looking down at the floor. He raised his head and nodded in agreement, while the rest looked on with concern and brows furrowed in lack of understanding.

"I suppose it has to do with what will happen when they take over our Mexican government?" asked Facundo.

"Yes, exactly, and there will be problems of land ownership. You people will need to protect yourselves somehow. Will the family be open to listening to Bryant and me? I don't want to scare anyone, but it is serious," said Lot.

"Oh yes, they want hear all. Maybe you help. Have ideas."

"Of course, we will help if we can," said Bryant, "but I will be helping Uncle Lot buy properties up north and assisting in setting up his businesses. At least, I know American land law well. When I return, I might be able to help them with that." He sat back in his chair, fiddling with his watch fob.

Lot nodded, running his fingers through his hair and thinking deeply, yet remained silent. The women also sat quietly, taking it all in. Prudence felt dumbfounded and ignorant. Facundo looked at María, raised his eyes, said a silent prayer, and then looked back to their guests.

"That be hard news for Sandoval family. Father die recent. Everybody and workers in big upset. We know nothing of new government, many *rumores*. We no like many strange peoples coming. Please, you talk with Sandoval family tomorrow. I think talk much on what you tell me." Facundo was feeling more anxious and worried. He paused for a minute while Prudence sat quietly, trying to absorb what Lot shared also.

"Thank you for warning, Señor Mullens. You have good ride tomorrow. We free from storm, one coming, maybe, but no see. We pleased meet you. Maria and I take leave now."

The two Mullen men together said, "We're so glad to have finally met you, and we are so grateful for your care of our much-loved Prudence. She was very lucky to have met up with you. We hope to see you again soon."

Facundo bowed formally. Maria curtsied politely. They turned and walked out.

People, who were observing, started commenting. One man said, "I almost didn't recognize Facundo and María. Look how handsome they are all dressed up. I'm used to seeing him behind the bar, and you'd never know María had birthed seven children. I'm tempted to whistle, but they'd toss me out if I did."

Everyone remarked at how dignified the couple appeared as they walked sedately out of the restaurant with Facundo's arm protectively around María's waist, their heads held high, as they returned home to their houseful of children. All eyes followed the obviously harmonious and handsome couple.

Prudence, her uncle, and cousin smiled at the audience still watching. Their looks turned serious as they looked at each other.

Prudence sent a swift glance towards her uncle and asked, "Do you really expect trouble over the land?"

"Prudence, my dear, we don't really know what might happen, but those government men seemed to be very interested in the land, overly so, especially one of them." Lot shifted his eyes away for a moment, heaved a resigned sigh and said, "Come on now, let's be happy we're together."

They retired with happiness filling their hearts. Tomorrow was enthusiastically looked forward to. The men prepared, packing carefully, because an adventure was waiting, and they knew it.

29
Lot and Bryant Meet the Sandovals

Prudence was up early in order to attend to her work in the cantina's office. Even though it was now the end of winter and spring was in full swing, mornings were still cold. The office was quite cold. She lit the small fireplace, which had been readied yesterday, and hoped it would hurry and warm up the room.

She left her wool hat on, tightened her coat, and thought about her family. *I know Uncle Lot and Bryant will enjoy the ride to the hacienda. They've never been out in the country where one owner owns all the land, for as far as the eye can see. I pray they get along with the Sandovals. Wait until they see the hacienda. It will be a whole new experience.* While her mind was wandering, she said a quick, little prayer, hoping her family and the Sandovals would get along. She let out a heavy sigh. *I'm not sure about Aldiana. She still looks at me as a servant and a foreigner.* Prudence knew that Lot and Bryant would be amazed seeing so much land belonging to one family. It's so different than back East where such large acreages were unheard of. *Uncle Lot owns a large ranch, but it is so small compared to out here.*

Prudence took off her hat and coat and prepared for her work by refilling the inkwell and searching for the correct book to work in. The bookkeeping for the cantina was not nearly as complex as for the hacienda, but, still, she would be working until noon or past.

A small knock on the door surprised her. She put her pen down and looked up to see Facundo walk in with Uncle Lot and Bryant.

"Oh, I thought you two would sleep late. Facundo, thanks for bringing them. Have you had breakfast?" asked Prudence.

"Oh yes," said Bryant with a satisfied look on his face, "and what a welcome breakfast after that ship's tasteless, monotonous food."

Lot confirmed the hearty breakfast with a pat on his full belly, "How long do you have to work this morning, my dear?"

Facundo interrupted, "Oh, Prudence, take day off. Visit family and new horse. If want, prepare trip. Go hacienda. Have good time." Facundo gazed at Prudence with a heart-felt connection, wanting the visit to go well for her.

"As long as Facundo doesn't mind, why don't you?" said Lot.

"Thanks, Facundo." She stood up with a happy grin covering her face and ran to hug her uncle and her cousin. She said, "Let me go and put on a long apron and my boots if we're going to feed and groom the horses. How many did you bring with you, Uncle Lot?"

"Two each, one hardy pack horse and one to ride. We left a lot of our things in San Francisco because, when we leave here, we're heading up north to look at properties. After I find what I want, we'll come back for everything, but we'll stop here first." Lot brushed his pants and headed out of the office, waving his hand to follow.

"Well, then, Bryant, will you help me with Cámila? She doesn't know me yet."

"Sure, we'll meet you at the stables. Hurry up and change."

"Thanks again, Facundo." She dashed over and gave him a quick hug.

Facundo blushed, "*De nada*, Prudence. Enjoy day." He stayed behind, as the others left, to ready the cantina for the regulars and any new foreigners. He was impressed with these Americanos and hoped, for Prudence's sake, the Sandovals would be, too. *That amigo mío had better declare his hand soon, or he'll lose her with them moving up north and all these new men arriving. I've noticed money is beginning to flow in, and I've heard a lot about the building and enterprises that are starting up in the Sierras. Too bad, but one cannot command the heart.*

At the stables, all three checked their horses' stalls for hay and water. They were comforted to see that the horses had been well cared for. Prudence always loved the many comforting smells throughout the stables, the fresh hay, the well-worn leather, and the horses themselves. They hollered at Pepe and asked if he would clean out the stalls and put in fresh straw while they groomed the horses.

"Sí, Señores, I get brother. He help. But first, I get brushes, curry combs," said Pepe.

Lot and Bryant brought out both of their horses and tied them. Bryant went with Prudence to introduce her again to Cámila and lead her out to be tied.

"Bryant, I'm surprised she is so gentle and cooperative in a new place, not knowing me," she said. She looked up at him, shaking her head in disbelief, "I still can't believe she's mine." Prudence began to brush her down. Cámila gave a deep snicker and a quick shake. "She really likes this, Bryant. Look how still she's standing."

While Pepe and his brother worked in the stalls, Lot, Bryant, and Prudence brushed, curried and untangled manes and tails. They checked and cleaned hooves. Their horses were all shod. Many local horses were not. Prudence explained that the hacienda had its own blacksmith and farrier to keep theirs shod, and that Jorge Luis, the oldest son, had a Peruvian Paso that had hooves so strong they didn't need shoes.

"Prudence, you haven't seen the saddle, bridle or the blanket, not even the chest and tail pieces. Come on, I want you to see them. I picked them up for almost nothing. You're gonna' love them," said Lot.

They opened the door to the tack room, and Bryant pointed to a black, handmade saddle with small pieces of inlaid silver over the cantle, the horn, and the stirrups. There were a pair of silver spurs dangling around the horn. The bridle, the chest piece, and croup carried even more silver in very small geometrical shapes: thin rectangles, tiny circles, and diamonds.

Prudence gasped, "Uncle Lot, these are precious. I've never had any-thing like this." She ran her hand over the saddle on the barrel and then picked up the bridle to examine every part of it. Next came the blanket of pure wool with blacks, grays, and reds woven into the design. She picked it up and shook it out, "My god, it is beautiful." *What will Jorge Luis think now? And Aldiana? Appearances are important to her. Maybe I'll finally measure up to their standards. No, probably not. I'm still a foreigner.*

Prudence never dreamed in all her life that she would have anything of such value. The beauty of the workmanship took her breath away, "Some-one put their heart and soul into making these. They appear almost new." Her voice lowered into almost a whisper, "It must have been a great loss to someone to give these up. I couldn't."

"I don't know the history. I never thought of asking, but I couldn't resist them. They're perfect for your horse and you deserve them," Uncle Lot came over to her, hugged her and gave her a kiss on her forehead. "You have no idea how proud your parents would be of you."

"I never thought to ask either, and, now, you have me wondering," said Bryant. "You know, Cousin, while I'm admiring your riding skirt under that apron you put on to help with the horses, you can't ride sidesaddle on Cámila. It would be way too dangerous, and she doesn't know the countryside or the animals. Anything could spook her."

"Oh, heavens, is that what you are thinking? Here, let me show you. This was my design," she said as she pulled back her skirt to show her riding pants.

"Good Lord, how clever. I didn't want you on a sidesaddle, either," said Uncle Lot.

Suddenly, the group heard footsteps approaching from behind and turned to see the two boys. Lot was the first to speak, "Well, boys, have you finished?"

Pepe gave a little head and shoulder bow, saying, "Sí, Señores, the stalls are ready now." A big smile crossed his face. "We finish," he said, while his older brother could not take his eyes off Prudence. That brought a smile and almost a chuckle from Bryant.

"Okay, boys, thanks for your help and here's a little something for you," said Lot as he gave each boy two coins. They looked down shyly and gave a quick bow. Their eyes were beaming when they left.

The horses were led back to their stalls, all spruced up for their upcoming ride. Prudence suggested they have lunch and eat well since dinner would be late.

"I would like a nap before we leave," said Lot.

"Me too," said Bryant, "Yesterday was long and tough. I could hardly walk by the time we arrived here."

Prudence gave a glance at her family members, tall and strong, and felt guilty. *I never thought about their trip here, nor that long journey by ship, either. They must be exhausted.* "We'll all rest. The thing is, though, the sun sets later now. The west wind may come in earlier from the bay, and it can be cold. Let's leave by three o'clock while it's still warm. At a walk, it'll take about an hour to reach the hacienda. I'll ask the cook to pack some food."

"Sounds great," said Bryant, putting on his coat to leave the stables.

"I'm turning in. See you later, dear," said Lot.

"Hey, don't forget your nightclothes and riding outfits for tomorrow," said Prudence, "They always like to take a morning ride before breakfast."

Feeling refreshed after a good, long nap, the three met at the stables, Prudence with her valise stuffed and a sack of food. The men had bedrolls. They decided not to attach anything to Cámila, since they did not know how she might react, but she did accept Prudence astride her with no trouble. They were off with half the town watching. Prudence knew they were murmuring, but she couldn't hear anything they said.

Within the small crowd, stood two young girls, entranced with Bryant. They looked at each other and pointed at him.

"He looked at me with those big, black eyes," sighed one of the admirers.

"He did not. He looked at me," said her rival.

"I don't care if he is an Americano. He is so handsome. We have to find a way to meet him," said the other with dreamy eyes.

They watched his well-formed figure, so in command of himself and his horse, until he disappeared out of the village.

Meanwhile, the riders rode quietly and slowly out of the village, unaware of youthful desires floating behind them.

"Uncle Lot, Cámila handles beautifully. It only takes the slightest touch of the reins." She leaned forward to pat her on the neck. Cámila shook her neck, flaring her mane.

They rode slowly to allow Cámila and Prudence time to become used to each other. At the top of the hill overlooking the pueblo, Prudence stopped, "Here's where we turn towards the hacienda, but look back. See the town? The Sandoval family own all this land, granted to them by the king of Spain." She swept her arm out in a wide sweep.

The two men raised up in their saddles, turning and staring in all directions. All they could see was endless land, hills rising off to the right with flatter land in the direction they were headed. Everywhere they looked was green yet. Not many wildflowers had bloomed yet, as only a few had popped up here and there. In the distance, they could see a long line of trees, which told them a river was there. Nearby was a field of mustard that grew as tall as their horses.

"Prudence, my dear," he said, pointing, "Look at that mustard. I was told that the mission fathers brought it and that most of them were trained botanists. I guess that was true. This expanse of land is incredible – beautiful. I am finding it hard to grasp what you're telling us."

Bryant was shaking his head in disbelief, "Pru, I am flabbergasted. It goes on forever, and I see nothing but open land." He lowered himself back down onto the saddle and said in a low, astonished voice, "Spectacular."

"How far is it now to the hacienda?" asked Lot.

"It's only about three more miles. You can't see it because of the trees, but soon you will see sheep and an apple orchard."

"What? An apple orchard out here? I might expect sheep, but – apples?" Bryant paused, glancing over the terrain, "By the way, where are the cattle?"

Lot, still upright in his saddle, kept surveying the land and shaking his head at the vastness held by one family.

Prudence answered Bryant when they started to walk the horses again along the dirt road, "The cattle are about a half-day's ride away from here. Wait until you see them. They are so different than ours, much smaller. They're called Corrientes."

Hearing that word with the r's pronounced so strongly gave Bryant a laugh, "Wow, Cuz, you sure got rolling the 'r' down. I'm impressed. I'm not good at that yet."

Uncle Lot added, "I never will be."

Spring was notably close, as the afternoon had warmed even though the night would still be cold. The ride was pleasant. They crossed the creek, and Prudence pointed out where the river ran in the distance. They could see the long line of oaks growing along the banks and the outlines of ponds and swamp areas. Suddenly, the men stopped in surprise. The hacienda came into view, "Look, Bryant, how different from our farms yet not too unlike what we saw in Chile and Panamá."

"I've always wanted to see inside one. I do hope we get a tour," said Bryant, looking at Prudence with a question in his eyes.

Prudence gave him a big smile and her eyes sparkled as she said, "I know they will. They are quite proud of the hacienda. You will be amazed, Bryant. We'll see it as soon as we pass through all these big oaks."

It wasn't long before they were out in the open.

"There it is," said Lot. "Look at the sign over the gate, *El rancho del viento fuerte.*"

They stopped and were impressed with everything they could see. The road to the hacienda was lined with olive trees on both sides.

They rode up to the entry steps of the veranda where three men appeared at once, ready to take the horses.

"Prudence, is it safe to let them take the horses? How about Cámila?" said Bryant, while Lot was taking it all in visually.

"I'm sure Cámila will be fine," said Prudence.

"Let's grab our things first," said Lot, untying his bedroll.

Bam! Bang! Went the huge front doors as they hit the walls, and Fiarela ran down the steps, shouting, "Prudence, Prudence, where did you get an Arab? She's gorgeous, a beauty," she stopped abruptly when she realized who was there. "Oh, sorry," she said, embarrassed.

Prudence laughed as she noticed Bryant's amazed eyes glued on her. Behind Fiarela came Aldiana, looking very dignified in a warm wool dress with a high collar. She was followed by her two sons. Both Jorge Luis and Edgardo had strong looks of astonishment on their faces and eyes full of admiration at the sight of Prudence astride a spectacular Arab. Neither knew what to think or say at first. She looked quite regal.

Prudence hurried to present her family to the Sandovals. Uncle Lot was quite perceptive. He saw at once Jorge Luis' interest in Prudence and felt it was almost to a point of ownership, but he could also see it was reciprocated. Fiarela couldn't take her eyes off the tall, handsome young man in front of her. Since she had known of them as foreigners, she could not imagine them as being so good looking.

Aldiana was in a state of shock. She never expected to see Prudence riding a top-quality Arabian, nor arriving with a very handsome uncle and cousin, both on excellent horses - a Morgan, and a Tennessee Walker. They were dressed in obviously expensive riding suits. She stiffened. Her mind went blank for a moment, not taking it in. Everything felt out of context with her expectations, and then the realization hit her. *These are people of quality*. Aldiana experienced a sudden intake of breath. Her eyes widened and her mouth remained open for a second. She stepped back and quickly composed herself. A wide welcoming smile appeared for their guests and her eyes sparkled, even though she was absorbing another unexpected view of Prudence, which was disturbing and irritating. Suddenly, right in front of her, Prudence's heritage was shown. She came from a family of means. Aldiana wondered, *Am I not to see her as a servant anymore?* She pursed her lips in displeasure. *I don't care who she is. She is still a foreigner and a heathen, and, as long as she works here, she will still be a servant.*

Aldiana knew the uncle was a widower, which irritated her more to see how handsome and presentable he was. He had presented himself to her with the best of manners. He was very respectful and did not let his eyes rest on her too long. Annoyed, she also noticed how her boys' eyes lit up upon seeing the guests. *Why didn't they light up like that when the Ochoas arrived? And Fiarela? I'm going to have to sit on her. Her behavior is deplorable*. Fiarela had not left Prudence's side.

"Prudence," began Jorge Luis, "Tell me, where did she come from? Is she yours? What a beauty." He couldn't get over this new view of her. His chest tightened with a welling of desire.

"Uncle found her in Chile," she said, beaming with pride. Now she felt a hope of being seen for whom she really was. "I'm so lucky she survived the trip on the ship. Uncle Lot told me they lost several horses on board from slipping, falling, and breaking their legs when the ship would roll. They had to be put down." She choked up and almost cried upon saying those words. She leaned over and hugged Cámila, "I love her so."

"I've heard how rough and dangerous those ships can be. Horses are easily damaged," Jorge Luis said, feeling Prudence's anguish and her gratefulness.

Edgardo had been rubbing Cámila's nose and inspecting her from her teeth to her tail. He turned to Bryant and said, "You certainly made a great choice. She's one beauty of a horse. You and your uncle are most welcome here. We have waited a long time to meet you."

Aldiana invited the guests to join her in the sitting room. She ordered the servants to take their belongings up to the guest rooms, and the workers to take the horses to the stables.

With the horses now removed, everyone followed her into the house. The expanse of the building, the veranda, and the gardens were almost overwhelming for Lot and Bryant. This was old money. They wondered how the Sandovals could afford to maintain it all.

The men looked around at all they could see and, then, at each other, pensively. Bryant, rubbing his forehead and letting a soft "whew" out, whispered to his uncle, "I sure hope they can hang on to all this for a long time and not lose it."

Lot nodded. "What a shame," he said, shaking his head. They were led to the sitting room, and as soon as they sat down on the antique European settees, they were offered a refreshing fruit drink, fresh apple with lemon and a touch of mint, which was greatly appreciated.

The conversation was social and polite, centering around the ride from town, a few questions about the ship, and San Francisco. Everyone commented on Prudence's Arabian mare. They knew of them, but only Jorge Luis had seen one. He had seen them in Spain while attending the university there for a year.

"Is everyone ready for a tour of the hacienda?" asked Aldiana.

"Oh, yes, Mamá, I know they will want to, don't you?" asked an excited Fiarela, who was quite taken with Bryant, glancing and smiling at him anytime she could.

Aldiana suddenly lifted herself from her chair, straightening her skirt as she did, patted her hair, and, looking at her new guests, said, "I'm going to remain here to check the rooms and the preparations for dinner. I think Benito is already waiting for you. Take your time and enjoy. There is a lot to see." She was relieved to not accompany them. The carriage would be crowded. She didn't need that. The thought that she was a little out of her perceived elite-element slithered in and startled her. These guests were worldly, educated. The men's manners were impeccable. She needed time to digest all that. She watched the family and visitors leave for the carriage, and then went to her room for a rest.

The carriage held the six people very comfortably. The three Sandovals were in competition to point out the different areas, such as where the wine was made. They could see the vats used for stomping the grapes as they rode past. They saw the outdoor ovens and cooking areas, the large vegetable garden, the blacksmith shop, and where the animals were killed, skinned, gutted, and hung. Then they rode by the stables, the working corrals, and the big arena for the charreadas. Lot and Bryant found it all fascinating and self-sustaining. But now, they wondered, with all the coming changes, how long can they keep all this together? They were taken to see the cemetery and then the chapel. Both men thought they might take advantage of the chapel while they were here.

"Señores," said Lot, "Is it possible that we may spend a little time in the chapel as we have been away from one for many months."

"Of course," said both boys, "Anytime you wish."

When they returned to the home, Aldiana sent the visitors upstairs to their respective rooms for a rest before the meal. "Please pull the wall rope to call the *mucama* to bring hot water, extra towels, or anything else you might need. We will eat at nine o'clock," said Aldiana.

Fiarela informed Prudence that she would be staying with her in her suite and that another rawhide bed had been ordered. Lot and Bryant ended up in a two-bedroom suite, nicer than the one at the hotel. Each suite had its own bathroom. They looked at each other in amazement. "This is one place I am going to enjoy," said Bryant.

"Amen!" agreed Uncle Lot.

But then, both men looked at each other. Both sighed and were silent for a moment.

"What do you think, Uncle Lot?" asked Bryant, slipping out of his jacket.

"I just don't know. It will likely become a big problem for the family, and we may have to help them. Somehow, we must get the complex land possibilities out into the open," said Lot.

"Okay," said Bryant, "but what about Señora Aldiana? How will she take it? She didn't seem too happy meeting us. I got a feeling she felt threatened by us somehow. Did you see how she looked at Prudence?"

"I sure did. No denying it, she was not very welcoming of Prudence. We may have some problems with her, my boy. Let's be careful until we know more," said Lot.

"I'll be discreet at the dinner table, and I'm going to observe Prudence and Jorge Luis, very carefully," said Bryant.

Lot nodded, walked over to his bed, sat down and said, "Watch your behavior with Fiarela. I know she is adorable, but keep your eyes on the señora."

30
An Elegant Dinner

soft knocking on the bedroom suite door woke both Lot and Bryant from a restorative sleep. *La mucama* wanted to know, talking through the door, if they were ready for a hot bath.

"Yes, please," Bryant turned to his uncle and said, "I could stay in that tub for an hour."

"I need to soak out this soreness from all that riding, but we have to be ready for dinner soon," said Lot.

Consuelo brought in the hot water for one bath, eyeing handsome young Bryant, and left sighing. He quickly disrobed, spending only a few minutes in the hot water and gave the tub over to Lot, who jumped in and out as quickly as he could.

"I'm so glad I put in my finest suit. We need to look our best, don't we?" asked Lot.

"Yes, Uncle, she is a beautiful widow."

"Stop that. I'm not trying to impress her. She is too recently widowed, and I certainly noticed your eyes all over the daughter -- cute young lady."

"Uncle Lot, she's more than cute. I never expected to meet someone so vibrant and alive. And, her eyes –," he turned to his uncle, saying, "I could drown in them. They are so big and dark. And did you notice her hair? So smart, not at all old-fashioned. I like that. Shows character."

"Don't jump in so fast, boy," said Lot, giving him a strong narrow-eyed look. "We have to respect their customs, which we don't know yet, and I was told that good manners are extremely important. Come on, get dressed. Let's get going."

"Okay," said Bryant, "but what about Señora Aldiana? To me, she appeared a little hostile. You saw how she looked at Prudence."

"I sure did. Let's be careful. Don't judge too soon until we know more," said Lot, walking over to his bed and sitting on it. "I admit, Fiarela is quite fetching with a personality to match, but keep your behavior impeccable with that young lady, and especially with the señora."

"Of course, Uncle Lot. I'll be on my best behavior and very discreet at the dinner table. I wonder if there is something between Prudence and Jorge Luis. I think I'll watch them for a bit." said Bryant. "Also, Uncle Lot, try to get a word in about the possible land problems."

"Of course, I will," said Lot, "I think it's very important that they be informed. I'll do my best."

Both men dressed, brushed their hair, adjusted their gold watch fobs, which hung across their vests, and left to find their way down the stairs to the formal *sala.* The laughter of Prudence, Fiarela, and the young men directed them. Lot and Bryant looked at each other, chuckled, and joined the gaiety.

Jorge Luis offered them a glass of homemade wine, which they both welcomed, but before conversation picked up, Aldiana entered and announced that it was time to dine. Lot had to be careful to keep his eyes off her as she was dressed in mourning. She was stunning in a black silk dress, material from the orient, with a large lace collar softly draped over a pleated bodice. Her skirt was fitted, but it swirled out at the bottom to allow for the ease of walking. He almost gasped and quickly felt guilty. No woman had commanded his attention since his wife had died.

Edgardo quickly took his mother by the arm in order to escort her to dinner with the others following. Aldiana was much too much the hostess to turn to see who was walking with whom, and it bothered her. In fact, it was eating her up. *Jorge Luis, my eldest son, should be escorting me. This is not proper etiquette.*

Aldiana's eyes flashed anger even more when Jorge Luis immediately placed himself at the table next to Prudence. And, to make matters worse, Bryant took advantage and sat by Fiarela, who just beamed. Aldiana straightened her back even stiffer and smoldered.

Evita, the servant, entered the dining room with her hair pulled back tightly into a bun with a ruff of white tied around her head, looking neat and attractive. She carried in a large bowl of *adobada*, chile soaked pork, and served each person. She returned in a few minutes with a platter of butter-flied lamb and another of grilled trout wrapped in fig leaves.

The family and friends sat quietly until Aldiana announced she would say grace. "As guests, you may join us if you like."

"Thank you, Doña Aldiana. We have missed hearing grace while sailing on that ship for so long," said Lot. "Grace was always said before each meal at home, and I miss that."

She blushed slightly, said grace, and added, "I hope you enjoy our cuisine."

The conversation was light until Jorge Luis brought up the possibility of a morning ride as their tradition, especially with guests.

"I'm most apologetic, but Bryant and I must leave for the north early in the morning. We will be headed for a small place up on the Sacramento river called Colusa. Do you know it?"

No one nodded. They all shook their heads, no.

"I'm going with Uncle Lot, since I'm a lawyer, to help him buy some properties," said Bryant. "We have an agent who said he found a large productive piece of land, far to the west of Colusa, about nine or ten thousand acres, which is huge for us. We Americans are not accustomed to working such large pieces of land like you are, but I understand it's needed if one is to raise great numbers of cattle and sheep," he said, turning to look at Fiarela.

"You know, I heard talk among the government land officials about not understanding the need for such large land grants. They seemed to think it rather show-offish and selfish. I heard one fellow say they need to be broken up. Frankly, I believe that is their intention," said Lot, taking advantage of the mention of land.

Jorge Luis and Edgardo shot glances at each other. Jorge Luis leaned over his plate, put his elbows on the table, and looked at Lot intently. His mother was horrified at his sudden lack of manners. Edgardo sat back in his chair with a dark look in his eyes and his teeth clenched.

Just as Jorge Luis was about to say something, Aldiana interrupted with, "Then it sounds like you are intending to settle out here?" She shot a glance at her eldest son and then at Prudence, with a growing resentment sparking from narrowed eyes. *I have got to give this careful thought. I cannot allow a heathen and foreigner into our family heritage.*

"Why would you want to settle so far from your home in Maine, may I ask?" said Edgardo.

"I couldn't face going home every night to a house with no one there yet full of memories. It was too empty and lonely. I needed to find some good investments, and everything I heard about California was positive. Opportunities abound out here since it was annexed from Mexico," said Lot.

Aldiana's eyes got large, and she sucked in her breath as she had not really understood that to be true. She covered her mouth with her hand. *Oh, dear God, what does that mean for us? I had better pay more attention.*

Lot glanced at Prudence and said, "Since Prudence understood our business, I sent her on ahead to meet my operator in San Francisco or is it called Yerba Buena? That's all I hear out here, so what do I call it? I'm never sure."

"It's pretty much called San Francisco now," said Prudence.

"Well, okay then." He paused and looked at his hosts before he said, "Unfortunately, on her way out here, Prudence had a very horrifying and frightening experience where she lost almost everything. We truly owe you people for helping her. I'm very grateful. I hope we can repay that someday," said Lot, with Bryant nodding.

Looking seriously at Fiarela, Bryant said, "In fact, after helping my uncle secure his properties, I would like to set up a law business in either Sacramento or in San Francisco." He looked at her with an expectation he had never felt before.

"I've never seen San Francisco, but I've heard what a lovely place it is," she said. Her big, warm eyes lay on him like a duck down blanket on a cold night. He felt a slight shudder.

"How about Sacramento? Have you ever been there?" As she shook her head, his thoughts assailed him, and his heart started to beat rapidly. He trembled lightly as he thought, *I can't keep my eyes off her. I've heard of love at first sight, but I never believed it. But how can I approach her? I don't think they would allow her to consider me, an American.* Bryant smiled with lips that quickly turned serious. He bent toward Lot.

Also turning to Lot, Jorge Luis interrupted, "I understand you had passage with a few United States Land Management Department men. I am curious to know if they mentioned land management law. How might it be different from Mexican land law?"

"Yes," said Edgardo, "I have heard they may come and confiscate all our lands. How true do you think that might be?"

Lot rubbed his chin pensively. He wasn't sure exactly what to say – or how much. He began with, "I don't like being pessimistic, but from what we heard, I believe that to be their intention."

Jorge Luis leaned over the table and spoke very clearly, "Señor, the Treaty of Guadalupe de Hidalgo guarantees us our lands. How would they do it?"

"I'm not familiar with that treaty, but when Bryant and I return, I'll have him read it, and I will too. I assume you will be required to prove your ownership. I think that may be the problem. What do you think, Bryant?"

"I believe that Mexican law requires you to record all your land with proper documentation, such as correct deeds. Is all the land properly surveyed?" asked Bryant.

"No, of course not," answered Jorge Luis with an edge to his voice.

Edgardo sat with a worried look, shaking his head no.

The women were now sitting up straighter and listening intently. Fiarela was almost bouncing in her seat. She could hardly contain herself, trying not to interrupt. Prudence didn't take her eyes off Jorge Luis and was beginning to feel the underlying, unsettled feelings. *Can this be true? How can our people do this? If they lose everything, what kind of person would Jorge Luis become? Would he be revengeful? What would he think of me, an American?*

"Señor Lot, the large acreage is measured by horseback," said Jorge Luis. "We have no trained surveyors. We use two horses. One horse stands where a stake has been placed, and the other goes ahead with a very long leather rope. When he comes to the end of the rope, he places a stake in the ground and then the other horseman rides up, and it begins again. They only record acreage as *más o menos*, more or less. That is considered legal here."

"Good lord," said Lot, "I think you may have trouble there. I believe the U. S. government is going to be very picky about documentation, especially if they intend to take as much land as they can. The government will call you into court. That costs a lot of money. Besides court costs, you will have to pay a lawyer, one who specializes in land law. Then, there are the costs of travel, food, and lodging. You will end up selling property just to pay the costs."

"How can they dare do such a thing?" asked Aldiana.

"I'm sorry, Señora," said Bryant, "but they can because they are the new government, and they will begin soon because the demand for land is growing rapidly. I see real estate prices going up already. The inflow of people increases weekly, and many want to stay and settle here."

"Yes," said Lot, "In fact, I understand the landing place on the Sacramento river called Colusa is turning into a small settlement. I hope to invest in a stable there, and I believe it will bring in a good business."

Aldiana looked at Jorge Luis and asked, "*Mijo*, would you and Edgardo agree to get out the old land documents and have Señor Lot and Señor Bryant look them over?"

"I think that's a great idea, Mother," said Jorge Luis. He looked at Edgardo, who nodded in agreement. He turned to Lot and said, "Señor Lot, is there any possibility that our land could be surveyed?"

Lot looked at Bryant, raising his eyebrows in question.

Bryant said, "Let us check the documentation first, and then we'll know more about what we can do."

Fiarela was so fidgety, moving around in her seat, that she could hardly control herself. If her eyes had not been so dark, the fire in them could have been seen. She slapped her hand on the table and had immediate attention from everyone, who were surprised into silence, "Why have we not been informed of all this?" Fiarela's voice was forceful and angry as she jumped into the conversation authoritatively, despite receiving disapproving looks from her mother. Her brothers were disapproving of such overt behavior, too, but remained quiet, while Bryant gave her a small approving nod.

"*Señorita*," said Lot, "What we overheard first was that new land management regulation isn't law yet. The government isn't stabilized out here. The Mexican military has a loose hand on it, but they don't have much authority, and they are too far away and barely accessible. I'm sorry to say that the man who was talking to us actually laughed when he told us that they were going to send out big posters to be placed in back alleys and up, under trees thick with foliage, so they can't be seen or found until too late." He pushed back his chair and got Bryant's attention. "Bryant - that is because there is no mail service here, no newspapers to speak of or a telegraph system. He also told us that the landowners will be required to speak English. Who speaks English in this country? And, if any discrepancies are found in any document, then the court would confiscate the land, and I don't believe the Indians have documents."

Everyone stared at Lot with disbelief, unblinking and wide-eyed.

"Uncle Lot," said Prudence, "I can't believe that. The rush for gold is bad enough, but a rush of greed to usurp the land from owners who've had their property for generations?"

"I'm afraid so, my dear, and it's not going to get any better. We'll check the documents when we come back, survey where we can, and if they are called to court, maybe Bryant can help since he speaks Spanish now."

"My god, I am glad Emiliano did not live to see this," sighed Aldiana.

Edgardo added, "This is depressing and unsettling. How about some entertainment? Mother, how about it?"

"I think it would be good for all of us. Let's retire to the *sala*. I'll send Eva for Genaro to bring his guitar and his brothers with the accordion and violin. Let's relax, have fun and forget all these bad things."

The young people's eyes lit up; smiles returned to long faces. They joyfully headed for the *sala*. They pulled the chairs up close to each other, enjoyed homemade wine and talked until Genaro and his brothers arrived. Another couple came with them and began to roll up the rug to prepare for the flamboyant Flamenco dance, which was a dance of mutual, physical attraction. The woman was clasping her castanets with long, sharp fingernails, and the man wearing loud heel-stomping boots -- the best for a wood floor.

Both performers were dressed in velvet, though the woman in red had many under skirts of various colors. She had on a low-necked peasant-style blouse with gathered sleeves and embroidery to match the colors of her skirt. Her waist was tiny, cinched in by a wide black band and tied tightly. The man wore black pants. His shirt and sleeves were of the gathered, loose type of white cotton with a velvet vest to match the pants. The woman wore large bone Spanish combs in her thick, chestnut hair but kept it loose to swing about her head. He wore the sombrero cordobés, a popular, flat-brimmed hat. He was quite dashing. She was spectacular. Ohhs and ahhs were heard from everyone. Some of the servants sneaked in to watch.

The music started. The dancers were mesmerizing. The woman held the castanets high in the air, clicking them loudly, as she swooped up and down in a precise, rhythmic ballet-type movement. Keeping in time, she also loudly tapped her heels, allowing her body to react to the rhythm of the music and the sensuous movements of the man. The flouncing of her many skirts pulled up were swirled around also, with the lifting of her knees and the tapping of her heels. Lot and Bryant sat entranced until the music ended. To show their enjoyment and astonishment, they clapped as loud as they could.

Afterwards, the lead musician announced a Tapatía dance. Fiarela offered to teach Bryant, and Jorge Luis offered to teach Prudence. Edgardo grabbed Eva while Lot and Aldiana, with Nito on her lap, sat and enjoyed watching the young people. At least, Aldiana gave the pretense of enjoying it while biting her lips. Edgardo was her only child comporting himself as expected. She smiled at him as he whirled by. He was dancing with a servant, which was always acceptable. No one thought anything about that, as he was always respectful, but what would Emiliano think of Fiarela and Jorge Luis dancing with these foreigners? The enjoyment emitting from their faces and their bodies was a flag, waving in the faces of everyone there. The servants had slipped in silently and were standing in the back against the wall, quietly watching. Aldiana wrung her hands, almost forgetting Nito on her lap. She glanced at Lot, wondering what he must think.

Lot seemed engrossed with the dancers, and she felt, maybe, he hadn't noticed that Jorge Luis' feelings were out of hand with Prudence - yet what could she do? She was not about to do anything that might appear unseemly. She must retain her decorum. She shifted Nito but couldn't shift her disapproving attitude. Her prejudices had once again infiltrated her thoughts and feelings, slapping her with her fears from the past. Her blood pressure began to rise with just a little nausea. She made every effort to look calm: not moving and looking straight ahead.

It did not go unnoticed by Lot who felt a sudden sadness for her and the children. *She is such a regal woman with good intentions, mainly. I will pray for her and maybe she can soften her heart.*

"Again, again," shouted the would-be dancers and their would-be teachers, Fiarela and Jorge Luis, when the music stopped.

"Doña Aldiana, I regret it, but Bryant and I must be on the road early, and we need to excuse ourselves to retire. Your entertainment has been most enjoyable. I don't know when I have had such a good time."

"Thank you. I am glad the evening was pleasing to you. I understand your need to leave early. I will tell Consuelo the time you must rise, and she will awaken you. Teresa will have something for your breakfast." Aldiana stood up and said, "Perhaps we will see you again when you return." She smiled but kept her eyes lowered and averted.

"Most assuredly, *Señora*. When we return, we will study the land problems and try to help the best we can. In the meantime, don't worry. You have plenty of time before things change."

Lot realized she was an elegant woman, stately, reserved, and quite concerned about her family. He wished he could know her better. He also noted her disapproval of Prudence, which he didn't fully understand. The cause of it puzzled him. Prudence could have had any eligible young man. She was brought up and educated in all the proper ways. She had every quality a man would want in a wife.

With reluctance, everyone said their good nights and left the festivities with a longing in their eyes, desiring more. No one had a problem sleeping that night.

The next morning broke early and was warmer than the morning before. The men had their gear packed and ready to go before breakfast, which Teresa served with gusto, "You need a good, full belly to ride all day. I think this will do it." They filled up on fresh fruit, bread, huevos rancheros, chorizo sausages, and delicious hot chocolate atole. Bryant and Lot complained about being too heavy to ride their horses because the meal was so filling. Both men left breakfast quickly to retrieve their horses and were surprised to find them waiting at the veranda steps. Juan had helped to ready them with the traveling packs and had seen to it that all four horses were taken to the house. Everyone came out with them.

"Doña Aldiana," Lot bowed, as he took her hand and lightly kissed it. "You have been most welcoming, and I hope to see you up north someday. Our entertainment won't be as lively and fun as last night, but we'll do our best."

He walked to Prudence and said with moist eyes, "I've barely had any time to spend with my dear niece, but the time will soon come. Come here, Prudence, and give your old uncle a big hug goodbye."

Prudence hugged her uncle with tears in her eyes. Bryant, who had been watching Fiarela with longing, stepped over to hug Prudence also. "Bye, favorite cousin, we'll be back soon," he said, glancing at Fiarela, who nodded, feeling hopeful.

"Jorge Luis, Edgardo, this has been a real pleasure meeting you. We'll be back soon and see how we can help with the land," said Lot. Both boys shook his hand and stepped back to allow them to mount the horses.

"Prudence, I wish you were coming with us, but next time we will take you up north to help with designing the house," said Lot.

"I would love that. I want to see everything you find up there. That is, if I can get away for a while from my work. I can't get too far behind," said Prudence.

Aldiana was wishing with her whole heart that this girl would leave with them, but she grudgingly admitted to herself that this family was one of means and standing - one to be admired. After meeting them and getting to know them a little, she began to look at Prudence with a new perspective. It was slight but there. *I never imagined that the Americanos could measure up to my standards. Lot is certainly a commanding, knowledgeable gentleman. Bryant is also. I don't know what to think now. Prudence is not just a servant.* That ate at her. The change in her perspective of Prudence was unsettling.

Jorge Luis was relieved that Prudence didn't just up and go with them but didn't dare say anything.

Edgardo was the one who did speak up, "Please, come back anytime, and tell us all about the new lands and investments you've found. Someday, I would like to see them. I've never been up north. We will all have to come up for a visit and give you a big fiesta for a housewarming."

Smiles were seen all around. Even Aldiana, holding Nito asleep in her arms, smiled at that possibility.

Nito had been allowed to stay up late, and last night he had thoroughly loved the music. He had tried to do some of the steps of the dance, stomping his feet, twirling, and falling down. Edgardo would lift him up and dance him around. Nito's eyes sparkled. He would call out "Ay, ay, ay, ay" with his arms waving about and laughing, which caused everyone to laugh with him. After a few dances, he climbed onto Aldiana's lap and fell asleep, but he was up early, outside with everyone, and started to wave his little hands as the men mounted their horses.

Lot and Bryant waved one last goodbye, threw a kiss to Prudence and rode swiftly out of the hacienda.

When the men, at last, were out of sight in the oaks, Fiarela said, "Prudence, we might as well get some more books done while you are here, or could we all go for a short ride?"

Edgardo shook his head at his sister and said, "Jorge Luis, we've got a load of work on our schedule." He paused, caught his brother by the arm, and said, "I forgot to ask more questions about that government guy coming to marry Elena. He sounded like a sleazebag, and we don't need someone like that as a neighbor."

"You're right. I didn't think about it either. We'll ask Mamá if she's heard anything," he said, looking at Prudence and wishing just the two of them could go for a ride together.

Edgardo suddenly recalled what had happened the night before with Nito, "Jorge Luis, I need to discuss a problem with you before we do anything. Can we talk in the office before the girls begin to work?"

"Sure. I'll be there in a minute. Girls, why don't you have a big cup of chocolate atole while you're waiting. In fact, how about bringing us some?" he asked, looking directly at Prudence.

His mother caught the look and fumed, but what could she do? Her children were adults, and now Jorge Luis was the owner of the Sandoval Legacy. She knew they would always take care of her, but she no longer held the power she once had. *I still have influence, and I am still the matriarch of this family,* she thought as she pinched her lips in disapproval.

"Come on, Fiarela, let's go get Teresa to prepare us a big pitcher full," said Prudence. The girls went to the kitchen while Aldiana took Nito and retired to her room. Teresa prepared a large, colorful tray. Prudence almost stumbled from its weight but managed to carry it to the office. They all sat together with Jorge Luis sitting close to Prudence, feeling warm and comfortable. To both, it felt natural. Although they avoided looking at each other, they both were sad when the chocolate Atole was gone.

"Girls, after you return the tray, please wait for a few moments. Edgardo has something on his mind, and we need to discuss it," said Jorge Luis.

"We'll wait in the entrance foyer until you call us, but make it short," Fiarela yelled down the hallway as the brothers took off for the office. Prudence put her hand over her mouth so she wouldn't laugh.

The girls sat down on a settee. Prudence spoke, "Fiarela, the chocolate was delicious. Teresa told me that the men often have it for breakfast before they go to work and nothing else. Is that true?"

"Yes, it's a good, sturdy drink. I can't imagine why my brothers are having a meeting now. I hope they hurry. I'm anxious to get to work," said Fiarela. She sat silent for a moment, twisting a strand of hair around her finger, debating about whether to say anything, "Pru, do you think your family will be gone long? Do you think Bryant liked me?"

"Frankly? Are you serious?" asked Prudence and Fiarela nodded. "It was obvious to me that Bryant is smitten with you. What do you think?"

Fiarela just sat with her head down, silent. Eventually, she lifted her head slightly toward Prudence, "Pru, I really, really like him. He is so handsome and nice. I want him to like me. I've never had a boyfriend. Do you think he would ever consider someone like me?"

Prudence leaned over and gave her a hug. "I'm sure he would. I saw how he looked at you. You might end up being my cousin," she whispered in Fiarela's ear as the men came back from their meeting.

31
Meetings

Inside the office, Edgardo paced and paced, annoying Jorge Luis. "Come on Ed, stop that. You're driving me nuts. I don't care what it is. Tell me what's bothering you, and get it over with," said Jorge Luis. Edgardo sat down and looked out the window into the vastness of the countryside, "Why is it so beautiful out when so much evil is occurring? The skies are a pure, heavenly blue, and yet, we have a blast of black wind blowing in on us."

Jorge Luis' face paled hearing those words. The words "evil is occurring" scared him. He reacted by jumping up from his chair and was about to say something. He felt like shaking the story out of Edgardo. He shook his head, closed his eyes, took a deep breath and sat back down to listen as Edgardo continued, "I'm asking you not to intervene or interrupt. Don't question or comment until after I tell the story."

Jorge Luis opened his mouth to argue but shut it quickly. He leaned a bit over the desk, picked up a quill pen and began to jab it into the blotter. He didn't like to give authority over to anyone, but this was his brother, almost his equal. Obviously, what he was going to hear was something he wouldn't want to. Edgardo kept crossing and uncrossing his legs, and shifting in the chair, which made Jorge Luis more uneasy.

"That bad?" Jorge Luis asked, sitting sat back further in the chair, almost as if he wanted to disappear into it. "I'll listen."

"Last night, a strange sound awakened me. It was Nito rolling around in his bed, crying out, 'No, no, bad.' Then more odd noises and tugging at the blankets. I realized he was having a bad dream. He'd never had one before. I didn't know what was happening. I went to the crib, picked him up carefully, and put him down in my warm bed."

Jorge Luis was now confused. *Nito? Where was this leading?* But he kept still.

"Nito woke and looked up into my eyes. It was like he was looking through me. He kept repeating, 'Bad man, bad man' and hit me on my chest.

He's never done anything like that before." Edgardo stopped, frowned and shook his head. "I calmed down and softly asked him, 'Nito, did you see a bad man?'

"Looking up at me, he nodded, and his eyes got bigger. Then he grabbed me and buried his head in my chest, and I barely heard him say, 'Him touch, touch bad.' I had to take a couple of deep breaths. I couldn't imagine what it was all about. 'Nito, what did the man touch?' I asked him, whispering near his ear and hoping he heard me.'

"Jorge Luis, stop staring out the window and listen. Nito said, 'Him touch hair, hair Papá. Him have knife, too. Bad man.'"

Jorge Luis gasped and sat up in attention.

"'Nito, what color was the hair?' again, I asked him slowly and carefully. He said, holding on to me tightly, 'Pru, Pru hair. Bad man - peu, peu.'"

Jorge Luis' eyes widened in fear. He became increasingly nervous as Edgardo told Nito's story.

"I wasn't sure what he meant by peu, so I asked if the bad man smelled bad. He nodded his head, Hermano, and then told me that the man stunk and touched hair again."

Jorge Luis sat up, rigid. All his senses were on high alert. He felt cold with fear. He clenched his fists and his face was a deep red. He felt he may blow up.

Edgardo looked at Jorge Luis, shook his head, told him not to say anything, and then said, "I tried to soothe him, and take away his fear. I told him that he had a good dream, not a bad one, and that the dream came to him from his angels. They wanted us to watch out for that bad man who stinks. I told him his dream was telling us to not let that bad man touch Pru's hair, and that we need to thank the angels for that dream. I made sure he understood he could stay in my bed, and go back to sleep with Papá," said Edgardo, looking over at Jorge Luis who was sitting stiffly.

Jorge Luis was almost paralyzed with fear and anger. He had learned to listen to his brother, but little Nito shocked him, "My god, Hermano, I knew he had your gift but that clear and so young? And to bring a warning that strong. It sounds like a warning about Rafa. What do you think?"

"That's what I'm guessing. I needed to tell you as soon as possible. Didn't the man who robbed Prudence stink? And isn't Rafa the leader of those bandits? We need to think how to protect her," said Edgardo.

"Let's get Facundo, Juan, Benito, and Gregorio and work out a plan," said Jorge Luis. His skin looked clammy. He felt jumpy, and when the wind blew an acorn against the outside wall, he jerked and darted his eyes, looking for danger there in the office.

"Jorge Luis, you've got to calm down and get a hold of yourself. We need you to think straight," said Edgardo. "I'll call the men and we'll meet tonight."

"That dirty little son of a bitch. The coward, he can't even come straight for me," Jorge Luis said, looking daggers at his brother. He spat out the words as if they shot out from his unerring gun. "So, Rafa wants to dance with the devil, does he? Let him try. I've got his number. If my eyes set on him, no matter where - he's done," said Jorge Luis with a tone of finality, patting his leg where his knife was kept, and then his hip, where he wore his pistol. His eyes became darker, cold, hard and flinty.

Edgardo knew he meant every word he said and worried that he might be putting himself in more danger than Prudence.

"Okay, okay, Brother, take it easy. We will have to be smart. With the men's help, we're sure to get him." Edgardo paused and took a deep breath, "I'm changing the subject for a moment so bear with me. I am going to ask a question that's on everyone's mind and has been for some time." He paused to let that sink in. Looking at his brother straight in the face, he asked, "Have you declared yourself to Prudence? Have you asked her to marry you yet? We all know you are in love with her."

"Are you crazy? Mother would never agree, and I'm not ready for that. I'm overwhelmed already with all this ranch stuff. I wouldn't be able to do right by her. Besides, I can't - especially now with this Rafa crap," he was wringing his hands, rubbing his knees and staring at the floor.

"You, dumb ass. Listen up. Who's marrying her? Who will have to live with her - you or Mother? Don't do to yourself what's happened to me. I'm only half of myself. I'm empty. I long for Ramona every day and night. You'll hate yourself and everyone else if you turn her away. You know she loves you and don't deny it!" said Edgardo, while pushing his hair back to front and front to back, pacing to the window. He turned, feeling shaky with deep emotion, "I want to see you happy more than anything. You two belong together. Fiarela considers her a sister. Don't be a fool. *Nadie tiene su vida comprada.*"

Jorge Luis had his mouth covered with his hand and said almost under his breath, "You're right. I admit I'm crazy about her. I want her with me all the time, but I never thought she could accept someone like me. When Lot and Bryant come back, I will ask for permission to court her." He looked imploringly at his brother for validation. His eyes begged for aid, "I'm too afraid she will spurn me. I can't face that and then Mother's wrath. I don't know what to do."

"Of course you know what to do, you stupid idiot! It's obvious that she already loves you. Talk to her first. You're both adults, for God's sake. And, Mother be damned. She's not the one who will be sleeping with her every night. Look, after her bad experience with that robber, that dirty-mouthed drunk in the cantina who mauled her, and that nightmarish episode with Alberto, she's scared of what might happen to her. She'll be better protected with you. Think about that." Edgardo was adamant.

Jorge Luis stood up, saying, "I never thought about that. I don't know how I could have been so insensitive. I feel like a fool. I never thought about how she might feel, being in a country that is so foreign to her and having to live where she does, especially being a truly educated lady. Oh God, Edgardo, now I feel unbearably guilty. I don't think I could ever be able to live without her. I want her in my life. I don't know how you do it."

"It's not something I will ever get over, but somehow, I will get through it for Nito's sake. He keeps me going. Let's get out to work. There shouldn't be any danger to Prudence today. She will be here all day working with Fiarela. Maybe you could give Benito orders to not take her home alone. Find someone to ride along but stay out of sight. And Benito should be armed. If you can, I would advise you to ride with her."

"Yes, good idea. Thanks, Hermano," said Jorge Luis, taking a deep breath, relieved. He walked to Edgardo and hugged him tightly. He opened the tall double doors of the office and yelled at the girls, "We're through. You can have the office, but don't go out unless you tell us, and one of us will go with you." The two brothers went out to the hallway and out the back door. Work was calling.

The girls looked at each other with furrowed brows, as they wondered what that was all about. Fiarela yelled back before they left, "Okay, my big brother protectors, we'll see you later." She lowered her voice and said, "We'll find out what he meant later. We'd better, anyway. Come on, Pru, let's go get to work."

The day dragged on for Jorge Luis, worrying about what to do about Rafa. *That bandido malvado, why's he got a vengeance against me? He's like a shadow. He's all over the place and we have no way to find that slippery vato. I have so much on my shoulders right now to have to waste time on him. I'm counting on this meeting with the men to come up with something solid that I can handle.* It was hard for Jorge Luis to concentrate on his work.

But the day did come to an end. Jorge Luis and Edgardo came in from work, cleaned up, and met in the office. They prepared the desk with a notebook, quill pen and ink in the inkwell for Jorge Luis. Edgardo took out a canter of tequila and glasses.

"Come on, Ed, pour me one now. I need it," said Jorge Luis.

"Agreed. I need one, too. Oh, oh, I hear boots down the hallway. Here's your drink," said Edgardo, as he handed it to his brother and the double doors opened. The men came in with serious faces, but the sight of tequila brought smiles.

"Come on in, take a glass, and find a seat. Thank God, you were all able to get here now," said Edgardo, as Jorge Luis went behind the desk to start the meeting. All eyes were on him, wondering what this was all about.

"*Buenas tardes, amigos*, sorry to call you here so unexpectedly. I think most of you have heard of Rafa - that dirty bandit," said Jorge Luis. Heads nodded, and the men turned and looked at each other curiously. "He's Elias' brother and has been here, threatening me and Prudence," explained Jorge Luis. Gasps were heard from everyone. "He's dangerous, and I'm hoping we can find a way to deal with this without frightening Prudence or Fiarela."

Facundo and his son, Pedro, Gregorio, Juan, and Benito listened intently. They were disgusted, shaking their heads. Soon, they jumped into a heated discussion on how to protect Prudence and take care of Rafa. Pedro sat very quietly, listening, but suddenly held up his hand.

"What is it, Pedro? Go ahead. Speak up," said Jorge Luis, who was leading the meeting with his elbows on the desk, holding and rubbing his hands in the air nervously.

"Señor, I discovered the General Store has a poster on their wall with a picture of Rafa. Some miners are offering five thousand dollars for him, dead or alive," he said. His eyes were large, as he glanced around at everyone, and he nodded as he spoke.

"Good," said Jorge Luis. The word was echoed throughout the room. Facundo gave his son a warm smile and a nod of fatherly approval.

Jorge Luis continued, "I don't want Prudence alone, coming or going from the pueblo. And, Benito, I want you armed, always. That Arab of hers would be an attraction anywhere. Please, don't allow her to be riding out on it alone."

"Jorge Luis," said Edgardo, "We have another problem. We shear sheep next week, and we can't postpone that. We're shorthanded, and all the men will be involved.

Facundo spoke up, "Don't worry too much. I don't think he will be here soon. I heard he was wounded in a big robbery up at the goldmines. I'll keep my ears open in the cantina. Pedro, you tell me if you see or hear anything."

"*Claro*, Papá," said Pedro, twelve years old, who was nodding and slowly moving back to sit out of the way of these adults. He didn't want to interfere with their ideas or options. He was very shy, and although he felt proud to have been included, he felt a little out of place.

Jorge Luis was up and pacing like a caged cougar behind the desk, which the girls had left in good order, but was now messed up. He had the quill pen in his hand, ready to record whatever ideas each man came up with. When he calmed down, he sat down again and said, "I'll talk to Andrés, the cook and Lizette. Maybe her girls will hear or know something," he noted on his list.

"I heard just two nights ago that Rafa's gang hangs out in a cave somewhere up high in the Sierras, past Angels Camp," said Facundo. He looked back in his memory and tried to sort through cantina conversations to see if he knew more.

"I haven't seen his horse tracks for at least two weeks out where they were rustling cattle. He's easy to track, unless he's got new horseshoes or a different horse. We're short men, and I can't check as often," said Gregorio, looking concerned. The lack of enough men was a serious problem.

"Yeah, I know that is causing us more trouble, but let me or Edgardo know if anything happens. From now on, I don't want anyone to go un-armed," said Jorge Luis, "And, I think we should not tell either Prudence or Fiarela yet. I don't want to scare them." He looked at Edgardo, who seemed disapproving. He then added, "Yes, I agree, Edgardo, we need to find a way to let them know about bandits around here and to always be armed and never alone."

"That feels okay for right now," said Edgardo, "but, we need to keep alert and," he emphasized, "DON'T LET UP!"

Benito suggested, "Boss, I'll try to have a man follow me, out of sight and armed - just in case."

"Good idea and Pru should not walk anywhere alone in the village, either. Rafa's bad news, so stay alert. Let me know as soon as you hear or see anything." Two hours had passed with much discussion. Jorge Luis brought the meeting to a close, "How about one more *trago*, and then we will call it a night. We'll meet again later. *Buenas noches*."

After the men left, Jorge Luis paced again behind the desk, pondering the spot he was in. *This is overwhelming. I'm not sure I'm doing the right thing. Maybe I should just take Juan, Gregorio, and Edgardo and go up to the caves and take him out. I don't think he'd stand a chance against us, but on the other hand, I don't dare take a chance with my men. We must get through shearing first. I'll go pray in the chapel and ask that Prudence be kept safe."*

"Hey, Hermano, I almost forgot," said Edgardo, "I asked Mother about that government official that is supposed to marry Elena. She said all she knows is that Elena will be married sometime during the summer when Father Serrano arrives, or if he arrives sooner, they would have it then. Mother felt he would be coming in June, which means for us the planning for Papá's funeral Mass - and your wedding."

"What? That's too soon. I'm not ready, and I don't even know if she will have me," said a desperate sounding Jorge Luis, rubbing his hands together. He looked around the room as if he was caged in an unknown place. He felt cornered.

Edgardo stood up and looked his brother closely in the face. He said, in a serious tone, "*Hermano*, you have one chance here and not a lot of time. If you fail to act, you will face, like me, a lifetime of heartache and an empty bed. Don't be a fool and don't wait too long."

Jorge Luis knew the message was true, but he agonized over how he could manage it all. There was too much responsibility, too many variables and unknowns with this hacienda and the land grant with the new government coming. *The Americanos and their laws are so different. How can I approach Prudence? What if she won't accept me, and how will Mother react? She's already upset about us. Where do I even start?* He looked around the office and realized how much it meant to him. He'd known that room since he used to crawl around his father's legs while he worked. He remembered how, slowly, over the years, he had learned the business management of the Sandoval family heritage.

Now what? Next week with the shearing going, I won't have time to see Prudence or talk to her. I've got to listen to Edgardo and find a way to act as soon as possible. But, being traditional, he wanted to formally ask for Prudence's hand from her uncle. He felt with approval from Lot, his mother could not interfere or say much. He walked quickly to the chapel with the heavy weight of fear for Prudence weighing on his soul. He slowly sat down and prayed. *I've got to get through the shearing, or we'll lose our wool and sheep market. Oh, Lord, please help me. I want to do right, but I feel at such a loss.* He felt caught tight within his pastoral and traditional heritage and its fixed traditions. So many sudden and incomprehensible changes seemed to be coming faster. And, now, he had admitted his love for a woman who came from those people, the foreigners, who were responsible for his nightmares. He was a man of deeply held feelings. He lowered his head, held it in his hands, and sobbed. He didn't see his father, but through his sobs, he heard him. His father's voice came from above his right shoulder. He clearly heard, "Son, you will know what to do. Always remember you are protected. Just be your own man."

Those words rang through Jorge Luis like a vibrating bell. *My God, I always knew that God worked in mysterious ways. He sent my father.* Jorge Luis sat up straight with a newfound strength and resolve. *Maybe I don't know right now, but I will when I need to.* He gave thanks and left the chapel, knowing all would happen in divine order.

32
Spring Shearing

The sun was rising earlier every day. Benito was already up, dressed, had his breakfast, had the carriage hitched up, and on his way to pick up Prudence in town. He was armed. One of the workers, young Danilo, who was well-armed, followed him at a distance, keeping out of sight. They were going to do this every time Benito went to pick up Prudence and bring her to the hacienda.

When he reached town that day, without anything untoward happening, Prudence was waiting by the kitchen door with a basket full of food. She didn't usually do that, but the day was so nice that she hoped she and Fiarela could have a picnic. Benito stopped the carriage, got out to help her up into the open buggy, but she handed him the basket, pulled up her skirts, and hoisted herself up easily.

"Benito, it is so beautiful out this morning." She looked at him with pleading eyes. "I really could ride Cámila and save you these trips. You know how I love to ride. And I don't believe that bandit, Rafa, would bother *me*."

Benito looked shocked, "How do you know about Rafa? No one was supposed to tell you."

I happened to catch a glimpse of Danilo following us. Remember? I asked you why, and you said that you didn't think he was. Well, when we arrived at the hacienda, I asked Jorge Luis about him and he told me the whole story. But, it can't be dangerous for me, Benito, and, if I had to, I would enjoy riding with Danilo. I promise that I would carry my gun. I've had years of practice and I don't miss."

"Prudence, I appreciate that, but, right now, we need to be watchful, very careful. I'm glad you were informed about these bandits. They are quite dangerous – especially the one called Rafa." He looked straight at her, getting her full attention. "Do you have your pistol? The one you brought out from Maine with you, the Colt forty-four?" asked Benito. "Jorge Luis wants me to make sure you have it on you, right at hand, loaded, no matter where you are - in the office, too."

"Yes, yes, I do, and I took my Colt Thirty-One Derringer and my ankle holster out of my trunk. I have them on. I've never needed them before. I only used them on the trip out here if we were in a small village. Is it really that bad, Benito?" asked Prudence, shaking her head lightly in disapproval. Benito nodded. Then she added, "I mentioned Rafa to Facundo, too, and he lectured me as well. I hate being lectured." Benito heaved a sigh and patiently waited for her to finish.

"It is too beautiful out this morning. The wildflowers are all over." She took in a full breath of fresh morning air and closed her eyes for a second. "Look at the lupine on the hills and the wild mustard. Did you know that the mustard was brought here by the mission priests? They must have dropped seeds everywhere they went or, maybe, the bay wind blew them all over because now they grow wild," she said. She bent forward toward the fields and waved her arm, pointing at the vibrant, colorful hills. "Beautiful, aren't they?" she paused, taking a deep slow breath again. "Phew, I love being out in the early morning, even with that scent of a skunk drifting from somewhere. Look over there," she pointed above a grove of oak trees, "See all those vultures soaring around? It must be a large carcass?"

Benito nodded, acceding to her, but said, "Sí, probably a cow, but we were talking about your guns and how important it is to be alert at all times."

Prudence turned to stare at her driver. "Benito," she began, "if this guy is such a bad bandit, why haven't they caught him yet? I understand there is a wanted poster of him in the store and a lot of dollars for his capture."

"He's slick," said Benito. "I hear he keeps his gang up in the mountains in a cave. No one has been able to find it yet. We really do have to be careful, Prudence. He has a vendetta against Jorge Luis, and we expect trouble."

"But, Benito, I haven't anything to steal. And, besides, aren't most of the bandits up at the gold mines?"

"I hope so," said Benito, "but some are creating more problems around here, and Rafa is notorious. We've got to take precautions." He broke off the conversation and gave the horse's big rear end a slap of the reins. They moved from a slow walk to a good trot.

Up on a higher hill, protected under a big oak, stood a horse and rider  with a spyglass, watching. He nodded with a smile of satisfaction. The man was not Danilo.

The ride to the hacienda turned out to be quite a pleasant one. The trees had blossomed. Now, they were sprouting lots of little budding leaves. The small creeks and depressions were still running, but at about half full.

"Benito, look, is that a grizzly bear up ahead, off in the distance? That's the biggest bear I have ever seen," said Prudence. "It won't attack, will it?" She crossed her hands up high on her chest as if to protect herself.

"It sure is a grizzly. No, it won't. It's too far away to be bothered by us. We'll stop," he said, pulling on the reins, "until he crosses the road. He's heading for the river. Grizzlies love the new, young tulle roots, so this time of year we watch out for them. They come down out of the hills, and they're dangerous."

The grizzly moved at a good pace and was soon at a safe distance. Benito urged the horse onward.

Danilo followed unobserved, but he spotted the horseman high up on the hill, watching with a spyglass. The man on the hill closed his spyglass, putting it in his pocket, while moving his horse slowly and silently down the steep, rocky ravine. Danilo made up his mind to tell Jorge Luis as soon as possible. *Could that be him, Rafa?* he wondered.

As Benito and Prudence passed through the trees and over a few running streams, they became quiet, listening to the sounds of the motion of the harness straps on the horse, his methodical steps on the dirt path, the swishing of his tail, and the occasional plops of excrement and farts. The crickets got louder as it got warmer, and Prudence enjoyed watching the jack rabbits speed away. They brought back memories of home. She remembered how, a few years ago, she had raised a wounded baby rabbit and then let him go when he grew up.

"Prudence, when do you expect your uncle and cousin to return? We're all impressed with them -- good people," said Benito.

"Thanks, Benito. It depends if the property my uncle wants is suitable. Bryant has to do all the paperwork. The land has to be surveyed and recorded so that he won't be swindled," said Prudence. "I really don't know how long it might take them."

"With this new bandit problem, you might consider going up north with them for a while," said Benito.

"I will, but maybe later. The bookkeeping keeps me very busy, and Maria still needs my help with the twins. Fiarela's not finished with her lessons, either."

"I understand," he said, giving her a sidewise glance, knowing it was really Jorge Luis who kept her there. "Keep your gun on you, don't forget." She rolled her eyes and nodded. "Look ahead, you can see the hacienda," he said. They both sat back silently in expectation.

Within minutes, they arrived and were surprised when Fiarela came bounding down the veranda steps, shouting, "It's shearing time! Let's go watch! Prudence, you should see it! Thousands of sheep. Please? Benito, can you take us, or can Prudence drive the small cart?"

"Fi, I've seen shearing at home in Maine, but, sure, I would like to see it. How far is it?"

Before she could answer, Benito spoke up, "*Chamacas*, calm down. You have to ask permission. I don't have time to spend all afternoon up there. I can't drive you." That worried him, but it would have to be up to Danilo to follow them. He was a good young man, and Benito felt secure that he would protect them.

Prudence and Fiarela both looked at each other, eyes wide, wanting to go.

"Fiarela, you go get permission. I will maneuver the small trap up the hills. You can direct us. I have a basket of food. Can you get some water?" asked Prudence.

"Oh, *que bueno*. Benito, you and Prudence wait here. I'll get permission."

Prudence had learned Spanish well by now. She and Benito enjoyed talking until Fiarela arrived with a big smile and another basket of food and water.

"I'll get the smaller cart, and you can drive, Prudence," said Benito. In minutes he returned with the small buggy, and the girls were off, but not without an admonition about being careful and keeping that gun handy.

The air, rushing over the two adventurer's faces, was refreshing. The view was equally delightful with the fields sprinkled with wildflowers, like the little yellow buttercups and the small, delicate, blue camursia.

Fiarela pointed out that if you put a buttercup under your chin, your chin would turn yellow. Prudence laughed and noted how lovely they were scattered around the countryside. "It feels so good to be out in nature doesn't it, Fi, and getting away from being inside all day?" she said.

"It makes me feel full of life. We're so lucky that the gnats are not out yet."

"Gnats? What are those? I haven't heard Facundo mention them."

"Oh, they're horrible. They're tiny, biting bugs. When they're out, you must be completely covered and wear gloves, or they will eat you alive. They're so tiny they get into your eyes, your ears, and hair," said Fiarela.

"Good lord. When do they arrive? Thank heavens you warned me."

"Probably next week, I think, and they come out early, when the morning warms a little. They invade everything - even the animals suffer," Fiarela answered.

Prudence cut in, "Look, over near that big oak, is that a coyote? It's going down into the ground."

"That must be where its den is. I've got to tell Jorge Luis. When they get into the sheep, they rip them up. He lost twenty-five sheep one night."

"I'm so sorry. I had no idea they did that kind of damage," said Prudence.

They were now in a flat area, but the shearing shed couldn't be seen yet.

"Oh, Pru, being out here with you makes me feel so alive. You're so bold and clever. I want to be like you. Teach me to drive. Please, please, teach me to drive. Will you?" begged Fiarela.

Prudence took a big breath in and thought about the implications of what she was contemplating. She said, "Fi, are you sure? How are you going to talk your mother into letting you – drive like a man?"

Both girls laughed so hard at their wild idea that Prudence almost ran off the road.

After they gained their composure, Prudence studied Fiarela for a few moments. She decided to think about it awhile longer. *How can I please Fiarela but still maintain my integrity with the family?*

"I appreciate your invitation. It's turning out to be a surprisingly fun morning," said Prudence.

"When I found out that they were shearing today, I thought that it would be a perfect excuse for a break. Boy, I wanted it. You really have kept my nose to the grindstone, but you've taught me so much, and I love it. I'll miss you terribly when you quit coming so often."

"I'll miss you just as much, but Jorge Luis will be happy when you can take over the bookkeeping. Will he be at the sheep shearing?" He hadn't been around since shearing started and she missed him more than she wanted to admit.

"Oh, yes," said Fiarela, looking at Prudence out of the corner of her eye. "He's in charge of the whole operation."

The soft plodding of the horse's hooves and the swishing of its tail brought a feeling of contentedness to both girls. They were quite relaxed, when, suddenly, they heard the bleating of thousands of sheep, barking dogs, and yelling *trabajadores*.

"Fi, listen to that. Wow, I forgot what chaotic music it was to my ears. Oh, what memories. How many shearers are there?"

"I don't actually know. Sometimes, I think, more than ten."

Prudence stared at Fiarela, "That's a lot. Is that the barn up ahead now? You said it was used for lambing too?"

"Yeah, it is. During the lambing season, they arrange pens inside for the ewes with birthing problems that have lost their lambs, and separate pens for lambs that have lost their mothers. The other ewes ready to lamb are outside in the holding field. There is another lambing barn far from here that is being used too."

"It must take incredible organization to work all that out with so many sheep. I can't imagine it. You know, back home when one of our lambs died, and the mother of another lamb died, the men would skin the dead lamb and wrap its skin over the lamb whose mother died. The mother ewe would smell her own dead lamb's skin scent and accept the orphaned lamb. Does your family do that?" asked Prudence.

Fiarela looked at her with wonder, "Really, I'm not sure. Oh, look. Here we are. There's the barn up ahead. A couple of more minutes and we can look for Jorge Luis." Fiarela gave a quick glance at Prudence, who slapped the reins against the rump of the horse to speed it up. She was careful to stay on the outskirts of the barn and pens to keep out of the way. She didn't want to create a problem or scare the sheep.

"Prudence, how about over there? We could park under the oaks near that little creek. We'd be in the shade and the horse could water," said Fiarela.

Prudence moved the cart and halted the horse. They both dismounted from the buggy, and Prudence unhitched the horse and tied it to a tree. The horse, free of its harness, gave a good shake and started nibbling grass.

Fiarela unloaded the picnic baskets and blanket. When she finished, she searched around, asking, "Can you see my brother?" Both girls looked to see if they could spot Jorge Luis.

"I can't see him in the holding field where most of the sheep are," said Fiarela.

"Maybe he's in the barn," said Prudence, "Wait, I see him. He's over at the branding chute. Let's wave at him."

At the branding chute, the sheep walked single file while Jorge Luis branded them and marked them with a chalk. The brand was carved from the end of an old wooden post, which he was dipping into tar. He looked up from his work, his eyes widened, and a look of surprise and joy crossed his face, but then, he felt concern and his anger swelled up, augmented by fear. He caught himself and decided he would not let the girls be frightened. They should have been followed by a bodyguard, but he did not see one. He would have to check on that. He gave the girls a big smile and yelled, "*Hola,* ladies. What are you two doing out here?"

"I wanted to show Prudence the shearing."

"I'll be right over. Give me a minute," yelled Jorge Luis over the din of the sheep, the shearers, and the dogs. He put down the brand by the bucket of tar and threw the chalk into its box. He covered the distance to the cart quickly, looked at Prudence and wished he could scoop her up into his arms to welcome her, but instead asked, "Prudence, you drove this buggy out here all by yourself? Did you come armed?"

"Oh, yes, I have my gun," answered Prudence. She stood straight and faced him directly to say, "I used to drive Uncle Lot everywhere. I loved it. I was twelve when I started driving, and I've never had an accident." She wanted to say that women are considered intelligent and capable and are not kept submissive in Maine but was polite enough not to.

Jorge Luis then remembered he had seen her drive around the barns. He looked her over again and was more impressed, his eyes full of admiration, but his thoughts of a deeper interest were interrupted by Fiarela, who said, "Hermano, can you show us around a little and then join us for a picnic?"

"*¡Por supuesto!* I would enjoy that. Come on over to the barn, but be careful, and watch where you are stepping." He turned to Prudence, who was caught again by the intensity of his eyes, and said, "Prudence, do you know anything about shearing?"

"Yes, of course, I used to watch the men shear in my uncle's barn, but you have a huge operation here. I'm amazed. How many sheep do you run?"

"We handle five thousand head or more here, and we have another crew working over at the barn where Edgardo is. It is a considerable distance from here. We have about another five thousand head over there. We'll finish in a week or more. Oh, here we are at the barn. You can watch the men work, but watch your step."

As Prudence stepped into the barn, she stopped for a moment, looked around, and noted that, although the organization was somewhat different, the behaviors were the same. She commented, "I see you use the same big hand shears we use. Do you get a lot of nicked-up sheep?"

"Oh, yeah, but the men are careful, and the sheep heal up quickly."

"What do you do with the wool?"

"Come with me, and I'll show you."

Fiarela, trying to step daintily, said, "Couldn't you, at least, have the men keep this ground cleaner?"

Jorge Luis laughed, "Come on Sis, you know better. I know it's sloppy and it stinks, but the sheep can't help it. All this confusion makes them nervous so they poop and they pee, and that is what happens. They don't stop just because you're coming. Besides, the men try to clean it up the best they can at quitting time."

Fiarela looked disgusted, but Prudence laughed and then looked around. "That platform up there. Is that where they throw the wool?" she asked.

"Yes. See that kid over there? He picks up the wool and throws it up to the guy on the platform."

"Hey, that's how we do it, too. He'll jump into the wool sack and stomp the wool down tight, right?" Prudence looked around and remarked, "God, what hard, dirty work." Now hungry for lunch, she asked, "Who feeds the men and where do they stay?"

Fiarela burst in, saying, "They have cooks, and the men sleep in their tents."

As they started to leave the barn, Prudence stopped, looked Jorge Luis directly in his eyes, and said quietly, "I hope you don't mind, but I want to know because in Maine we always had to do this." Both Fiarela and Jorge Luis looked puzzled and intrigued. "Do you castrate your little bucks?" she asked.

Jorge Luis was taken aback, and Fiarela blushed from what they considered was a topic for men only.

"Yes, we do. Then, we either sell them or butcher them," Jorge Luis managed to say, without stumbling over his words from embarrassment.

Prudence realized she was enjoying this conversation. She was toying with him and had never done that before. She had noticed how embarrassed he became, and she had never seen that. She knew being bold was not considered ladylike, but she couldn't stop. She pushed him further just to see how he would react, "How do you do it? Uncle Lot had to bite the skin, then suck out the testicle, and then he would spit it into a bowl. We considered them a treat for breakfast. Do you eat them?"

"Yes," said Fiarela, "We usually eat them for breakfast, too, mixed with scrambled eggs. They are a once-a-year treat for us, too." She gave a little smirk, as she was aware of what Prudence was doing.

Prudence turned to Jorge Luis and questioned, "I supposed you bite them out with your teeth also?"

Jorge Luis turned a deep purplish hue when he answered yes and quickly changed the subject, "Come on, ladies, I'm hungry. Let me wash up, and I will join you for the picnic." He wasn't sure what to make of Prudence right now. She always acted like a lady but seemed to have no boundaries when it came to proper ladylike questioning of certain things. He wondered about all foreigners. *Are their women all so forward? Do they all project themselves into men's business? I've always enjoyed her outspokenness. She speaks her mind. I admire that, but can I trust her to be discreet? Mother insists we be very discriminating when we choose a wife.* His heart began to sink a little.

"Let's prepare for lunch, Prudence," said Fiarela. "*Hermano,* come over as soon as you can."

"I'll finish running that last bunch of sheep through the chute and be there." Once again, he thought about Prudence and her forwardness and curiosity about the shearing here, comparing it to Maine. On the one hand he admired it, but it was not what his culture expected of a woman, and in front of Fiarela. He had seen enough of Prudence to know she would be an excellent mother. His heart told him so, but his mind was doing a number on him. Doubt had raised its ugly head.

"Okay, we'll see you in a few minutes. We'll have everything ready. I know you have to go back to work soon," said Fiarela.

The picnic blanket had been laid under a big oak near where Prudence had tied up the horse. The girls laid out the food and sat admiring the countryside with all the wildflowers, which were scattered over the green grass - white, lavender and yellow ones.

Prudence picked some flowers for the blanket and put them in a little bowl. She looked at Fiarela and smiled, saying, "Back home we call those little yellow ones scrambled eggs, and, yes, I did try to eat some when I was very young, and, yes, I liked them. They were mild and sweet." She laughed at Fiarela, whose eyes had widened in surprise and, almost, disbelief.

Jorge Luis arrived quickly and, for the first time, after he sat and started to eat, let his guard down and relaxed. His previous doubts slipped away on the welcoming breeze. It took the bite out of the early afternoon heat and his worries. He ate gustily. The three of them chatted easily. His gaze was fixed on Prudence. His doubts disappeared and he knew exactly what he wanted.

Noticing, Fiarela felt her brother was more than impressed. He was enchanted.

"Jorge Luis, back in Maine, we mark our sheep with chalk, which tells which field that sheep goes into. Is that why you do it? I saw that you branded your sheep with a big S and a small six-pointed star. I could see it on the sheep. I assume the S is for Sandoval. What does the star represent?"

He paused a moment, "Well, first, the chalk does tell us in which field to put the sheep." Now, he was beginning to feel nervous, "You're right, Prudence, about the S. The brand is so old that I think the star is just decorative. It helps identify our brand from other brands with an S. In fact, my grandfather once said our brand came with the family from Spain." He looked away, feeling guilty about telling a lie. That did not settle well and gave him a small stomachache. Fiarela sat, holding her breath and diverting her eyes.

"I was curious because back in Maine the six-pointed star is a symbol of our Jewish people," said Prudence.

Jorge Luis' mouth dropped open. He looked quickly away until he regained his composure. Fiarela, surprised upon hearing that so unexpectedly, gasped, coughed and covered her mouth, turned her head away and looked off into the distance, while Jorge Luis spoke a little too rapidly when he explained, "Well, we're all Catholic out here. But, that's interesting. I've never heard of any Jewish people in California." He looked down at his boots, so she couldn't see his face, and rubbed the dust off them with a sinking feeling. *Jesus, give me strength. By blood, I am considered Jewish, but I know nothing about it. What would Prudence think of me if she knew?* "Ladies, I've got to get back to work. Before I go, Prudence, is there anything else you would like to know?" he asked, hoping she'd say no.

The girls were both sitting down on the picnic blanket again, quite comfortably, so she did not get up, "Yes, I forgot to ask. Do you cut the tails off your lambs?"

This time, taken by surprise, Jorge Luis laughed and said, "Yes. It helps keep them cleaner and safer from maggots and screw worms. And, you might be interested to know we eat them fried." *That was too close. What else might she ask? I believe there should be no secrets between a man and his wife, but, I think, Mamá is right. People knowing about our Jewish roots would bring fear, and they might ostracize our family. Oh God, I don't want to live with this always eating at me.*

Before she was going to get up to say goodbye, she spoke to him one last time, "By the way, Jorge Luis, since Fiarela is close to finishing learning the financial books, I won't be coming out like I have been. What would you think about her learning to drive the small carriage? It might prove to be a big help if she could. What do you think?"

"Well, I," he looked from one to the other, "I'd never thought about such a thing. You should get permission from Mother, I suppose. On the other hand, I am in charge now, and I see nothing wrong with it. Go ahead but be discreet and don't over-do it."

Fiarela jumped up and gave Jorge Luis a big hug, "I love you, big brother! I've wanted to learn so badly. I can hardly wait."

Prudence stood up and held her hand out to Jorge Luis, saying, "Thank you. I will be very cautious with Fiarela, don't worry. It's been a wonderful day." She could hardly take her eyes off him, wanting him to hold her hand, not just shake it.

Taking her hand, Jorge Luis felt a jolt he could not deny. He had a hard time letting go. Her hand was so tiny compared to his. Hers was warm, soft, yet strong. To Prudence, his hand was large and rough, but carried a feeling of protection. She wanted to walk into his arms, but felt she needed to remain polite and ladylike.

Prudence, seeing a different side of Jorge Luis during the tour and the picnic, took her leave, demurely stating, "I'm very appreciative, seeing the shearing, and I hope it did not disturb your work too much."

"No, no, *mi placer,*" Jorge Luis responded, and he meant it. He hitched up the horse for them and watched them take off. *Those two make quite the pair,* he thought, smiling to himself, but his eyes were only on golden hair, glinting in the sun.

He walked back through the barn and was met with a male cacophony of teasing catcalls, whistling, sexual innuendos, thumbs up, and the men rolling their eyes at him. He tried to ignore them, but finally turned, faced the men and yelled, "¡A trabajar!" With a smirk on their faces, the men went back to work quickly. But all day, Jorge Luis would feel that little hand in his. That touch gave him a deep warmth he had never felt before. He felt it had to be a fantasy. Prudence was still off limits to him. Or was she? That feeling was his, and he would keep it. His world began to crumble again, but this time softly and warmly. He held onto a little bit of it. *Edgardo's right. I admit it. I don't want to live without her. What the hell am I gonna do?*

Although the afternoon had warmed considerably, it was still pleasant, and Prudence came away filled with contentment. *Jorge Luis was hard-*

working. He was happy and thoughtful. I do want him with all my heart, but he will have to let go of his mother and her prejudices. No, Aldiana, I am no longer a foreigner. I am in American territory. I am not a heathen. I am a Christian.

They had only gone a short distance but were out of sight when Prudence stopped the horse. She turned to Fiarela and suggested that if she wanted to learn to drive the trap, she should do it now on the way home. "We don't have permission from your mother, but Jorge Luis gave you his. Fiarela, I think you could get your mother's later, and we may never have another chance. I know it might be a risk. Do you want to do it?" she asked.

"Oh, yes, yes. Can I? Please show me how. What do I do first?"

"Here, take the reins, and I will teach you." She taught her how to hold the reins, how to use one to turn the horse, how to use both reins to halt the animal, and then taught her how to use both reins to speed the horse up. Fiarela was ecstatic and a fast learner.

"Pru, this is wonderful." Her face beamed with happiness. "I don't understand why I couldn't be allowed to do this. Driving is so easy, and the horse so well trained. I want to drive all the way home. May I?"

"I don't see why not, but, Fiarela, I do hope I haven't created a problem for you. Will you tell your mother or Edgardo?"

"No, no, not yet. I won't even tell Jorge Luis yet. I need more practice. I don't know how they will react, and I am not taking a chance. Besides, Pru, if I marry an American, he might expect me to know how, wouldn't he?"

Prudence gave a chuckle, thinking of Bryant, and said, "Maybe our excuse for you to practice could be that you want to show me something around the hacienda that I haven't seen, like the orchards." Prudence looked slyly at her and reminded her that Jorge Luis will be at the shearing barn all week. "He won't be coming into the office interrupting our lesson to see if I am teaching you properly, so maybe we could slip out then," she said.

"Oh, that would be perfect. But, you're wrong, Prudence. He comes in to see if I am paying attention and learning, and," she paused a bit, "to get a good look at you."

"Fi, you are just being kind." She felt a flush creeping up her neck, which she began to rub. Her face became flushed, and then the crushing doubt crept in. "He – he - I know he sees me as that strange, foreign woman most of the time," she dropped her head down and said softly, "I don't think he sees me as a real woman, and I won't be a doormat, either, for any man."

Fiarela was horrified to hear her say that, "Pru, you're wrong. He would never do that to any woman. We love you because you are strong, independent, and so competent."

Fiarela realized she had grasped the reins too intensely, as the horse was coming to a stop. She had to shift her weight on the seat to relax herself. "I love being around you," she said, "and I'm envious. Sometimes you may appear a little wild and bold, but you have a different background. I wish I could be more like that. We've never known a woman like you. You are educated and stunningly beautiful, and I know my brother sees all of that. He is quite taken with you. Edgardo sees it, too. Mother, too, but she has a hard time with it."

Fiarela looked directly in Prudence's face and leaned over closer to her, as she reached up with one hand and caressed Prudence's face, saying, "The attraction between you two is more than obvious. It is like lightning. How can you deny it?" Fiarela pulled the reins, stopped the horse, grabbed and hugged her. "I want you for my sister."

Prudence turned quickly to hide the tears that ran down her face, while she was blushing at the same time. She had hoped that Fiarela had not seen how strong her attraction to Jorge Luis was. Her usual negative dialogue sneaked in and began to run through her mind. *I have nothing to offer him. I live in a cantina with the brothel. I would never be accepted.* Suddenly, she realized that was no longer true. *They met my family. They know we are people of substance.* She turned to Fiarela and said, "I would love to be your sister. Wouldn't you like to be my cousin?"

Now it was Fiarela who turned red. But she did get the horse moving again and showed she would become a good driver.

Prudence wiped away her tears and pointed out, "He certainly was not as distant and cold with me at the picnic. His company was truly enjoyable."

At that moment, they arrived at the edge of the hacienda. Looking around, they hoped that no one saw them. Fiarela pulled in the reins to stop the horse and handed them over to Prudence before anyone saw her driving. They had not noticed the young rider, Danilo, sent by Jorge Luis, staying out of sight behind them. They rode up to the veranda steps, leaving the buggy for Benito.

The girls waited inside in the foyer sitting area. Both were full of an enchanting day, happily chatting until Benito showed up. He felt the joy. It was palpable. To his surprise, he had an experience he'd never had. In the air above Fiarela he saw a luminescent six-pointed star. The shock left him gasping for air. The girls did not notice, and instead of commenting, Benito went silent. He'd had hunches that were right many times, but didn't most people? A few of his dreams had come true, too, but he'd never experienced a vision like that. *I'd better ask Edgardo about it. I know he has the gift, but I don't want it. What is a six-pointed star and why over Fiarela?* He made the sign of the cross and thought, *why me?* He held out his elbow for Prudence. He left a curious question hanging in the air about Fiarela, as he escorted Prudence out.

33
The Americano

"I'm sick and tired of these damned gnats. I hate standing up inside this carriage and holding the reins through this little window," said Benito.

"I thought Fiarela was pulling my leg about the gnats, but they're even worse than she said. I hope she's right about them being gone in another week. Thanks, Benito, for covering the windows," said Prudence.

"Maybe the west wind will come up sooner today," Benito said, shifting his weight. Standing so long was setting his back off, and he was getting uncomfortable, "Oh, oh, Prudence, hang on, I'm slowing down. There are riders up ahead, three of them. They're covered up, but the big one looks like an Americano."

"Is it that bandit?" asked Prudence. She sat straight up on the edge of the seat, looking intently at Benito, her eyes wide and alert.

"I don't know. They don't look like bandits, but I'm not taking a chance. Get your gun ready and stay quiet. They're waiting and watching us. When I stop, I'll get out, but you stay very quiet. Have that gun ready but hide it," whispered Benito. "I don't think they are bandits. Facundo told us that nobody had seen or heard anything of Rafa for quite a while. There haven't been any robberies anywhere or any cattle rustling. No one knows why. Jorge Luis told us we have to keep up the surveillance until we find out more, and I am to keep an eye on you." Benito reached for his rifle, but remembered it was outside up by the seat. "Prudence I can't get my rifle until I'm outside, and they will see me so stay very alert," he warned.

She nodded and stayed silent. She had taken out her gun and hidden it in a fold of her skirt. She was so tense that she had to remind herself to breathe. "Do you know Rafa, Benito?" she asked.

"No, but I know his brother, and the tall man up ahead can't be him. He's also too big, but one of his men might be," said Benito. "Peek out of the curtain on the window and be observant. Don't hesitate to shoot." He stopped the horse and dismounted from the carriage slowly, watching the riders' every move. *Okay, let's find out what these men want. I've never seen them before.* He protected himself by placing himself with the carriage and the horse between him and them, and as near to the rifle as possible.

"Hey, there," yelled the largest man, "We're looking for the hacienda Sandoval. Are you headed there?"

"Yes," said Benito, slapping his face, as he was bitten by several gnats. He looked over the men, especially the well-dressed, tall one, obviously an American, and noted their behavior. Then, decided to say, "Señores, follow me. We are headed that way, and it will only be ten or so minutes more." He knew it wasn't his place to ask questions, but he would remain alert.

Prudence stayed inside, quiet. She did hear one man's Spanish with an American accent, but he was not from New England. *Who could this be? Will Jorge Luis and Edgardo be at the hacienda? Please, Jorge Luis, be there.*

Benito grabbed his rifle and entered the carriage. He tried to carry on a simple conversation to ease Prudence's obvious anxiety. He wanted her to stay alert but not be overly uneasy.

"Prudence, I think we are safe, but keep watching out the curtain, will you?"

"Of course. That scared me. Jorge Luis is really serious about that Rafa bandit, isn't he?"

"Yes, he's a brutal, vicious man and cares about no one," said Benito.

"Benito, why is he after Jorge Luis? That doesn't seem possible," she asked.

"I don't know except something occurred at the hacienda awhile back, and Rafa has a grudge against him." He stopped talking for a couple of minutes, "Prudence, it must have been lonely for you and Fiarela with the shearing going on longer than usual, and, by the way, have you heard anything from your uncle and cousin?"

"No, and it's been a month since they left. I thought they would be back sooner. Poor Fiarela has been sighing, rather listless, and not paying attention at work like before, so we've had more corrections to make in the books. I think her mind is lost on Bryant."

"And, you, Prudence? Who is your mind lost on? I've noticed you aren't quite as lively either." He turned his head over his shoulder and gave her a little smiling wink.

"Watch what you are saying, Benito," she said, blushing.

By the time they arrived at the hacienda, to everyone's relief, the west wind came up and blew away the gnats. The men dismounted, and the tall Americano walked over to the carriage when he saw Prudence stepping out.

"Señorita, may I help you and introduce myself? I am Austin Balde-mar Jarrod, at your service. I'm from Texas here as a government representative for the Land Management department. I'm here to discuss matters with a Señor Jorge Luis," he stopped, taking a second look at Prudence. "Say, you're an American, aren't you? What is such a beautiful, young woman like you doing out here in this god-forsaken wilderness? You can't be Señora Sandoval?" he spoke, in a low suggestive tone. His hand raised hers to brush it with a slow, sensual kiss while looking directly into her eyes. Her eyes were bewitching. He wanted to feel her hair full in his hands. Her figure - so alluring - such a slender waist, pulled at him. Her beauty was a magnet. His eyes glinted with greed, and he felt the inner drive to conquer take over. *I'll have to plan well on this one, I think. I need to find out who she really is and why she's here. She's a prize.* He could feel deep in his gut what it would feel like to conquer her. *I am a patient man. I get what I want.*

Prudence was aghast. *This American has to be Elena's fiancé. He's obviously a philanderer. Wait until Jorge Luis and Edgardo meet him. I'm giving him the cold shoulder.*

He let go of her hand, gave her an intense look, and asked, "And you are?"

"I am Prudence Mullens from Maine," she spoke, enunciating each word calmly and coldly. "Have your men go with Benito. Come with me. I will show you where to go and introduce you to the family. You are here on business?" she said politely but a little curtly, not looking him in the eyes.

"Yes, but this is a get-acquainted visit and information gathering, so to speak."

Prudence used the large wooden knocker on the door, and soon Donaldo had the huge doors open. He looked up in surprise at the unknown man, obviously an American. Prudence promptly said, "Donaldo, Señor Jarrod is here to see the family. Is Señor Jorge Luis here or Señor Edgardo?"

He did not answer the question but said, "Please, come in. You, sir, may wait in the foyer. I will find Señora Sandoval," he looked at Prudence and added, "Fiarela is in the office, waiting for you."

"Over here, Señor Jarrod," said Prudence. "Sit here, and, hopefully, Donaldo will find her soon." Prudence, without excusing herself, turned her back to him and left for the office.

Austin watched her for a moment until she turned to go down a hallway. *That is one nice, little ass.* He then stood up and perused the room slowly, taking in the antique settee, the chairs, the table. *Jesus, those are real antiques sent from Spain. They must have cost a pretty penny.* He checked the paintings and the tapestry on the wall, the carpets, the vases. *Those vases are from Asia - big money.* He ran his hands down the drapes and fingered the decorations. He assessed all of them. *This is just the foyer. What must the rest be like?* He felt a deep envy hit his gut and he almost staggered.

The Ochoas don't have this. They have a nice place, a good functioning hacienda but nothing that can equal the Sandoval's. They don't need all this land. I could make a mint by selling it. Land is becoming a real premium now. What about Prudence? What is she doing out here? I'll marry Elena. I need a good wife if I am to gain socially, but I'd sure like to have a little piece of that luscious, little Prudence. He took in a deep breath, almost feeling her body against his, and that was pleasurable. There was something about a woman's body that invigorated him. Who needed anything else, he believed.

He brushed his hair neatly with his fingers and cleaned his mustache, of which he was very proud. It was thick and glorious. His hair was black, but his mustache had come out a burnt red, which he felt was quite distinguished. He also brushed the dust off his hat, having suddenly noticed how dirty it was from riding. *This damn country is nothing but dust.* He bent over and brushed his boots also. *I fit in here. The Sandovals will notice I am no cowboy. I'm considered a gentleman, a man of means. And - no dust settles under these boots.*

He had just sat down when Donaldo arrived with Aldiana whose eyes widened as Austin stood up to his height of six feet and six inches. She had to bend her head back to look up at him. Donaldo quietly left, raising his eyebrows, unseen by Austin.

"May I present myself, Señora Sandoval? I am Austin Baldemar Jarrod the third." He added "the third" to doubly impress her. She was duly impressed and gave him a warm smile.

"I represent the United States Department of Land Management. And, I'm sure you know, I'm here to marry your neighbor's daughter soon. I am at your service with pleasure, Señora Sandoval," he bowed.

Aldiana, in politeness, reached out her hand, which he took and placed a respectful kiss upon it, not lingering as with Prudence. Aldiana was more impressed.

She is one striking woman -- a woman of culture. She must have been a beauty in her youth. I know she is a widow. I wonder how lonely she is. He took in her comfortable stance with him, a stranger, and yet, in total control.

He felt welcomed and even admired. *I belong with these kinds of people.* He squinted his eyes, visualizing himself there, and in his mind he had already been accepted. *I will do my best to cultivate them. They're people who noticeably have influence.*

"Señor Jarrod, welcome to our home. I am very happy to meet you. Elena is a dear, one of our favorite young people. I wish you every happiness. Now, how may I help you?" she asked.

"Actually, I am here to become acquainted with you and your family. I have heard many good things about all of you, and I will soon become a member of the Ochoa family. I don't want to be considered an interloper but a real member of their family and a neighbor of yours."

Aldiana stood, studying him for a moment. She was not sure what to do with him as her sons were still working. "Sir, since the men will be working for some time yet, perhaps, you would like to take your things to a guest room, and then Benito can give you a tour of the hacienda?"

His eyes lit up and a lopsided grin passed over his face. "Thank you, Señora, I would be most grateful. You have a beautiful and very impressive home here, and you are certainly a reflection of its perfection. I will wait here for Donaldo. Thank you again," he bowed and sat down.

Donaldo and Austin carried the suitcases and bedroll to a guest room suite. Immediately, Donaldo took Austin out to the carriage barn. He introduced him to Benito, who was not impressed with this tall Americano. He had watched this man try to suggest himself into Prudence's favor. He guessed Austin was to marry Elena, the Ochoa's daughter. *Pig*, he said to himself.

"Pleased to meet you, sir. Felicitations on your coming marriage. Elena is one of our favorites, a lovely girl. Which carriage would you like to ride in?" asked Benito.

"Thank you. Maybe the small, open one. I want to see everything. And, Benito, I will have questions about everything I see, especially since I am an official representative for your new government, the United States of America. I expect that you will have the answers to them. I know you have been here a long time." He raised and tilted his head, looking down on Benito as if confirming his place as nothing more than an old servant.

That stuck in Benito's craw, but he said, "Naturally, sir, happy to." Benito turned his back and walked to the carriage, squinting his eyes, pursing his mouth, and gritting his teeth. He wasn't about to tell this *extranjero* anything. Benito's teeth were set on edge.

34
The Women React

rudence slammed through the office double doors, which startled Fiarela, who jumped up, knocking her record book off the desk.

"Prudence - you look frazzled. What's going on?" Fiarela said, picking up her book.

"Fiarela, I just met the man Elena is going to marry. I don't know Elena, but he's not a nice guy. Benito and I just now met him and two of his men on the road while we were coming out here," she put her hands on her hips, looked Fiarela straight in the face and said emphatically, "He came right onto me. I felt like slapping him." Prudence, with her fists clenched and her green eyes flashing, sent daggers to Austin.

"My god, Pru, should we do something?" asked Fiarela as she moved towards Prudence, her eyes wide as she placed her hands over Prudence's shoulders. "I thought all Americans were like your Uncle Lot and Bryant," said Fiarela, naïvely.

"Good heavens, no. They come in all shapes and sizes. This Mr. High and Mighty is a real womanizer, a skirt-chaser." Prudence clenched her teeth and sat down.

"Oh, Prudence, that's - that's - should someone go tell Elena? I would want to know if it was Bryant," Fiarela said, feeling shocked at hearing something she would never have thought about. She watched Prudence in disbelief. She didn't know any men like that. Shaking her head, still not comprehending how anyone could do that, she finally said, "Let's go find my brothers and warn them to keep an eye on him."

"Okay, but I don't want any trouble. I don't want him to see us if he's out looking around the hacienda with Benito," Prudence spoke as she jumped up, shook her skirt, went to the doors, and pushed them open, looking down the hallway. "It's clear, come on."

The two girls, careful to walk without clicking their heels on the parquet floor, sneaked down the hallway and out the back door. They stopped to look around.

"Look, there's Danilo, walking toward the stables," said Fiarela. "He might know where they are. Dan-i-lo," she shouted.

"Shh, don't yell. Come on. He's stopped and waiting for us."

Fiarela felt ashamed she had not been more careful. She wondered if that Americano really was that bad, but she totally trusted Prudence and would not take a chance.

Danilo had stopped and watched the girls approach him. The girls seemed to be looking around surreptitiously, talking, but not loud enough to be heard. He wondered what were they whispering about and why? What was up with them? He'd never seen them act like that.

"Hi, Señoritas, what can I help you with?" Danilo asked, carefully brushing back his hair and pulling at his mustache. It was important to look good before these two ladies. Although he was only nineteen, he intended to keep his reputation of being the most handsome and dashing young man at the hacienda.

"Danilo, do you know where my brothers are?" Fiarela asked, cautiously looking around, which Prudence was also doing.

"If you see that American, don't say anything important to him. Be careful of him," said Prudence.

"An Americano? What Americano? Where?" Now Danilo was not only curious but worried.

"He's in the house, or he's out touring the hacienda with Benito, and he's the one going to marry Elena Ochoa. We need to warn Jorge Luis and Edgardo. Are they in the stable?" Fiarela asked.

"No, they're up at the reservoir cleaning out the drains. You'll need to take the horses. Do you know where it is, Fiarela?" *Need to warn? What's with this Americano?*

"Yeah, don't tell anyone you saw us and watch that guy. Don't let him around any of the ladies," said Fiarela.

That opened his eyes. "I won't. I won't. Is he dangerous?" asked Danilo, glancing around himself.

"I think so. I know he's a skirt-chaser, a real pig," said Prudence. She and Fiarela dashed off for the stables, leaving Danilo astonished.

The girls found Juan repairing harnesses. He led the horses out and helped them saddle up. "Girls, be careful riding out there. I saw two rattlers out this morning. Watch where you're going. Prudence, do you have your Colt 44 with you?" he asked.

"No, I don't, but we'll be watchful, and we won't be gone long, either," answered Prudence.

While the girls were saddling up, Danilo ran over to the blacksmith area where his horse was tied in the shade and jumped on. He had orders to follow Prudence no matter where she went, but that was due to the danger of the bandit, Rafa. But, this? An Americano? Nevertheless, he meant to be very diligent. This was his first big responsibility. He was still young and inexperienced, but good looking and solidly built. He wanted to show Angela, his girlfriend, that he was a competent man. He wanted most of all to marry her. He waited outside the gate of the hacienda until he saw the girls pass through. Danilo would follow them anywhere on the big *rancho.*

The ride for the girls was pleasant. The path led across two of the lower hills. The green of the hills had now changed to a yellow-brown. The grass had dried out. No wildflowers could be seen anywhere. Below the hills was a flat land that needed irrigating for growing hay. The reservoir that received rainwater during the winter was still almost full and would be used to send water down to the field when needed.

"Look, I can see them. They're cleaning out the big drain. It always plugs up, now and then, especially during the winter with leaves, twigs, and even dead animals. Once there was a live skunk caught in there, and the boys had to pull it out," said Fiarela, chuckling. "I sure enjoyed that. Mother made them go sleep in the barn!"

Prudence had to laugh at that tale, and she knew the smell of skunks was most difficult to remove.

The air had warmed up a lot, but the wind was blowing enough to keep away what few gnats were left. The first part of July's hard-hitting heat had killed most of them off. Because of the heat, the men were working without their shirts on. Prudence held her breath as she looked at Jorge Luis with such a well-developed, muscular upper body. Seeing his muscles flexing and swelling as he worked gave her a feeling of excitement and longing. *Someday I want to be in those arms.* She could almost feel them, strong and protective.

"Hey, ladies, we saw you coming. What are you doing out here? Aren't you working today?" yelled Jorge Luis.

"We need to talk to you," yelled back Fiarela, as she dismounted and let the reins fall on the ground. Her horse was trained not to move. Prudence noticed and did the same. She was impressed by such good training. She showed horses in Maine and appreciated a well-trained horse.

"Can you come over here?" Fiarela called loudly.

The men wiped the dirt and sweat off. They slipped their shirts on but left them open and walked over. Jorge Luis' face became more radiant the closer he came. Prudence almost forgot why she was there. Fiarela watched the two of them, believing they were about to embrace, but they didn't.

As he neared Prudence, the scent of him, the sweat of labor mixed with his own odor, heightened her desire. She quickly pulled herself together and said, "We came to tell you the land management man Uncle Lot talked about is here. We felt you should know."

"Yes, Prudence was worried because he was rude to her," said Fiarela.

Both men reacted, eyes narrowing. They both stopped, muscles tensing, "What? How dare he. What did he do?"

Jorge Luis, watching the gold in her hair sparkling in the morning light, demanded an answer, "Prudence, tell me exactly what happened." Edgardo nodded strongly.

Without preliminaries, Prudence started in, "Don't trust him. He's a pig. He's supposed to marry Elena. I don't know her, but I feel sorry for her."

Edgardo looked at his brother darkly, as he knew what was coming. So did Jorge Luis, and he was already fuming.

"What did he do to you? Did he touch you?" Jorge Luis had his fists clenched and his nostrils were enlarged with anger.

Edgardo stiffened. He knew that she hadn't been touched but, obviously, the Americano was unpleasant.

"No, no, he didn't touch me except for a disrespectful and very suggestive kiss on my hand."

"That's it, Edgardo, we better stop work and go set a few things straight with him," said Jorge Luis, his eyes flashing anger.

"No, no," said Fiarela, waving her hands with Prudence, shaking her head strongly. "He's staying for lunch. I think you should wait 'til then."

"Benito was going to give him a tour, so he won't be around. Please, I don't want any trouble over this. I just wanted to warn you," spoke Prudence and with a serious tone of voice added, "Don't trust him and don't believe him, but pay good attention to him. He is quite full of himself, too."

"Just what we need, a skirt-chaser and a government agent with a swelled head. Let's finish here, clean up for lunch, and while you interrogate him, I will take a deeper look at him. Make it clear women are respected in this country," said Edgardo, who waved at the girls and started to take off for the reservoir.

"You two go back and don't let him see you," said Jorge Luis. "We'll join you at lunch. Wait up, Ed. Let's talk about how to set him in his place."

Fiarela and Prudence remounted and rode carefully back to the stables, followed by an unseen and bored Danilo, who wished he knew what was going on. *This is just plain crazy*, he thought.

Benito, meanwhile, kept Austin busy, showing him everything he could until the time to eat. He offered no answers to any direct or specific questions. That didn't sit well with Austin, but he admitted to himself that Benito was a loyal worker. He understood Benito's refusal to give him any information. Still, he asked a lot of questions, observing Benito's face closely, which told him the answer to only a few of his questions. *I've played enough Poker to read faces quite easily, but this guy, Benito, knows how to hold his hand close. I'm not getting much out of him.*

Back at the house, the girls worked hard on the financial books. They discussed Austin and decided to be as polite as possible and not divulge anything important.

Aldiana kept busy with Teresa, seeing that the lunch would represent the family status and impress an important agent of the United States.

Jorge Luis and Edgardo agreed that they did not want to antagonize a government land official, who probably knew nothing about managing land. However, they both wanted to put him in his place and keep him there.

They all gathered outdoors under the grape arbor and introduced themselves. It was warm but pleasant in the shade of the lush grape foliage and its full clusters of immature grapes. Nevertheless, most everyone felt a bit tense, sitting down together for lunch, except Austin. He was in his element -- a powerful government agent and a conqueror of this new land. He was here with a family of means -- one he hoped to gain from, eventually.

"Doña Aldiana, what a delightful outdoor place to eat and a perfect day for it under your bounteous grape arbor. Look at all the grapes you will have soon. I imagine that you designed all this grandeur," he said, speaking an understandable Spanish while looking deep into Aldiana's eyes, with an ingratiating social smile, which was not missed by the young people.

"Thank you, Austin," she said, surprised to hear him speak a fairly good Spanish. She would never be presumptuous and ask why. "We do love it out here and want you to enjoy it too," she said. She sat up very straight, looking quite regal in a light, cotton summer gown of a soft ochre color. She turned to Eva, who brought out enchiladas de pollo with red chili sauce and asked her to bring her grandson, Nito, to join them.

"Of course, Señora. Then I will carry out the *tostones*," spoke Eva, who turned to Austin and, in slow, accented English, said, "Potatoes in chili sauce with bread and watermelon juice."

Austin was impressed and gave her a big smile, intensifying his eye contact. Eva glanced at Prudence, who had taught her the simple English, with a proud smile. She was unaware of Austin's suggestive tone nor his look of intention to conquer.

The Americano was suddenly distracted when he noticed the child, Nito, who came out, running straight to Edgardo, crying, "Papá, Papá."

Edgardo leaned down to give him a kiss and said, "Here's your chair. Get up and sit by me, Nito. We have a guest today." He pointed at Austin, saying, "His name is Austin. Can you say Austin?"

Nito, acting shy, looked down, shook his head, and would not say anything. He started jabbing his food and kept his head down. His eyes were scrunched tighter and, once in a while, would give a sly upward look at Austin with furrowed brows. Edgardo looked at him expectantly, as did everyone else.

"Sorry, he does talk a little and is usually very friendly. Just an off day, I guess," Edgardo explained.

"What a handsome young man. I didn't know you were married," said Austin with an obsequious smile, which was not lost on Prudence.

"I'm not. I'm a widower," said Edgardo. "I understand you will soon be married to Elena Ochoa. I suppose Elena is busy with wedding plans? She is one of our favorite people, and we are most anxious for her happiness."

"Oh, sorry for your loss, Edgardo. I didn't know," said Austin. "Yes, Elena is under a lot of pressure. We expect the priest to arrive soon, possibly in another week or two, and he can't stay long. That's why I wanted to come and meet all of you beforehand, as my time is limited. I will have to meet with my colleagues soon to get our United States Department of Land Management going. This is a big country, and there's lots of work ahead of us."

Jorge Luis picked up on the information about the priest and then spoke up, "I imagine, Austin, your position with the government will be time-consuming, considering everything is new and must be organized, and, then, opened up and set in motion; however, here in California, families are held in highest esteem. Our first loyalty is to our loved ones. They come first, and our women are always treated with respect and protected. You may find that to be one of our greatest differences." He looked at Austin, unwaveringly and forcefully intending to get his point across.

Austin could see that Jorge Luis' dialog was aimed right at him. He took it as a warning. He could easily see that Prudence was Jorge Luis'. Anger pushed his thoughts across his mind. *I never let that stop me before.*

Thank god I speak a good, passable Spanish, even though it is Texan Spanish. That mestizo doesn't know who he's up against. I'll show him who owns this country now. Austin decided to brush aside the content of Jorge Luis' speech. He really didn't care. With his eyes squinting, he took a breath in through his nostrils like a *toro r*eady to make his charge, but he let go of that almost overpowering, furious feeling. He looked back, nodding. "Of course," Austin said, "but I will have to be away a lot in the beginning. I hope Elena can understand and forgive me for it." He spoke sadly, but the steeliness in his eyes betrayed him as he stared at Fiarela, which caused her to feel uneasy.

"Why can't she go with you? We like our families to be together, and, I think, she would want to see that you are properly taken care of," said Edgardo.

"Oh, yes, she would," said Prudence, leaning over her plate and looking at him directly in his face. "Being together with one's husband is so important to a woman. Life here can be terribly lonely. I know that Elena would bring stability and prestige to you as an official government agent," she said, emphasizing her last words.

Fiarela couldn't stand it. She patted the table with her hands for attention, stating, "I would never want to be away from my husband. He would need to be loved and cared for properly, and I want to do that. I intend to be a very good wife." She emphasized her last sentence.

Aldiana was somewhat taken aback by the direction of the conversation. She had no clue as to why they were discussing all this. Was there something she didn't know about Austin? She sat forward and listened, forgetting to continue to eat.

Austin felt subtly attacked, with his back to the wall. *I'll have to be careful with these people. They aren't ignorant peasants. I may have to find a way to give them a good scare. That daughter is quite an attractive little thing for a Californio and a better catch than Elena, but – I'd rather have that beauty sitting by Jorge Luis. She's an American.* His thoughts turned back to the conversation.

"You're right. I must consider finding suitable housing in Sacramento or San Francisco, or wherever they decide the department will be. I do hope Elena will want to go with me. I really want her to be happy. Her family's *rancho* is so isolated. I will certainly consider her first," said Austin, hoping to put an end to the attack on him. He felt very unsettled for a few minutes, and Nito's behavior had captured his attention.

Nito was wielding his fork and spoon as if they were weapons, fighting a food enemy. He would stop and stare at Austin, casting dark looks at him for a minute before attacking his plate of food again. Edgardo was aware of his unusual behavior but chose to ignore it. He decided to try and remember to talk to him later. He knew something was bothering him about Austin.

Aldiana interrupted to ask Austin how he liked their Californio food since it must be quite different than what he was used to. She hoped the conversation would distract and move into a safer subject, but it didn't. Jorge Luis decided to just jump in.

"Say, Austin, the Treaty of Guadalupe de Hidalgo guarantees our land titles. How do you see that working?" asked Jorge Luis, trying to modulate his voice.

"Yes, we hear all kinds of rumors and have real concerns," said Edgardo. He suddenly leaned forward, putting his weight on his elbows on the table. That brought a strong look of disapproval from his mother, which he ignored. It was all he could do to not reach over the table and grab Austin by the neck.

Prudence wanted to verbally lash into him but held her tongue. She tried to remain cold and calm when occasionally translating for him. Her emotions were close to spilling over. She had not expected Austin's kind of news. What she heared pushed her fears to the extreme.

"Señores, I am not familiar yet with that treaty. I'm not sure it is valid since the United States won the Mexican war, and I have heard no decision about it," said Austin.

The hair on the back of the necks of the two Sandoval men stood up and their breathing became tighter, tenser.

"Also, I've been told," said Austin, "Mexican grants often seem to have vague boundaries and other odd types of irregularities. We'll have to check into each grant and make sure all of them are correct and legal." He nodded authoritatively with his last statement. *And it will be right down to the last crossed t and the last dotted i.* Looking at Jorge Luis, he found it impossible to believe he was the owner of such an outlandish amount of land. *You arrogant, backward, Mexican. Just wait until I pull you into an American court.*

Jorge Luis and Edgardo felt their whole life, and their family's stability and hope, sinking. Edgardo looked down at his feet and sighed. Jorge Luis simultaneously felt numbed and angry. His teeth were clenched tight. His eyes narrowed with disgust.

Aldiana spoke up authoritatively, "We have been here for four generations. That should make us legal." She lifted her head and looked down her nose at him as if asking what right he had to question her family's ownership.

Heaving a sigh and pressing his lips together, he looked at her and said, "Unfortunately, Señora, it is much more complicated." *I suppose I must explain every little detail to them. Why do I have to deal with these Californios? The court judge should take care of them.* He felt disgusted and bored. "Besides the irregularities of the old deeds, we have a population explosion," he said, "More than sixty thousand people have arrived here so far just this year, and we expect more every day. Those gold diggings act like a magnet, and most people will want to stay and have their own land. We have to check all grants for occupancy and improvements, too. Witnesses must be found. On top of that, everything is being changed. Most likely, the Department of Land Management will be held in San Francisco instead of Sacramento. That may change my position. I'm not sure how it will end up."

"Sir," said Edgardo, "a problem has developed with people called 'squatters.' They're moving onto our land and refusing to leave. There have been a couple of shootings. How do you plan to solve that?"

"Since these people are Americans, I would think that you, an American government official, would have these people immediately removed," said Prudence, shifting in her seat. Her voice had an underlying tone of hostility. She was horrified. She couldn't believe he was an American. He was an embarrassment, and she was becoming angrier and angrier.

"That is a problem," said Austin, throwing up his hands, "I do admit that. Unfortunately, we have our hands tied. Those squatters don't respect the laws and don't care. They say no one needs that much land and they have a right to some."

Aldiana could not believe her ears. She stroked her cheeks and massaged the back of her neck, feeling at a loss. She suspected they may possibly face a bigger loss. She listened even more intently.

Fiarela didn't totally understand what was being discussed, but she began to realize that things looked bad. She wished Bryant was there. He was a lawyer - he'd understand and know what to do. She twisted and turned in her seat, looking from one person to another. *Why does everyone defer to Austin?* she wondered. To her, he sounded like a know-it-all, a big bag of wind. She had to say something.

"What happens when you do find something faulty with a claim, even though it might be something simple, like a little mistake?" she asked.

"I'm afraid the landowner must prove his innocence," said Austin, looking Fiarela straight in the face and gesturing with his hands, as if he were saying that's just the way it's going to be.

"And if the person who made the mistake is dead?" asked Jorge Luis.

"I'm afraid it's the same. You must prove innocence which, I know," he said, shaking his head and shrugging his shoulders, "might be impossible to prove. Another thing," he paused, looking at everyone slowly around the table, "even if your land has confirmation of title, that doesn't mean it will be accepted. You may have to defend it up to five or six more times."

The words "five to six more times" were heard repeated around the table. Everyone's brows were furrowed, and their eyes were full of concern.

"Okay, what are the five or six other agencies we might have to deal with?" asked Jorge Luis, more than disgusted with this example of a government official. Now he was wondering about Austin's two colleagues. *Will they be as power-seeking and nasty? We need to be very careful with this guy. I can see now how much power he does have, and he likes to wield it.*

All eyes were locked on Austin except Nito's. He had lowered himself down out of his chair and, with his head down, gave a sideways, long, dark look at Austin. He walked to his grandmother and climbed up onto her lap. Austin watched Nito, thinking, *I'd like to have a son but not like that spoiled kid. My son will not ever be allowed to be a sissy boy.*

Austin pulled out of his thoughts and sat back in his chair, stretched his legs and began, "There is the Board of Land Commissioners, the Surveyor-General and Land Office, again the District Court, and there is the Supreme Court."

"Oh, good god, that is outrageous - using technicalities and legalities to grab land," said Jorge Luis. His fists were hard on the table, and he felt ready to punch that uppity son of a bitch, Mr. Power Hungry.

"Somebody is going to make a mint of money," said Edgardo. His sleek Indian knife of razor sharp obsidian, in his pant leg, crossed his mind, and he shuddered.

"In any case, I do hope you can get all your deeds and documents in order. Furthermore, whoever appears to defend the property in the courts must speak English. The judge doesn't speak Spanish."

"Nobody in California speaks English. Can we use an interpreter?" asked Edgardo, while Jorge Luis bit his tongue to keep from whipping Austin with a stream of *palabrotes.*

Aldiana felt as if her breath had been sucked out of her. She had to put an end to this. She looked over at Eva, standing at attention by the kitchen door, and motioned her to come over. She handed Nito to Eva and asked that she take him upstairs for a nap. She shook and wiped down her skirt, tilted her head, and leaned back a little in order to look up into the face of the tall Texan, who was now standing and preparing to leave. "Señor Austin, I was very happy to meet you. I wish you much happiness in your coming marriage and hope you might join us again sometime, with Elena, of course," she said, with a hint of sarcasm. She started to turn away to retire into the house but paused for another minute, listening.

"Thank you, Señora, I have thoroughly enjoyed the tour and your sumptuous luncheon. And, of course, meeting everyone. I hope to see all of you at my wedding soon." He turned to Jorge Luis and added, "I intend to stay at the hotel tonight. I'm meeting a businessman there. Is there any problem with that? I was told you own the hotel. Also, in a couple of weeks, I will be back again from Sacramento and will need to stay there. Then I'll be on my way to the Ochoas for my marriage."

"Yes, we do own the hotel, and you should have no problem staying there. Here, let me send a note with you with my signature," said Jorge Luis, who pulled out a small notebook from his pocket, wrote on it and signed the note with the dates. He would be sure to be there and see how much he could find out about this tall, arrogant Texan. He had never hated anyone, not even Rafa, but this man he considered more and more dangerous, and he was feeling a greater hostility toward him.

"Thanks again. Please give my compliments to your magnificent cook, Señora." Austin bowed politely to Aldiana, who did then turn and retire into her home. But Austin gave Prudence a lingering look. He was lucky he wasn't on the receiving end of Jorge Luis' fist, which was ready to explode.

When Austin started to leave the outdoor eating area, both Sandoval brothers stood up too. Jorge Luis said, "We'll walk out with you to the stables and make sure you and your men are properly taken care of."

Austin rolled his eyes and said, "Thanks, but it isn't necessary." *These damn fools. What now?*

On the way, Edgardo brought up the subject that he should be careful while riding in this country, "This can be dangerous country at times. We have a lot of big rattlers that often spook the horses. We lost a couple of men due to being bitten."

"Worse are the grizzlies when they're wandering through," said Jorge Luis. "They can knock a horse down with one swipe. Kill it, too." He looked at Austin to see how he was taking it, and it was obvious from his pursed lips and looking off to the side that he wasn't appreciative.

Edgardo added, "We've got a big problem now with marauding Indians and a notorious bandit. Best be on guard. We don't want anything to happen to you or your men out here so far from any help."

At the doors of the stable, Jorge Luis did not offer his hand but said, "We'll see you soon." Edgardo gave a crooked smile, nodded, and they walked back toward the house.

Austin was humiliated and angry. *Just wait, I'll give those two greasers sopa de su propio chocolate. They don't fool me for a minute. I know all that nonsense was a warning.*

In the stable, one of Austin's bodyguards took a look at his face and remarked, "What happened? *Tienes cara de huele-pedos, really pissed.*"

"*¡Cállate, miserable!* Shut up, you miserable bum," Austin spat. He slipped back into his reactive angry thoughts. *Well, that's over. Now I know them, but they don't know me yet. Things are going to change fast around here. Just wait and see. And, yeah, you deadbeats, I understand and speak a pretty good Spanish because my grandmother was a Mexican, so you can't pull a fast one on me.* He almost bit his lip, admitting that to himself.

Juan already had his bedroll, his two hired men, and the horses ready to go. Juan did not like the energy he picked up from those bodyguards of Austin's. They were arrogant, men who knew-it-all, and their prejudice against the Californios was obvious. He didn't feel they could be trusted. When the three of them left, he felt relieved. *Good riddance.*

The two brothers sat down again at the table for a few minutes with Fiarela and Prudence.

"I'm going into town to keep an eye on him and see if I can get his two bodyguards to talk," Edgardo said, "Prudence, I hope your uncle and cousin return quickly. We need them."

Prudence nodded and mouthed the words, "I hope so," but did not say anything.

"Okay, what I'll do, then, is finish the reservoir work," said Jorge Luis. "Afterwards, I need to get out all the old documents and deeds and start getting them in order. Prudence, your relatives will be here in a few days, and I need to have everything ready for them. We need to fix whatever documents are ambiguous before we are hauled into court. I would give you a ride to town and join you, but that will have to wait until another time." His longing for a possible romantic ride to town had to be set aside. "Edgardo, take Prudence with you and go ahead and stay in the cantina. See if you can find out what we're up against."

Prudence was disappointed as her dreams for a ride with Jorge Luis slipped down the drain, but she understood. "Edgardo," she spoke, "I am ready to go. Just let me know when you want to leave. I'll be with Fiarela."

Edgardo decided to talk to Nito before he left. He found him napping in his bed with his nana, who was sitting and sewing. "Would you kindly leave for a moment? I need to be alone with Nito," he asked.

When she went out, he woke Nito, who was excited to see his father. He jumped up and down in his crib bed and tried to climb out. Edgardo lifted him out and sat on the bed with him, "Nito, I want to ask you something. Did you like Austin?"

Nito bowed his head and said, "No."

"I didn't either, Nito, but what did you think about him?" asked his *papá*.

Nito looked up into his dad's face and said, "Him bad. Hurt people. Him like hurt people. Him have gun. Him have big knife, too. Me 'fraid, *Papá*." He grabbed tightly onto his father and buried his head into his chest. Edgardo held him tighter.

"You're right, Hijo. He is a bad man. But, don't be afraid. *Tío* Jorge Luis and I are going to stop him. We won't allow him to hurt anyone. Thanks, *Hijo*, for telling me. Now, thank your angels for showing you the truth about Señor Austin at the table. You have been a big help for us, Hijo. I am proud of you. Now, go back to sleep, and you can have more fun dreams."

"*Sí, Papá*, fun dreams," repeated Nito.

The nana was called back. She settled Nito once more into his bed to finish his nap. Edgardo left, found Prudence, and they left for the pueblo.

Aldiana had left the table immediately after the exit of Austin in order to go up to her room. She carried a heavy heart. She was glad Emiliano was not there to have received the frightening news, that they may lose their home and property. She retired to her room, slipped into something more comfortable, and went to stand before her altar, feeling weak with emotions.

Emiliano, why did you leave me? She began weeping. *I miss you so, your joy of life, your strength and knowledge, your warm body next to mine. My bed is so cold now. Even though we grew old, I still wanted you. I need you now.* Her grief was flooding her body, her mind, her spirit. She was finally letting go. Her grief, held so quietly, was pouring out in loud gulps and little cries. For the first time, Edgardo's loss hit her physically and mentally, and she understood, at once, her son's deep pain. *He's so young to have suffered such a loss, even if she was an Indian. My heart goes out to him. You were right, Emi. My pride and my prejudices are the obstacles that you said would bring down this family. Emi, help me. You always knew what to do.*

Help me give them up. You always told me that our children's hearts would lead them well, and that I should welcome that. I will try.

She stood in front of the niche in her room that held her altar with the statue of our lady of Guadalupe. She thanked God with a profound gratefulness for putting Emiliano in her life. Then her thoughts shifted to the Americano who was to marry Elena. *She is never going to be happy with that man. I don't know what to think of Austin after all those horrible things he told us. Please, God, help me, I want, in the depths of my being, for my children to find happiness and comfort with companions of their hearts, like I did.*

Her weeping stopped. She made the sign of the cross, went to her bed, and climbed in. In seconds, a deep sleep slipped over her.

Emiliano suddenly appeared to her for the first time. She felt the energy of his love flow over and through her. She heard him say, "I love you, my dearest. You have a great strength and capacity for love that our family will need. You will now be able now to give fully with an open heart. We will meet again. He threw her a kiss and was gone." Aldiana woke up feeling infused with gratitude, love, and a new beginning - a new chapter of her life.

35
The Return

rudence was sitting and checking the receipts at the cantina's office desk, checking receipts, but she was unable to keep her thoughts from intruding. *I admit I am worried to death about Austin. I had such an awful dream of him last night. I know if I complain about him, he will make it miserable for the Sandovals. Austin would take everything away from them if he could.*

Prudence tried to keep her focus on the financial figures in the record book in front of her but couldn't. *What he said about land laws will make it impossible for Californios to keep their properties. He's just a cheap crook. I am so ashamed that he is an American. What will others think about me?*

The office felt claustrophobic, stuffy, and smelled a bit musty to her. She left her desk and opened the wooden shutters of the window. Bending over the three-foot deep sill, which kept the room cool in the summer and warm in the winter, she stuck her head out the window and took in some long breaths of fresh air. That helped a little, but she still felt queasy. Prudence walked to the water cantor and drank a cup, but she decided she needed a walk outside until she felt better. *Maybe May's got her dog, Peggy, outside the hardware store with her two little puppies. They are so cute. I'll go in and see if she has any new fabric.* She thought she'd cut through the cantina since it was empty, but as soon as she started to open her office door, she heard the big double cantina doors from the street begin to open.

Peeking out her office door, the sounds she heard caused her disgust of Austin to augment into a real fear of being assaulted by him. Prudence knew that Austin and both of his men were upstairs in the hotel. She heard two men at the door. Maybe the third man was behind them. She held her breath, but then, to her joy, in came her family.

"Uncle Lot, Bryant! Thank god it's you. I'm so happy to see you. You're here just in time. You have no idea what's been happening," she said, as she ran towards them and embraced them both. Her words were fast and jerky. Her face was obviously flushed, and, to them, she was much more emotional than usual.

"Prudence, Prudence, we're happy to be back, but why are you so upset? Come, come my dear," said Lot, hugging her.

Bryant, seeing his cousin obviously upset, became agitated and began shuffling his feet, while thinking about Fiarela. He waited to give Prudence a hug. "Prudence, is Fiarela all right? What's happened? You're making me very nervous," he said.

"I'm sorry. Fiarela is fine, Bryant, don't worry. I want to hear all about up north, and then I will tell you about everything here. Come on, let's go to the restaurant," said Prudence. She started to walk but then said, "Oh, wait. I need my purse and my jacket." She picked up the jacket, slipped it on, grabbed her purse, and held it up to show it off, "My purse was stolen before I arrived here. This is what I made as soon as I could, but I'm still lacking any identification. Uncle Lot, maybe you could help me with that?"

"Of course, dear one, I'll help you. Your purse is delightful. How clever you are. Your aunt taught you to sew and embroider beautifully, didn't she?" commented Lot with Bryant shaking his head in agreement.

Bryant said, "Oh, Cousin, it is so good to see you as talented and creative as ever. And, I'm so sorry how that bandit treated you when you were traveling out here, but, here, let me take your arm, and let's get going." Prudence brushed her hair back with her hand, straightened her skirt, and took Bryant's arm.

On the way out the front door, they ran into Jorge Luis and Edgardo. "Hey, what a surprise," said Lot.

"Good to see you again," said Jorge Luis. He went quickly to shake Lot's hand while Edgardo was shaking Bryant's. He gave Edgardo a hopeful glance before he added, "I have all the old records and deeds out for you to look at when you are able to come out to the hacienda."

"Good to see you two and you look well. That's great about the records. We'll put Bryant right to work on them," said Lot.

"I'm anxious to see them and find out what I can help with. Maybe we can ride out there tomorrow," answered Bryant, looking at his uncle.

Edgardo added, "Before we talk about that, I want to hear all about your new properties. Later, we need to let you know about some difficult problems that have come up."

"Had breakfast yet? Let's have it brought up to our bedroom suite," Jorge Luis said, before they could ask about the problems. He then leaned into Bryant and lowered his voice, "We need privacy."

Lot and Bryant looked at each other with raised eyebrows and a rather dismayed look.

"I don't like what this portends," said Lot, rubbing his chin and shaking his head.

Bryant looked at the brothers, asking, "I'm concerned about your sister. Is she all right with whatever is going on?"

"None of us are, and it's obvious that she's been pining for you, Bryant," Jorge Luis said with a bright smile, which gave Bryant a feeling of pleasure - with a little embarrassment. Edgardo gave a chuckle, which broke the tenseness they were all under.

The others went up to the bedroom suite, while Jorge Luis headed to the hotel kitchen to order breakfast.

They sat at a small, round table covered with an embroidered tablecloth done by Aldiana. Her exquisite work was copied from her sketches of spring wildflowers. Prudence kept running her fingers over the stitching, feeling the flowers and admiring the colors. She wished she had spent more time learning the more advanced stitches of embroidery.

Lot was admiring the suite's living room and remarked, "You have a very comfortable room here. Makes it nice for privacy." When Jorge Luis returned with the food, Prudence helped serve breakfast.

Bryant looked at the food and said, "Nothing like a good steak to start the day." They all agreed and started to dig in.

Prudence was reticent about dumping all the bad news too fast on her uncle and her cousin. She knew they would be highly upset. She waited until they had spent a few minutes eating and then said, "Uncle Lot, why don't you start by telling us about your trip?"

"Well, okay - to start off, we actually met Sutter at his place in Sacramento, which turned out to be a little discomforting because he had his two black mistresses from the Sandwich Islands with him. And, we knew he had left a family behind in Switzerland." He looked around the table at everyone and saw that they were following his story with rapt attention. "Sutter suggested that we stay there in Sacramento in his building, which we agreed to do. Unfortunately, it was jam-packed with men. Each man was allotted only eight hours for one mattress and then had to be up and out. They were on their way to the gold fields. With so many men in and out, it was too noisy. The bed pads were lumpy; the blankets were dirty. It was just too uncomfortable for an older man like me," said Lot.

Bryant interrupted, "That's why we left early and made our way to Colusa. I helped Uncle Lot arrange his stable business. I think he'll have good luck with it. Colusa is growing fast. Believe it or not, there are a lot of immigrants arriving from the southern United States."

"Bryant also helped me secure a wonderful piece of property, ten thousand acres, west of Colusa. It's a valley in the foothills, and if you ride up to the top of one, you can see the whole Sacramento valley. That's what I hear people call it, anyway. The property has a salt lake on it where the Indians used to mine salt, a good creek, and a lot of acreage for dry farming. I can hardly wait to get started. I plan on putting in wheat, oats, and barley. But, Prudence, I need you to help design a home for us. How about it, dear?" asked Lot.

Bryant added, "Maybe you guys can help us with procuring some sheep and cattle. There are, probably, about five thousand acres for livestock grazing."

"Sure, no problem," said Edgardo, while Jorge Luis nodded affirmatively.

Lot stopped and looked at Prudence, Edgardo and Jorge Luis, one at a time, "Okay, now what's going on here?"

Bryant sat up straight, shoving his plate aside and paying close attention.

Prudence began the tale with the first encounter with Austin and his men. From there the story degenerated with each of the brothers recounting everything they had experienced.

Lot and Bryant listened with a growing feeling of fear. Lot kept rubbing his hands and Bryant, feeling deeply disturbed, often looked away, worrying that Fiarela might be upset, too, like Prudence visibly was.

Bryant gave a deep sigh, wringing his fingers. He finally interrupted the conversation, "Now, I understand something that happened on board the ship that I couldn't believe. I didn't want to admit what I saw one night when I couldn't sleep. It had to do with Austin, and after what I've heard from you and seen myself, I must tell you that he is a most dangerous man."

The others were shocked to hear that and leaned in closer, their attention riveted upon Bryant. Prudence was almost holding her breath. Again Jorge Luis' fists were opening and closing. Edgardo, restless and unaware of what he was doing, was fingering his knife in his pant leg. He would protect his family to the end, if necessary. They all were waiting in anticipation and suspense to hear what Bryant could have experienced. Lot sat up and said, "Okay, Bryant, now what? Out with it."

"Austin played poker with the seamen constantly and seemed to win easily. The men would become quite angry at times, and I remember one sailor calling him out and accusing him of cheating. Austin reacted by jumping up and grabbing the guy by his shirt front, lifting him up to face him.

He called the sailor a drunken fool, and if he didn't keep his mouth shut, it would be shut for him."

"How disgusting, but I believe it. That doesn't surprise me," said Prudence. "I'm glad Fiarela is not here to hear this. She was upset enough." She looked at Bryant to make sure he heard her. She said, "I'm assuming there's more?"

"Yes - well, I was shaken, of course, but the men did become on edge and easily angered after so many days at sea, so I just overlooked it - until it happened again, and then something worse occurred that I can't dismiss. One night I was restless, couldn't sleep, and I didn't want to wake Uncle Lot, so I went up on deck where I saw, to my surprise in the darkness, two silhouettes against the sky. They looked like they were tussling. I definitely did not want to be involved. I didn't want them to see me. I ducked down and stayed out of sight where I could watch. I knew one had to be Austin because of his height and the other, I believed, to be the poker player. He had the same body type, very muscular and short. I saw the glint of a knife from what little light there was, just a quarter moon. I watched when the tall man picked the sailor up, shook him, and started beating him mercilessly. The man went down. He pulled him up and cursed him. I could hear that. Then I saw the glint of the knife again, and a swift movement. I swear he slit the man's throat, lifted him up, and tossed him overboard. I stayed there frozen until Austin left. That scared the hell out of me. I was afraid to breathe for fear he might hear me or see me. I was petrified. I knew he would quickly do the same to me. As soon as I felt safe, I retired as fast as I could back to my bed. I couldn't prove anything, so I stayed clear of him after that and never told what I had seen to anyone. Uncle Lot, I didn't even dare tell you."

"I'm upset you never told me, Bryant," said Lot. "We could have left him in some port somewhere, maybe, but then he would have come, eventually. I want all of you to be extremely careful around him. Don't trust anything he might say and watch his every move."

Silence settled on the group until Jorge Luis said, "To think he will be one of the government's agents for land management. He's got to be stopped somehow."

"It doesn't bode well for anyone with land or, for that matter, standing in his way no matter what it might be," said Bryant. "Don't you think so, Uncle?"

Lot removed his fingers from his pursed lips, "Yes, and he's the kind of man who usually gets someone else to do his dirty work. Don't ever forget that."

The table was quiet as everyone sat in silence, trying to digest the horror, until Bryant changed the subject.

"I want to see all your land records," said Bryant. "We're going to save every bit we can. We did see the other two agents in Sacramento. We had to record Uncle Lot's properties and, since we had known them from the trip on board the ship, we got together - except for Austin. He wasn't there. They shared with us how pressured they were by the government to get things going and how the large land grants would have to be broken up. The agents didn't particularly agree with that, but Austin did. They said they didn't want to change things too fast, but Austin intended to. Both government men felt he was overly ambitious and hard to get along with."

Lot sighed and said, "I am sorry, boys, that you and your family have to be subjected to such treatment. Nobody deserves that. I would suggest that Bryant and I meet with you right away and get started. We'll need time to go through everything and have it all prepared for you. At least, as much as we can do."

Both Sandovals were more than upset. Jorge Luis had his elbows on the table, fingering his mustache, thinking that this was a bigger problem than they realized. He nodded in agreement with Lot. *It is obvious to me now that Austin is a serious adversary. We're up against conquistadores with a system that has no intention of respecting or honoring us as human beings, our society, or our way of life. This is going to take more effort to overcome than I thought.*

Edgardo leaned harder on his elbows on the table, but he nervously lifted his hands up and down, sometimes tapping his fingers. He looked at Lot and said, "I think we should meet as soon as possible. You're right, Lot, this is more serious than I thought."

Prudence was pale. She rubbed her forehead. Jorge Luis glanced at Prudence, concerned. He noticed her agitation and reached over to take hold of her other hand, which was resting on the table. Holding it, he could feel her underlying anxiety. Jorge Luis leaned over and said compassionately, "Prudence, we are going to take care of this. Please, don't let it frighten you." He kept hold of her hand.

Prudence had been feeling overwhelmed with fear of what was in store for Jorge Luis and his family. She knew the implications of loss for the Californios. She worried what was coming would be disastrous for them. She knew what it was like to have lost everything - the bottom had been pulled, literally, out from under her. These people didn't understand what they were in for.

Prudence realized that Jorge Luis was setting aside his own fears to comfort her. She squeezed his hand gratefully. She didn't care who noticed. She felt honored, validated, and protected. She looked him in the eyes with a sense of relief and acceptance of his offer of help. Deep in her heart she felt a complete trust for Jorge Luis, and, even though she knew that tall Texan was dangerous, she let go of most of her fear. No matter what that horrible man did, she knew she would stand by Jorge Luis if he would let her.

She grasped Jorge Luis's hand tighter and held on. Jorge Luis could still feel her uneasiness through her hand. He looked down at her and whispered, "Don't worry, I'll help you."

His face softened when he felt her hand squeeze his again, and she said, "I know you will, and I'll do everything I can for you." But there was still a deep part of her that was unsure of her future with him, especially now that the Americans had taken over, and he stood to lose everything. *Unfortunately, I am an American.*

36
The Land Meeting

Back at the hotel the next morning, Lot and Bryant woke up with feelings of inadequacy and sadness.

"Listen, Uncle, I'm worried about how much we can save of the Sandoval property," said Bryant.

"I agree, and I can't imagine trying to survey all of it. I hope their documents are in good order. I won't be surprised, though, if they aren't. Most old deeds aren't accurate. You know the kind: start at the creek, walk to the first oak tree, which might not even be there anymore. Some of my old deeds are like that," said Lot.

Bryant stood looking out the second-story window of their bedroom suite in the hotel. "You know, Uncle," he said, while Lot was putting on his boots, "This is a quaint, little town, and I love the hacienda. Let's eat and get out there. Hey, I can see Facundo's home from up here. One of his boys is carrying firewood, and the other is sweeping the porch." He paused, watching the two boys, and then turned to Lot and said, after a pensive pause, "Uncle Lot, I'm really ready for a home and family. Do you think Fiarela would have me?"

Lot raised up from pulling on a boot, gave Bryant a long, thoughtful look and said, "It's pretty obvious to me that she would, but since her father is dead, you'll have to deal with her mother, Aldiana. Get your courage up, Son."

Bryant stepped back from the window, gave his uncle a crooked smile, and said, "I'm sure going to try." He grabbed his jacket, his small valise full of working tools, and walked to the door to wait.

It didn't take long before Lot was ready. They met Prudence at the stables, and the three of them were off to the hacienda. The morning was cool and their ride most enjoyable. A red-tailed hawk was making his rounds, a skunk was waddling along with three babies off in the field, and a flock of blackbirds, their flight forming organic shapes, seemed to be leading their way. How comfortable the three of them felt and how fast the trip seemed when they arrived.

Prudence went to the office to work with Fiarela, who was showing a financial record book to Jorge Luis. Lot and Bryant went along to the office to discuss how to get started. Lot admired the formal room, which obviously ran efficiently by the looks of the organization. Books lined the wall, which were neatly placed on polished wooden shelves, plus a table and chairs for visitors.

"You have an excellent working office here, Jorge Luis. I envy you, but when Prudence designs me a home, I will have one, too," said Lot. Prudence and Fiarela looked at each other, each smiling, and nodding with approval.

"Thank you, but today we have all the documents and deeds laid out on the dining room table where we have more room," said Jorge Luis. "Edgardo is still putting everything in order by dates. That way, you can see the progression of the acquisition of the land."

The men went on to the dining room where all the papers were laid out. Lot and Bryant worked their way slowly around the table checking the papers, while Jorge Luis and Edgardo stood aside, waiting with bated breath.

Aldiana entered the room and smiled at her guests, "Welcome back. I'm glad to see you again, and deeply grateful that you will be helping us. I'm having some coffee sent in for you."

"Thank you, Aldiana. That will be most welcome. It is nice to see you looking so well," said Lot, who knew he was taking a risk calling her by her first name, without Doña or Señora, but he felt they knew each other well enough now and took the chance. Aldiana smiled, gave a nod, and retreated from the room.

In the office, Fiarela was impatient, "Come on, Prudence. Can't we run down to the dining room for just a minute to see what they're doing?"

"I suppose so. I know Bryant was anxious to see you, but he didn't have a chance to talk to you when we arrived," said Prudence, wishing that Jorge Luis might be longing to have more contact with her. She tried not to get her hopes up. She knew they would be very busy.

"You really think he was anxious to see me? Hurry, let's go," Fiarela said, as she pushed the doors open to leave.

"Wait for me," said Prudence. She quickly wiped the quill pen clean, put it away, and closed the ink well. Out of habit, she shut the record book.

The men looked up with smiles when the girls entered the dining room. Bryant went immediately to Fiarela and began asking if she was all right. It was obvious to everyone that they were in love and meant for each other.

Jorge Luis watched his sister, thinking, *He's a foreigner, but he's a lawyer with a big future. How will Mother react to that? I hope she doesn't think less of him like she does of Prudence, who certainly doesn't deserve it.*

At that moment, Aldiana came in with Eva, who carried a large tray with coffee and slices of freshly made bread. Aldiana stopped in her tracks when she saw Fiarela and Bryant together. She had not been paying attention to her daughter. *Obviously, there is something between them. What is happening to my family?* She and Eva placed everything on the tea cart kept in the room. Aldiana poured a cup of coffee and walked over to hand it to Lot, who thanked her profusely. She sat down carefully, arranging her black mourning skirt, pushing back her hair and began observing her daughter with the lawyer, Bryant. Seeing them together like that surprised her, which triggered a wide range of confused emotions. Her old judgmental feelings swelled up and assaulted her. This time she recognized what was happening and caught herself. *I must be rational and not let my emotions get the best of me. He is a fine young man, and obviously in love with her. Anyone can see that. I do want to see her happy and safe.*

Fiarela and Prudence both had a slice of bread with their coffee. "Fiarela, the men are really busy. We should go back now to our own work," said Prudence.

Fiarela stood up, her eyes on Bryant, and told everyone that she would see them later. She left with Prudence and Aldiana, following. The two girls went to the office, and Aldiana went to check on Nito.

"Edgardo," said Lot, "While we're sitting here, I want to address a concern you had about people you called 'squatters.' I honestly don't think you can remove them without support from the United States government, which, I know, you won't get. I've given it a lot of thought, and, I believe, all you can do is offer to sell them the land at a very reasonable price. They may not accept, but I would give it a try. Is there any way you can build fences to close them off from the rest of your property?"

"Good god, are you serious?" said Edgardo, with Jorge Luis looking intently at Lot and then at Bryant.

"Yes, I most certainly am. You have no private army to fight them off, and I understand you are shorthanded now due to the Gold Rush, so what can you do?" said Lot.

Jorge Luis and Edgardo looked at each other and each looked off into an unexpected dim view of devastating loss. Their shoulders dropped, but they said nothing.

"Maybe we can survey the land with some of the more ambiguous deed descriptions," said Bryan, who spoke a good Spanish and made sure they understood, "But there is too much acreage. I don't think we have enough time. We'll do everything we can to see that all the documents are correct, and when you are called into court, I will gladly represent you. Hopefully, it will be fairer and simpler since I am an American.

"We are incredibly grateful to you," said Jorge Luis. "If you have any questions about some of the old deeds, perhaps, Mother might know some of the background information."

"By the way," said Edgardo, "Juan grew up with Papá. They were like brothers. He might have some memories, too."

At that moment, Aldiana entered again, quietly, leading Pedro, Facundo's son, "Sorry to interrupt, *hijos*, but his father sent him with a message for you." She put her arm around the boy, smiled, and said, "Go ahead, *mijo*, speak freely. They will listen." She walked softly out of the room.

"Señores, a ruffian came into the cantina, and he started drinking. My father told me to watch him closely. He started talking with another rough-looking man, and then they sat down to play poker. I grabbed the menu that Prudence had written in English for us, and when I brought it to them, I heard him brag about a lot of money they would get, and what they would do with it. Then I heard one man laugh and say that Rafa - Father says he is a bad bandit - that he has a donor, an American gentleman who is paying him, and he laughed again and winked his eye. I heard the other one say that Rafa hated Señor Jorge Luis, but I didn't hear why or what they were going to do. Sorry, Señores. I came as soon as I could to tell you."

"Oh, *Pedrito*, you did well, and if you hear anything else, please, come tell us. Would you like a cup of coffee before you leave?" asked Jorge Luis.

"Yes, sit down a moment with us. Keep those ears of yours open while you're working. You've been a big help for us and be sure to thank your dad for sending you." Edgardo gave him a full cup of coffee with plenty of cream and sat down by him. Pedro beamed and felt quite grown up.

Lot and Bryant glanced at each other, puzzled. They had no idea who Rafa was, but this information did not bode well.

When Pedro got up to leave, Jorge Luis slipped a couple of coins into his palm, and told him, "We'll have to get you a real horse now instead of Old Flojo, if you are going to be our messenger." He received a wide admiring smile and a thank you as Pedro left. "There goes a good kid, just like his father," said Jorge Luis.

Jorge Luis turned to Lot and Bryant to explain, "Rafa is the brother of one of our workers on the hacienda. He's a notorious bandit who hides out in the caves up out of Murphy's. It's high up in the Sierras and not too far from the gold mines. I threw him off the hacienda once, so now he has a vendetta against me. We've had Danilo follow Prudence wherever she goes to protect her, but now I think we need to talk to everyone who lives and works here to keep their eyes open."

"But what about this donor?" said Lot, "Do you have any idea who that would be?"

Edgardo interrupted, "My guess is that he would be Austin, but how he got together with Rafa is beyond me. He must have met his brother Elías when he was here. I know Austin has it in for us and, probably, for all us Californios. We know they want to break up our large landholdings."

Bryant felt almost defeated as a lawyer as he thought about the ramifications of what he had just heard. *I can see the writing on the wall. Please, God, support me in helping this family. None of this is fair to anyone. I must find a way to protect Fiarela. I'm so in love with her.*

"Listen," said Bryant, rubbing his hands. He had hoped to help guide the family through the adjustment of the United States taking over with their new rules. But, now, he realized he couldn't save them. They would be very lucky to keep anything. He wanted to grab Fiarela and hold her tight and keep her safe. "I will do everything possible, but I advise you to have an alternate plan of what you can do. Do I understand, correctly, that you own the pueblo, the cantina, and a new hotel?" clarified Bryant.

"Yes, we own the entire town and both hotels," said Jorge Luis.

"If they are money making, I suggest we do everything to save them. Possibly, they will be easier to prove ownership. What about the river? Do you own that, too? It could be a valuable asset," said Lot.

"Yes," said Edgardo, "We also have a business supplying beef to the diggings along with some mining equipment. If the bandits don't hit us on the way up to the Sierras, we always do more than well. It's a lucrative business right now."

"Let's start with those businesses. I believe they will be accepted as legitimate, whereas the land itself would be wanted for real estate, and some of those shyster land lawyers stand to make a lot of money buying and selling."

Bryant rubbed his chin in thought and cut in, "I almost forgot. The other two land management men, Richard and Peter in Sacramento, said they believe California will be a state next year, and by the next year, 1851, the Land Management Law will be ready to go into effect. I think that is when the court will become very busy and persistent."

Everyone was dismayed to hear that.

Lot let out a big sigh and leaned back into his chair to say, "Sorry, I forgot all about that. That doesn't give us long to get things corrected and in better order. It gives us only a little more than a year. These documents will require a considerable amount of time, and I must be back up north. I'll try to come back and forth as often as I can."

"Okay, let's get going," said Jorge Luis, giving Lot a grateful smile. "We should prepare what we have a possibility of saving. Then, let's deal with the rest. Lot, will you go over these deeds for our outside businesses?"

"Yes, Son, gladly," said Lot.

"Bring them on," said Bryant. "Now we have something to get our hands on and can get to work. I know you're starting to cut hay tomorrow, but if it is acceptable, we will be out tomorrow to start."

"The brothers shook hands with Lot and Bryant. "We are deeply indebted," said Edgardo.

"We'll leave everything out for you. I'll inform Mother that you will be here all day and to see that you are fed. Help yourself to the wine canter, too, with our pleasure," said Jorge Luis.

"We'll walk out with you. Benito will have your horses ready," added Edgardo, "Meals are on the house, and you are welcome to stay as long as you need to in the hotel. Anything you want, just ask Facundo. He will see that you are taken care of, and of course, he knows the business. We'll be cutting hay for most of next week. It's quite a distance from here, but one of us will try to make it home now and then."

Ranch work, with its constant and heavy demands, was becoming more and more difficult as the younger men took off for the gold fields in the Sierras.

37
Elena's Wedding Invitation

ord arrived at the hacienda, to Aldiana, that Elena's wedding would take place at the Ochoa's family hacienda the next weekend. The wedding would be held in their chapel at eleven o'clock in the morning. Following the wedding, the festivities would begin with barbecues and an abundance of food. Fiarela was asked by Señora Ochoa if she would perform the horse dance during the afternoon. Aldiana was informed that there would also be an agility cock race, horse races and a bullfight with a grizzly bear would be held in the evening with much gambling. The Ochoa family expected everyone to attend.

Aldiana had just entered the foyer from the hallway when she caught sight of Jorge Luis descending the stairs. She rushed over to the stairway to stop him and let him know about the wedding.

She told her son, "Jorge Luis, *Hijo*, this morning, I received a wedding invitation from the Ochoas. The wedding will be held next weekend on Saturday, and they want all of us to be there. I am still in mourning. The year after Emiliano's death isn't up yet, and I don't feel right about attending any social event. I know that Elena is like a daughter to me, but I just can't disrespect Emiliano. You know I must take charge of all the preparations for Father Serrano's visit here in another week, and I'm just not up to trying to do both. I wish I could. Elena will have the wedding that every young girl dreams about. However, I just don't feel I can go, and I am worried about her marrying a man like Austin. He sets me on edge. It makes me nervous thinking about it. Elena's always been like a second daughter to me and loved by our whole family." She paused with a long slow sigh, "I'm sorry. By the way, Jorge Luis, the Ochoas requested that Fiarela do the horse dance in the arena." She looked with askance at her son.

"Mother, I understand about your reluctance to go, and I am sure Señora Ochoa would, too. Don't fret over it *Mamá*. The horse dance? What an opportunity for Fiarela. She should do it. She will be excited. Have you told her yet?"

"No, no, not yet. I will soon. We need to check the dress she will wear, and she must practice the dance again, of course, without the casta-nets. That would frighten the horse." She started to leave but remembered something else, "Wait, *Mijo,* the Ochoa's also invited Prudence's family since Austin knows them so well. Will you inform them, please?"

"How nice of them. Elena's wedding should be an interesting experi-ence. Wait 'til they watch Fiarela in the arena with the horse! I'll bet they've never seen anything like it. What an honor for her," said Jorge Luis. "You know she is quite the young lady now. I think it's time she be thinking of marriage, too." He gave her a quick hug and turned to leave, "Ma, I have to be at the cantina tonight. Let me know the wedding details later." He started to walk off.

Aldiana felt she needed to share her new insights and feelings. She moved quickly before he could get a way. *Here I go again, but I feel I've got to say it and let Jorge Luis know his happiness is important to me.*

"Wait, Jorge Luis, I want to tell you something." She reached up to put her arms around his neck, smiling, "Your father and I were so happy to-gether. I want more than anything for you to have that, too." Unfortunately, she fell back into her old dogma, saying, "Jorge Luis, you are an older man now. You need a wife and a family." She started to continue, but Jorge Luis interrupted her.

"Mother, I do love you, but don't start that again. I've heard it too many times. I'm not leaving my responsibilities here to go to Mexico or Spain to grab some unknown woman to be my wife. I've got work to do." He strode off. *Mother just won't let up will she. I won't allow her to pressure me.*

As she stood there in her tracks, holding her breath, she realized that she had caused disgust and anger in her son. She knew, in her heart, that this time she needed to work harder at letting him be his own man.

She felt frustrated and guilty by how badly she had missed the mark. Jorge Luis had always shown great capacity for responsibil-ity. Now, with his father's death and with him receiving the entire estate under the Primogeniture law, she knew he must feel overwhelmed. The responsibility for every-thing and everyone weighed heavily on him. She was not helping. *He is so much like Emiliano. I saw that stand out as he walked down the foyer stairs. His father would be so proud to see that his first son has become the competent, honest, and stalwart new hacendado. Mijo, my dearest son, I so want you to be happy.* She walked out to the chapel to pray.

Jorge Luis left with each step building frustration and resentment. *Why do I place so much need of approval from Mother? Right now she made me feel I need to avoid Prudence when I want to be closer to her. Doesn't Mother understand that we all must accept the reality that we will live in a new world, and we are expected to be Americans? Does that mean we give up our deepest values? Never! How important is it to be a Catholic? I don't know. We're Catholics, but we weren't to begin with. My god, what does it all matter? It does matter. I know it, and I won't give in. I'll stand face to face with you, Austin, y que te rompe la cara, if need be.* His boots hit the hard-packed dirt path harder.

Halfway to the stables, he ran into Danilo. He calmed down and asked him about his surveillance of Prudence.

"Señor, I have seen no one so far, but- " Danilo paused, bringing the image to mind, "I did see some strange horseshoe prints in the damp ground by the creek, where someone let his horse drink and then cross over. That's all I've seen."

"*Maldito sea*, those strange prints are sure to be Rafa's. He's one dangerous bastard. What did they look like?" asked Jorge Luis.

"The left hoof was shod with a crude horseshoe. It had some odd, chipped marks on one side and there was a crack in one place, which would be bad for the horse. The right hoof was not shod, and the two back hooves had better shoes on them, really strange. Never seen nothin' like it," answered Danilo.

"That's him. If you ever see him or those tracks again, tell me or Edgardo immediately. Juan might be able to track him," said Jorge Luis.

"Yes, Patrón. I'm sorry this is all happening," said Danilo.

"Keep up your good work. I appreciate it. By the way, if you intend to marry Angela, the priest will be here soon after Elena's wedding next weekend. He won't be here long, and when he leaves, he won't be back for a long time, if ever. The mission is selling off its land, and he may have to leave, so think about it."

"Thank you, *Patrón*, I will. I do want to marry her," said Danilo, his face lighting up and his body relaxing. He left with a feeling of worthiness.

Time passed quickly, working with Juan at the stables. Jorge Luis had to hurry back to the house and return Prudence to the pueblo. Jorge Luis needed to see Facundo and talk to him about Austin. He wanted to ride with Prudence with all his heart, but, now, with his mother stirring up all the emotional conflicts, he was slipping down into darkness. He began to feel a need to avoid Prudence and all she represented. A vision of Austin entered his head. *Ese condenado, he'll override all our rights and our needs just like Mother just did to me. Why can't she let go?* He breathed in deeply and relaxed his solar plexus as he let the air out. *Come on, get a grip, pull yourself out of this. I want what my parents had - a lifetime, loving partnership. I don't want to be empty and hurting like my brother.* He shook his shoulders to get the stiffness out, straightened up his body, and walked faster.

By the time he had worked through those thoughts, he was at the office door. He took a deep breath and entered. His heart nearly dropped. His sister and Prudence weren't there. The office was cleaned up and in order. *Don't tell me she's gone already.* He ran out and down the hallway. There they were, waiting in the foyer.

"Girls, I couldn't get here any sooner, sorry," he said. "I'm still taking you, Prudence. I'll go tell Benito and bring the cart around, but first, I do have to change. I won't be long."

More sitting and waiting made Fiarela antsy, "Prudence, let's wait outside. I'll go out with you."

Prudence felt as if she were in a trance, thinking for a while that Jorge Luis didn't care enough to want to take her to town, but now she knew he did. She beamed, feeling a flood of warmth through her chest.

They sat on the veranda and watched the sun cast long shadows across the grounds. Some of the shapes melded into one another, giving an appearance of otherworldliness. It was late in the afternoon. The sun might drop behind the hills before they reached town, leaving streaks of oranges and reds against a darkening sky.

While they were waiting, Fiarela jabbered on. Prudence, lost in her own thoughts, didn't hear much. The words went in one ear and out the other, but she did notice the changing colors of the world around them.

The veranda's huge wooden doors finally opened, and Jorge Luis appeared, taking Prudence's breath away. He was dressed in black leather pants, which were embroidered with a floral motif down the sides, and all hand-sewn with silver thread. A short jacket matched his pants. The outfit was set off by a red scarf tied around his neck under a white shirt collar. His wavy, chestnut hair was held back by his dress hat and black bolo under his chin.

Fiarela reacted immediately, saying, "How handsome you look, doesn't he Pru?"

"Yes, quite," said Prudence, thinking that he would have most of the women all over him at the cantina tonight. She felt like a second-class citizen in her work clothes. *What has he got planned? Is he going to throw me under the cart? He knows that I'm not allowed to go into the cantina alone at night.* Her underlying fear was turning into resentment, and her expectations of a romantic ride were sliding into a sad nothing.

"Fiarela, Prudence, wait here while I go get Benito. We're taking the carriage, and he'll drive us," said Jorge Luis. He left for the carriage barn.

"I wonder why he wants Benito to drive. Maybe he doesn't want to get his fancy clothes all dusty," said Prudence, sarcastically.

Fiarela didn't know what to say to that remark. She remained silent but was more than curious about what may have happened. That was not like Prudence at all.

Benito arrived, driving the one-horse carriage. Jorge Luis was inside. He opened the door and offered Prudence a hand up, but she retorted, "I am quite capable of getting in by myself, thank you."

Now what on earth is going on with her? wondered Jorge Luis. There went his plan for a romantic ride to the pueblo. He felt like his desires had been thrown into the trash heap.

They were sitting opposite each other in the carriage when Benito started off. They waved goodbye to Fiarela out the window, which forced them to be close, but both sat back fast.

Prudence started a conversation by stating, "I know Edgardo went to town to keep an eye on Austin, but what are you all dressed up for? Do you have special plans for the evening?" It was noticeable to Jorge Luis that there was no smile forthcoming.

"Yes, I did have plans. I was going to ask you if you would dress up and join me for dinner in the restaurant and then for dancing at the cantina. Would you?" He crossed his fingers as if he were a nervous teenager again. "Today's lunch was maddening. I need to relax with someone I feel comfortable with. I always feel at ease with you, Prudence. What do you say?" he asked.

Prudence hesitated for a minute, as she felt guilty for reacting so childishly. But his last words sounded so sincere she couldn't refuse, "Yes, I would like that, and I agree about the lunch. I don't trust Austin at all. Be careful of him."

"You're right. We're in serious trouble." He was shaking his head, "I'm praying that your uncle and Bryant will be able to actually help us. I know they are certainly trying, and we are grateful. You have no idea how much."

"I heard that the meeting went well this morning," said Prudence, "but all the work left me drained and too tense, and then Fiarela and I had to work extra hard to catch up. This day has been a long one, and I am exhausted," said Prudence. As her voice became slower and slower, she finally said, "I hope you don't mind. I'm going to put my head down for just a minute." She put her head down on a cushion, succumbed to exhaustion, and didn't awake.

She had been emotionally drained after listening to the possibility of an irreversible loss of the Sandoval family land. The land had been loved and cared for over generations of hard work, sweat, and sometimes tears that had been put into it, as well as given appreciation, gratefulness and love, which was so obvious. Prudence had grown to love the people, and the slower pace of the pastoral lifestyle. She loved the uncrowded vastness and beauty of the land. A crushing blow hit her each time she thought about it. She, the American, represented a new, sudden conquering - an unrelenting force. But, as a woman, she was also the victim as she watched her loved ones face disaster.

Jorge Luis moved carefully to her side of the carriage and placed her head on his lap. He leaned down and kissed her hair lightly. Her sleeping gave him the chance to simply hold her. *If she will have me, I want to hold her for the rest of my life. Would she have me? With the situation we are in right now, I may have nothing to offer her.* He rode that way until Benito pulled up in front of the cantina's back door. "Give me a hand, Benito, will you? Help me get her down. I don't want to wake her. Be careful," said Jorge Luis.

"Sure, Boss." He helped lift her down and held her without waking her. When he handed her over to Jorge Luis, she sighed heavily and shifted her body but did not wake up.

Benito opened the kitchen door, went up the stairs, and opened the door to her room with Jorge Luis right behind him. "Okay, Boss, you be careful." He paused a moment and said, "I mean it. I'm going over to the stable and see if I can find out anything. Then, I'll be in the cantina as just another cowboy. I won't know you, and you won't know me," whispered Benito.

"Good," nodded Jorge Luis as he carried Prudence to her bed and laid her softly on it. He covered her with a blanket and softly kissed her before walking out and downstairs to the cantina.

Jorge Luis stood in the entrance to the large public room of the cantina, surveying the room. His eyes swept slowly over everything that was going on. *Looks like a good crowd. The gambling tables are full. That's what I like to see.* He noticed several young couples dancing. *I wish I had Pru-*

dence here. I feel like dancing tonight. Diós mío, there's that hijo de puta, Austin. His body tensed, and he felt like he was going to explode with anger. *He's got a pile of chips, probably from cheating. I've got to control myself, or I will tear him limb from limb. Why isn't he at the Ochoas preparing for his wedding?*

Suddenly, he had been noticed, and all eyes were on him, including the eyes of Austin, who sat at the poker table playing cards. People whispered around the tables, "He's the new *hacendado*, but where is that hot dame he's usually with?" Austin turned his back. The others quickly returned to the game. Gambling was in the men's blood, and they would be there until the place closed up - except for two or three who might be tossed out on their bums. Facundo didn't put up with violence or drunks who could not hold their liquor.

Facundo was quick to grab him, "Hey, Boss, what the hell's going on? Edgardo's here and told me not to know him? He's been making the rounds, and he told me to watch that Americano. The place has been full so that's been hard to do, but he doesn't seem to drink much. Been spending his time, so far, playing poker."

"Thanks, Faco, keep watching him. He's dangerous. Don't let him pull any smart stuff." Jorge Luis began to tell Facundo about him, yet found it hard to keep his eyes off Austin at the poker table. His body stiffened from anger.

Jorge Luis' mounting agitation was disturbing to Facundo. This man was his childhood friend, like a twin brother.

Facundo felt taken off guard listening to the detailed information about Austin's arrogant behavior at lunch, plus the nasty story that happened aboard ship. He simply stared at Jorge Luis. He couldn't think of anything to say except, "My god, *amigo,* does that mean we may all be in danger?" He needed time to mentally absorb the story. He had not thought about all the negative aspects of being under a new government, especially under someone like this American official. Fear welled up for him and his family.

Jorge Luis shook his head but didn't explain further, "I don't know. I'll talk to you more about it later."

"I'll keep watching and keep my ears open," said Facundo with a sharp gut ache. "Anything I can do, let me know. I've got Pedro surveying the poker table. The man does seem to tend to lose it if the others have been drinking too much and complain they've been cheated. He hasn't punched anyone yet, but I don't want any trouble in here."

"I don't want any trouble, either. Keep your eyes on him. He's a big government land agent and very aggressive. He's a rounder, so watch how he treats the women," said Jorge Luis. He went over to the poker table and sat down to play, wondering how Austin would react with him at the same table. Then his thoughts turned to Prudence upstairs. *Will she wake up? Will she come down? She was totally exhausted, but I hope so.* He picked up his cards, and the game was on.

38
The Cantina Date

Prudence stirred and woke feeling surprised and disoriented. The room was pitch black. *Where? Where am I?* She felt around her and realized she was on top of her own bed. The blanket on her was one of her own. *I've still got my clothes on - Jorge Luis – he brought me up here. I fell asleep in the carriage. I can't believe how stressful it was today. I'm still exhausted.* She sunk down into her bed, rubbing her arms and her back. *Oh, dear, I've got to get up. I'm supposed to go to dinner with him and then dancing in the cantina. I ache all over. How can I do it?* She lay for a moment, listening to the music wafting up from below. She began to feel the rhythm. It stirred her feelings and her body relaxed. *The music coming up from the cantina sounds wonderful. I want to go.*

She slowly moved off the bed with her body less stiff and sore, lit the candle, and washed her face. *Oh agony, I'm a mess. What gown? I need to look my best.* She picked out a lime green dress that set off her golden hair. She left it loose and full except for her ivory combs. Her earrings were simple gold hoops. When she looked in the mirror, she was pleased. She gave a twirl in her gown and felt enthusiasm begin to grow into real anticipation. She could almost feel Jorge Luis' arms around her. He was so handsome in his outfit that she could hardly wait. She put out the candle and opened the door to the stairs.

She almost skipped down the stairs as she gained back her strength, feeling more and more empowered and expectant. She heard a few "Mama mías" from the kitchen staff and a couple of whistles, which picked up her spirits. She looked forward to seeing this night through. She passed down the back hallway to the cantina, but stopped at the door and hesitated. *How should I do this? Maybe I can just walk in, but I'm never supposed to go in there alone at night.* With a touch of anxiety, she knocked on the door softly and waited, holding her breath.

The door was opened by Pedro, Facundo's son, "Oh, Miss Prudence." *Wow, does she look gorgeous.* "Please wait a minute, and I will inform Señor Sandoval."

There must be a big crowd tonight. Pedro looks exhausted. Poor kid, he should be home in bed, but, oh, listen to that music. I can hardly wait. Where is Jorge Luis, I wonder?

Pedro went to the poker table and whispered in Jorge Luis' ear, which caused him to sit up, turn his head toward the door where he saw her. She took his breath away.

"Tell her I'll be right there. Thanks, Pedro." He put his cards down, turned in the chips, gave Austin a studied eye, and wove his way through the crowd. He came up to her and bowed. He emphasized each word he spoke, "You are beautiful tonight. Let's dance, shall we?" He held out his arms. There was not a handsomer couple in the room.

By then all the partiers knew he was the *hacendado* and the owner of the cantina -- a commanding presence. Even the poker table stopped for a while to watch. The players couldn't help but watch with their own dreams in their heads.

Austin sat up straight. His neck tightened. *She's ravishing. She'll be in my arms soon. She'll find out what dancing is all about. He can't come close to me when it comes to holding a woman and moving her with my body and hands. A tango is what she needs. Jorge Luis will split a gut. I'll bide my time.*

Austin didn't drink while he played poker so that he could easily read the other players' faces the drunker they became. He was winning regularly, which inflated his ego each time he scooped up the chips. *I know how to beat these hicks.*

Edgardo surprised Jorge Luis with being dressed, talking, and acting like a cowboy out for a night of carousing on the town. He looked worn down with his hair unkept, rundown shoes, and faded old clothes.

Edgardo had been keeping his eyes open for miscreants and trouble-makers. The majority of men in the cantina were mainly new people, except for one of Austin's bodyguards. Edgardo recognized him from the hacienda. He wondered where his other man was. He hadn't seen him tonight. Most of the other men were passing through on their way to the diggings and needed a place to stop. The Sierra mountains were a long way off yet. No one recognized Edgardo except his brother, Facundo, Pedro, and Marina, who entered at that time to entertain the men by singing.

Instead of entering on the small stage, she made a grand entrance, appearing through the private door to the bordello. Marina came in swinging her magnificent hair back, raising her head dramatically and walking to the front of the crowd with sensuous movements, wearing a tight, alizarin crimson gown. Her cleavage was deep and cut in a long V -- very revealing. The back was pulled up just below the hips with a big bow, framing her perfect derriere with rustling pleats, which swished as she walked. Hands reached, begging to touch.

The crowds hailed her, hooting and calling, but they all went quiet as soon as they heard her deep, husky voice. The first song she sang, "El ángel de amor" brought tears to many drunken eyes. Then she moved among the men, singing "Levántate, joven divina." Both songs were favorites of the local Californios, and some sang along.

She suddenly saw Austin and made for the tall, handsome Texan and sang straight to him. He invited her to sit on his lap, but she ignored that. As she angled off, she ran her hand through his hair slowly and suggestively, her gold and silver bangles jangling. She made her way back to the front with the men throwing kisses and shouting, "More, more!"

She started her final song, "El último adiós," with outstretched arms to the men. She ended by throwing out her arms wide and flashing her hair over her head and back again. The applause was thunderous, with foot stamping that nearly brought the house down. She left with a flourish of hip and skirt, stopping at the door to bow and throw a kiss and sing the final words again. Silence reigned behind her as she shut the door. Her last words, "El último adiós" – "The Last Goodbye" rang in their hearts.

Even though most of the men did not understand Spanish, they felt the emotion behind the words and knew what the words meant when Marina went through her dramatic actions in shutting the door. Those lonely men, homesick for the arms of loved ones and hearts so far away, felt that the words of "The Last Goodbye" were meant just for them. They sat soaking up the feeling for a few minutes before returning to the regular cantina energy. But Marina would stay in their dreams that night.

Jorge Luis and Prudence had stood off to the side to listen to Marina and watch her entertain the cantina public.

Prudence watched Jorge Luis closely when she said, sighing and trying to let go of her long-held jealousy, "She's so talented. The men are glued to their seats when she sings, enchanted."

"Yes, she packs them in when she sings and holds them until she finishes," said Jorge Luis.

Prudence still felt a sliver of jealousy, a feeling of not quite measuring up, but Jorge Luis had seemed matter-of-fact in discussing her, and, at least, Marina had not sung directly to him, as she had done before - deliberately causing an uproar. She respected them, and that was a relief to

Prudence.

Jorge Luis put his arm around her tiny waist and maneuvered her out onto the dance floor again. The musicians were playing a waltz. He swirled and whirled her around the room until they felt as if they were swirling as one, in another dimension, in which neither wanted to end. Their altered reality stopped when the dance ended, and they faced each other with wonder. Each felt as if they could have gone on without end. Jorge Luis wondered how had that experience happened? *Is this what my brother feels when he has his visions? Pure bliss?* He looked into the eyes of Prudence, and saw that she, too, had experienced what he had. Prudence, with pure elation shining from her eyes, nodded silently when Jorge Luis said, "With *you* in my arms, I could waltz forever - all over California - with *you* in my arms," he whispered.

At the poker table, Edgardo watched everything with interest. Austin's bodyguard was playing cards and swigging his liquor down, as if he were lost and dying of thirst in the desert. His tongue was loosening. He was stumbling over words in broken English, as if he had a whiskey throat. Edgardo noticed Austin becoming tense and staring at his hired man. Austin had not recognized Edgardo, who tried to keep his head turned away, looking down at his cards.

Austin heard his bodyguard start bragging and cringed at what he was hearing. "Just wait 'til you see what we have in store for those stupid Beaners and dumb Indians," said Austin's man. He started laughing, "I'll show 'em what it means to be a landowner." He spit on the floor, waving his arms drunkenly, "Many servants, too, many – right-here-in-my-arms." He pointed to his chest, laughed again, and smacked his lips. He leaned back and almost knocked over his chair. "You'll see. Y-e-a-h. I'll have a wife as beautiful as that singer, and it won't be long, either," he picked up his cards, but his hands fumbled, and they sprayed over the table. He nodded to himself, appearing as if in a stupor. He looked around the table, pointed back at Austin, repeating, "Wait and see." He gave a somewhat derisive, low laugh and almost under his breath said, "I – know – things."

That did it for Austin. He pushed back his chair, stood up, and cashed in his chips. He strode around the table, jerked his man up and out of his chair.

"Wha – what're you doing? I'm playing here," he said, blinking with confusion and stumbling. "Wait, Boss. I'm okay."

"You're coming outside with me, you piece of shit," growled Austin. He grabbed him, pushing him out the door where he beat him mercilessly.

He tossed him into the water trough to sober him up some.

After a few minutes, Austin pulled him out and dragged him to his room across the street in a dump. Only he would stay in the hotel.

"You're going to your room and stay there and keep that loud mouth to yourself. I don't know how I got talked into hiring you. You're nothin' but a drunken bum." Austin threw his man into his room and slammed the door. If he'd had a key, he would have locked it, but he knew this *mosquito muerto* would pass out soon. He'd take care of him later. He straightened his clothes and ran his hand through his hair. He was grateful that his other man had found a woman to spend the night with, causing no problem. He walked back into the cantina, feeling fired up with anger and frustration. He wasn't about to let some two-bit cowboy bodyguard with a big mouth ruin his plans.

Once he stepped back inside the cantina, he calmed himself, put on his best social smile, and headed for Prudence and Jorge Luis. He didn't care who Jorge Luis was at this point. He was too fired up and he had the power. Just wait, he'd bring down this so-called elite *hacendado* show-off in due time. He stopped in front of them and requested a dance with Prudence, putting on his most gentlemanly manners. He now felt back to his suave self.

"Prudence, how lovely you look tonight. May I have the pleasure of a dance?" he said, bowing to her but looking at Jorge Luis for approval, which stung Austin to lower himself before someone he considered beneath him, but he did it for the sake of propriety.

Prudence looked at Jorge Luis, who looked daggers at Austin, yet nodded. "Yes," he took Prudence's arm and, gritting his teeth, directed her to Austin. In seconds, a woman came up to Jorge Luis and claimed him for a dance. While they danced, his eyes were on Prudence whenever he could see her in the crowd. Austin was easier to follow on the packed dance floor with his height of six feet, six inches, but Prudence was difficult to see behind him. He gave up and paid more attention to his dance partner.

Austin had chosen the timing purposely. The dance floor was full of couples- each one absorbed with their partner. He would usually stick out like a sore thumb because of his height, but not so on a crowded floor. Austin was a smooth, accomplished dancer and planned his moves to not call any attention to them.

"Austin, I'm sorry. I'm not a very good dancer. I apologize. Where did you learn to dance so well?" said Prudence, surprised by his dexterity and natural rhythm.

"In Texas. My uncle was a dance instructor. I found I love to dance, but out here, unfortunately, there are few opportunities," he said.

"I'm sure you will have an active social life with Elena, and, I know, she will love dancing with you," said Prudence.

"I want *you* to," he whispered as he bent down, so that she would have to draw a little closer in order to hear him. "I will see you again," he said as the music stopped. On the last note, he leaned down, unseen by the others, and in one swift move he pulled her toward him, kissing her passionately on the lips - to her shock and disgust. She was left speechless. She quickly looked around, hoping no one saw them. She hit his chest with her fist, hard, and felt an adrenaline rush when she tried to push him away, but he stepped back, moved swiftly through the crowd, and was gone. Humiliation and anger surged through her, flushing her face.

Prudence stood, still in a state of disbelief and barely breathing, with her eyes rapidly blinking. She was trying to regain her composure before Jorge Luis returned. Bursting with emotion, she wanted to tell Jorge Luis how foul Austin was and what he had done, but fear held her back. She kept smoothing and straightening her skirt and reaching up nervously to fit her bodice and sleeves. *What am I going to do? If I tell him, he might beat the tar out of Austin regardless of how big he is, or – or - Jorge Luis' gun never misses. No, no, Austin is too powerful and mean. He would ruin Jorge Luis and his family.* Fear gripped her with the idea. *I wonder if Edgardo saw what he did? I hope not. He wouldn't hesitate to use that Indian knife of his.*

She spied Jorge Luis coming toward her and took his arm, shaking slightly, saying, "I can't stand that man, Jorge Luis, and I am tired. I'm so glad I came. I loved the music, and our dancing was more than enjoyable." She moved closer and hugged him. "Thank you for a wonderful evening. I would like to do it again sometime, but I do need to leave."

"I'm sorry, Prudence. I understand. I know you have to work in the morning, but I'm so happy you joined me. I hope you enjoyed it as much as I have. I'll escort you back to your room right now, if you like." he said, hoping, when they reached her room, she would invite him in.

But she didn't. Prudence told her thank you and good night and entered her little home up above the cantina, alone. She felt so vulnerable and needy. Sitting down at the little table, she bent over and rested her head in her arms over the table. *Nothing seems to be working out. I didn't dare ask him in tonight. I wouldn't have been able to resist him.* Her vision of a long, romantic evening with dancing, was sucked away by a cruel, two-faced, smooth-talker, and advantage-taker. *I must keep Austin away from me. I hope someday he gets his come uppence.*

Jorge Luis went back to the cantina, disappointed but understanding. He entered with the intention of getting together with Edgardo and Facundo, now that Austin and his poor excuse for a bodyguard were gone. It cut him to the quick to let him dance with Prudence, but it seemed to him to go all right.

Facundo was closing the cantina a little early, but it was his call. Some of the men had staggered out into the night, others complained and moved into the bordello, but most understood. They were grateful that there was a cantina available. The gold fields were a long way off.

Edgardo had gone into the office to wait, so Jorge Luis joined him there. Facundo came in quickly and informed them that they would talk in the morning, "Tonight was plain tiring - big crowd, big money, but I'm bushed. See you in the morning. Lock up for me?"

"Sure, we will. We're leaving right now, too," said Edgardo as Facundo hurried out. "I'll bet he helps out María with the twins at night, too," said Edgardo. "When I would stay with Ramona, I remember what it was like at night with just one baby."

"You're right. Let's retire to our two-bedroom suite. I suddenly feel done in, too. It's ready for us, isn't it?" asked Jorge Luis.

"Yeah, I asked earlier. I'll tell you tomorrow what I know," said Edgardo.

Jorge Luis reminded Edgardo that they had to plan for the trip to Elena's wedding next weekend and, "Oh, yeah, and don't forget Facundo in the morning."

Edgardo just nodded. Halfway up the stairs, he paused and said, "I hate to see Elena marry that piece of trash. She deserves better. You know, *Hermano*, I feel so empty and lonely. I know Nito is lucky to have a grandmother, but he really needs a mother. I wish things were different."

Jorge Luis rubbed his mouth in thought, remembering Elena and Edgardo as children and how close they were. He had known how Elena had adored his brother, and later had seen that she was in love with him, but he remained silent. To Jorge Luis' astonishment, he began to feel an emptiness and loneliness slowly settling deeply in his being. He understood his feeling matched Edgardo's.

The two brothers went up the stairs together, deep in thought, both wondering what tomorrow might bring.

39
Wedding Shocks

iarela staggered out of bed at 3:30 a.m., still half asleep. "Thanks, Consuelo, for waking me. I can't believe it is time to leave for the wedding already. I'll get Prudence up."

"Señorita, do you need help with your bags or bedrolls? Breakfast?" asked Consuelo, the *mucama*, rubbing her own sleepy eyes.

"How about a good breakfast with a basket of food to eat on the way? Has anyone gone out to wake up Benito? I hope my brothers are up. Is Bryant up?"

"Don't worry, Señorita Fiarela, I will see that it is all taken care of," said Consuelo.

Prudence was stirring in her bed before finally opening her eyes. She was surprised to see Fiarela up and half-dressed. "Why didn't you wake me? I've got to hurry. Good thing I laid out my clothes last night, and my valise is packed," said Prudence, hurrying to wash in the basin, and dress quickly in comfortable riding clothes like Fiarela.

In good time all was in order. Beds were hastily made, the windows and drapes closed. The bedrolls and valises were carried downstairs to wait in the foyer. A full breakfast was eaten with gusto, when in walked Jorge Luis, Edgardo, and Bryant, who had also spent the night.

Big appetites were obvious when the men sat down to eat. Bryant remarked, "Man, look at this food. I am starved." He filled his plate and then leaned over to his cousin and said in a low voice, "Prudence, I slept on a rawhide bed last night. I'd never heard of such a thing. Do girls sleep on them? Don't they have real beds?"

Prudence wiped her mouth with her napkin, gave a soft laugh, "Everyone sleeps on them. I'm used to them now. Come on, eat. We have to hurry."

The young people were just finishing the meal with a drink of chocolate atole when Benito arrived, ready to load up the carriage. The small suitcases and wedding gifts were all packed into traveling boxes and tied tightly on the roof except for the water and food. They would need that during the long ride.

Aldiana and Nito, still in their nightclothes and bathrobes, came out to watch and wave goodbye as the carriage left the hacienda carefully and slowly.

The big hacienda wagon, full of families and children with a few horseback riders following alongside, had left by four in the morning in order to arrive on time for the wedding. The Ochoas were their closest neighbors, but the wagon would be slow, and it would take almost a half day's ride to reach the Ochoa hacienda.

Everyone would be staying a few days for the celebration. The wagon carried guitars, violins, an accordion and a small harp. There would be lots of singing and telling stories, with laughter all the way. Plus, there was an abundance of wine available. It took four of their biggest and strongest horses to pull the wagon full of people so it would be slow going, but fun. Many people came in the large wagons from far away, which were pulled by teams of oxen.

Jorge Luis, Edgardo, Bryant, Fiarela, and Prudence were cozy in the two-horse carriage. Jorge Luis had his guitar, Edgardo his accordion, and the rest had their voices full of joy. They would have as much fun as those in the wagon. The trip to the Ochoas would be quite festive and full of laughter. Time passed quickly. However, they did miss Aldiana, who was still in mourning and had to prepare for the arrival of all the same people from the Ochoa wedding, plus the possibility of many more from afar next week. Uncle Lot had never met the Ochoa family and simply did not want to make such a tiring trip. He decided not to attend the wedding but to instead continue to work on the old documents and deeds, which the Sandoval family was grateful for.

In between singing favorite songs, Fiarela remembered something that no one knew yet. She started waving her arms, opening her eyes wide, and putting on a big smile, chanting, "Listen, Listen, Listen!" She started bouncing in her seat, "Listen, the Ochoas requested that I be the one to perform the horse dance in the big arena – with everyone watching." She sat back into the cushions. Her faced carried a proud smile.

"Hey, Sis, that is a huge honor. Why did you wait until now to tell us?" said Jorge Luis.

"You'll be the hit of the afternoon, for sure, but why not let us in on it?" asked Edgardo.

"*Mamá* told me not to say anything until she knew I could do it. I had to practice all week. She didn't want me to be embarrassed or get too nervous. I am, though," she said.

Bryant and Prudence didn't have a clue of what they were talking about. They sat with a puzzled look, especially Bryant, who wasn't sure at all what a horse dance meant. He understood it to mean that Fiarela would be performing something in front of everyone. He wasn't sure how he felt about that. All the men's eyes would be on her out there in the middle of the huge arena full of people. A small pang of jealousy stabbed him.

"What on earth is a horse dance?" asked Prudence with Bryant, staring at Fiarela, not knowing what to think.

Jorge Luis cut in, "I'm not missing that. Prudence, you will love it. I'm proud of you, my little sister. You will be the star of the afternoon."

Prudence leaned forward to hear the explanation more clearly above the noise of the carriage. She listened with her mouth open from surprise and curiosity.

"It's really quite simple," said Fiarela, "I just walk out into the arena with the music, greet the crowd, and stand in a dance position as the horse and rider enter, prancing and dancing until he reaches me. The horse bows to me and we start dancing."

"My word, I can't wait to see that. You never told me you could do something like that," Prudence said, turning to Bryant, "She'll be beautiful out in the middle of the show ring in a colorful, flamenco dancing dress, won't she, Bryant?"

"I – I – don't know what to say. I know she is a marvelous dancer. I've never heard of a woman dancing with a horse. I can't imagine it. I'm not missing it, either," said Bryant, not quite sure what it all meant, but he didn't want to be what he had been hearing a lot about - a controlling *macho*.

Danilo, with a bedroll on the back of his horse, rode shotgun, and remained hidden as much as possible. He would stay over if the others stayed. *Sure wish Angela were riding with me, but she's in the wagon.* He could hardly wait to have a whole day of fun with her.

The trip was long but great fun until Prudence noticed Edgardo, sitting, staring out the window as if he were somewhere else. She tapped Jorge Luis on his arm and pointed with her eyes to Edgardo. Jorge Luis took one look and surmised his brother was having one of his spells. "Edgardo, ¿Qué te pasa? What's wrong?" he said in a soft voice.

Edgardo took his time shifting in his seat to face Jorge Luis, with a faraway look. He began to share what he had seen and felt, "It's Elena. Something has happened that feels wrong, really off. All I could see was a big, heavy darkness hanging over her." He looked away again and sat in silence for quite a while. No one knew what to say, so silence reigned for a short time until they all began to relax. Jorge Luis pulled out a wine bottle, uncorking it with his teeth. He found some delicate cups and saucers in a case, and soon their nervousness flowed out into boisterous singing and loud laughter.

The Ochoa hacienda inhabitants could hear the visitors coming from far down the olive tree lane. They knew a very enthusiastic crowd was about to descend on them. When they did arrive, Benito parked as close to the house as he could in order to carry everything into the home easily. Everyone helped. Benito finally went out and unharnessed the horses. He led them off to the corrals. The big day was here. What could go wrong with such organized, enthusiastic people, and bustling activities taking place all over the hacienda?

"Señora Ochoa," called Fiarela. "We're all here and everything is in the house. Can I go upstairs and help Elena? I can't wait to see her," said Fiarela.

"Yes, my dear, please do. She needs you," said *la señora*, in a voice that choked halfway through her sentence. She pointed up the stairs. Fiarela heard her voice and, feeling something was wrong, sprinted up them, ran down the hall, and entered Elena's bedroom without knocking. Elena was in bed almost hidden under her blankets and all alone.

"Oh, my god, Elena, are you sick? I'm here. Can I help you? We need to hurry. The wedding starts soon," said Fiarela.

Elena pulled up the blankets, covering her head for a minute or two and, then, with a burst of energy, she sat up looking hallow-eyed, hair mussed, and burst out sobbing.

"Elena, Elena, what happened? What's the matter?" Fiarela rushed to the bed, sat down, and clasped Elena in her arms. Elena's head came down on her chest, as she told her story between intermittent sobs.

"Oh, Fiarela, Fiarela, he's a horrible man. I can't. I won't marry him," said Elena, between gasps of breaths and burst of sobs. "He got drunk last night, mean drunk, and came into my room. He told me that I was his wife now. I said no, I wasn't, until tomorrow. He said that tomorrow was only the ceremony. Fiarela, - he – he violated me." She buried her head and in almost a whisper continued, "I couldn't stop him. I tried to scream, but he muffled me, and I fainted."

Fiarela was horrified. She didn't know what to say or do. Her eyes went big. She mouthed the word 'what?' before speaking, "My god, Elena, how could he? I've never heard of such debased, brutal behavior like that."

And the night before her wedding? "What can I do, Elena? How can I help you?" And then, she remembered Edgardo and what he had told them during their carriage ride. "Elena, I'm not sure I should tell you this, but I am going to. Edgardo had mentioned a vision to us on the ride here that he didn't know if he should tell us or not. He kept seeing a black cloud over your home. He didn't see you at all with Austin anywhere. He told us, 'Maybe that's me wanting better for her.' We all looked at him and agreed we felt sorry for you, Elena, and we prayed for you to have a chance at happiness. Marrying an official of the new government could give you many advantages for your life, we all agreed. But Edgardo kept looking off to the side, out the window. He seemed to be looking beyond the wide-open space. He shared that he felt nothing but a huge, dark energy surrounding you, a maelstrom that might eventually destroy you. He grabbed his stomach as if he were in pain. He shook his head, dropping his chin to his chest as he emitted a long sigh. We didn't know what to say."

Looking up into Fiarela's eyes, Elena said, "He is such a dear, isn't he? He always has been. Thank you for sharing it with me. I always loved him." She shuddered and swallowed her sob, "He was my first love. Did you know that, Fi? I am so thankful I am not marrying that – that - . I hope he gets what's coming to him. Edgardo has always been so good to me, even at my silliest. Oh, - good heavens - he will kill Austin." She put her face in her hands and started to cry again, bursting out in loud laments.

Elena lifted her head and said, almost in a whisper, "Fiarela, that's not all, he was caught this morning in the bed of a servant, against her will, too, and he still expected me to marry him!" She was pounding her knees with her fists. "He's gone. My parents threw him out." She buried her head in her hands, "There's no wedding, and all the guests are here. They don't know anything yet." She let out a long wail, "If they find out, maybe they will turn their backs on me. Why me? I don't care if I become an old maid. I want to marry someone as kind, sweet and fun as Edgardo always has been with me." Before Fiarela could answer, they heard footsteps approaching the door.

La Señora Ochoa knocked quietly and entered the bedroom, wringing her hands, "I am so thankful you are here, Fiarela, to comfort her. This has been beyond belief. We must decide what to do. No one really knows about this yet. We don't want anyone to know. This was not her doing. We don't want her ostracized or disrespected."

"Señora, please, help her into her robe and let her sit in the chair." Jorge Luis took Prudence to show her everything going on for the celebration.

"I'm going to get Edgardo. He foresaw something bad coming but didn't see what it would be. He will help you," said Fiarela.

"Yes, yes, please, and hurry," begged Elena's mother.

Fiarela ran downstairs and caught Edgardo as he was carrying supplies into the house. He dropped them when he saw the state that his sister was in. "Oh, no, Fiarela, don't tell me. Is she all right? What's happened?" he asked. He felt a weight hit him in the chest. *That Austin, if he's done anything, I'll kill him with my bare hands.*

Fiarela grabbed him and whispered in his ear.

"I knew it!" he said aloud, "I knew it. I felt it all along." They both started running up the stairs but halted before the door. Fiarela knocked softly and they entered. Edgardo ran to Elena. Elena stood and fell into his arms. He held her tight and kissed her on her forehead.

"Elena, Elena, my dearest. You must sit down." He gently helped her sit and pulled up a chair next to her. She leaned her head on his shoulder and hid her face in his chest. He turned to Señora Ochoa with a request, "Señora, please, can you have some calming tea and light food brought up for her? She needs nourishment. And don't worry, we *will* find a solution."

After she left, he looked at his sister and asked, "Fiarela, can you find Jorge Luis and Prudence? I think we need their help, too."

Of course, I will." Fiarela had been crying, too, rubbing her knuckles and fingers, not knowing what to say or do. She straightened her collar and her hair and left the room.

When they were alone, Edgardo started to talk in a soft low voice, "Elena, we've been friends forever. We've grown up together. I'm alone now, Elena, and terribly lonely. I'll love my wife forever, but I have a heart big enough for another, one I've been very fond of all my life. We've always had good times together, haven't we?"

"Yes, Edgardo, we always have, and you know that I've always been in love with you, but you were never for me. I knew that. I believed that, in time, I would grow to love Austin. Edgardo, I made up my mind to learn how to be a good wife. I've been taking cooking lessons." She lifted her head to look at him. "I'm learning everything I can about running a household, and it's been exciting, but now," she shuddered and grabbed Edgardo's shoulder, laying her head down again and weeping.

"Elena, dearest, I'm so proud of you, a stalwart heart. I always saw the goodness in you. Elena, I am asking you to marry me. I know this may seem inappropriate now, but I am serious. No one need know what happened to you."

Her sobbing stopped. She put her arm up around his neck and said, "This couldn't be a worse time. You've always been my hidden love. I want to marry you. I always have. Yes, yes," but then she hesitated and said, "But what do we do after what has happened?"

"I'm going to talk to Jorge Luis and then we'll talk to Father Serrano and get permission to hold the wedding. If he agrees, then we'll talk to your parents. I know they'll be happy. Would you agree to that, Elena?"

"I want to, but," she paused and put her head in her hands and spoke through them, "I'm afraid. After what he did to me, I don't know if I can be your wife." She started crying again.

He held her closer and assured her, "That is not a problem. We have all the time we need. We have wonderful memories together, and we have always enjoyed each other's company. We'll be good together, and Nito will love you."

"Oh, he is such a darling boy. You are so lucky to have him." She paused for a moment, breathing deeper now, "Edgardo, I've been in love with you for years. I can't believe this, and, to think, I might have married him." She agonized over the thought. "Oh, my God. What if I am pregnant? Edgardo, don't say anything, but that happened to my mother when she was young. It was a military man. She said she will never forget his heavy, drunken body pounding on her, the pain, and his foul alcohol breath spewing in her face. She thought she was going to die, and then afterward, later, she found out she was pregnant. She told me she couldn't face having a baby that would remind her every day of him. It would kill her not to be able to love her baby. She wanted to die, but then an Indian woman came to her, and gave her a drink, and she lost it. My parents really love each other. I always wanted that, too." She buried her head in his chest again and hid her face. Edgardo felt like he was sinking into a bottomless abyss. His heart went out to her. He held her tighter.

After knocking on the door, Jorge Luis and Prudence came into the room. They both stopped, shocked at what they saw. Things looked worse than what little bit Fiarela had told them. She came in behind them and stood off to one side, unashamedly weeping.

"Edgardo, Elena, what's going on here. I knew something was wrong when Fiarela came to get us, but she wouldn't tell us. What? Come on, tell us," said Jorge Luis, becoming fearful and impatient.

Prudence stood silent with her hand over her mouth and Fiarela by her side. She felt tense and her breathing was shallow. It was apparent to her that this was something serious.

Edgardo related the sad, disgusting, and frightening story. Both Jorge Luis and Prudence stood silent. Then Jorge Luis burst out with, "We'll hunt him down. He'll never do that to another woman. I'll swear to that, Elena!" Then it hit him - what had happened back in the carriage. "Edgardo, you hit the nail on the head again with your vision about Elena's marriage, but next time ask for the details, and we'll stop it before it happens. You were right, he would have ended up destroying her. She's always been a sensitive and naïve young girl."

"*Hermano*, I wasn't shown that or what he would do to her on purpose. If I had seen that, I might not have been able to come up with this solution. Everything would have turned out differently. Sit down all of you, and I will tell you what we're going to do." He had their rapt attention, but a knock at the door was heard, which interrupted them.

They thought for a moment it was the servant, Fermina, coming to pick up the tea tray. Fiarela opened the door to find Bryant confronting her. He looked at her, concern filling his face, and said, "Fiarela, I've been so worried. I couldn't find you. Is everything all right?" He glanced around and said, "It isn't, is it?"

She stepped quickly out the door, saying in a very low voice, "No, it isn't. Let me ask if I can tell you and have you come in."

"Yes, you've been crying. Please, let me help you. I can't stand seeing you like this," he begged.

She moved back into the room and asked if he could be a part of helping. They all looked at each other, not quite certain what to say.

Jorge Luis spoke up, "Look, Elena, Bryant is Prudence's cousin. He's a lawyer and, although it isn't formal yet, he will soon be our brother-in-law."

Elena lifted her head, eyes big with surprise and said, "Fiarela, really?" She burst into tears again, but said, "Let him in. He might as well be here, too. He's family, almost."

Jorge Luis and Edgardo took Bryant aside and explained what had happened. The shock showed in his face. His cheeks tightened, and his eyes narrowed and flashed with anger. He glanced at Fiarela, thinking, *If he ever comes near her* - "If I ever come in contact with him, I'll beat the living daylights out of him. I'm almost his size. I would take great pleasure in doing so." He looked at Elena and shook his head at such depravity.

"Not this time. We have a different solution - if you all agree," said Edgardo. "I know time is running out, but we do have one."

Everyone straightened up and stared at Edgardo.

"If Father Serrano agrees, Elena and I will get married. There will be a wedding after all," said Edgardo.

"What? Are you kidding us? *¿En serio?*" asked Jorge Luis.

Bryant looked at Fiarela and moved closer to her. He took her hand and held it tightly.

"No, we're not kidding. You know what my life's been like without Ramona. I always admired and felt close to Elena. She's been in love with me all along." He looked at her, and she nodded. This time with a smile.

"Wait, wait, give me a minute," said Bryant, while all stood with their mouths open, not knowing what to expect. "I've got to say this. I know this is a strange time, but I must." He knelt in front of Fiarela, "I fell in love with you the first time I saw you. I love everything about you. I want to spend the rest of my life with you. Will you marry me?"

"Bryant, Bryant, my love. I love you like crazy. Yes, yes," she cried, falling into his arms as he stood up. Suddenly, she held imploring eyes on the rest, "Can I? Can I? I love him so." The two brothers looked at each other and smiled.

"Of course, little sis, we knew this was coming," Jorge Luis said. He grabbed Bryant, hugging him. "Great to have you in the family."

"Amen to that, *cuñado*, welcome," said Edgardo from his seat while holding Elena.

"Say, is there any chance the priest would marry both of us?" added Bryant, with Fiarela clinging to him.

The unexpectedness of that question left the room in a breathless silence until, finally, the eldest Sandoval looked around and announced, "Okay, we three are going to speak to Father Serrano right now and pray he will say yes. I'm sure he will. He knows that I am the hacendado now," said Jorge Luis, "You girls get your dresses ready and everything you have to do. We'll talk him into it."

The room became a flurry of activity. Part of it was pulling out things from the huge antique wardrobe and dresser drawers, searching for clothes, shoes, and accessories for the wedding, and trying to get Elena's face back to normal after suffering such a brutal trauma.

"You'll need to keep the veil over your face during the ceremony, Elena, but you still look gorgeous in that dress. Do you have an appropriate one for Fiarela, just in case?" asked Prudence.

"Oh, I'm so selfish, only thinking of myself. Here, Fiarela, look through my other wardrobe and pick one."

Prudence shifted through a few, "Here's one. It's not quite white, but it is a very pale blue, almost white, a lovely color for you." Prudence felt happy for the girls but had been feeling left out, saddened it wouldn't be her walking up the aisle to the altar in the chapel.

"How does it look?" said Fiarela, turning in front of the mirror, "Elena? Prudence?"

"Perfect, perfect, it's lovely. Two gorgeous brides," said Prudence.

"I wish the men would return. I'm so nervous and afraid that the priest may not grant us our marriage. I hope no one finds out what happened to me. I was so humiliated, and now, I am so angry I could kill Austin myself," said Elena.

"Just forget about him, Elena. Think about Edgardo. His heart may stop when he sees you walk up that aisle in that dress. You look divine," said Prudence. "You too, Fiarela. Bryant's knees will go weak. I hope he doesn't fall. Come here, let me fix your hair, just in case."

The two hopeful brides turned and posed in front of the mirror and Prudence. When they heard a knock at the door, they looked at Prudence, at each other, and held their breaths.

Prudence hesitated, but then, with a questioning look, took a few steps toward the door but turned back. Fiarela and Elena quickly pushed the air with their hands as if coaxing her and whispered, "Go, go, open it."

Prudence moved forward and reached for the doorknob with a prayer in her heart.

40
The Wedding

$\mathcal{P}$rudence reached gingerly for the doorknob. She looked back at Elena and Fiarela in their wedding dresses and peeked through the crack in the door.

Meanwhile, Elena's mother, Fernanda, had been called upstairs to Elena's bedroom and told everything. She listened intently to their solution while she stood, holding her breath, and praying for her daughter. She felt a great relief to know Edgardo would marry her daughter. He would take care of her with compassion and dignity. *I'd always hoped she'd marry one of those boys.* As she watched Prudence almost hesitating to open the door, she prayed again. *Please, God, please, open Padre Serrano's mind and heart. I desperately want my daughter and Edgardo to marry. I am praying for their happiness.*

Prudence pulled the door open. "It's them!"

The three men were barraged with questions, "Can we? What did Padre Serrano say? Will he allow both of us to get married? Tell us."

Fernanda was on the point of fainting for lack of breathing with her anxiety and expectation.

Jorge Luis stepped forward with a big smile and a "Yes!"

Fernanda hugged and kissed her daughter. She hugged Edgardo. Excusing herself, she ran from the room to find her husband, Ignacio, and get dressed for the ceremony.

Fiarela bounced up and down with excitement. Bryant rushed to her, holding his arms out to embrace her.

Edgardo went to Elena and kissed her more passionately than he ever believed he could after the loss of Ramona. He knew then that this was what he needed and wanted. To Elena he said, "I will love you as you deserve to be loved, always." He clung tightly to her. She looked up at him, adoringly. Tears of happiness and gratitude were leaking from her sparkling eyes, but Edgardo wiped them away with tender hands.

"Listen," said Jorge Luis, "we have to hurry. People are filling the chapel, and Father Serrano expects us to start right away. Do you have the rings?"

"No, we don't," said Bryant. "What should we do?"

Elena grabbed a ring from several on her fingers, and said, "Here, we can use this one. It was my great-great-grandmother's. I think it will do."

"Let's see," said Fiarela. "It's beautiful. Look at that little silver cross on the top. The ring looks like it opens, does it?" asked Fiarela.

"Yes, it does." Elena started to open the ring while everyone huddled around her to see it. Inside was a gold six-pointed star. Fiarela, Jorge Luis, and Edgardo gasped, looking at each other with wide-eyed, questioning stares.

Prudence spoke up, "That's beautiful. Does that mean that through the cross they get to the stars in heaven?"

"Maybe, I'm not sure, but maybe. Maybe that's what it means," said Elena.

The three Sandovals said nothing, as they stood quietly - almost in a state of shock.

"Fiarela, what about you? Do you have a ring?" asked Bryant.

"Yes, yes," she said, coming back to herself and regaining her composure. "We can use this one." Her hand shook visibly as she removed the ring, "It's special. My father gave it to me when I turned fifteen. He said it was his mother's."

"Okay, we're set. I'll take the rings and you follow me," said Jorge Luis, heading for the door.

"Wait – wait! - We've forgotten Mother," wailed Fiarela, both hands on her mouth and her eyes tearing. "What are we going to do? I shouldn't be getting married, you either Edgardo. We're just being selfish." She burst out crying, feeling a deep shame. In their enthusiasm, they had completely forgotten their mother left at home.

The others, with open mouths, tried to catch their breaths.

Finally, Jorge Luis spoke, "This is a predicament." He paused a moment and then said, "But, wait, no one here knows about Austin. We don't want to ruin the Ochoas' wedding festivities if we don't have to." He turned to look directly into Fiarela's face, saying, "You don't need Mother's approval to marry, Fiarela, dear. I'm the hacendado, and I have full authority, but you're right. We don't want to hurt Mother. That would be a terrible blow for her if we don't let her know right away. She may understand Edgardo more, but you are her only daughter."

Prudence moved over to put her arms around Fiarela's waist and asked, "Jorge Luis, is there anyone that we could send back to talk to your mother and prepare her for the shock?"

"I don't want to miss this chance to marry Elena. We don't know what the future will bring," said Edgardo, "I know that sounds selfish, but when Padre Serrano arrives at our place, he can't stay long. He has marriages to perform, many baptisms, and Father's funeral to preside over. He said he would be coming in two days after this wedding. That's not enough time to organize everything. Did Gregorio come? If he did, let's send him."

"I'm pretty sure he did. I'll write a note and catch him right after the ceremony because right now they're waiting for us in the church. Let's pray that Mother will forgive us and understand. I'll take the blame if she doesn't. Fiarela, I know how you are feeling, but Father Serrano may never come back. The mission will be closing soon, and he's going to retire," said Jorge Luis.

Edgardo said, "Let's go, but I am concerned about Mother. Afterwards, please, find Gregorio as soon as possible and have him hurry." He reached for Elena's hand and said, "But, I am getting married."

"Fiarela, I don't want guilt to eat at you. I'll abide by whatever you decide. You know how much I love you," said Bryant, looking deeply into her eyes. He felt her consternation and shame.

She glanced quickly at her brother with pleading in her voice, "Are you sure you can fix it with *Mamá*, Jorge Luis?" asked Fiarela. He nodded yes. She took a deep breath and said to her brother, "I'm getting married."

"Okay, come on. The chapel is close, and you can change your minds if you feel the need. No one is going to be upset by it," said Jorge Luis, not believing what he just said, as they headed to the chapel. *If they change their minds now, everyone will be upset and outraged. Please, God, may all this go well.*

The day was warming up. The adobe brick chapel, with a small bell tower, was clean, bright, white, and shining in the overhead sun. All the guests had entered, and only the musicians waited outside. The priest waited inside at the altar.

Jorge Luis placed Ignacio at the church door to wait for the two brides he would escort to the altar. Meanwhile, Prudence walked up the aisle, escorting Elena's mother, Fernanda, to her seat. Prudence went on to stand by one side of the altar. Jorge Luis followed and took his place at the opposite side of the alter. After they took their places, the two grooms walked down the aisle, ignoring the buzzing gossip and the stares of the guests. Each stood on one side of the altar.

The people were murmuring and whispering. Nobody knew what was happening. Why were there two young men beside the altar? Why was Edgardo Sandoval up there? Where was the Americano? Is that strange man him? The guests were very curious to see him. Rumors ran through the crowd from mouth to mouth swiftly.

The musicians moved inside and lined up against the back wall with their guitars, trumpets, violins and an accordion, waiting to play the processional piece. They started the music as soon as they saw Ignacio with a bride on each arm. Elena's father walked them slowly up the aisle and to the alter to the hauntingly beautiful and spiritually inspiring "Ave María." Silence reigned in the chapel, even with the sight of two brides, both stunning in their wedding gowns. Bryant and Edgardo struggled to breathe. They went weak in the knees watching their beautiful brides approach the altar to become their wives. Neither could believe this was happening – right now.

The Ochoa chapel, rectangular in shape, appeared more church-like. On each side of the central and only aisle, were highly polished, handmade oak pews. They were tightly filled with family, friends, and the hacienda workers' families.

Colorful geraniums were tied to the ends of the pews, bringing a look of gaiety to the room. On each side of the room was a door leading to another room. Outside, the building gave the appearance of a cross. Behind the priest, standing at the altar, was a hanging crucifix. On each side, framing the crucifix, was a stained-glass window depicting biblical scenes. The entire wall represented the Holy Trinity. The window to the left was a depiction of large, swirling clouds with the sunrays hitting the earth, which was a standard representation for God. After the middle stained-glass window with Jesus on the cross, the window on the right showed the symbol of the Holy Spirit represented by a white dove. The high sun, through the stained-glass windows, sent rays of color that played across the tiled floor and sprayed across the back of the Father's robe. For those who sat watching, the scene was calming and deeply reverent.

Edgardo radiated a smile full of pride. Everything felt as if it had been previously ordained in heaven. *I do love Elena. Not the same as I did Ramona, but it will be good.* While he was thinking, he noticed the aura of Padre Serrano very close to his head and murky in color. He realized that the murkiness was because the priest had just come in from being involved with his mundane work. His thoughts had not been in the heavens.

Jorge Luis, watching Ignacio walk up the aisle with the two brides, slowly and dignified, filled him with a feeling of profound pride. Looking out over the crowd, he could see the surprised looks and watched them whispering. He simply kept a happy smile on his face. *I can't believe my little brother and sister are being married today. I hope that Gregorio can carry the letter to Mother as fast as possible. It will be a huge shock to read that her two youngest children will arrive home married. I explained in the letter that Father Serrano had approved, and we hoped she would be happy for the newlyweds. I said that I would explain more in detail when we arrive home, and that we would leave as soon as Fiarela finishes the horse dance.*

Ignacio deposited the two brides in front of the altar where Edgardo joined Elena and Bryant went to Fiarela's side. Jorge Luis remained on his side of the altar, as he and Prudence were the witnesses. *Prudence and I should be in front of this altar. I'm the oldest. Fiarela's marrying an American. Why can't I? Why is Mother so opposed to her?* He looked at the two grooms whose faces were lit up with happiness.

That should be me.

A deep sadness hit him through his chest, but he only allowed it to last a minute. *I am truly happy for them.* He glanced at Prudence with a look of longing. He straightened his posture and affirmed: *I will be next.*

Father Serrano raised his arms in welcome to all and as a direction to stay standing as they sang the "Gloria." He followed that with the opening prayer. Everyone sat down, and the two couples knelt for a reading from the Old Testament. Bryant recognized the reading from his Congregational Church Bible teachings at home in Maine. He began to feel more at ease with something familiar. He wished he knew the group responses to the Psalm that was sung. He liked being part of a service.

After singing the "Alleluia", the priest began using a sacred text to expound the Mystery of Christian Marriage, the dignity of conjugal love, the grace of the Sacraments and the responsibilities of married people. Everyone was asked to stand while he questioned the couples about fidelity, children, and more.

As Edgardo responded to the questions, he noticed that the aura of the priest had changed considerably. His energy brightened as he became involved in the sanctity of the marriage ceremony, the prayers, and the sacred music. The colors of Father Serrano's aura had become clear, vibrant, and flashing out from his head and shoulders two to three feet. Upon seeing that change, Edgardo felt blessed. He felt the Holy Spirit was telling him that their sudden, unexpected marriages would be blessed, also.

Edgardo listened with one ear as he thought about spirituality in his marriage. There was no church they could attend. They only had the family's little private chapel, but, maybe, he could plan a simple ritual for he and Elena. *Perhaps, before bed, we could have a short meditation and prayer time together. That would clear up our energy from everyone else's scattered work energies and all the different kinds of problems we have faced that day. I think that would calm and unify us.* He looked at Elena and smiled.

Bryant felt a little embarrassed that he did not know all the things he was supposed to do during the ceremony and worried that Fiarela might be disappointed in him. But when they recited the Lord's Prayer, he regained his confidence. He did know that. He looked at her and smiled. He would learn.

The priest extended his hands over the kneeling couples and offered a nuptial prayer. He then asked Fernanda to bring up the *lazos*. The cords were shaped in the form of a large eight, the symbol of infinity, which were placed over the heads of the two couples. The rings and the coins were exchanged. The marriage license was signed by Prudence and Jorge Luis. Afterward, the priest declared the two couples married with an admonition to "go in peace to glorify the Lord with your lives."

"Thanks be to God" resounded through the chapel as a response.

The priest announced the couples as married. They kissed softly and sweetly, and left the sanctuary sedately but hurriedly.

Both Edgardo and Bryant felt exhilarated, though a sense of responsibility descended upon their shoulders, like the dove in the stained-glass window, representing the Holy Spirit. Both saw their marriages as sacred, and their wives to be loved and protected.

Outside, Jorge Luis stopped the group, "Quick, you guys go back to the house and stay there. I'll find Gregorio and send him to Mother."

They all moved back into Elena's bedroom suite and waited solemnly until Jorge Luis came in. Everyone looked up at him expectantly, not knowing what to expect or do.

He smiled, but then the smile faded, and he spoke with a sense of urgency, pointing with his hands and waving them about, "Listen, Elena, I think you should change into something comfortable and pack to come home with us to avoid all the questions and comments. Okay with you, Edgardo?"

"Yes, I agree. That's the smart thing to do, but what about Fiarela's horse dance?" asked Edgardo.

"Oh, yeah, I forgot. There's no reason why she shouldn't do the dance. Everyone expects that. We'll all be sitting up in the covered family and judging stand. No one can confront Elena there. We'll leave immediately afterwards. Prudence, I'm sorry you will miss out on all the food and singing and dancing. I feel badly, but I don't know what else we can do," said Jorge Luis.

"Please, don't worry about me. I'll go along with whatever you think we need to do," said Prudence, admiring Jorge Luis' leadership, his decisiveness, and his clarity. She saw that he came into his inner authority easily with this situation. She felt a sudden sadness and cried deeply, *Why couldn't we have been married, too? Maybe it's just not meant for us.* Even though she felt sorry for herself, she was pleased and happy for her cousin, Bryant, and for Edgardo – two sweet, kind men.

Jorge Luis spoke, "I'm going down to the kitchen to see if Señora Ochoa can find someone to bring some food up here for us and pack some for the trip. I'll explain our plans to her and then hunt up Benito. I want him ready to take us home immediately after the horse dance. Fiarela, can you have some clothes to change into after the dance? You can do that in the carriage. After all this trauma and excitement, we need a comfortable trip home."

Elena's small, walnut antique table was covered with an oriental silk tablecloth which was very exquisite with embroidery, and ready for the food to arrive. Barbecued meat and a bowl of the juices came in from the Barbecue Master, Joaquín Ochoa, Elena's grandfather. Crusty bread was carried in for dipping in the juices, along with bowls of red enchiladas and frijoles, a salad, and some corn on the cob, which were devoured in minutes. They were all starved due to the stressful energy all morning.

Jorge Luis soon joined them again, telling them that everything was taken care of, "Fiarela, they want you at the arena in an hour. Can you do it?"

"If Bryant will go with me, I can do it. Nobody will bother him," she said, glancing up at him. Bryant threw her a little kiss and nodded yes.

One hour later, Elena was packed, clothes changed, and she walked out with the rest to the show ring - after the guests had seated themselves. The wedding group sat, in anticipation, up high in the stand and alone.

Soon the musicians came out from one side of the arena, stopped, and waited to play. All eyes were on the gate where Fiarela would enter. The bleachers were full of murmurings, "It was just yesterday, she was running around everywhere. Look at her, all grown up. How did she ever catch that Americano? I hear he's a famous lawyer. And, Elena, so lucky to get rid of that nasty foreigner. Edgardo Sandoval, what a catch." The musicians raised their instruments, ready to play. The crowd went silent, waiting. The gate opened with welcoming music, and a loud round of applause was heard from the audience when Fiarela appeared in the middle of the gate.

She was costumed in a Flamenco-type dress, quite colorful. The dress was white with front and back necklines embroidered with bright roses. The balloon sleeves were yellow to set off the roses that were yellow. The flounces of the skirt were done in primary colors. Her hair was lifted up on the back of her head with flowers.

She stood in the gate with one arm raised high and the other in a ballet pose across her chest. The music started. Fiarela lifted her knees to move the flounces of her skirt and, with a flourish, walked gracefully to the center of the show ring. She bowed to the crowd. With more applause, she turned to face the gate.

The gate opened again. A stunningly beautiful horse, white with a black mane, tail, and lower legs, entered with its rider, dancing. The crowd roared. Fiarela could not believe her eyes. She stood posed as he danced to her. The rider barely touched him with a very thin rod, and the horse bowed before her. The crowd went wild. The horse rose, and Fiarela began her dance. The horse danced continually around her while she responded sensuously to his every move.

Bryant was nearly out of his mind watching his wife. "I've never seen anything like that. She is incredible – and, she's my wife! She's gorgeous. I can't believe I'm so fortunate," he said to the others. He did not feel jealous, only immense admiration and pride.

Everyone agreed, and they all left the stand as soon as Fiarela began her finale, walking gracefully to the gate. Ignacio and Fernanda beamed, feeling so proud of Fiarela and sad her mother had not been there to see her. They left early to avoid the people.

Benito was waiting with the carriage. After the others had stopped hugging her and praising her performance, Fiarela retired to the carriage to change as quickly as possible.

The spectators left the stands feeling terribly disappointed to see the carriage leave so fast, but they didn't stay sad long. Dancing, singing, and sumptuous food awaited them with plenty to drink. The sun was setting low, and the bull and grizzly bear fight would start soon.

That night money would change hands rapidly among the watchers. Betting was big. Mainly men would attend the fight, as the women considered them too gruesome and barbaric.

No one paid much attention to the carriage that whizzed down the olive tree-lined lane. Elena's parents hurried back to the house and sat alone in their bedroom suite, bereft, and sad. However, they both were grateful and happy for their only child.

"Ignacio, Edgardo is a blessing. We are so lucky," said Fernanda.

"We could not be luckier. We will only tell people that we would never allow our beloved daughter to marry a man who did what he did with our servant and nothing more. Don't worry, Fernanda. Elena will be very happy, and we will see them soon. Now, I'm off to the barbecue and a glass of my best wine."

"You mean several, don't you?"

They both laughed.

41
A Deadly Return

enito kept the horses at full speed all the way out the olive tree-lined lane. At the end, he turned on the dirt road that led back to the Sandoval hacienda. Danilo, on horseback, and quite unhappy to leave Angela behind at the festivities, followed until he could ride hidden off to one side in the woods.

Fiarela and Elena were wives now. They were allowed to sit on their husbands' laps because the carriage was small and crowded. They felt cushioned by strong arms and warm chests against the rough jolts of the carriage. The regular rhythm and noises of the carriage and horses soon soothed the rough nerves of the day's upheaval, the sudden changes with the upside-down wedding, so that the newly weds slipped easily into a deep, healing sleep.

Prudence, sitting on the same side as Jorge Luis with a basket of food between them, commented to him, "Aren't they sweet? Look, they're falling asleep."

"No wonder, after all that stress and excitement, I think I could sleep. Aren't you tired, Prudence?"

Prudence nodded and smiled, but said, "I'm exhausted but I'm okay. I've been praying for Elena. Edgardo is so patient and loving. I have real hope for them." She yawned and then sighed, "I think I'm letting go of the strain, finally."

The carriage was crowded and uncomfortable. Jorge Luis suggested that they put the basket on the floor. He rolled up some coats and put them behind him as he leaned over on one side. "Prudence, here, lean on me. You'll be more comfortable," he offered.

It didn't take long before they, too, slept, relaxing into the rhythmic bumping and jerking.

Benito realized that all was quiet behind him inside. He slowed the horses, yet he managed to keep them at a steady pace, slipping through the darkening night. He was fine. He knew the road and so did the horses. He even dozed occasionally.

The carriage, below the pale light of the rising moon, rolled through the night, a black shadow against the pieces of scattered moonlight that peeked through the trees. They were about an hour away from the hacienda. When -- crack! A shot echoed in the air. Benito screamed, and all hell broke loose.

The riders woke disorientated from sleep. More shots came quickly. They heard Benito fall from the carriage and heard him scream again.

"My god, my god what's happening?" Shouts came from the men and screams from the women. "Are we being attacked? Is Benito shot? Is he dead?"

The two couples grabbed each other. Jorge Luis grabbed for Prudence just as the horses bucked, kicked and fought their harnesses and the traces to get loose. One fell. The other had its hooves stomping the fallen horse – each loudly screeching. The carriage jerked, bounced and rocked violently until it flipped over. The passengers were thrown around, flailing their arms and crying out. They all landed in a pile against the roof of the carriage and were hit by all the baskets and things packed along with them. The blankets were tangled around them. "Is anyone hurt? Who is hurt? Be careful when you try to move! Girls, girls, are you all right?" Everyone was yelling - frightened.

The fallen horse righted itself, while the other snorted, stamped its hooves trying to jump, but they did not break loose.

Inside the carriage, the young people tried to untangle themselves without hurting each other or their loved ones. The girls were screaming. The men yelled. Everyone was trying to grab something to pull themselves up.

Outside they heard a loud moan and a stream of obscenities from Benito. At least they knew he was alive but obviously hurt. More shots and hoof beats were heard off in the distance. The men were calling out, "Is everyone all right? We've got to get out of here!" The darkness added to the problem.

The carriage door was jammed, badly bent and dented. It would not open. The men quickly decided to break the window that was now at the top and pull them all out. One by one they helped each other out. They quickly ran to Benito.

"I'm over here. I'm shot. Who the hell was that?" asked Benito. His voice was low with pauses when he breathed in gulps of air.

The girls knelt at his side. They could see he had already pulled off his belt, using it as a tourniquet. A bullet was lodged in his leg.

Edgardo had banged his knee and was limping, but he managed to start a small fire to light things up, as the women began to help Benito. Edgardo noticed that the moon was only up two hands. It didn't give them the light they needed. The trees were tall and thick, which blocked much of the moonlight.

Just then, Danilo came galloping out of the darkness. He could see the overturned carriage, and his heart gave a leap until he saw that everyone was out. He slid his horse to a stop and jumped off, "You're safe! Is Benito okay? I was afraid he was shot. I thought he was dead. I shot the one who hit Benito, but sorry, sorry, I couldn't get the second man. Oh, God, Jorge Luis, I killed a man, and I let the other one get away. It's all my fault." He ran up closer and grabbed Jorge Luis, pulling on his arm, crying, "I killed him! I couldn't get the other one!"

Danilo was as pale as a ghost. His whole body shook from shock. The others looked stricken, and no one knew what to say.

"Who, who was it? Danilo, do you know who it was?" asked Jorge Luis, removing his hand from his arm. Jorge Luis' heart was still pounding. He felt somewhat bruised all over. It was hard now to put his attention on Danilo, with what was going on, but forced himself to clear his mind and focus on this young man.

Prudence tried to control herself, though she felt herself still shaking while kneeling by Benito, trying to comfort him.

Fiarela, with tears running down her face, tried to help Prudence with Benito who was close to passing out and moaning with pain.

Elena stood sobbing, paralyzed from fear.

Bryant and Edgardo were with Jorge Luis as he tried to talk to Danilo. Jorge Luis asked again, "Did you recognize him?"

"Yes, yes, I know him. He's one of the Americano's men. Why would he do such a thing? Why? I didn't mean to kill him. I only meant to wound him. What do I do now? Is Benito dead? Oh, God, I let the other one get away. What have I done?" Danilo was almost incomprehensible.

"Calm down. You were only acting to protect all of us. Benito will be taken care of as soon as we get to the hacienda. Take Jorge Luis to see the man's body. Edgardo and I will look over the carriage for damage. When you come back, we'll set it upright," said Bryant.

Jorge Luis' head was still ringing from hitting the wall as they were thrown about the carriage and then hurled on top of each other. He didn't complain but walked off with Danilo, leading his horse. His mind raced with worry. *After what Austin's done, he needs to be strung up in the village square and let the vultures have him. I've got to get us home. Benito needs care. That rough attack will set in with the gals soon, too. Thank God they are not hurt, just shaken up. Mother will be in a worse state than ever now.* He was locked in a tumble of worries.

Prudence yelled after them, her voice quivering, "Be careful. That other guy may still be around somewhere."

Poor Danilo was almost useless, but they checked the body to make sure he was dead, and when they returned, Bryant and Danilo had unhitched the horses. They did not want the horses to panic while they tried to upright the carriage for fear they might overturn it again. The damage was minimal, and it would receive a complete overhaul later in the carriage barn.

The dark didn't help, but the moon had moved up higher, above the trees, sending more light. The fire illuminated the scene clearer. Danilo was still agitated and mumbling, but he joined in helping pull up the carriage and righting it.

Fiarela held Benito's head on her lap as she and Elena kept trying to ease his pain and keep him comfortable. Benito whispered, "My little *Princesa,* I used to help you when you were all scratched and bruised up, and now you're helping me." He let out a big sigh and closed his eyes, scaring the girls.

Elena whispered quietly, "He's still breathing. He's okay."

Jorge Luis took charge, "Girls, you three get into the carriage and sit together on the seat. We'll lay him on your laps. You can hold him. He'll be safer during the ride. Now, we have to do something with Austin's man."

Benito was almost unconscious, but he overheard them and said, "Bury him. Don't let that dirty Americano know. He's out to get you, Jorge Luis, and he's powerful. Bury his man."

Hearing that inflamed the men. They looked at each other and agreed, "*De acuerdo,*" they whispered together.

"Danilo, listen kid, you did well. This took you by surprise. It won't be the last time you'll kill in your lifetime. Come on, buck up. You go back and stay with the body, but stay hidden. The other one may be around. We can't afford to lose you, too. If you can, go through that guy's pockets. He may have something we should know about. We'll get help for Benito, and we'll return to take care of the body. Keep your eyes and ears open."

"Oh, oh, I – I, sí señor," said Danilo, starting to tremble again at the thought of seeing the corpse again, and touching it. But the words spoken by Jorge Luis gave him relief. He began to pull himself together. He disappeared among the trees.

Jorge Luis sat up in the driver's seat and drove them back to the hacienda. He kept the horses moving carefully and quietly, not wanting to call attention to themselves with any untoward noise.

Elena sobbed quietly, "It's all my fault. This wouldn't have happened if it weren't for me. I'm so sorry."

But the others did not accept that from her nor allowed her to continue. "This was no one's fault but Austin's," they said.

At the hacienda, Jorge Luis went directly to his mother's room while the others waited in the foyer. They looked afright with their hair all messed and clothes with rips and tears. Jorge Luis told his mother quickly about the day's ordeals and the frightening assault. Aldiana almost fainted but got a hold of herself.

She came out and broke out in tears, welcoming her new daughter-in-law and son-in-law. They all hugged each other. She had to leave quickly to hunt up Teresa to work in the kitchen. She came back and asked Fiarela and Elena to help Teresa.

Jorge Luis thought that they might have to go for Shadowhawk to get that bullet out. He sent Edgardo and Bryant to find Gregorio and send him off to the Ranchería. He gave orders to prepare a room, bring in a bottle of tequilla, and have a cauterizing instrument prepared at the Blacksmith shop. He insisted that Benito be well cared for. He left his mother and Prudence in charge, with Fiarela and Elena working in the kitchen.

Edgardo and Bryant found Gregorio. They woke him up from a dead sleep, frightening his wife. Gregorio was informed that he had to ride in haste to the Ranchería for Shadowhawk. By the time Edgardo finished telling him the story, he was up, dressed, and ready to go.

They, then, both went to rouse up Juan to go with them and check out the footprints of the second man. They all left with Jorge Luis to go back to Danilo, who was waiting alone with the body. He had gone through the man's pockets but still felt fearful.

"I didn't mean to do it, God. Please forgive me, please. I will go to confession and do whatever you say I need to do," pleaded Danilo. His stomach was turning upside down and sideways. He was nauseated but managed to control it. *What if that Americano finds out? He'll know when this bastard doesn't return to the pueblo. The other one will tell what happened. Austin'll hunt me down and kill me for sure.* He felt like his well-planned life was in tatters. *I never understood how any man could kill a fellow human being and now I've done it. I only shot at him to wound him and protect my boss and the others. I've never killed a man before. He was shooting at Benito. I only wanted to wound him and stop him from shooting someone else. This villano, laying here on the ground, deserved what he got, but now I'll be on the chopping block with that Austin.* He wrung his hands, bending over the saddle. Danilo raised his head up. Hoofbeats could be heard. *There are four horses, surely, Jorge Luis and Edgardo. Bryant and Juan, too?* He stiffened up, more alert.

"Everything okay here?" asked Jorge Luis while Juan, Bryant and Edgardo got off their horses to examine the body.

Juan, bending over the dead body, looked up and said, "Yeah, he's dead. Where you gonna hide him?"

Tears began to flow from Danilo's eyes. He pursed his lips and began to feel anger surfacing unexpectedly. His guilt had subsided. He looked imploringly at Jorge Luis.

"What do you think, Juan?" said Jorge Luis.

"This is a bad business," said Edgardo. "He probably thought he could get away with killing Benito and you, Jorge Luis, by people believing it was only a robbery -- maybe a kidnapping. Prudence would bring a lot."

Jorge Luis' heart gave a lurch as he thought about Prudence and 'what if' scenarios. "Come on, think, you guys," he said.

"How about taking him to the hacienda and throwing him in the pigpen?" said Juan.

"Oh, God." Danilo gagged and covered his mouth with his hand.

"Danilo, get a hold of yourself. You literally saved us all." He turned to Juan to say, "No, no, we can't do that. Let's dig a hole. If we cover it with rocks, it will look like an Indian burial. Juan, throw him over your horse. Let's go up in that ravine," said Jorge Luis, pointing off to the left where it looked like all the rest of the ravines. "Up there is heavy brush and a lot of trees."

The job took a while. Danilo did try to control himself and helped out by sitting on his horse to watch for anyone approaching unexpectedly. Jorge Luis, when the grave was finished and covered with rock, took time to say a few words, "Lord, take this man unto your arms. Maybe he will learn with you what he couldn't learn here. He walked the wrong path and paid the consequences." He bent down and took a handful of dirt and tossed it over the protective rocks. Edgardo did the same, but Juan spit on it.

There was no galloping back to the hacienda. Each was lost in his own thoughts. Nothing like this had ever happened before. Was this an omen of things to come? The horses plodded on in silence.

Once back at the hacienda, Jorge Luis dismissed Juan and Danilo. Juan went home to his wife, who prayed while she waited. Danilo rushed into the arms of Angela. Jorge Luis with abated breath went immediately to see Benito. Prudence was sitting with him, holding his hand. Shadowhawk had arrived and prepared him for surgery in a small room off the kitchen. He sterilized his knife with fire, the wound with tequila. Benito had finished off a bottle of tequila as an anesthetic and was almost unconscious. Aldiana, Fiarela, and Teresa were in and out checking on any needs. Elena stayed in the kitchen, helping. Extra servants came in to help. By now, almost the entire hacienda had heard about Benito.

After Shadowhawk had everything prepared, the recovery of the bullet was started. He was deft, competent, and fast. He soon had the bullet out, the wound cauterized and sewn up. Benito would recover well. Jorge Luis stayed to help clean and then went out to get the horse and help send Shadowhawk back to the Ranchería.

Prudence left to go sit in the foyer and wait to tell everyone that Benito would heal perfectly with time. The others all arrived quickly, and, upon hearing the happy news, the married couples went off to their respective rooms, leaving Prudence sitting alone.

Aldiana noticed Prudence after the others retired to their bedroom suites. She felt Prudence looked somewhat forlorn, and her heart went out to her for the first time.

She had realized that when her two children came home unexpectedly married, their lives had truly and completely changed. Her heart, tired from the long night, suddenly filled with joy at the thought of her new prospective role - becoming a grandmother. *Elena has matured into a lovely young woman, and I am so grateful for Bryant. He will be a marvelous husband for Fiarela and a saving grace for my family.*

She paused, watching Prudence. Not only her heart, but her whole being told her that Prudence had so much to offer. She could see the deep love between her and Jorge Luis. This time, there were no old prejudices surfacing, only her love for her family. *Oh, how much I want Jorge Luis to be happy. I will give him my blessing. I am seeing her pure, honest beauty. How could I have been so blind and selfish. I'm going to her right now. I pray she will be understanding and forgive me.*

Prudence sat there wondering what was she going to do. The sun would be coming up very soon. She was dead tired and needed to sleep, but how would she get home? She was surprised, looking up, to see Aldiana coming over to her, and when she offered her a guest room, she accepted gladly. Aldiana took her to the room herself, which surprised Prudence, who thought the servants must have all gone to bed. She was thankful for Aldiana treating her very kindly and making sure she would be comfortable but wasn't sure why. Aldiana even gave her a quick kiss on the forehead when she said good night, which astonished Prudence. She welcomed the kiss and wished it could be a part of her life.

However, she still felt she was the odd one out amongst the women and their husbands. She had always slept in Fiarela's room but not anymore. It's all changed now. Fiarela was a married woman. She climbed into the guest bed, feeling grateful, but, at the same time, felt left out and very much alone. She wasn't sure she even still had a job. *I must have faith, I must,* she thought. She said a prayer for Benito's recovery and then added a feeling of profound gratitude that, after all the chaos that had occurred, everyone was safe and sound.

Jorge Luis felt at loose ends. Everything had been taken care of, but he felt lost and lonely, with an emptiness in his heart. He still had aches and pains all over from the wreck. Finally, he fell asleep and dreamed he was proposing to Prudence, but he kept losing her. He couldn't quite find her anywhere. When he did see her, she was just out of his grasp. He woke, restless, rolling over and then back again. Suddenly, his inner-voice said, "Patience, patience, you're almost there." With that, he fell into a deep, dreamless sleep.

42
The Chapel

From the day Aldiana had received the invitation to Elena's wedding, she began arduous preparations to ready the hacienda for Padre Serrano's visit. She expected him to arrive late on the Monday after Elena's wedding and stay one or two weeks - if they were lucky. His daily schedule was full, and all the events had to be prepared and ready on time. Once he left, he would not return for another year, if at all. The mission was failing fast. Its lands were almost sold off, and most of the Indians had left. The missions had not been receiving the help they were accustomed to from the Presidios, and Father Serrano was on the verge of retiring.

At the Sandoval hacienda, there were already four weddings for him to officiate. Aldiana had to remember to check with Danilo about his wedding. How she would have loved to have had a huge, prestigious wedding for Fiarela but that would not have been proper so close to her father's death and, besides, preparations would have taken months. The church banns would have been difficult and required too much time. Fiarela would have had to wait until next year. *Oh, Lord, help me. I couldn't handle that and who knows what is going to happen to us in the meantime. I am so thankful that she is safely married.* Aldiana shifted her attention to her lists.

There would be nine baptisms and everyone was looking forward to watching the baptism of Facundo and María's twins. Prudence was curious to see the babies in their new, long baptismal dresses. How would they react to the Holy water or oil poured on their heads and what formal Christian names would be given to them? Lastly, the funerals would follow. Only two would take place and Emiliano's would require a full Mass, more extensive and longer than the other one. Flowers needed to be placed on his gravestone in the family cemetery. The grounds would have to be cleared of weeds and all the headstones scrubbed. Even though Emiliano had been buried months ago, family, friends and workers who knew him would want to walk out to the old family cemetery and pay their respects after Mass.

Many families would arrive from all over. Sleeping quarters had to be arranged. All the hacienda guest rooms would be filled, but a good many of the visitors would sleep outside under the stars.

Food had to be provided. At least a couple of the fatter steers would be killed and butchered, along with several sheep and many chickens. The children were expected to help with the chickens by chasing and catching the ones that ran and flopped around when their heads were cut off. They also had to help pluck the feathers after the chickens were dumped into boiling water. The older children gutted and cleaned the chickens. Everyone pitched in.

The barbecue had to be cleaned and readied for the master barbecue chef. The older boys would scrape, clean, and ready the barbecue. The master chef would be working from dawn until late that night. Sometimes they dug a deep hole in the ground and prepared to cook a pig.

Most of the people would be there for three or four days, which required tables and more tables, all covered with white tablecloths for the food.

The hacienda would be upside down with hustle and bustle until that Monday when Padre Serrano and his assistants, all men, arrived.

Aldiana was working from sunup to sundown, handling all the hundreds of details and the many workers who came to her, requesting help with all kinds of problems. She fell into bed at night exhausted but with a feeling of real accomplishment. Jorge Luis had allowed her the freedom to make decisions even though she was still somewhat taken aback by the unexpected marriages.

Monday arrived very quickly, and Aldiana was still recovering from the shock of two of her children coming home married. She was beginning to adjust due to the numerous demands and preparations helping take her mind off them. Seeing them so happy melted her heart. It also helped her emotionally that Jorge Luis had not come home married. That would have been too much.

When Padre Serrano and his men arrived, she greeted the party and welcomed them to her home. Padre Serrano was escorted to a bedroom suite, whereas the living room had been converted to a dorm room for his assistants. Padre Serrano would have the bedroom area to himself. He could pray and meditate in silent solitude and comfort. A second tub was brought to the bathroom and extra chamber pots, one for each person. Plenty of towels and washrags were added along with pitchers and bowls of water. They were well taken care of. At dinner, the padre would dine with the family and his assistants with the servants.

Because the bookkeeping was extensive, with hosting so many people, Fiarela asked Prudence if she would come to the hacienda again for one or two days and stay overnight to help make sure that all the information would be recorded into the correct record books.

"I don't mind at all, but I'll have to check with Uncle Lot. He's all alone in the hotel now that Bryant is here with you. He was quite shaken when Bryant arrived a married man. He didn't expect that so soon nor under those circumstances, but he understands, and he's more than happy for Bryant," said Prudence.

The next morning, when the girls were talking, Prudence asked, "Fi, don't you want to attend some of the events in the chapel, too? I want to see the twins get baptized."

"Oh, I do, too," Fiarela looked up, shaking her hair in place. "Of course, I'm attending my father's funeral Mass, but I am really worried about being able to keep up with all of this. Look at these piles of papers I must contend with. Prudence, thank God you're here. Listen, I asked Gregorio to take you home and then bring you back in the morning. Maybe you could stay overnight for a couple of nights? Pru, it's going to be so exciting around here. Do you think Uncle Lot would like to stay here as well? He's been so alone in the hotel."

"I'll plan on staying and helping. I'll let Uncle Lot know what I'm going to do and ask if he wants to come with me. I'm sure he will. By the way, when I arrived, on my way to the office, I stopped by the room off the kitchen and peeked in on Benito. He was sitting up and looking better again. He looked like he was ready to go back to his own home and family. Fi, I still have bad dreams about that horrible shooting that night, do you?"

"Once in a while. I think it would be much worse for me if Bryant weren't with me. I feel so safe with him. I wish you and my - oh, here comes Gregorio. I'll see you in in the morning, Pru," said Fiarela, as she leaned over and gave Prudence a hug and kiss as Prudence went out to meet Gregorio.

As Prudence was leaving the hacienda, a feeling of sadness swam slowly over her. She forced a smile on her face to hide it, but it was tight and drawn. *I want so desperately to belong.* While she sat, with a deep sigh, she reorganized the things she placed on the seat to take home, and then sat looking out the window.

Once at the cantina, she put all her belongings away in her room and then sought her uncle, who was waiting in his hotel room alone. To Prudence, her uncle Lot looked tired and stressed after a day's work with the old deeds and documents that he had worked with in the hotel room.

He felt there were too many interruptions when they worked on the dining room table, and Aldiana was overwhelmed with preparations for Father Serrano's visit.

Prudence hugged him and asked if he felt all right.

"No, my dear, I really don't. I feel like all this work is almost a waste of time. I'm not sure we can do much to save the property, but I will certainly keep trying. It's heart-wrenching to see the possibility, really a certainty, of the loss of it all. They are a lovely family, and I hate to see them hurt."

Prudence was shocked to hear him speak in such an emotionally wrought manner. His words were so straightforward but tremulous with feeling. They gave her cold chills. She had no response. Instead, as she watched him sink down in his seat and seem to drift away, she turned to look out the window, staring, not seeing the lovely countryside.

A sad thought about the Californios and what was in store for them jolted her from the window. She thought about Benito – still recovering. She glanced at her Uncle Lot, but he had not reacted. It was as if he weren't there. *I miss Benito and our wonderful talks on our way to and from the hacienda. Uncle Lot is obviously very tired and not talkative. Gregorio was very nice bringing me home, but Benito treats me like a father would treat me. I think he has recovered enough to be with his family, in their little casita among the workers' bungalows, but I know it will be awhile before he can drive again.*

The next morning, Gregorio dropped her and Lot, who had documents to return, off at the back door closer to the hacienda office. Lot went down to the dining room to continue going over deeds and documents, feeling quite pessimistic where the land and the fate of the Californios was concerned.

Prudence, before she stepped into the house, watched, in the distance, people scurrying around with many tasks. She noticed someone pushing a wheelbarrow full of wine bottles to lay in the cold water of the creek, while thinking about how nice and cold the wine would be. Suddenly, she saw Danilo ride in. He stopped Gregorio, and when she saw Gregorio point out toward the barn, she assumed Danilo must be looking for Jorge Luis. She went on in to help Fiarela with her curiosity piqued.

Danilo rode out to the barns and found his boss talking to Elías. "Boss – oh, good morning, Elías." He turned back to Jorge Luis, saying, "Boss, can I speak with you?"

Jorge Luis nodded, without interrupting his conversation, and pointed his finger to one of the corrals, "Elías, don't leave. I'll be right back. I need to talk to you." He swiftly connected with Danilo at the corral and asked, "What is it, Danilo? Did you see someone while you were following Gregorio and Prudence on your way here?" asked Jorge Luis. He was looking at him intently, his brows and eyes tensed, hoping for the best but expecting the worst.

"I did. Up on a hill by one of the rock piles, I saw the sun glint off something, so I stopped for a good look." He pointed up the hill, which had a grove of oak trees covering the top and a rock formation that snaked down the hillside into a ravine. "It was a man on horseback with a spyglass watching the carriage. He followed the carriage with the glass. I watched him leave and head back in the direction of town. The extra tracks we saw at the shooting that night were Rafa's. Do you want me to go up there and see if they are the same as the man on the hill?" he said it without thinking. Suddenly, fear gripped him, and he frowned. A fast memory of Angela in his arms last night brought a grimace to his face. *What if? What if Rafa shoots me?*

"No hurry," said Jorge Luis, "but, go get Juan to go with you and track him. See if he does go to the pueblo. Edgardo, Juan and I have made plans to trap him and take him up to the gold mining in the Sierras. We'll hand him over to the Vigilantes. I hear they are tough and act fast. They'll hang him for sure." He paused for a moment before speaking forcefully, "You - you - be careful. Don't take any chances." He wiped his hands on his pants and reached over to pat Danilo on his shoulder. "I'm going back and talk to Elías and see if he knows anything about his brother. I don't want him to know about this, though," said Jorge Luis, pointedly. Danilo got the point, nodded, turned, and left.

Prudence had entered the back door and went immediately to the office to find Fiarela already working with several piles of papers and invoices. "Fiarela, wow, I feel overwhelmed seeing all those piles. I know I can't recognize many of those signatures. Can you actually read them?" asked Prudence. Fiarela rolled her eyes and shrugged her shoulders, shaking her head. "Oh, Lord help us. We'll have to be extra careful to see that everything is entered in the correct book," said Prudence, lifting one pile of the papers. "Man, this is a huge undertaking, Fi. Your mother must be going crazy with it all." Prudence set the handful of papers down carefully to avoid scattering them all over. She realized that everyone was expected to hand in their invoice or written note of what they had provided. All the food, wine and juices, butchering of the meat, and labor costs had to be accounted for.

"Oh, no, mother loves it. Nobody's better at organizing all this than she is." She paused and sighed, "But, Prudence, I'm shocked at how much the hacienda has to provide for Father Serrano's visit. This is more than a big deal. We're expected to provide anything that is needed, not just for him and his men but for everybody."

Back at the corral, after reporting to Jorge Luis, Danilo pursed his lips, pulled at his mustache, and left to look up Juan. Jorge Luis walked back to Elias and asked sternly, "Elías, I know everything is upside down with Padre Serrano here, but I want to know if you've had any contact with Rafa?" Looking intently at Elías, he thought, *He'd better not lie to me.* "Tell me everything you know and right now. You understand me? Elías!" Jorge Luis stood straight and stiff. His eyes never wavered from Elías with his downcast and guilty look.

Fear embraced Elías, "Uh, well, uh, not, not much..." His eyes were on the ground, as he shifted his feet back and forth nervously while fingering his beard. After a minute, he made up his mind to tell his boss what had happened. He took a deep breath and lifted his eyes to Jorge Luis' face, saying, "I hate to admit it, Boss, but he showed up last night and threatened to make a big stink if we didn't let him in. He left his horse about a mile away, so he could sneak in with no one hearing him. I'm sorry, but we can't control him. He just does what he wants to. I know he's no good, but he is my brother," said Elías.

"Yeah, I understand, but damn you, Elías! Don't you understand he's dangerous? He has threatened me and now, Prudence. God help him if anything ever happens to her!"

"¡Qué no! She's a nice lady. We all admire and respect her. That no good brother of mine," he answered with a sigh and a helpless look. "I'll talk to my boys and see if one of them can sneak out to warn you if he shows up again. He took me by surprise, Boss. I'm sure sorry. It won't happen again. I promise." Elías looked downcast, shook his head and wrung his hands in obvious distress.

Jorge Luis said, "Thanks, but you be careful as well. He's impulsive and treacherous." Jorge Luis left and returned to the barns.

Elías stood for a few moments, looking forlorn. He knew now his brother's days were numbered. He had heard that Rafa had hooked up with that Americano government man and that gave him a pain in his stomach. He couldn't understand why Rafa had turned out so bad and refused to change.

Meanwhile, in the office, the girls worked feverishly. Finally, Prudence said, "Fi, I need to stretch my legs and get some fresh air. If the chapel is empty, I would like to go in for a few minutes. Is that allowable? I know Padre Serrano is very busy."

"I don't see why not, if it's empty," said Fiarela. "I would join you, but I need to finish up with these figures, so they don't get mixed up. I must attend my father's funeral Mass, which will take a lot of time. Besides," she said with a big smile, "Bryant wants to eat lunch with me in my suite." She gave Prudence a sly look with a little snicker.

"Oh, how sweet," answered Prudence, in a teasing tone and rolling her eyes with a knowing smile. "Really, I'm so happy for you both. You're perfect for my cousin." She hugged Fiarela and gave her a kiss on her cheek, "I'll be back soon - Cuz."

"Wait, Prudence." Fiarela's voice had softened and her expression turned somber. She looked straight into Prudence's eyes, "I know deep down in my heart that Jorge Luis really cares about you. And I know that you care about him. Heck, everyone does. Even *Mamá* finally caught on." Fiarela looked at the ceiling and her brows furrowed. "I just don't understand what he is afraid of," said Fiarela with sudden seriousness.

"Sometimes, I know it in my heart, too," Prudence said, shaking her head, but, then, with a sad frown, she continued, "but it seems he's just not ready or, maybe, he's not willing. I don't understand it either, Fi," she whispered, pausing. Her face became set, appearing hard and full of determination. She said, almost to herself, "I will not be anything but a proper wife." She turned her face to look across the room and out the window, sighing. She fingered her hair, pushing it behind her ears and fidgeted with her belt and skirt. Nothing helped, and tears began to sneak down her cheek. In front of her stood Fiarela, the young, beautiful woman madly in love with her husband, who certainly responded. She looked at Fiarela and shook her head, saying, "You, Fi, a Californio, married my cousin, an American. I'm an American. Why can't I marry your brother, a Californio?"

Her emotions were surfacing like a volcano, so she walked out quietly into the darkness of the hall, which began to smother her feelings until she choked them back. Opening the back door, the warmth of the outside air wiped across her face, and the brightness of the sun almost blinded her. *What am I doing out here? I can't fall apart now. I won't. I'll pull myself to-*

gether once I can meditate in the chapel and calm down. Contemplating the powerful yet tender words she just heard from her new cousin, she realized that Fiarela had just confirmed once and for all Jorge Luis' feelings for her. *Why was it so different for a man – no, not just any man but a hacendado, a man who was responsible to carry on the legacy of the Sandoval family. He had to retain the utmost respectability in order to maintain discipline with so many workers. He would always respect his mother's feelings and that might keep an invisible, yet very tangible, wall between us.* But she knew that, with her knowledge of bookkeeping and her experience plus the help from her family, she could be a tremendous advantage to him.

I know with tenderness and softness, and my reliability, I can break open Aldiana's heart. I'm sure of it. Doesn't he understand that? Even though she continued her thoughts that tended to pull her down, she began to reach deep within to begin dragging her courage up from the depths.

Prudence trudged slowly, but with more determination toward the chapel, praying it would be available. She still felt as if hope had been sucked out of her. She woke a little from her reverie and noticed the sights of people hustling here and there preparing for the festivities. *Why do I feel so left out? I'm not really. I'm included, but I don't feel that I truly belong. I'll sit for a while in the quiet of the chapel. I've missed my church and all the activities I was a part of.*

Meanwhile, Fiarela shook her hair back and forth and pushed it behind her ears before sitting down again to make notations in the record book. Prudence had cleaned up her ink pens and straightened up the desk before she walked out. *Just like Prudence, always so neat and considerate. Why doesn't that stupid brother of mine wake up? I want her for my sister.* Fiarela shook her head, letting her hair fall into place. She rubbed her chin a moment, pondering what it would be like to have a sister. Finally, she stood up, stretched and walked over to the water canter and drank the fresh, cool water. *I just needed to move a bit. I'm determined to plug away at all this,* she said to herself. Her reward of being with Bryant alone in their suite for lunch made all the work worthwhile. Her husband was one in a million, and she knew it.

The night before had been long and torturing, as Jorge Luis had tossed and turned all night long in great distress. *It's time – time to make a decision. I can't live in this place of vacillation any longer. I can't take it. I'm not dealing with all this like I should. I need to talk with Padre Serrano.*

When morning arrived, and after Jorge Luis had addressed his men with their work orders, he strode to the chapel where the padre performed his rituals. More than six months had passed since his last visit and there was a long waiting list for him. The pueblo had no church, being so small. All ceremonies had to be held in the small chapel on the hacienda.

The chapel could seat about fifty people. The building was horseshoe in shape with big, carved, wooden double doors in front, which let in the bright light when open. The pews were in the center with the aisles on the sides. At the entrance, there was a small table with sand for the many prayer candles. The candles were made by the inhabitants of the hacienda, and it was always open for anyone with a need. The back had windows that could be opened for air. In front of the windows, there was a statue of the Holy Family and the altar - a very simple chapel but well used.

Upon entering, Jorge Luis would always feel peace, but not today. He was not at peace. His mind was full of worry and apprehension for the success of the talk he hoped to have with the priest while he was there. He felt full of confusion, with his feelings wounded and shaken, almost fearful. He could no longer shove them down and deny them. They pushed too hard with needs and wants mixed, yet lacked clarity. He felt he was shattering like a glass thrown on the floor. He desperately needed to talk it over with Father Serrano.

Jorge Luis entered the chapel and dipped his finger in the Holy water. He hurriedly made the sign of the cross, knelt in front of the alter, and began to pray. *Please, God, please, soften the hearts of Padre Serrano and my mother. I want them to understand how much I love and need Prudence. Our lives are being turned upside down, but with her, I would be able to do anything. I beg you, have piedad.*

Padre Serrano, hearing someone enter, came in from the side room where he worked while he was there, "Jorge Luis, *mijito,* how good to see you. I wondered when you would come in."

"Padre, it's good to see you again. Do you have a moment for me?"

"Of course, do you want confession? It's been quite a while."

"No, no, Padre. Please, I need to speak with you, not as a priest, but man to man. I have never felt so tormented. Please, Padre, man to man."

Padre Serrano sat down by him, looked at him intently. He slowly responded, "Ah, sí, you seem quite conflicted. Not like you, *hijo.* What is it or who is it? Is it your father?"

"No, not my father," said Jorge Luis, looking startled. "My father was a wonderful parent. He had no part of this. Padre, you know I am responsible and well-respected. I have tried to be an exemplary Catholic. But,

I can't stop feeling the way I do. I have never felt so tortured. My heart has never been full of pain like this before."

"Yes, Jorge Luis," he nodded, taking his hand and holding it for a moment. "You have been a good son. The kind every parent would hope for." He leaned over and patted him on the shoulder, "Your pain, then, must be for a woman, but not Marina, I think."

"Marina?" he jerked back with a deep frown, giving the Padre a dark look. "*No, Diós mío, no,* her name is Prudence. Prudence Ann Mullen." As he spoke her name, he lost focus on Padre Serrano. Prudence Sandoval y Mullen– that was the first time he had consciously, in the silence of his own mind, spoken that name. *Señora Sandoval, my wife.* Chills rushed over his entire body. There was no doubt now, no doubt at all.

The padre was watching intently. He had witnessed that reaction many times -- the breaking wide open of protected hearts. Jorge Luis regained his secure attention.

"She is a foreigner, an Americana. She comes from Maine, far, far away. She's independent, competent, and rides a horse like a man!" His nervousness made him speak too fast. He looked at the priest to see his reaction to that last statement, but Father Serrano was intently listening. "She is educated and has learned Spanish already. She's our bookkeeper, and she is teaching Fiarela, who adores her. I have contact with her often. It's killing me," he said as he looked straight at Padre Serrano with pleading eyes. His fists were clenched in pain.

Padre Serrano glanced at Jorge Luis. A slight smile appeared on his face. He held back a little chuckle. He had seen this pain many times before.

"She is honest and forthright. Father, she's not a Catholic and not of our class, but her people are obviously well to do. You married her cousin, Bryant, to Fiarela. He's a lawyer who is quite well off and up and coming out here. But, Prudence? Mother considers her a heathen! And an outsider."

"Ahhh, and you are in love with her. That is obvious. Jorge Luis, you are a mature man and at the age to be thinking of forming a family. Does she reciprocate?"

"Padre, I'm sure she does. I feel it, but I have never dared to approach her. I would never do that to her. Our relationship is - is sometimes so wonderful. We are compatible, but, then, at times, it becomes frustrating, especially when she speaks her mind and acts as my equal. I'm not used to that. But, I admit, I admire that quality in her."

"Son, if you care that much about her and truly love her, go after what you want. Don't let her slip away. She may, also, feel as you do and afraid to let you know how she feels. I watched you two in the Ochoas' chapel and felt that."

That remark surprised Jorge Luis, but he went on, "But, Father, I feel guilty, as if I am betraying my family and my heritage. I think about her night and day. I've never met a woman like her. She has such integrity, honesty, and loyalty." Jorge Luis broke down into tears, "I can't live like this. I don't want to live without her."

"*Mijo*, you have always had a true and open heart," said Padre Serrano with a reassuring yet commanding tone. "Do not fret over worldly things. If she loves you, love will sustain you through all the many trials you will face. Pray on it. Do what your heart tells you. Do not let others influence you. Have you talked to your mother? Fiarela married an Americano. She seems quite accepting of him."

Jorge Luis agreed but shook his head. "But you don't understand, Padre, my brother-in-law is a well-known lawyer. He adores her and can give my sister a very good life. I'm facing the possibility of big losses here and may have nothing to offer Prudence. That frightens me, and Mother still considers Prudence a foreigner and a heathen. She wants me to go to Mexico or Spain to find a wife. I won't do it. I'll stay single the rest of my life if I have to."

"*Hijo, hijo*, that cannot be. If need be, go to your mother, respectfully, but explain to her that you are the *hacendado*. You have made up your mind to marry Prudence, if she will have you. I can marry you while I am here if you want." He placed his hands on the shoulders of Jorge Luis and looked him straight in the face, "You deserve happiness. You will find a way. Again, pray on it. Let me bless you, Son, and then I must prepare for the next ritual." Padre Serrano stepped back, smiled, made the sign of the cross and said, "*Diós te bendiga, mijo*." He turned and left the chapel.

Jorge Luis knelt again, praying with an easier mind and a quieter heart, settled about what he would do. But Prudence? Behind him he heard soft footsteps entering the chapel. Whoever it was sat down and was silent. He continued to pray for some time. He felt the love of the Holy Mother descend upon him so strongly that his eyes teared up. He could almost hear her whisper to him, "Don't be afraid to love, my child, for love is all there is." He bowed his head and let out a deep breath, gave thanks and said amen. He rose up, turned to leave, and froze in surprise. His immediate thought was, *How can the Lord work so quickly?* His breath came hard. He blurted out, "Prudence, what are you doing here? Are you all right?"

"Yes, I am. I didn't know that was you. I thought you were out working somewhere. I'm sorry if I disturbed you." He furrowed his brow and shook his head while she said, "I saw the priest leaving, and asked him if I, a non-Catholic, would be allowed to enter the chapel to pray. He assured me that God's house is always open to all, and I would be most welcome, so I came in. He didn't mention you were here. What are you doing here? Are you all right?"

Jorge Luis moved closer to her and said, "Yes, yes, I'm fine."

He reached out to touch her arm as she continued, "I miss my church. It's been a long time since I have been to it, and I was always very active in ours." Her voice softened and lowered as she said, "I'll leave if you want me to."

"No, no, I was just surprised to see you. I have been very thoughtless, Prudence, never thinking about your spiritual needs and how homesick you must have been at times. I apologize for that."

Prudence's eyes blurred with tears, "Thank you for that. I missed my family so much, my home, my friends, and our church, too. Please, I apologize for feeling sorry for myself because I have my uncle and my cousin here now, and I am truly grateful. Your family has been kind to me, even your mother who looks askance at me. I'm just a stranger, a foreigner to her."

"Good heavens, no!" He sat down next to her, and drew her to his shoulder, where she cried unabashedly. "Prudence, no one thinks of you that way. You are a heroine to Fiarela. Edgardo admires you and finds you fascinating. Facundo holds you in the highest of respect. Benito adores you - so do I, Prudence. I would give my life for you." He kissed her forehead. "Please, Prudence, I know, at times, I've been cold and distant, but don't be afraid of me. I did not know how to deal with my feelings for you. I have never felt this way before. The idea of me being with *you* was too overwhelming. The feelings I have for you are so different, confusing, and frustrating, and yet so incredibly amazing, all at the same time. You've been in my thoughts and my feelings ever since that first time I laid eyes on you at the river. Remember the river? That first time we met? I'll never forget that big Colt forty-four you held on me, and, yet, I'll never forget how gorgeous you were. Yes, Prudence, even in those baggy men's pants." He smiled softly and pulled her closer, "I have always wanted you." He let out a big sigh, "Oh, Prudence, how I love you."

Prudence sat back with a teary face and stared at Jorge Luis. A minute passed before she could digest what he said. The words that left her mouth shocked him, "I felt the same toward you. I refused to acknowledge my feelings at first. You were too frightening to me. I could barely handle the situation that I was forced to live in," she paused, while lowering her eyes before she continued, "When I first arrived, I was in a state of severe shock. My normal middle-class life was destroyed, and I found myself in a strange culture that was incomprehensible. I didn't speak the language, and I was forced into a poverty-stricken life. Here – here - in this country, I have absolutely nothing to give but my knowledge. Look where I live - in the hotel upstairs next to a bordello. What must you have thought of me? I tried not to think about you, the owner. I felt there was no hope for someone like me – not in a million years."

"I, too, felt the same, but, my love, there is hope for you and me isn't there?" implored Jorge Luis.

They sat silently for some time – he, holding her and protecting her. She, being held and feeling protected. Neither had ever felt this intensity or mutuality of love before. Now what? Neither had an answer.

Jorge Luis tenderly lifted her chin, peering directly into those wide, questioning eyes and said, "I love you. I walk *loquito* over you. I want to marry you. Prudence, will you have me? Will you marry me?"

Prudence stared up at him, wanting him more than anything, "Yes, yes, I love you," she said, feeling herself trembling and her heart beginning to race, "I've always loved you. I – I've wanted you for so long. I love you. I want to share my life with you."

She accepted his proposal with her whole body and soul, but then, a little fear crept in and she felt a tinge of reluctance. *How would his mother react?* she wondered. "Jorge Luis, I'm concerned about your mother, and since we haven't been what you call '*novios*' or '*prometidos,*' you must ask my uncle for my hand in marriage, and you must do it formally," she said.

Jorge Luis was left too stunned for words. He looked at her and paused to collect his thoughts, "Of course, *mi querida,* I will do that formally. I must find a way to approach my family and our people. They will not approve of me marrying an Americana, and, even worse, not of our culture. My sister married an Americano, Bryant, your cousin, and Mother has taken that well. But, I'm just not sure…" Doubts and a feeling of insecurity crept in. He didn't like that feeling. He felt a band of tightness crushing his heart.

"I will have the same problem with my family and friends, but not Uncle Lot or Bryant. They like and respect you," said Prudence.

"*Diós mio.* I did not think of that. I am not thinking straight. Even Edgardo had to go through serious marriage formalities with Shadowhawk to marry Ramona. I am so sorry." He felt a deep guilt. Why had they all been so insensitive? Why hadn't they recognized her situation as a foreigner, with nothing in a strange land where everything and every person was strange? "How could I have been so blind and selfish. I should have realized that you would have marriage traditions too. I promise you, Prudence, I will never forget again," he said.

Her thoughts did not travel as far as his. She had already lived through a huge jolt of life and a complete change being an immigrant in a foreign land, alone with nothing. She had adapted. She had to. She would again if she had to.

They sat in silence for a few minutes. "What are we to do?" worried Prudence.

"I want to marry you right now while Padre Serrano is here and let the chips fall where they may. I want you now, Prudence. I don't want to wait," said Jorge Luis. His hand slipped behind her neck and pulled her head to his. Her hands quickly found their way around his neck while he kissed her passionately. He drew back his head and whispered, "Will you marry me now? I mean right now?"

"Yes, yes, please talk to the priest. I don't want to wait either. Maybe he will allow us like he did Bryant and Fiarela. I'm so afraid, though. I don't want to give you grief with your family."

"Prudence, *mi amor*," Jorge Luis took a deep breath, "I will announce to my mother that I will marry. She will be astonished and, maybe, not approve. Then I will discuss the date of the wedding with our priest. I am not going to wait. We'll have only a couple of days to get ready. If he returns, it won't be for another six months to a year or never."

"What? That's impossible," Prudence was taken aback. Her head was spinning, "At home I would need time to organize a big wedding. But here, well, maybe all I need would be a little help from your mother's seamstress to sew a dress. I have nothing else to plan, so that would be simple." She held his head in her hands and looked into his intense, dark eyes, "I am worried about you, Jorge Luis, and your family relationships. Can we marry simply and quietly?"

Jorge Luis pulled her closer. He whispered, "Prudence, I want to kiss you again. May I?" They kissed fervently and passionately, interrupted only by a masculine voice behind them.

"Well, well, it is about time you woke up, *Hermano*. Finally, you recognize what has been right in front of you this whole time. Welcome to our family, Prudence," Edgardo said with a huge smile. He leaned over and gave Prudence a big kiss on her cheek, "Have you talked to Padre Serrano yet, you two?"

"No, we haven't talked about a date, not yet. He knows about us, though. I talked to him earlier," responded Jorge Luis, feeling a bit embarrassed.

"I will get him for you," said Edgardo. Before they could respond, Edgardo was out the door. Prudence sat trembling with excitement. Jorge Luis sat, thinking, *Damn that brother of mine*, while holding his breath -- afraid Prudence might get up and leave.

Padre Serrano arrived and stood in the entrance watching the young couple sitting in silence, with their backs to him. His thoughts encompassed them, and he wondered why the human condition had to be so painful. He wondered how he could help them and felt he must as he walked forward to greet them.

He reached them quietly and surprised them. They both flinched and looked at him with eyes full of hope. They rose and stood before him. He said, "I can marry you four days from today. Is that enough time for you, Prudence? And you, Jorge Luis?"

They gasped, both nodded and said, "Yes, yes, of course, we will make it work."

"All right then, go inform your mother, Jorge Luis, and you, Prudence, your uncle. I would suggest Fiarela and Bryant as your witnesses. I will have the ceremony right after the lunch at two o'clock, about three. Can you do that?" When they both nodded, with a little smile, he walked out of the chapel.

Jorge Luis pulled Prudence to him once more and kissed her softly and tenderly, "Come with me to tell my mother, and I will go with you to tell your uncle. He's here, in the dining room, helping Edgardo with documents."

"Uncle Lot will be very happy for us. Please, don't worry about your mother. She really loves you. I think she will come around. I know she wants you to be happy. I'm sure of it," said Prudence, staring him in the face and trying to speak in a convincing tone of voice. "Besides, she can see how happy Edgardo and Elena are and Bryant and Fiarela are just delirious." She raised his callused and rough hand to her lips, kissed it warmly, and held it to her chest with both hands, mouthing the words, "I love you."

Jorge Luis looked at her with a loving yet unsure and quizzical expression. "I think, maybe, we should call a meeting of everyone here and announce it that way. What do you think?" said Jorge Luis.

"Good idea. After all, you are the *hacendado*. You don't need to ask permission from anyone. I'll go and check on Fiarela in the office and then get Elena in the kitchen. Maybe Teresa will mix up some chocolate atole for us. Wouldn't that be good? Don't tell anyone what it's about," said Prudence. They both felt a sense of relief that their announcement would be with everyone in a meeting. There would be strength in numbers. Prudence leaned up to kiss him and lingered for another.

After being told about a meeting, everyone hurried to the office, wondering what was happening. Only Edgardo knew. Settling in their chairs, whispering could be heard, "What's going on. No more problems, I hope."

Everyone quieted down when Jorge Luis went to the front and stood in front of the desk. They all watched him intently with some trepidation, not knowing what they might hear.

"I've got some news to share with you," he said, smiling like something big was about to happen. "Don't worry, it's all good, very good. I'm as happy as I can be. Prudence, *mi amor*, come up here, please." He put his arm around her and looked at his mother, "Mother, Uncle Lot, everyone, I finally found the woman I want to share my life with, and she has said yes. We've talked to Padre Serrano, and we're getting married in four days."

Edgardo started clapping, "Finally, he's done it. There isn't anyone here who didn't know you loved her, even Mother."

"Well, I certainly did," said Lot, "and, my dear, I couldn't be happier for you both."

"Glad to have you in the family Jorge Luis," said Bryant.

Elena joined in with giving each of them a kiss and a hug. Having come in from the kitchen, she patted Prudence's face as if she were feeling a leg of lamb, "Oh, excuse me. I've been in the kitchen too long," she wiped her hands on her apron, and added, "I do love you both."

Aldiana was speechless, but just for a moment. There was no ignoring her son's sincere, deep feeling, his determination and excitement. She jumped up and hugged her first-born son and then kissed Prudence. She looked at her family. "I can't believe that all of you will have been married within a week of each other, all three of you. I will be having all kinds of *nietos* soon. I am so happy for all of you, and Jorge Luis, you truly have chosen well," she said, looking at them and speaking with deep affection in her voice, "You have my blessing." Jorge Luis and Prudence, both, hugged and kissed his mother.

Fiarela had run to them, hugging them both, but waited anxiously until after her mother finished talking, to say, "Jorge Luis - Jorge Luis, I have something so important to tell you. Papá told me, on his deathbed, that I could tell you this *only* if you chose Prudence to marry. He told me that he admired her and felt she was perfect for you. He wanted you to have his blessing, but only if you married her."

Jorge Luis teared up as he bent over to hug and kiss his sister, "Bless you for telling me. You don't know how much that meant to me." He felt his father's blessing enter his heart and was strengthened by it. He fully accepted the leadership of his family now and rejoiced. He felt whole with Prudence by his side. He could face his country falling apart around his ears with fortitude.

"This calls for a celebration," said Edgardo.

"Amen," said Lot. "Prudence, we can make plans in the carriage on our way home later."

"Bryant," said Edgardo, "let's you and I go find the best house tequila. Elena, dearest, will you and Fiarela take the crystal glasses out of the cabinet, please?" The women, including Aldiana, were already talking wedding plans, clothes, and food. The family was now one, united in love. That would sustain them through what was to come.

My past life, which was so predictable and comforting, is almost gone, but with Prudence at my side, I can gladly face any unknown. I can manage change. I have hope again.

Jorge Luis looked around at his solid, stable, and growing family, feeling full of pride and with the warmth of love, announced, "I propose a toast" - everyone raised their glasses - "to Prudence, the love of my life," and to himself he said, *My dreams and my prayers have been answered, thanks to God and the Angels.* He thought of the words he had learned, studying at the university in Spain, from old Sophocles:

"One word frees us of all the weight and pain of life. That word is love."

Epilogue

Jorge Luis considered himself the luckiest man in California. He was more than proud of his wife, Prudence, his true love and business partner. Every time he looked at his children his feeling of completeness increased.

Prudence felt as if she had the most fulfilling life in the world. Not only was she with the love of her life and her three adorable children, but she was able to take a large role in the family businesses. She received all the support she needed from Edgardo and his family, Elena's parents, the Ochoas, who lived with them, and, above all, she gained Aldiana's complete approval.

Fiarela was the happiest woman in Sacramento, and still very much in love with her handsome husband, Bryant. She loved their children, her home and her full social life. They spent time often at the hacienda, where Aldiana had a fun and exhausting time with all her grandchildren.

The Sandoval Family was hard hit by the many rapid changes, but with Lot and Bryant's help, Facundo's insight and creativity, their own initiative, hard work, and optimism, they faced and overcame each obstacle, gaining in strength and forming a solid, integral family.

Historical Overview

The Californios' loss of land was a simple fact of life. Under mind-boggling circumstances, and in basically two years, the pastoral and predictable lifestyle of the Californios was pulled out from under them, and, for all intents and purposes, faced extinction.

I wrote my story ending for a particular purpose. I wanted to reflect my belief in the importance of knowledge and education, and that love is the energy that holds the fabric of human lives together, with a spiritual under-pinning, and brings the strength to face whatever life throws at us.

Education at that time was virtually nonexistent, but the rancheros did know Mexican land law well. The majority of Californios lost their land and ended in dire poverty. An example was the famous Californio Apolinaria Lorenzana. Although she owned two ranchos and one other piece of property, and served her fellow man all her life, sacrificing her own needs, she ended up living off the generosity of other people.

The fast changing political, social, cultural, and economic environment created massive confusion, especially in that faraway frontier country of California where there was no communication - only a minimum of contact with outsiders at San Diego, Monterey, and San Francisco harbors. The Gold Rush brought everything to a head due to the flood of Americans and other foreigners. It overwhelmed the Californios. They had no time to adapt to lifestyles preferred by New Englanders and other strangers. Those strangers now owned the country that had been theirs for generations. They were no longer Californios, but they were not yet Californians. They were stripped of their core identities. Who were they now?

The American Department of Land Management placed unreasonable demands of proof of ownership on the grant land holders, involving them in court actions. They kept most in litigation for an average of ten to fifteen years. General and Governor Mariano Guadalupe Vallejo was in court over a period of seventeen years, which cost him his land except his home in Sonoma. The landowners piled up legal expenses that cost most of them the bulk of their property. The Californios were deprived of any security or certainty in land titles, no matter how correct and complete their documents. The families lived under this frightening threat with no way of knowing what the decision might be for them. Their lives were disrupted with frustration and anger by the energy of greed that flowed over their land. They were helpless and left without hope. No Californio escaped the suffering. It is difficult to explain how quickly these things happened to both the

Californios and the Indians. They were just simply run over.

Everyone was required to travel to San Francisco to present their documents, which added to the court costs. There was no public transportation yet, unless some of the people from San Diego and the Los Angeles area were able to take a ship to San Francisco, if one was available. The rest walked, rode in a wagon, or traveled on horseback. This placed a great hardship and more suffering on the Californios. Someone had to run the *ranchos* while the owner and family were gone. Who? They were already shorthanded due to the call of the gold mines taking their younger workers.

The previous life experiences of the arriving Americans created a huge problem, which was not solvable. Their previous experience, with only small land allotments, had not prepared them to understand the need for such large land grants as were customary in California for an economy based on cattle, hides and tallow. The settlers had no concept of the fact that one cow needed many acres for grazing. Many Californios owned a large number of cattle but were poor. The old saying was "Land rich, but cash poor." The immigrants also didn't understand the concept of free-range cattle and horses. Since there were no fences, if a man needed a horse for any reason, he could just catch one and use it. Many innocent Indians were hanged as horse thieves because they took a horse when they needed one - a tragedy due to ignorance, which caused more suffering. The prejudices against the Native Californians continued and gained force with the arrival of so many foreigners with their own prejudices and ignorance.

Because of the lack of cultural, economic, and social understanding, it was argued by government land management and other groups that the land acreages should be reduced to the American norm before confirmation, approval of deeds, and land for the Californios.

Beneath the everyday life of many of the old Californio families, existed the Jewish legacy which remained hidden until nearly the 2000s; however, even though there had been an intervening four hundred years since the families had become Catholic, there was something about Judaism that seemed to maintain a deep underground hold, which kept it somewhat alive even if no longer really understood. This long-held fear of the Holy Inquisition was ever present in these old families. They had to protect their loved ones by keeping it all hidden.

The arrival of thousands and thousands of people in 1849 into a country that had nothing caused food prices, along with everything else, to triple. The result was that many got rich and many starved.

In 1849 the sourdough bread of San Francisco was becoming famous. Another interesting fact was that the Hudson Bay Co. leased Alaskan glaciers to bring ice to San Francisco to be kept in ice boxes. An interesting cultural addition in 1849 was the first library in California, which was established in Monterey. Eight hundred books were shipped to it. These examples show how fast changes came to the long-isolated frontier with a small population, long out of touch with the rest of the world.

Squatters were a continuing problem. They refused to leave the land even if the courts decided in favor of the grant holder. In 1852, a squatter proposal came about which allowed them to "homestead" eighty acres on the Mexican land grants with no compensation to the landowners. Much resentment was caused by the tendency of the courts to decide land cases on what appeared to the layman to be trivial technicalities.

The 1850 migration was a repetition of 1849, but different in detail. Relief agencies were formed that saved thousands of travelers, who came over-land, from disasters that occurred up high in the Sierras.

To show how fast and extreme the changes were, here is an example: Before 1848, San Francisco was a village of eight hundred and twelve inhabitants. When gold was discovered, by early that summer, the population of San Francisco dwindled to almost zero. Everyone left for the mines. In 1849 there was a huge boom with forty thousand people settling in San Francisco within that one year. In the next eleven years, the population grew to 380,015 people. It was so crowded that ten to twenty men lived in one room, paying exorbitant rent. Building construction could not keep up with the explosion of the population. Neither could the Californios. They were run over again.

California acquired a new political setup, a new social structure, and a new economy. They arrived so fast it seemed like it all had dropped out of the heavens. Businesses sprang up quickly due to the lure of gold, such as stores along the diggings, as well as professional gamblers and freighters that came up the river to Sacramento and Stockton to replenish their stocks. Cattle and sheep were driven up to the mines to be butchered. Even entertainers arrived, like famous Lola Montez, who lived in Nevada city, and Mario Lanza, the international singer from Italy. They played in the newly built theaters. Daguerreotype studios appeared almost at once to take pictures of the miners to send home to their families.

More businesses of all types were set up quickly. Wagon and carriage making and leather works flourished due to cowhide being so plentiful, and a business in explosives filled a big need. Cotton and woolen mills were lucrative. Lumber became a huge business. Iron working was important.

The businesses popped up like mushrooms to fill all kinds of needs for new settlers.

Due to the miners' demand for meat, the cattle and sheep markets expanded. By 1860, cattle had grown to 3,000,000 head and sheep to over 1,000,000.

Tens of thousands of Chinese miners came to escape famine and poverty, but suffered a lot of mistreatment and prejudice.

The missions, after being secularized and losing their subsidies from the Spanish monarchy and the church, could not meet their costs. They had to sell off their land, let the Indians go, and because of that went into decline. They were no longer under the protection of the Presidios. The mission markets were lost by the Californios. More losses and suffering.

The 49ers' inrush of such huge numbers of people changed the complexion of the province. They wanted direct action like they had known at home and did not want to be under any military governance.

September 9, 1850, California left behind its chaotic province standing and put on full statehood. The new California settlers were up and running. They ran right over the Californios.

Several generations of agricultural, self-sufficient, and pastoral lives ended with a few swift and unexpected blows, but people like Jorge Luis and Prudence faced the challenges and carried on.

Glossary of Spanish

This is not a dictionary. These words are taken from the context of the story and can have more than one meaning. The words translated into English are meant to fit the situation and the common use in dialogue.

A

Abue = (abuela) grandmother

Adobado = pickled

Adorada = adored, adorable

Alta categoria = high class

Ama de cria = baby caretaker

Amiga = friend (feminine)

Amigo = friend (masculine)

Amor = love, (an endearment)

¿a solas? = alone, private

A sus órdenes = at your orders, service

Atole (Champurrado) = a favorite breakfast, picnic and fiesta drink made from a blend of corn, chocolate and milk plus other ingredients.

¡A trabajar! = To work! Get to work!

¡Ay caray! = Alas! Hah! Strange etc. Used like caramba.

B

Bandido malvado = nefarious bandit

¡Basura! = Trash! A very strong, harsh word when aimed at a person.

Bienvenida = welcome (to a female)

Blanca = the horse's name (color white)

Bordello = house of prostitution

Buenas noches = good night

Buenas tardes = good afternoon

Bueno = good

Buenos = short for good morning

Buenos días = good day, good morning

C

¡Cállate! = shut up!

¡Caramba! = an expression to cover almost anything from "Wow!" to "holy shit!"

Cara mía = my dear (an endearment for a female)

Cariño = love, (endearing)

Caro = dear, beloved (affection)

Chorizo = Mexican sausage

Chamacas = girls

Chamaco = young man, boy

Charreada = rodeo

Claro = of course

Claro que no = of course not

Cobarde = coward

Compadres = friends, buddies

Conquistadores = conquerers

Con placer = with pleasure

Corriente cattle = a small, hardy breed common to California of that time

Cucaracha = cockroach

Cuñado = brother in law

D

De aquerdo = agreed or I agree

De nada = you're welcome

Desgraciado = disagreeable, ungrateful person, etc.

Dios = God

Dios mío = my god!

Dis-par-e = dispare = shoot

Doña = reserved for an older woman, well respected, generally owns property.

Dueña = female boss

E

Edict of Expulsion = also known as the Alhambra Decree. Publicly announced by the Spanish monarchy to expel Jews from Spain as composed by Torquemada, the Grand Inquisitor. Note: In 1968 Spain formally revoked the decree and edict. If a person can prove their family members were victims, Spain awards them citizenship.

El angel de amor = The Angel of Love, a Californio song

El Campo de Los Angeles = Angels Camp east of Stockton, CA

El extranjero = the foreigner

El más allá = The world of spirit

El Rancho del Viento Fuerte = The Ranch of the Strong Wind

El roble = the oak

El último adiós = The Last Goodbye, a Californio song

Encantada = enchanted (used in introductions)

Enchiladas de pollo = chicken enchiladas

¿Entonces? = Then? Well?

¿En serio? = Seriously? Are you serious? Are you kidding? Etc.

Ese condenado = That damned

Es necesario = it is necessary

Está bién = okay, good (it is well)

¿Está leyendo? = She's reading?

F

Faco = short for Facundo

Flojo = slow, lazy, name of the horse

Frijoles = beans

G

Gracias = thanks, thank you

H

Hacendado = land holder

Hacienda = landed property, estate

Hermanita querida = dearest little sister

Hermano = brother

Hija = daughter

Hijo = son

Hijo de puta = son of a whore/bitch

Hola = hello, hi

Huevos Rancheros = a favorite breakfast dish – eggs with a Ranchero sauce on a flat quesadilla.

J

Jefe = boss

Jesucristo = Jesus Christ!

Joven = young man, kid

L

La cena = dinner

Ladrón = thief

La gente prohibida = the forbidden people

La mucama = upstairs maid

Lazos = cords, ties, ropes

Levántate, joven divina = Raise Yourself Up, Divine Young Lady – a Californio song

Linda = pretty

Loco borracho = crazy drunk

Loquito = crazy

Los Sandoval = The Sandovals

M

Macho = male

¡Madre de Diós! = Mother of God!

Madre mía = mother of mine (like holy mother)

Magnífico = magnificent

¡Maldición! = God damn!

¡Maldita sea! = damn it!

Mañana = tomorrow

¡María Purísima! = Maria of truest purity

Masa = flour made from corn

¡Más le vale! = he'd better be

Más o menos = more or less

Me ba-jo (me bajo) = I'm getting down

¿Mejor? = better?

Mestizo = mixed blood

Mi compañera = my companion, female

Mierda = shit

Miserables = miserable, a harsh word to call a man

Mija = my dear daughter (an endearment)

Mijo = my son

Mi placer = my pleasure

Mi querida = my dearest, darling etc.

Mosquito muerto = bum, no good etc.

Mucama = upstairs maid

Muchacho = boy, kid, (adolescent)

Mujer = woman

Muy delicado = very delicate

N

Nada = nothing

Nadie = no one

Nadie tiene su vida comprada = no one has their life bought and paid for

Nerviosa = nervous

Nietos = grandchildren

No lo sé = I don't know

No me dis-par-e (no me dispare) = don't shoot me

Novios = boyfriend/girlfriend, going steady

Nuestra casa es su casa = our home is your home

O

¡Ojalá! = I wish, god grant, I hope, hopefully

¡Oye! = Hey! Listen! Listen here! Listen up!

P

Palabrotes = bad, coarse words

Paso Llano = four beat lateral movement in cadence – a Peruvian Paso gait

Patrón = boss

Pésame = condolence

Piedad = mercy, pity

Pobrecito = poor guy

Por supuesto = of course

Presentimiento = presentiment, premonition, an intuitive feeling about the future

Princesa = princess

Prometidos = engaged

Pronto = fast, quick, soon

Pueblo = town, village

Puta madre = M----F---er

Q

¡Qué barbaridad! = how rude, bad, etc.

¡Qué Bueno! = how good, great, neat

¿Qué diablos! = what the devil!

Qué Diós te bendiga = (May) God bless you

¿Qué necesita? = what do you need?

¿Qué te pasa? = what's wrong? What's happening?

Qué te rompe la cara = I'll break/smash your face

¿Quién sabe? = who knows?

R

Ranchería = village of huts for the Indians

Rumores = rumores

S

Sala = living room

Santa Atocha = A saint that some pray to or use in an expression

Santón = name of a Peruvian Paso horse

Señor = Mr., Sir

Señora = Mrs., (here, like mam)

Señorita = Miss

¿Se puede -? = Can one? Like "May I" sometimes

Sí = yes

¡Sí, claro! = Yes, of course!

Siesta = in this case – time to take a nap

Sí, por supuesto = yes, of course

Sopa de su propio chocolate = A threat to do you one better, or give you a taste of your own medicine

Soy una tumba = I am as silent as a tomb

T

Tienes cara de huele-pedos = you look really pissed etc.

Tienes razón = you're right

Tio = uncle

Todo = all

Toma = take

Toro = a bull

Tostones = potatoes in chili sauce

Trabajadores = workers

Tra-ba-jo (trabajo) = I work

Trago = a drink

U

Un buen día = a good day

Un fantasma = a phantom, ghost

V

Velorio = a church service for the departed

¿Verdad? = True? Really?

Viejo = old man

Y

y = and

yo = I

Selected Bibliography

These are the writings that have been of use in the making of this book. This bibliography is by no means a complete record of all the works and sources I have consulted. It indicates the substance and range of reading upon which I have formed my ideas, and I intend it to serve as a convenience for those who wish to pursue the study of this era.

Alfassa, Shelomo. *A Quick Explanation of Ladino (Judeo-Spanish)* Foundation For the Advancement of Sephardic Studies and Culture/Ladino Preservation Council 1999.

Allende, Isabel. *Daughter of Fortune.* New York, HarperCollins Publisher 1999.

Ashley Griffin: *Horse Breeding Behavior (University of Kentucky).*

Beebe and Senkewicz: T*estimonios: Early California through the Eyes of Women, 1815 – 1848.* Berkeley, Heyday Books 2006.

Bouvier, Virginia M. *Women and the Conquest of California, 1542-1840: Codes of Silence* Tucson, The University of Arizona Press 2004.

Bruno, Lee: *Misfits, Merchants and Mayhem: Tales from San Francisco's Historic Waterfront, 1849 – 1934.* Petaluma, Cameron & Company. No date.

Caughey, John Walton. *California: a 1951 University of California Berkeley textbook,* New York, Prentice Hall 1940.

De Mente Boye Lafayette*: NTC's Dictionary of Mexican Cultural Code words: The Complete Guide to Key Words That Express How the Mexicans Think, Communicate, and Behave.* Chicago, NTC Publishing Group 1996.

Edwards, Peter. Translator. *The Edict of Expulsion of the Jews.* Foundation For the Advancement of Sephardic Studies and Culture. Date unknown.

Fernández-Armesto, Felipe. *Our America*: *A Hispanic History of the United states,* New York, W. W. Norton & Company, Inc. 2015.

Freidenreich, David M. *Making it in Maine: Stories of Jewish Life in*

Small-town America. Colby College, free and open, 2015.

Garcia, Charles: *Was Columbus Secretly a Jew?* Special to CNN 2012.

Garcia, Yvonne: *A Brief History of Crypt Jews of Spanish and Portuguese Descent.* The Association of Crypto Jews.

Gray, Vykki. 2008. San Diego Friends of Old Time Music, Inc: *Los Californios ¡Que viva la ronda!* Transcriptions and Arrangements.

Harlan, George. *San Francisco Bay Ferryboats.* Online.

Hellman, Judith Adler: *Mexican Lives.* New York, The New Press 1994.

Heslinton, Courtney: *The Peruvian Paso* Online.

Hurtado, Albert: *Cultural Assumptions, patterns, and changes related to marriage and the 1800s.* Publisher unknown.

Jackson, Helen Hunt. *Ramona.* Written in 1880. Made in USA, San Bernardino, CA. August 2016. ISBN: 97811467964456.

Kolatch, Alfred J. *The Jewish Book of Why.* New York, Jonathan David Publishers, Inc. 1981.

L'Amour Louis: *The Californios.* New York, N.Y. Bantam 1985.

Levoy, Fay Lavender: *My Personal Jewish Resource* Irvine, Ca.

Library of Congress: *California as I Saw It:*

1. *Spanish California*   2. *The Missions*   3. *Mexican California*
4. *The United States and California*   5. *The Discovery of Gold*
6. *The Forty Niners*   7. *Government and Law*   8. *The Mines*
9. *Towns and cities*   10. *From Gold Rush to Golden State*

Library of Congress: *Mexican American culture Differences.*

Marks, L. Afassa: *The Jews in Islamic Spain: Al Andalus.* Foundation For the Advancement of Sephardic Studies and Culture 2004.

McMahan, Jacqueline Higuera: California Rancho Cooking. Seattle, Wa. Sasquatch Books 2001.

Orme, Wyatt. *"Cryto-Jews" In the Southwest Find Faith in A Shrouded Legacy.* Online.

Paso on the Web!: A Brief comparison: *The Peruvian Paso Horse versus The Paso. Fino Horse.*

Pitt, Leonard: *The Decline of the Californios.* Berkeley, University of California Press 1966.

Read, Ethel Matson: *Lo, the Poor Indian: A Saga of the Suisun Indians of California.* Fresno, Panorama West 1980.

Romero, Simon: *Hispanics Uncovering Roots as Inquisitions 'Hidden' Jews.* New York Times 2005.

Sanchez, Ph.D., Dell F. *The Sephardic Awakening in America.* Temple city, Hope of Israel Ministries 2000.

Shorris, Earl: *The Life and Times of Mexico.* New York, W.W. Norton & Company 2004.

Unknown. *Background: Mexican-Americans in California in the 19th Century.* Anneisaacs.com.

Unknown. *Caballo peruano paso, The Trail rider, The Peruvian Paso Horse.* Wikipedia.

Unknown. *Californio: Society and Customs,* Animal Corner: *Reproduction: Horses.* Wikipedia.

Unknown. *Hispanics Uncovering Roots as Inquisition's "Hidden" Jews.* Online. Code Switch 2014. New York Times.

Unknown. *Rancheria, AAARancheria, California Tribes, Rancheria Indians, Peruvian Paso.* Wikipedia.

Unknown. Jewish History Series: *The Spanish Inquisition.* Aish.com.

Unknown. *1840s in Western Fashion, Los californios.com, Los Californios, Info. Wikipedia.*

Biography

Sadye Reddick was raised on a sheep ranch which was isolated, with no electricity, no telephone, and no neighbors except a French Basque family that worked for her father. The isolation led her to become an avid reader with an appreciation for language. Until seventh grade, she attended a small country school where she learned to love learning, which has never ended. The love of language was stimulated by a lifetime of living with, working with and teaching immigrants.

She attended the University of California, Berkeley and Davis where she received her degrees: a Bachelor of the Arts in Spanish and a Lifetime Teaching Credential. She became a Primary school teacher, Reading Director, Reading Specialist, and Early Childhood tester and trainer. With her background, personally and academically, she taught many Spanish-speaking children each year. She offered the only Remedial Reading class in Spanish for the bilingual classes. She developed a complete testing program for reading skills in both languages for the teachers.

Sadye has five children and is a grandmother, a great-grandmother, a great-great-grandmother and loves huge family gatherings.

She lectured and presented workshops for sensitivity development and leadership training for adults through the Americana Leadership College. She gave back to her community by becoming the president of the Dixon Teacher's Association -- always working for the benefit of the children and teachers.

She remains active by teaching English, citizenship, art, Spanish, and by offering her knowledge, skills and experience to help with the Healing Clinic at the Unity Spiritual Center. She is also an artist and illustrated a children's book that doubles as a parenting aid, with her daughter, Yvonne Read, R.N., N.P. titled *Parenting Through the Power Within*.

Made in the USA
Monee, IL
22 July 2020